DEMON MOON

meljean brook

BERKLEY SENSATION, NEW YORK

THE BERKLEY PUBLISHING GROUP
Published by the Penguin Group
Penguin Group (USA) Inc.
375 Hudson Street, New York, New York 10014, USA
Penguin Group (Canada), 90 Eglinton Avenue East, Suite 700, Toronto, Ontario M4P 2Y3, Canada
(a division of Pearson Penguin Canada Inc.)
Penguin Books Ltd., 80 Strand, London WC2R 0RL, England
Penguin Group Ireland, 25 St. Stephen's Green, Dublin 2, Ireland (a division of Penguin Books Ltd.)
Penguin Group (Australia), 250 Camberwell Road, Camberwell, Victoria 3124, Australia
(a division of Pearson Australia Group Pty. Ltd.)
Penguin Books India Pvt. Ltd., 11 Community Centre, Panchsheel Park, New Delhi—110 017, India
Penguin Group (NZ), 67 Apollo Drive, Rosedale, North Shore 0745, Auckland, New Zealand
(a division of Pearson New Zealand Ltd.)
Penguin Books (South Africa) (Pty.) Ltd., 24 Sturdee Avenue, Rosebank, Johannesburg 2196,
South Africa

Penguin Books Ltd., Registered Offices: 80 Strand, London WC2R 0RL, England

This is a work of fiction. Names, characters, places, and incidents either are the product of the author's imagination or are used fictitiously, and any resemblance to actual persons, living or dead, business establishments, events, or locales is entirely coincidental. The publisher does not have any control over and does not assume any responsibility for author or third-party websites or their content.

DEMON MOON

A Berkley Sensation Book / published by arrangement with the author

PRINTING HISTORY
Berkley Sensation mass-market edition / June 2007

Copyright © 2007 by Melissa Khan.
Cover illustration by Franco Accornero.
Cover design by Lesley Worrell.
Interior text design by Laura K. Corless.

ISBN: 978-0-425-21576-0

BERKLEY SENSATION®
Berkley Sensation Books are published by The Berkley Publishing Group,
a division of Penguin Group (USA) Inc.,
375 Hudson Street, New York, New York 10014.
BERKLEY SENSATION is a registered trademark of Penguin Group (USA) Inc.
The "B" design is a trademark belonging to Penguin Group (USA) Inc.

PRINTED IN THE UNITED STATES OF AMERICA

10   9   8   7   6   5

To all of the Missys out there—
may you never grow up.

Special thanks to Megan Frampton,
slayer of semicolons and guru of music;
and to Jennfer-with-an-i, for everything.

CHAPTER I

Pray do not press your Guardian dictum upon me again. "Appearances are almost always deceiving"— how preposterous! I am beautiful and charming, and that is all my appearance promises. Any in Society who are disappointed when they do not find more cannot fault my countenance. The deception is not mine; they have deceived themselves. But let them continue to look, whether they are fools or no; I rather enjoy it.

Colin Ames-Beaumont, in a letter
to Dr. Anthony Ramsdell, 1813

No club should be so crowded at nine o'clock in the evening; drinking and dancing should never reach such animated heights until one o'clock. Two, if it were summer. Any earlier, and it gave the appearance that one came to drink and dance, as if such things were to be pursued for themselves rather than as a means to more pleasurable activities.

It was almost vulgar, and Colin Ames-Beaumont watched with no small measure of dismay as the early crush of people became a smash. Perhaps buying Polidori's had been a terrible mistake. Restoring the nightclub had been an obsession that had quickly burned out, and whatever lingering interest he'd had was quickly snuffed when a human woman with waist-length ebony hair and a horror of a black leather dress slithered up to his private table.

A techno beat pounded through the club, reverberated through his chest. Sumptuous golds and reds enfolded the lounges; the dance floors vibrated with energetic blues and greens. The music was good, the décor excellent; becoming a cliché was not.

Colin resisted the urge to glance down and confirm that his charcoal-gray trousers and ivory cashmere sweater had not been transformed into a tuxedo, complete with satin-lined cape.

And to think he'd been charmed the first time he'd seen Bela Lugosi sweep onto the stage.

A smile curved the woman's blood-red lips, but it failed when her gaze ran over his face. He heard the startled catch of her breath, the sudden increase in her heartbeat.

Colin loved it when they did that.

The male vampire who'd been observing her from one of the second-level lounges did not; Colin heard his growl between the pulses of electronic music. More black leather, a studded collar—he blended with half of Polidori's human clientele, and most of the undead.

Though she didn't move, the woman in front of Colin seemed to flail about, trying to reclaim some of the seductive posture with which she'd started. He'd disrupted her without effort, without expression, but now Colin's smile came easily.

As he intended, she regained her confidence, if not her sense. Bracing her palms on the tabletop, she leaned forward and gave him a view of her ample cleavage. "May I buy you a drink?"

Oh, good God. Could they not have come up with something more original? How did they expect him to respond? *I never drink . . . wine.*

"No," Colin said, "but if it's free, I will take a sip." He slid his fingers across the back of her hand. She shivered, and his smile widened.

There was lust in her involuntary response, but also fear. Very good. It was foolish of them to approach him this way. Grasping her wrist, he pulled her around the table. After a brief hesitation, she sat on the cushion next to him. Her gaze never left his face, and her tongue flicked out to touch her lips. Her breathing deepened and slowed as she lifted her hair away from her neck.

Colin brushed his thumb over the pulse beating at her throat. "I can make it very good for you," he said softly, and rasped his teeth against her skin. Her lips parted on a gasp. How long would it take?

Not long. The vampire abandoned his post in the lounge.

Only a short lesson, then. Colin's fangs sank deep. He controlled his descent, contained the pleasure of it—and sent the bubbling ecstasy back to her, let it course through her bloodstream. She stiffened and shuddered as the orgasm hit her, tiny cries breaking from her throat.

Ah, humans. Unable to experience the rapture in any way but sexual. He drew back before the bloodlust could rise, not bothering to close the punctures. Let her partner do that; he'd scent Colin on her skin—and hopefully, wouldn't forget.

She would.

Colin affected a bored expression as the vampire swept the still-quaking woman to her feet. After a furious glance at the streaming wounds, the vampire's head dipped, his mouth closing over the punctures. His dark head against her pale skin made a fascinating study in contrasts.

Colin sighed. It fascinated others as well, though for different reasons; the odor of blood was generating quite a bit of attention from the other vampires in the club. Perhaps it was for the best; he'd only have to explain this once.

"I could have ripped out her throat," Colin said pleasantly. The male lifted his head to stare at him, shaking with rage; the woman's hands clenched on his shoulders as if to hold him back. Good girl. The flush of orgasm had left her cheeks, replaced by pale apprehension. "You don't know me, yet you sent her to me."

The male's shame apparently left him speechless—or he'd finally taken a good look at Colin. If it was the latter, Colin might have had pity on him.

Her eyes luminous, the woman replied, "It was my idea. We'd heard you don't kill." She swallowed. "Don't kill humans."

Colin lifted his brows; his smile mocked them. "And from whom did you gather this intelligence?"

"Everyone knows," she said, but some of her bravado deserted her. She glanced up at her companion, as if for assistance.

The vampire had been young when he'd been turned—twenty-five, perhaps. Judging by his late-1980's hairstyle,

Colin estimated his transformation had been fifteen or twenty years previous. How unfortunate that so many of the undead clung to the fashions of their youth.

But then, so did humans.

"You are Beaumont, aren't you?" the vampire asked.

"*Ames*-Beaumont," Colin corrected. "My grandmother bought the hyphen, and paid dearly for it delivering an earl; I should hate to see her sacrifice wasted."

After a brief moment of disconcertment, as if he did not know what to make of Colin's reply, the male pulled out the chair tucked beneath the opposite side of the table. "May I?"

Amused, Colin inclined his head. The Goth façade had dropped from the vampire in all but appearance; out came the Midwestern farm boy. The woman settled into his lap.

"I'm Paul, this is Fia." He paused, and uncertainty flickered over his features.

Was he afraid that he'd inadvertently given Colin power over them by telling him their names? Alas, if only. Colin didn't deny or confirm his fear, though, and gestured for him to continue.

"We've recently returned to San Francisco," Paul said, and clasped his hands over Fia's. "Last year, when the . . . the . . ."

It wasn't pity that led Colin to help him out. "When the nosferatu began slaughtering us?" he supplied, and grinned as terror spiked the psychic scents of the vampires around them. None of these had fought the nosferatu—if they had, they'd not have survived. Nor had they been inside Polidori's when the cursed creatures had set fire to it, trapping seventy vampires inside . . . many of them the community's elders. But they would have seen how the nosferatu ripped their human victims apart; photographs from the rituals Lucifer and the nosferatu had performed had leaked into the news and online. A few might have witnessed firsthand their unbelievable strength and speed.

"The nosferatu. Yes." The vampire's pallor deepened; both he and his human guarded their minds well. If not for the physical response, Colin would have had difficulty reading him. "Most of us fled seven months ago, right before they burned this place down."

If fear of the nosferatu had inspired them to flee, they were more intelligent than the elders had been. "A wise decision, I daresay."

"Most of us lost our sires," Paul added, and Colin suppressed his grimace of distaste. One did not *sire* vampires as if they were animals. Of course, the elders had acted as animals, allowed themselves to be herded into Polidori's and then massacred. Against the nosferatu, there had been no safety in numbers, and they'd only presented a larger target. "But you survived."

"Apparently," Colin said.

Fia shot a quick glance at Paul before she said, "There are rumors that you had protection from a demon. Perhaps a werewolf. You've frequently been observed in the company of a woman who isn't . . . isn't human, nor vampire." She reached up and slid her hand self-consciously over her hair, and Colin almost burst into laughter. The dye and the leather had been an attempt to simulate Lilith's appearance?

He wasn't certain what was more ridiculous: their obvious assumption that the halfling demon was his consort, or that this human thought she had hope of mimicking Lilith in presence or personality.

"And you've been focusing your hunts on dark-haired women," Fia continued.

They'd discovered that?. But Colin's expression reflected none of his surprise as he said, "There is no such creature as a werewolf."

A psychic ripple of disappointment and disbelief from the vampires met his statement. Had their elders taught them nothing? Then again, the elders might not have known the truth about their origins, or the other beings that stalked the Earth.

Very few did.

"But there are demons? And they can offer us protection if the nosferatu strike again?"

Colin's humor fled. "No," he said flatly. "And entering into such a bargain with one would be more foolish than sending a human in an attempt to soften an unknown vampire."

Embarrassment emanated from both members of the couple, but they were determined. Paul said, "We've also heard that a few vampires have been recruited by a government agency—and that those vampires were all connected with you in some manner. With Polidori's." He waved his hand in a sweeping gesture, as if Colin couldn't see the vampires around them, the club. "Do you intend to lead us? You are the eldest among us."

Fia touched her neck and said quietly, "The most powerful."

More vampires gathered near, and Colin's gaze swept over those assembled. Had they all planned this, or were they simply taking advantage of one couple's daring? He leaned back and rested his arm along the top of the sofa. A sword lay behind a panel in the wall; he hoped he would not have to use it.

Establishing superiority through bloodshed was as outdated as their clothing, and better suited to beasts.

Colin's gaze didn't move from Paul's, but he directed his statement to them all. "I am pleased that you noticed," he replied. "Though I find it unfortunate that you assume my power has an obligation attached. Your elders were satisfied without having me as leader; you should follow their example in that—if only that. In their constant fighting amongst themselves for position, they killed each other as successfully, if not as quickly, as the nosferatu did."

Paul pressed his lips together and shook his head, clearly unhappy with such an answer. "But this club was the center of vampire activity before the nosferatu arrived. You've purchased and reopened it. For what purpose, if not to reestablish the community here in San Francisco?"

"John Polidori was a friend of mine; I didn't want to see his legacy—such as it is—in ashes. If you are seeking a leader, do not look to me. If someone else wishes the position, he need not fear I'll challenge him."

"We don't need just anyone," Paul said. "We need strength. The nosferatu massacred the elders, yet you remained in the city and lived. My consort was one of those killed; I won't lose another."

Colin glanced at Fia. The only humans brought into the community were those a vampire intended to turn. A human could not be fed from daily for long; it became too dangerous. Yet she was comfortable among them, and obviously familiar to many. Either she had known of vampires before Paul had lost his partner, or she'd absorbed knowledge from him and entrenched herself in the community very quickly. "Then you'd best learn to protect her better. I've little interest in leading a group of vampires who would use a human as their weapon and shield."

"Yet *you* feed from them?"

And another had grown bold. Colin barely glanced at the speaker—dark and tall, shaven head, his leather vest exposing his muscular arms and a tattoo of a wolf. There were advantages to his extraordinary—*nosferatulike*—speed; Colin memorized the vampire's appearance in that swift look, though to the vampire, it would seem as if Colin hadn't given him the slightest acknowledgment.

As an insult, the cut direct had been much more effective in London's drawing rooms—instead of being silenced the vampire's voice rose and rang with challenge. "You endanger all of us. The elders should never have allowed such as you to roam the streets."

Such as him? Colin's amusement returned. "They attempted to stop me . . . once. Will you try to do the same now?"

"You fought them?" Fia's question was echoed by uneasy murmurs.

Colin raised his heel to the sofa cushion, rested his elbow on his knee. His smile was as lazy as his posture. "I'd no need for such drastic measures," he told her. "Would *you* kill such as me?"

Her lips parted as her gaze slid over his features. For an instant, she stopped breathing . . . then shook herself out of it. "Yes. If you didn't follow the community's rules."

Delighted by her response, Colin laughed softly. "Your elders found that they could not kill me. And why should they? When I first came to this city, there was no vampire community here, and worldwide the requirement of partnerships and bloodsharing was in its nascent stages; our numbers weren't high enough to warrant it."

As the vampire population rose, it became a requirement of most communities that each vampire have at least one bloodsharer, so that they'd not feed from humans. Almost all vampires paired up in twosomes or threesomes and exchanged blood between themselves. It was an arrangement that had evolved from the need for secrecy; even a single vampire would be found out if he needed to hunt each night.

But for Colin.

He agreed with the reasoning behind bloodsharing, though he could not do it—and he would not tolerate being *told* how to live. "Why should I submit to a rule that didn't exist when I was born?"

"For our protection," Paul said, as if it were that simple.

"You've been watching me feed for months; have my activities drawn human notice?"

"No." Once again, the bold vampire with the wolf tattoo spoke. This time, Colin caught a hint of frustration and bewilderment in his psychic scent. From his inability to understand how Colin could feed undetected, unremembered?

Even Colin did not fully understand it.

"But that doesn't mean you won't be discovered in the future."

"I have not in two hundred years," Colin said with a careless shrug, and returned his attention to Paul and Fia. "I've no intention of bloodsharing, or discontinuing my hunts. I've no intention of leading you. I fear I don't have what you're looking for."

"You have answers."

Yes, but most of these vampires were too eager to fall into line, to follow. He couldn't imagine what they'd become if they received some of the truth. Individually, it might be safe, but a group would likely become a cult, speculating on realms they'd never see: Caelum, Hell, Chaos.

Participating in rituals, carelessly playing with curses and symbols.

"I also have a tan," he said as he rose to his feet. Several vampires took a step back; Paul and his human did not flinch. "If there is anything else I can provide you, do ask it of me."

Fia's mouth flattened with her disappointment. "Maybe you could lower the thermostat? You've got the air-conditioning on at the bar and in the DJ station, but it's blasting heat everywhere else."

"I'd hate for my employees to suffer discomfort. Are *you* uncomfortable?"

"No, but—" She waved toward the vampires, her partner. Their skin glistened with perspiration.

"I daresay no human here is. More to the point, neither am I—so I'll not likely adjust it. I find that seventy-two degrees is a near perfect temperature." In the nightclub, at any rate. Colin lifted her hand from the table, pressed a kiss to the back of it, and left a folded business card in her palm.

She looked up, startled. He only smiled and walked away through the gyrating bodies, toward his suite of rooms.

He didn't bother to turn on the lights. Though he'd only moved in a month previous, he was as familiar with these rooms as he'd been with his house. He'd lived in the Victorian mansion in the Haight for over a century—now he waited for *its* restoration to be completed.

The soundproofing around the suite erased the heavy electronic heat. Three symbols were carved into the door frame, and he might have used them only to silence the noise from outside, but the spell they cast also prevented any communication from being sent or received. The form of communication did not matter; a phone call, an e-mail, or sign language were equally useless.

His computer screen glowed softly in the corner of his office. His message to Lilith was short: **My dear Agent Milton, you may soon expect a call from Paul and Fia. She's human, but he'll likely transform her soon. She is the brains; they share the bollocks. Your compliments had best be poetry to my exquisite ears, because your sodding little experiment is a bloody pain in my arse.**

Lilith could interpret that as she pleased.

Christ, what a nuisance this had all become. After Lilith and her unlikely partner—Hugh Castleford, a former Guardian, knight, and composer of horrid prose—had out-wagered Lucifer and saved Castleford's students from the nosferatu seven months before, the nosferatu had been teleported to the Chaos realm and the Gates to Hell closed for five hundred years.

With such a resounding success, Colin had never imagined there'd be a need to recruit vampires to fight rogue demons, that Lilith would continue playing secret agent under the same Homeland Security directorate as the FBI—within the newly established and vaguely named Special Investigations division—or that she and Castleford would head operations from a dilapidated warehouse in Hunter's Point. The agency had three primary functions: to slay the demons and nosferatu who remained on Earth, to conceal from the human population and cover up all otherworldly activity, and to train novice Guardians and vampires.

Which, Colin supposed, suited Lilith and her partner well—she liked nothing better than to lie, and Castleford nothing better than to lecture.

Still, it was absurd. But nothing equaled the absurdity of the Guardians and their blasted Ascension, which had left the angelic corps reduced to a few dozen warriors—a force incapable of containing the hundreds of rogue demons who'd escaped from Below before the Gates had closed, or the nosferatu who'd yet to crawl from their caves. Even Castleford, for all he lacked in style, had the grace to Fall and give up his Guardian immortality, rather than Ascend and leave Earth defenseless.

Nor had Colin imagined that he'd involve himself in SI's operations and become part of that defense. He hadn't resisted Lilith's suggestion that he appear in public to gauge the vampire community's knowledge of things Above and Below, and to enlist those who could be of use to her. Initially, it had been an amusing diversion, but the level of attention he'd garnered from the vampire community had been . . . unpleasant.

They should look and admire; they shouldn't expect anything in return.

Colin leaned back, stared up at the ceiling. He'd known that others had watched him and his movements over the past few months, but he hadn't realized they'd catalogued his victims and analyzed the results. Statistically, dark-haired women would be his primary source of blood—but statistics wouldn't account for the trend they'd observed.

An obsession, fueled by guilt. This one would burn out soon, as well.

A chime from his computer alerted him to the incoming mail. Lilith, likely with an effusive description of his beauty. He wasn't in the mood for it.

But he stayed his hand from closing the program. It wasn't from Lilith, but Savitri Murray, who lived in the apartment above Castleford's garage. Who played with her electronic devices and kept the books at her grandmother's restaurant. Who never looked at anything with fear, but instead a wide-eyed curiosity. Dark, lovely Savitri.

The message was probably a mistake—something in which she'd accidentally replied to all of the original recipients instead of just Castleford or Lilith.

The subject line said only, **A question . . . Help?**

His lips twitched. Always questions with her. Endless questions.

She wouldn't look to him for answers. His smile faded, but he opened the e-mail, intrigued.

Is there any *good* reason for a nosferatu to take the overnight flight from London to New York?

He stared at the screen, dread freezing an icy knot in his chest. No idle question, this. An airliner from Heathrow had crashed into the Atlantic the previous week, the cause of the malfunction unknown. And Colin knew Savi was scheduled to return from India via London that evening.

Oh, bloody hell.

❧

The probability of this ending well was a big fat zero.

Savi went back once, just to make certain her eyes hadn't deceived her—she wished they had. There, in the aisle seat, near the starboard wing: a pale face with liver-slice lips. No eyebrows. Huge, muscular form. Cap pulled down over its ears to hide their pointed tips.

Nosferatu.

She quickly glanced away.

The flight attendant smiled apologetically when Savi returned to the cabin, as if good flight attending should have included the power to prevent Savi's bladder from reaching the breaking point while the two restrooms in first class were in use. "Is there anything I can bring to you, Miss Murray?"

Do you have a sword in your little beverage cart?

Savi shook her head. With luck, this would be over before Nani woke from her nap. She would be disappointed; Savi had promised her grandmother she wouldn't use the computer on the long flight home.

But then, Nani was often disappointed in her.

"Asha looked very beautiful," her grandmother said without opening her eyes.

"Yes, Nani," Savi said automatically as she sat down and checked her e-mail for replies. Thank god the airline provided Internet access through a LAN connection—it would be easier if she could use a phone, or the microphone in her headset, but the nosferatu might hear her speaking. E-communication was her safest option.

"Her hair was exactly as a bride's should be. You should grow yours out. No suitable boy is searching for a hedgehog to be his wife."

"No suitable boy is searching for a college dropout, either," Savi muttered, and glanced away from the screen.

Nani's face was drawn and tired; the trip to Mumbai had been difficult for her. Like Savi, she had delicate bones and a slim frame—but she'd not had Savi's luck in avoiding the parasites and bacteria that were so easy to pick up abroad. She'd spent a good portion of the month dehydrated, unable to eat or drink without losing it later.

Despite her frailty, Nani's voice was steady, strong. "You're twenty-six, *naatin*. You are beautiful, but if you wait much longer you will have only divorcés and shop owners to choose from."

Savi fought the hysterical giggle that rose in her throat. The nosferatu wouldn't leave much for a divorcé or a shop owner to marry.

Her instant messenger connected, and she scanned the list of online friends. No one she could trust to call Lilith or Hugh, or even the vampire. What time was it in San Francisco? Nine in the evening, but perhaps Lilith and Hugh were near their computers at home.

Just in case, she duplicated the e-mail and sent it as a text message to their cell phones, then surfed to find a news article about the plane that had gone down the previous week. She'd only caught the headline during their trip. Now she needed details.

Overnight flight—the *same* flight. No survivors. Preliminary inquiry suggested it hadn't been a mechanical failure, nor an explosive—and there were rumors the bodies found had sustained injuries inconsistent with a crash.

How easy would it be for a nosferatu to kill everyone on board, then leap out mid-air? It could fly quickly enough to reach Europe again before the sun rose, or go west to America—or simply dive into the ocean and wait for the next evening before emerging.

What time had the flight gone down?

Twelve fifty-eight Eastern. Savi's heart stopped. Less than an hour. Would the nosferatu keep the same pattern? Most likely; Hugh had once told her they hated change, hated to veer from a familiar course.

Nani sighed. "You've been so difficult since we returned from that place."

Caelum. Savi's throat tightened, but her voice was light as she said, "I was difficult before that."

A messenger window popped up. **No, my sweet Savitri. Are you in the air?**

Colin. She'd avoided the vampire for seven months, but now her eyes flooded with tears of relief. Except for brief meetings in which his affectations had known no bounds, she hadn't spoken with him. And he'd never been the least bit apologetic, as if he thought she didn't remember what he'd done in Caelum. A few times she'd caught him watching her—probably wondering why she hadn't said anything of it to anyone. It must prick his vanity to be ignored.

It pricked hers knowing how stupid she'd been to trust him. Now she had no choice but to trust him again.

Yes. She added the flight number and a link to the news article.

She didn't expect an immediate response. Colin would be trying to reach Lilith and Hugh, or one of the SI agents who handled this type of thing.

This type of thing. Again that hysterical laughter threatened. Seven months ago, she hadn't known this type of thing existed. Had known nothing of Guardians, who protected humans from demons and nosferatu. Nothing of vampires. What she had known she'd considered little more than a fantasy, spun from books into video and card games—and she'd profited well from it.

Now she'd probably pay.

It only took two minutes for Colin to get back to her. **Lilith is sending a fledgling to the Gate to collect Michael or Selah.**

Michael or Selah. Both Guardians could use Savi as an anchor, and they could teleport from Caelum directly into the airplane. But the Gate nearest to San Francisco was in southern Oregon. How quickly could a young Guardian fly?

E.T.A?

Forty-five minutes.

Oh, god. Too close. She stared at the screen and willed the number to decrease. But wishing had never helped her before; it wouldn't now. She didn't have time, she didn't have a sword or a hellhound or a gun—what did she have?

Hellhound venom. Hugh had given it to her along with a few other methods of protection. It was in a perfume vial—a significant payload, enough to paralyze the nosferatu, but she had no way to deliver it. Stabbing wouldn't work; the creature was too fast. And even if she managed to cut it with a venom-laced blade, it wouldn't slow it enough to allow her to get away. Not a lot of damage could be done with the few items she had—a plastic fork to the eye?

The big fat zero was growing morbidly obese.

As if concerned by her lack of reply, Colin wrote, **Do not be afraid, sweet Savitri.**

I'm not. Not for herself. But Nani, the other passengers?

You should be. A round yellow face suddenly winked up at her.

"Shh, *naatin*," Nani admonished a moment later. Savi stifled her laughter; it had too sharp an edge, anyway. "You waste too much time with those friends online." The rest lay unspoken: Had Savi not spent so much time on her computer, she'd have passed her classes, finished her studies, obtained the almighty degree. It did not need to be spoken; it had been said a million times. Nani meant well, of course—it was just that Savi's idea of what was good for her conflicted with her grandmother's.

But it was hard to blame it on a generation gap when a two-hundred-year-old vampire finished a sentence with a smiley.

She closed her eyes, tried to imagine his expression at that moment. His features were impossible to forget: his short hair, like burnished gold; the darker, slashing brows; thick lashes around wintry gray eyes. A blond god, with a deity's careless cruelty; the firm line of his mouth suggested it, and his smile was a predator's.

Was that wink to reassure her or to mock her?

Talk to me, sweet. Can you see it?

Savi turned, leaned out over the aisle. **The top of its head.** It took only another minute to locate the seating plan from the airline website and send him the link and seat number.

You're in first class?

Nani's with me. And the reason she'd chosen the ridiculously expensive tickets. Savi had insisted over Nani's protests, citing reasons that ranged from her grandmother's age to the fatigue of the endless flight and multiple connections.

Did it accomplish anything? Is she impressed by what you've made of yourself, or does she think you more reckless than ever, tossing away money?

Ah, there it was. She could almost hear the aristocratic accent, the lazy viciousness.

Are you deliberately trying to piss me off?

Yes. The nosferatu will eat your fear. It's ambrosia to such as us.

She sighed. Surely he realized that seven months of living near Lilith had inured her to such melodrama. And he didn't need to convince her that the nosferatu was terrible, evil—she knew what it was.

I'm not afraid, she repeated.

She didn't add that if he asked again in forty minutes and Michael still hadn't shown, he'd get a completely different answer. Colin took as much pleasure in producing fear as he did in his appearance. And Savi was easy—but not *that* easy.

CHAPTER 2

Caelum is ... beyond beautiful. A fitting home for once-humans who call themselves Guardians, and who claim their powers have an angelic source. I've heard Hell described exactly as you imagine it: fire and brimstone, cities crawling with demons, and torture pits. But Chaos—no one will tell me anything about Chaos. I've had to guess most of it.

—*Savi Murray, in a secured e-mail to Detective Taylor, 2007*

❧

Colin tore his hands through his hair and tried to ignore the voice yelling at him through his speakerphone. "Make sure she stays calm, Colin, or I'll rip your balls off! Tell her to get into that bathroom right now and use the fucking symbols."

Shut up, Lilith. He didn't say it aloud, because she would rip his balls off. They'd regenerate, but he liked that part of his anatomy too much to lose it, even temporarily. He said through clenched teeth, "Agent Milton, my dear, you are *not* helping. Where's Castleford?"

At times, it was much easier to deal with the former Guardian; his self-control was near legendary, his focus unrelenting. Lilith's was ... not, and the more she cared for the person threatened, the more demonic she became.

Colin had no intention—*no time*—to manage her fear over his own.

He heard the deep draw of her breath through the speaker, the buzz of her motorcycle. Her tone was slightly more even when she continued. "Training the newbie vamps over in the

Mission. He's on his way now. I'm almost to our place. That plane—I *knew* it. The bloodsucker probably thinks it's an abomination for humans to fly. Goddammit, I've been stonewalled for a week by the FAA and the British—"

"Lilith!"

Another deep breath. Then softly, "This is going to kill him, Colin."

No, the only thing that might kill Castleford would be losing Lilith; but Colin realized it was something he could use to convince Savitri to hide. Her relationship with Castleford echoed that of a brother and sister—she might not fear for herself, but she might do as Colin asked for Castleford's sake.

"Get her in there, Colin. I don't care what you have to do or say. You're beautiful; promise her use of your glorious body for the next fifty years."

"You don't have to manipulate me, Lilith," he muttered. Recollection of Savitri's caramel skin, her scent, and the taste of her blood might tempt *him*, but he doubted he would have the same effect on her.

Castleford wants you to take Auntie to the washroom and use the protection of the symbols to keep the nosferatu out.

He waited restlessly for her reply, rubbing at a spot of Prussian blue on his palm. Caelum had become yet another obsession, but it slipped away with each stroke of his brush. And as with all that was elusive, he only pursued it the more. Soon his memory of Caelum would be a pale imitation of the images on canvas.

Run, Savitri. Hide.

"Is she going?"

If Michael and Selah arrive before the nosferatu begins killing everyone, there's no need to hide. And if I use them to put the spell around the restroom and hid inside, Michael and Selah wouldn't be able to teleport into it to save us if they arrived after the nosferatu killed everyone. So unless Michael can carry an airplane, we'd die anyway. The symbols couldn't protect us from a crash.

She had to be logical. "Can Michael carry an airplane?" Colin asked aloud. It wouldn't surprise him if the Doyen could. Michael could heal injuries, transform humans into

Guardians, and teleport across realms. All other Guardians possessed only one unique Gift in addition to incredible strength, speed, and the ability to shape-shift and create clothing with a thought—but their leader was an exception to that rule.

"What? No." Lilith paused, and the sound of the motorcycle died. "I don't think so. It doesn't matter, Colin: lie to her. Hell, give me two minutes to get inside and online and I'll do it myself."

I have venom. I have an idea—just in case.

He typed his response with inhuman speed. No, Savi. Whatever it is, don't try it. Lilith's almost ready to talk to you. Wait for her.

She'll lie to me. I'm giving Michael until 9:50. I can't wait longer than that. There are four hundred people on here, Colin.

His gaze fell to the clock in the corner of his screen, and his gut twisted. He tried to think of a lie, tried to think of anything that might convince her.

Tried to think of anything he could say that she would trust.

I have to close my computer. Give my love to Hugh and Lilith.

Suicide. No question where she'd learned it. Just like Castleford.

You're human, sweet. Wait for the Guardians. And to make her smile, even if he could not: You must wait to see me again, if nothing else.

They'd better hurry, vampire. Even you aren't pretty enough to stop a nosferatu. But perhaps I'll flash a picture of you at him first, just to see.

A smiley grinned up at him. He stared at it, unable to believe she'd be such an idiot. He had been attacked by one of the nosferatu two centuries before; the result had not been as lovely as his face suggested. Three people—two of them Savitri's friends—had been mutilated and killed earlier that year. Did she think because Castleford and Lilith had pulled off the impossible that she had gained some kind of imperviousness by association?

What the bloody fucking hell was wrong with her? Did she have absolutely no sense of self-preservation? Had she learned nothing when she'd been in Caelum? She'd evaded his presence so well since they'd returned he knew she'd not forgot *all* of it. Why would she be so stupid and careless, taking another risk with her life like this?

The messenger logged her out.

"I'm going to kill you, Colin." Lilith's voice was low and dangerous.

He bit his tongue. Blood filled his mouth, and he rang off without a word.

❧

Savi decided that she wouldn't need protection from the nosferatu—it would either kill her or it wouldn't—but she would from the other passengers. Did Britain have anything similar to the U.S.'s Federal Air Marshal program? Would there be armed guards undercover on international flights? Savi had been shot before; she didn't want to repeat the experience. But it would take too much time to find out—better to just look after herself and Nani as best she could after she'd killed the damned thing.

The battery pack slid out easily. Not much room to maneuver, but her hands were slender, her fingers long. Her lovers had often complimented them, as if she'd come by their design through accomplishment instead of genetics.

Her other tools were in her checked luggage; it was impossible to carry on screwdrivers and clippers. They'd have made this easier, but they weren't necessary.

She smiled to herself. A screwdriver to the nosferatu's eye—*that* would have been interesting, though probably no safer or more effective than a plastic fork.

She reached into the empty battery slot, and paused. Not smart to let anyone see her do this. Though most of the passengers reclined in their seats and slept, a few were reading or using their computers. The flight attendant might pass by at any moment, and would be justifiably suspicious if she saw Savi tearing out the guts of her laptop.

No, it's not a bomb that I'm making, but I do intend to maim—and hopefully kill—a cursed bloodsucking fiend. Do you mind holding this penlight for me?

That wouldn't go over well. Nor would Savi's assurance that it would all be unnecessary if Michael and Selah arrived. *I know a couple of humans who've been given angelic superpowers and*

Gifted with an ability to teleport; they can pop right into the plane and teleport the fiend away faster than you can blink. You probably won't even notice.

No.

A blanket over her lap hid evidence of her not-quite-terrorism, if not the movements beneath it. Perhaps the flight attendant would think she was masturbating.

Dammit. That's what she should have told Colin she'd be doing in her final hour: imagining Michael's face as she brought herself to multiple orgasms.

The insult to his vanity would've probably made his head explode.

"What are you doing, *naatin*?"

"Trying to find my power inductor, Nani." Savi ignored her grandmother's exasperated sigh and waited until she closed her eyes again. Nani had the ability to nap anytime, anywhere—within moments her breathing deepened, and a soft snore came from her throat.

Savi hooked her fingers in the gap between the battery housing and the power supply, clenched her jaw, and pulled with steady pressure. The plastic was the same as the outside casing, resistant against impact.

It finally cracked; she gasped in pain, then worked loose the small, flat piece and removed it. Her nail had torn in half. Fighting tears, she sucked on her fingers until the sting eased.

At least the injury was useful; she'd need the blood later.

The inductor retained the heat from its use, and it was probably better to unwind the wire while it was warm. No time to let it cool, anyway. It must be done slowly and carefully—a single kink in the thin length would ruin everything.

Another steady pull around the inductor's copper coil; this one was more difficult. Tiny screws held the inductor in place. They wouldn't give, but the iron bobbin in its plastic seat would.

Maybe. If her hand didn't give first; it already cramped from the awkward position and the force she applied. The edge of the broken casing cut into her knuckle, then suddenly sliced deeper as the bobbin snapped free. *Oh god, oh god.* She could barely move her fingers, so badly did they ache.

Breathing shallowly between her teeth, she used the nail of her left forefinger to find the end of the wire. It had been sealed, but she picked at it until the tip came free of the spool. Twenty-four gauge copper wire, seventy-five wraps around the bobbin. Almost two meters. She'd ordered it to those specifications less than two months before. The wire was thicker than a typical inductor coil, but she'd wanted to see how it performed with international voltage.

Not well; it fluctuated and overheated too easily. But it was as thick as piano wire, if not as sturdy—the tensile strength one-tenth that of steel.

It *should* work; the only real question was if she was strong enough, quick enough.

Probably not. But she had to try.

She gingerly placed the laptop beneath her seat and began unrolling the wire. Glanced at her slim gold watch. Twenty minutes.

❧

Savi knew very little about magic. She knew nothing of how the symbols worked, only that they did. *Silence. Surround. Lock.* Hugh had shown them to her for an emergency and explained the rules: the lock was keyed to the blood of whomever cast it. That person could go in and out as they pleased. Anyone else inside when the spell had been cast could leave, but not return. If no one remained inside or the symbols were destroyed, the spell broke.

And no one outside could hear through, enter, or break through the surround. No *being* could—but fire, flood? The structure was not impervious to damage from natural sources, including gravity and the crushing pressure of the Atlantic.

She wound the copper into a huge coil, slipped it over her neck. It had taken her five more minutes to prepare it than she'd anticipated.

"Nani!"

She didn't wait for her grandmother to come fully awake before pulling on the older woman's arm.

"*Naatin*, what—"

"I cut myself," Savi said quickly. "Help me in the bathroom?"

The restroom was vacant, thank god. She'd have hated to walk past the nosferatu bleeding like this. She pushed her grandmother in ahead of her, turned, and locked the door. Her earring post barely made a scratch in the plastic, but it was enough. She finished it with a dab of blood over each symbol.

Silence. The hum of the engines disappeared, though she could still feel the vibration beneath her feet.

Her heart pounded. It must have been doing so for a while, but this was the first she'd noticed its rapid pace, or the clammy perspiration on her face. Gooseflesh raised the fine hairs on her arms.

She took a deep breath to steady herself, to rebuild her mental blocks. Hugh had been teaching her to guard her mind since she'd returned from Caelum; she'd put the shields into place as soon as she'd recognized the nosferatu, but the toll of pain and stress might have weakened them.

No psychic emissions could penetrate the spell; before she exited, she'd make sure her shields were solid.

"*Naatin?*" Her grandmother's query held an edge of fear.

"Nani, there's a nosferatu on board—those things that killed Ian and Javier, you remember?" She lifted the hem of her long linen skirt and dabbed at her upper lip, her brow. Her fingers left a stain on the pale green.

It was going to be a bitch to run in.

Nani's mouth set in a thin line, and she shook her head. "Hugh destroyed them—"

"No, not all of them. There were a few that weren't part of Lucifer's bargain, and there's one here." Savi turned on the tap, clenched her teeth as the water washed away the blood. The wounds still seeped, and she wrapped tissue around them. Added more around her palms. "You're going to be safe in here—but you can't leave, okay? I'll be back in a minute or two."

"No, *naatin*. I forbid it."

She met Nani's gaze in the mirror. The same dark eyes—the same features, but for Savi's wild, spiky hair and slightly lighter skin. "There's no one else."

"Yes, there's no one else. You are the last, Savitri. I can't lose you, too."

"You won't," Savi said, her voice thick. "I promise you won't."

Nani's braid fell over her shoulder with the force of her headshake. Savi tucked it back. "You'll make me cry. You are too impetuous, too unsettled."

"I know." She bent and kissed her grandmother's forehead, then turned.

"Savitri! Make a promise you can keep." Nani gripped her forearm. "Promise you will let me find a husband for you, so that you marry this year. Let me know you are in a good position before I die. Make an old woman happy for once."

She hesitated only for a moment. "Will you stay here if I promise?"

"Yes, *naatin*."

A short laugh escaped her, and she closed her eyes. "Alright, Nani. We'll find a suitable boy."

❧

Michael didn't come.

Despite everything, Savi had waited another two minutes, leaning back against the lavatory door and pasting a smile on her face as if nothing was wrong, as if her grandmother wasn't locked inside a toilet and surrounded by magic made from symbols Lilith had learned from Lucifer.

Savi had been rescued by a Guardian once before; perhaps that one time was all her karma allowed. Perhaps every bit of good had been used up when she'd been nine years old and Hugh had thrown himself in front of her, attempting to shield her from a pair of bullets.

Even then, velocity had almost triumphed over virtue—one lead slug had passed a millimeter from her spine, the other an inch above her heart. Small distances in a small body, but had Hugh not been there, had his flesh not changed the bullets' speed and trajectory, she wouldn't have survived; the gunman had aimed for her head.

Her parents and her brother had not been so fortunate.

The flight attendant gave her a sympathetic smile. *Yes, they've been in India. Oh! Their poor intestines. The grandmother will be in there for some time. And there goes the younger, stretching her legs as she tries to settle her stomach.*

At least that's what Savi hoped she thought. Surely she wasn't thinking of breaking strain, force per square inch, friction, James Bond villains, and magical venom. But it was hard to determine; maybe those things did occupy the mind of a woman who spent most of her time thirty-five thousand feet in the air between Britain and America, surrounded by a thin shell of aluminum.

But the flight attendant probably didn't think about the venom. Savi didn't think about it much, either—she knew that Lilith had to cut into venom sacs beneath her hellhound's tongue to collect it, and that Sir Pup was awake when it happened.

It wasn't an operation that Savi liked to consider, and she was grateful she'd never seen it.

Down the portside aisle, past the sleeping businessmen and -women, to the coach class. Two blue seats near the windows, four in the center. The nosferatu was in the second row; she didn't look at it as she made her slow circuit, crossing to starboard behind the last line of seats in the cabin. Most of the passengers slept.

Michael? Selah? Now would be really, really good. The nosferatu's arm hung over its armrest, its fingers flexing. In anticipation? How had it afforded the flight? Where had it obtained identification? Had it simply slipped in with its inhuman speed? Was there a body in the cargo hold—or in the airport—belonging to the person who was supposed to have been in seat 29B?

She shook her head. It took some effort, but she quieted the portion of her brain that screamed for answers. Some things were very simple: Gravity made airplanes fall out of the sky when pilots and passengers were dead; a long distance divided by a short time made a fledgling's speed *too slow*; nosferatu were Evil, with a hatred of humanity, and no Rules preventing them from murder.

Worse than demons. Or vampires.

Or suitable boys.

She uncapped the hellhound venom and poured it into her

mouth, held it on her tongue. It tasted oddly sweet and heavy, like nectar from a sun-warmed peach. It was too bad her face had to be the delivery system.

The passenger behind the nosferatu had reclined his seat. Hopefully asleep—and hopefully he wouldn't mind that Savi was going to sit on his lap for a few seconds.

She lifted the wire coil from around her neck. Made a single loop.

Then she stepped into the row behind the nosferatu, dropped the loop over its head, and fell into hopefully-sleeping-guy's lap.

She didn't have to pull much; the nosferatu's powerful surge to its feet did most of the work. It yanked her forward, and she smashed into the seatback, almost swallowed the venom. The wire slid through her left hand, providing enough friction to tear and rip—her fingers, and judging by the sudden spray, its throat. Like pomegranate juice.

The copper snapped. *Oh god, oh god. Please let it have cut the carotid artery.* It wouldn't kill it, but it would give her time. Sleeping-guy yelled and struggled beneath her. She leapt up, her stomach against the headrest. Blood was everywhere. She sealed her lips against the side of the creature's gaping neck, the pumping blood, felt its hand come up, its nails digging into her right shoulder and she expelled the venom.

Like blowing up a balloon, Savi. A wet, cold, disgusting balloon.

Screams rang in her ears. The hand fell away from her shoulder as paralysis set into the creature—maybe it would be enough. It would have to be; it was all she could do.

She ran. A passenger managed to grab her skirt—but he couldn't hold on. That was the thing about momentum and velocity: it often won despite good intentions.

Locking the door was unnecessary, but she did anyway. Nosferatu blood covered her chin, was *in* her mouth, her throat. She gagged and spat into the sink, splashed at her face. Her right arm and her fingers were numb. Nani sat on the commode and quietly sobbed into her hands.

Savi smiled weakly, forcing out her words through the

chattering of her teeth, the sudden shivering that had overtaken her body. "A surgeon? A neurosurgeon. Ivy League.
Fair-skinned. Tall and handsome."

But not too handsome.

§

". . . so . . . beautiful . . ." The blonde moaned the words as
she came. The third woman that night, but he could not stop
drinking. A dull ring in his ears—his cell phone, Colin realized dimly. Lilith.

He didn't want to know. Neither Selah nor Michael had
been in Caelum; the fledgling Guardian Lilith had sent had
been forced to wait until one of them had returned. It had taken
more than an hour and a quarter before the fledgling alerted
Selah. Colin had flipped on the television once, only to hear of
"Terror in the Skies."

Then he'd left to hunt.

He broke away and pushed the sleep onto her. She fell
limp, unconscious in his arms. He sliced his lip and mixed his
blood with hers to heal the punctures. He'd almost taken too
much, but she was strong, young. She'd recover quickly.

He let her slide to the linoleum floor in a boneless, quivering heap. Her groceries still sat on the counter. He paused to
inhale the scent of oranges, then shoved the bags into the refrigerator and carried her to her bedroom. A nice, tidy flat. A
moderately intelligent woman, but she shouldn't have invited
a stranger up, no matter how lonely she was, nor how handsome and strong and helpful he'd seemed.

She'd not learn a lesson from it, however; she'd forget
him by the morning. Or, at best, remember him as a very
pleasant—and very beautiful—dream. Perhaps she'd question the haphazard placement of the groceries in the refrigerator, but she'd never think a vampire had fed from her in
that kitchen.

No, she'd likely blame her job, or her exhaustion, or tell
herself she was being fanciful.

Small wonder they needed the Guardians' protection.

He pulled her blankets over her; she sighed and rocked her
hips against the mattress. He contemplated waking her, but
he'd indulged that lust with the first woman.

And it was not bloodlust that had driven him to the third.

His phone rang again as he walked through the living room. A mirror hung over the sofa. He'd closed his eyes and refused to listen when he'd passed it before, loaded down like a footman. Now he stared into it. Perhaps the screams would drown out Lilith's voice when he answered her call. She wouldn't hear them, though she was no stranger to their like.

"Yes, Agent Milton?"

"I'm not going to kill you after all. I need a favor."

"Do you?"

In the mirror, a human body was devoured, torn apart by a flying beast. The human's face remained, frozen into the glacial sky, shrieking.

Chaos.

"Damage control. I'm flying to New York with Michael; Hugh's there with Selah, and she's ready to jump in, but we need her back as soon as possible. That means you have to handle . . . Colin, what the fuck is wrong with you? You should have asked me to call you beautiful by now."

"I was feeding," he said, his voice flat.

"And her declarations were enough? That's revolting. Listen, I need you to take Savi out, let her be seen by as many people as possible. Preferably a cop or two, as well. Auntie, you can leave at home with Sir Pup."

He looked away from the mirror, massaged his eyelids with thumb and forefinger. "She killed it?"

"Garroted it with a wire from her laptop, then pumped it full of venom," Lilith said, and laughed. Colin thought he detected a note of pride beneath it. "It's not dead, though, just paralyzed. Michael teleported it to the holding cell at SI. Savi's in the bathroom with Auntie; Hugh says Savi will wait until there's no other choice before she lowers the symbols' protection. But we're going to have to deal with the mess, spin a story—there must be a lot of witnesses, and the body disappeared mid-flight. The plane lands in half an hour. Selah will bring them to our house then, so be there. We should arrive in New York just after that; we're over Nebraska or some godforsaken place now."

He'd have Savi to himself for the entirety of the evening? A slow grin slipped over his mouth; Colin walked out of the flat, careful to turn the lock on the doorknob. He couldn't engage the dead bolt from outside, but it wouldn't have kept something like him out anyway. "You're flying there with Michael; is he *carrying* you? How primitive, Agent Milton."

"Yeah, and I'm fucking freezing. A garrote!" She burst into laughter again.

A masculine voice rumbled in the background. Lilith must have covered the mouthpiece with her hand; Colin could only hear the sharp tones of her reply. He stepped outside. The clouds had thinned into pale ribbons, and the moon hung round and heavy above the skyline. A block away, his Bentley sat by the curb; it'd take most of the half hour to drive across the city to Castleford's house in Merced Manor. Much faster to run, but not half as stylish.

"Michael says to tell you that he found something of yours by the fountain. What the hell does that mean?"

He almost stumbled over the curb. Why hadn't the Guardian killed him? Castleford would have. "It means that Savitri is going to have a very, very good time," he finally managed.

Ridiculous, to think of this as a second chance with Savi. A second chance for what? He'd only spoken at any length with her twice: fifteen minutes in her grandmother's restaurant, and a few hours in Caelum. She was a bright young woman, certainly, but one he'd vowed not to pursue. His temporary obsession and their mutual enthrallment in Caelum was hardly reason to risk his friendship with Castleford and Lilith.

The motor roared to life, but its growl was nothing to Lilith's. "Colin, it's not just Hugh anymore—she's my sister now, too."

As if he could forget.

❧

The vibration of the engines stopped. Savi lifted her head from Nani's silk-covered lap. Only two and a half hours had passed; the pilots must have continued on to New York instead of returning to England.

A swipe of wet tissue across the symbols erased the blood. From outside, she heard orders to come out, threats of armed agents and lethal force.

"Michael, Selah," she said softly. "We're ready."

Selah immediately appeared in front of her—all golden skin and blond hair. A white flowing gown. No wings, but they probably wouldn't have fit in the bathroom.

And then she and Nani were home.

CHAPTER 3

I do not see any danger in telling P—— the truth, but for the details regarding the sword. We should not let it become known our family harbored your Doyen's dragon-tainted weapon from the time of the Crusades. It is not the curiosity of humans I fear, should the connection be discovered, but we ought not to risk the attention of the horned and winged set.

—Colin to Ramsdell, 1814

Somehow, Selah managed to avoid the piles of hardware and wiring materials littering Savi's apartment. Despite the successful landing, Savi had to help steady her grandmother—though she wasn't too steady herself; teleportation was disorienting.

Their luggage appeared on the wooden floor next to them, along with her laptop, and Savi sighed in silent envy. Guardians, demons, nosferatu, and hellhounds had the ability to hold items in an invisible pocket of space . . . or something. No matter how many questions she'd asked, Savi had never been able to determine exactly what it was, but it resembled the hammerspace in a video game: it didn't matter the size or shape of the item, the Guardians could shove it into their cache, carry it around without effort, then make it reappear with a thought.

Selah gave a quick smile before shifting her form. For a moment, Savi stared at a mirror image of herself, down to the clothes and jewelry. Then Selah altered it slightly, darkening her skin, widening her face, narrowing her eyes, thinning her lips.

"Colin will be here in a few minutes," the Guardian said, and her voice was also like Savi's—perhaps a bit lower in tone. "Follow his instructions. I need your clothes; I can't return them. Tomorrow, take the files you need off the computer. I'll come back for it then."

Lilith must already be at work, changing the story, creating lies, and destroying evidence. Savi nodded her permission for Sclah to take them; her skirt, sandals, and shirt vanished into Selah's hammerspace, and Savi stood barefoot on the cold floor in her underwear.

Nani shook her head. "You won't leave me nude," she said in her accented English.

"We'll worry about yours later. With luck, they won't get past Savi to look at you. I've got to get back before they charge the bathroom. I hope they don't shoot me."

Savi winced. "Sorry." Bullets wouldn't kill a Guardian, but they'd still cause considerable pain.

"No worries; I'm tough." Selah disappeared.

Nani sank onto the sofa with a sigh, kicked off her sandals. "Dress yourself, *naatin*. You'll become ill."

Savi crossed her arms beneath her breasts, shivering. Not just clothes—a shower was a necessity; she didn't want to stink of fear and blood and nosferatu when Colin arrived.

She found her bathrobe in her luggage and shrugged it on, wincing as the rough terry slid over her shoulder. She had to tie the belt one-handed.

A scratch sounded at the door connecting her apartment to Hugh's house. Sir Pup. And the vampire, if the knock accompanying it was any indication.

Dammit. She glanced around the apartment—the silk paintings, the DemonSlayer posters, the jumble of mismatched furniture—and sighed. No time to straighten anything. Nani would likely spend the entire meeting apologizing for Savi's clutter.

She opened the door, and the hellhound streaked through and almost toppled her over in his eagerness to welcome her home. Then he stopped and growled, each of his three heads swinging around as if to search out the source of the nosferatu scent.

"It's okay, Sir Pup," Savi told him. "It's just Nani and me.

I had an adventure." Smiling wryly, she lifted her gaze to Colin's face.

Oh, god. It wasn't fair. She'd prepared herself for it, yet still her breath caught and her heart began to hammer in her chest. And he knew it. Her psychic shields blocked her emotions, but couldn't hide her physical reaction.

Yet there was no mockery in his eyes as he looked her over. His perusal was quick, intense. "Invite me in, Savitri," he said quietly.

The request startled a laugh from her. "Vampires don't need an invitation." She pitched her voice low as well; Nani knew Colin wasn't human, but probably assumed he was like Michael and Selah. Perhaps even Lilith. No one had disabused her of the notion—her fear of the nosferatu was too great. She had accepted Hugh's friends and background, but she wouldn't like knowing Colin was basically half-nosferatu. Demons, Guardians . . . they were tolerable. Nosferatu were not.

"No," he said, and the tips of his fangs showed when he smiled. "But I am a gentleman, and a gentleman doesn't enter a woman's house uninvited."

She willed her heartbeat to return to its normal pace. She needed to step away from the door, put some distance between them, but it was difficult not to stare. That golden hair, artistically messy. His sculpted cheekbones and angular jaw. The lean, elegant length of him in his tailored trousers and soft, clinging sweater. How did he manage it when he couldn't even see himself in a—

There, a reason for escape. She swallowed and nodded. "Alright, but give me a second?"

His smile widened. "Of course, sweet Savitri."

She felt his gaze follow her as she walked across the living room to the cheval mirror that stood in the corner. Nani rose to her feet and narrowed her eyes disapprovingly. "You cannot leave him at the door, *naatin*," she said in Hindi. Then added in English, "Mr. Ames-Beaumont, please come in."

"It's okay, Nani." Savi turned the mirror to face the wall, and looked around for any that she'd missed. "I'm just making sure he'll be good company, instead of ignoring us in favor of admiring himself."

"Savitri!"

"Don't scold her, Auntie," Colin said, laughing. "She has the right of it. There is another by the kitchen, Savi. Sailor Moon?"

She shot him a surprised glance as she flipped over the small frame depicting anime characters in schoolgirl uniforms.

"A short obsession . . . with their equally short skirts," he added as if in explanation, then turned his attention to her grandmother. "Mrs. Jayakar, you are as beautiful as ever."

She blushed and patted her hair. "And you are too kind to an old woman."

His brows rose. "Hardly old." He bent and kissed her cheek. "If it weren't akin to cradle-robbing, I'd steal you away and ravish you so completely you'd never leave my arms."

Savi couldn't stop her grin as her grandmother swatted his arm and protested his audacity, laughing. Even Nani was not immune to his looks and charm. After the tension and fear of their flight, this was exactly what she needed.

But unfortunately, they couldn't stay there. "I'm going to get ready," Savi said. "Where are you taking me? Any dress code I should follow?"

His assessing gaze swept from her bare feet to the tips of her hair. "Not a tattered housecoat."

And that easily, he declared her inadequate. Her mouth flattened, and she bit off her automatic reply. Nani did not approve of *gaalis*.

"You're going out?" Dismay filled her grandmother's voice, and Savi sighed.

"I have to be seen, Nani, so that no one can say I was on that plane. No suitable boy is going to marry a girl who's a terrorist."

She ignored the sharpening of Colin's expression and waited for Nani's reluctant nod before she headed for the bathroom.

"Savi," Colin said, and she glanced back over her shoulder. "Anything you put on will be appropriate."

"Only because they won't be looking at me anyway."

His delighted grin warmed the room—or her blood. It just wasn't *right* for a man to be that beautiful. Even Guardians and demons who could shape-shift into ideal forms couldn't equal Colin when he smiled.

"They will," he said, ". . . after a while."

§

Colin angled the lamp, shining the light more fully onto the painting. His masterpiece, if he'd ever had one. But it had not been his brushstrokes, the color, nor the composition that made it beautiful: it was the subject.

Caelum. The realm the Guardians made their home.

Seven months before, only Guardians and their angel predecessors had ever seen Caelum. But when Lucifer had threatened Savitri's life, Michael had teleported her to his temple in that realm, out of the demon's reach. Several days later, the Doyen had taken Colin so that Lucifer would not discover Colin's link to Chaos.

Lilith had not been able to escape as easily: a symbol on her chest anchored her to Hell and prevented her being teleported to Caelum. Moments before Michael had taken Colin to Caelum, before she and Castleford had left to face Lucifer, Castleford had requested that Colin bring Caelum back to her, and the painting Colin had created filled one wall in Castleford's living room.

He'd chosen the prospect from outside the doors of Michael's temple. It had been from that spot Colin had first seen the splendor of that realm; he didn't know if he'd managed to capture the effect for Lilith, but it still overwhelmed *him*.

He traced his fingers over the rough canvas, followed the curve of a spiraling tower in which the anterior edge of the lower spiral was the same as the posterior edge of the higher. What had Savitri said of the shape? He pondered for a moment. That it was the result of the Gestalt effect, he suddenly remembered; that they couldn't truly see it and their minds completed the form with the most rational interpretation. He'd painted what he'd seen—but she was correct; there was no sense in such a structure.

And she'd been as awestruck as he, naming most of Caelum's forms irrational. Indeed, the spires seemed too tall and thin to hold their weight; the sky too blue and the sun too bright; the waters surrounding the city too still.

How many times had she stopped him to point out a physical

impossibility? How many times had he pulled her along to show her another sublime arrangement of shape and shades of white?

She'd had to leave the day after Colin had opened the doors of the temple. He'd had two months; time given by Michael so he could paint—and recover.

But had she seen it better than he?

The click of Savi's heels sounded quick and light on the stairs. He resisted the urge to shut off the lamp, to give himself the advantage of darkness. In the months since his return, he had never observed her reaction to the painting.

She'd always run too quickly; the moment he arrived, she'd fled for the safety of her flat or the dark little office she kept downtown.

Savi stepped through the entrance to the living room, and paused. Her gaze slid past him. Her eyes darkened, her lips parted on a sharply indrawn breath.

And it was the only time in his long life he'd been pleased that something other than his face had caused such a response. Would that he could read her emotions as well, but as usual, her shields were firmly in place.

He smiled, and the change of his expression must have caught her attention; she narrowed her eyes at him. "Did you put my grandmother to sleep?"

"Yes," he said.

"I didn't know you could do that."

"You've never asked me, Savitri. I did not take her blood."

Oh, but to have Savi's again; to have the whole of her. He settled for looking, though he shouldn't have taken so much pleasure in that, either.

She'd chosen low-waisted, black trousers and a crimson silk top with sleeves that split at her shoulders, leaving her slim arms bare. Her skin seemed the warmer for the blue tones in the crimson; it shouldn't have. A long cream coat was draped over her forearm.

He didn't look at her shoes for fear that he might fall to his knees to examine the contrast of strap against ankle, the arch of her foot.

She glanced at the painting for an instant, and her mouth tightened. "Can other vampires? Can nosferatu?"

"No. Yes, if the human has little psychic resistance or if the nosferatu drinks the blood."

"Does Nani have resistance?"

"Not to me."

"Do I?"

"Yes."

She walked slowly into the room, circled the sofa, and leaned her hip against the upholstered back. "Why?"

"Why do you have more resistance? Or why did I suggest she sleep?"

A wry smile touched her mouth. She'd slicked clear gloss over her lips; they glistened as if she'd eaten a ripened fruit and forgotten to lick away the juice. "Both?"

He gave a small shake of his head.

"Why did you suggest she sleep?"

Was she aware of how much she gave away with that decision? Concern for her grandmother rather than protection for herself.

He had only six feet to cross to her side; he did it in an instant. She blinked, and he lifted her right hand. "I didn't want her to see me do this," he said. The scent of her perfume eddied around them: vanilla, jasmine. His mouth watered, and he swallowed before adding, "I can't heal it in the same way as Michael, but I can accelerate it and ease some of the pain."

His thumb smoothed over the raw tip of her forefinger, the gash on her knuckle. She winced and tugged her hand from his grip.

She shifted her coat to her opposite forearm and opened her left fist. "This?"

His breath hissed through his teeth. Deep, straight cuts across the first bend of her fingers; shallow slices over the center of her palm. They'd been cleaned, but they must be stiff and sore. "From the garrote?"

"Yes. I didn't have piano wire in my gold watch, unfortunately."

He chuckled softly. "The nosferatu is no 007. What are these?" Faint mahogany lines formed an intricate design on her palm. He gently turned her hand over, saw the same on the backs of her fingers. "Henna?"

"My friend's wedding."

A sudden image of those decorated hands sliding over his skin made him ache. He glanced up; she was staring at his mouth.

Would her lips taste as she smelled? Sweet Savitri. He'd only had her blood and her body—her tongue had been busy speaking of beauty that wasn't his. "Do you trust me?"

"No," she said. "But I'll let you, as it is your blood that will be spilled this time."

He stared at her for a long moment, his jaw clenching. Why hadn't he healed her in Caelum, and immediately put her to sleep? Whatever vague, lingering memory produced this continued resistance could have been prevented with little effort—but he'd not made it.

It didn't matter. This obsession *would* fade.

He viciously scraped his tongue beneath his fangs, and brought her hand to his mouth. She gasped as he painted the blood in short strokes over the wounds, then spun her around and pulled down the neckline of her shirt to do the same to four punctures on her shoulder. They were surrounded by livid bruises; the nosferatu's dark scent clung, despite her shower.

He lifted his head, fought to control his breathing, his arousal, his bloodlust. Her pulse raced in the hollow beneath her jaw.

"Colin—"

He closed his eyes at the tinge of fear in her voice. Wasn't that what he'd wanted? "Clean it off, Savitri. I'll wait in the car."

§

A cop pulled them over on Sunset. Savi wordlessly gave Colin her driver's license, and he handed it over along with his license and registration.

"I apologize for speeding, Officer," he said pleasantly. "I was distracted by my companion's sparkling repartee."

Savi squinted as the cop shined his flashlight over her face, and tried not to laugh. Silence had reigned between them from the moment she'd slid into the passenger seat, but in the midst of this absurdity, it was impossible to hold on to her anger or her fear.

"You were going ninety in a forty."

"Sparkling Savitri Murray," Colin said. "Like champagne. Sweet Savitri, my sparkling wine."

Two sobriety tests and a warning to install rearview and side mirrors later, Colin pulled back into traffic and sent her a sidelong glance. "Do you have credit cards?"

"Yes, but it's not necessary. I can fake the charges."

He shook his head. "We need more than a paper trail."

He took her to a convenience store, where she debated longer than necessary over the candy bars, making certain her face showed to the camera aimed down the aisle. A fast-food restaurant, where she argued with the manager about the temperature of her French fries.

"I feel like a bitch," she told him as she returned to the car with a free apple turnover. "Here I am, in a Bentley with Ramsdell Pharmaceutical's primary shareholder, and I'm complaining about a dollar's worth of food to a guy who probably makes less a week than I spent on my coat."

His smile didn't touch his eyes; his gaze was fixed on the red box in her hand. He inhaled deeply, then turned to look out the windshield. "We've done enough for now. We can go to a sit-down, if you're hungry."

She wasn't. "Are you?" Once, she'd seen him eat food at her grandmother's restaurant.

A smile hovered around his mouth. "I ate."

"Polidori's reopened when I was away; I'd like to see it." After a brief hesitation, he gave a stiff nod. She watched him steadily, trying to discern the reason for his tension. She opened the box and pinched off a bite. "Do you want some?"

"No."

"Do you like food?"

"I can't taste it. But the scent . . ." His lips firmed. "I remember some, particularly fruits and sweets. The cinnamon, the apples. Oranges—I had them several times." He looked at her, then away. "The privilege of aristocracy."

"Too exotic for the plebs?" As the younger son of the seventh earl of Norbridge, he'd have had access to a variety of luxuries a commoner could never have afforded.

"Yes. We had—have—an orangery at Beaumont Court. Though my nephews had transformed it into a fort upon my last visit."

"Do they know what you are?"

"Yes. I'm their beloved blood-drinking Uncle Colin, as I have been for generations."

"They don't think it's weird?"

"My youngest niece's response upon learning the truth was, 'Brill!'" Colin shook his head. "She was not a bit disturbed, though I'll admit to some dismay at her vocabulary. Worse, that the longer I visit, the more I adopt their speaking habits. That is the true horror, my sweet Savitri."

"Do they know about your sister and Anthony Ramsdell?"

He heaved a long sigh, but the amusement crinkling the corners of his eyes belied the harassed sound of it. "Yes. Indeed, I have to recount the events every Christmas season; the children especially enjoy it when I linger over my part—bedridden and starving, attacking Emily and trying to drink her blood until Castleford and Ramsdell arrived at the penultimate moment and rescued her from my evil clutches."

"Evil?" Grinning, she popped another bite of the apple turnover into her mouth.

"Quite, though they do not seem to believe it." His voice lowered dramatically. "Instead I must tell them stories of the evil demon Lilith, and of how Ramsdell thwarted her and returned Michael's magical sword to his possession after centuries in Beaumont Court's library. So, yes, Ramsdell has become a family legend, Castleford and Lilith slightly less so; alas, despite my exquisite appearance and the immortality I gained from their actions, I'm neither legend nor villain."

"I guess it's more exciting to hear tales of winged Guardians and demons than a mere vampire." She caught her tongue between her teeth to stop her laughter when he turned his head to stare at her, an aggrieved impatience creasing his brow. But his lips twitched slightly as he looked back toward the road.

"It's *most* disagreeable."

"And I suppose it also helps that his medical practice was the basis for Ramsdell Pharmaceuticals," Savi said. "Your family still reaps the benefit of it."

"Yes. When creating legends, possessing both virtue and money is an unbeatable combination. I have one, but have no inclination to acquire the other." He smiled briefly. "You do not have the history or familiarity with such things that my niece does, yet you have adjusted very well. Particularly considering your pagan roots."

"I don't know if that helps or hurts—have you seen Detective Taylor lately? Since she found out about all of this?" She shook her head when he arched a brow and replied in the negative. "Never mind. Despite all of the stuff in the restaurant, even in my apartment, I can't really say that Nani and I are pagan—or much of anything. Between Nani and Hugh, my upbringing was completely secular."

"Perhaps it is more shocking, then, your adjustment."

"Well, I'm not convinced anything I've learned is faith-affirming or -destroying; at most, a shifting of a paradigm. We don't really know."

Colin gave a short, disbelieving laugh. "Savitri, don't be absurd. You've not seen enough evidence? You've a rational explanation for Caelum, and its effect on us? For the symbols' protection, and the spell's prevention of communication of *any* form, as if it can recognize intent?"

"No. I don't," she admitted. "But what's the reason behind it? We have an explanation that it all derived from Heaven, that demons were created when they followed Lucifer in his rebellion, that the nosferatu were cursed with bloodthirst and vulnerability to the sun when they refused to take sides in the First Battle—but who witnessed this? The demons and nosferatu, who *say* they were once angels."

"Ah. But they're all liars, so you assume they lie about this as well."

"Well, I don't *know* that they do; I just don't rule it out as a possibility. And doesn't it benefit them to say they came from Heaven? Maybe they're just capitalizing on things people already believe, and they change the details of their story according to the culture. It inspires more power, more fear—is more impressive."

"And what of Michael and the Guardians? Do you doubt his word as well?" His fangs gleamed when she shifted uncomfortably. "Do you think his story of the Second Battle is a lie?"

"No. Demons are real; I'm not questioning that—or that they probably were jealous of the angels who were on Earth, protecting it. I live with a hellhound, so I don't doubt Lucifer bred them, and used them to massacre the angels during that battle. And I've seen what Michael can do."

"So you are willing to believe that he really did lead an army of men who fought against the demons, and killed a Chaos dragon with his sword?"

"Yes."

"How generous of you, Savitri." His voice was teasing. "And what about afterward—that the angels gave him the power to transform other humans into Guardians, and take their place as protectors in Caelum?"

"I'm willing to accept that, too. I just don't necessarily think it has to all come from some huge, ineffable source. There might be other explanations. Stop laughing, it's not that funny," she said, but when he glanced at her and sucked in a long breath as if he was trying to suppress it, then failed and burst into laughter again, she had to join in.

"Oh, Savitri," he said. "You are incredible. Still a skeptic."

She shrugged. "They—you—do things I have no explanation for, but maybe in three hundred years, there will be one. A thousand years ago, the world was flat, gravity didn't exist, and lightning was a sign from the gods. And no one's studying Guardians or demons—except for the quacks, scientists don't even know they're supposed to be figuring this shit out. They don't have terms for most of it. But once people take a look at it, pull it apart . . . demystify it all, maybe they'll find a reason for it. So I'm not saying it isn't true—but I'm not ready to say it is, either."

"Do let me know when you are; I think I shall very much enjoy hearing your conclusions, however convoluted they may be."

"I may take a long time."

He grinned. "I'll wait."

The turnover had almost completely cooled; she took another bite. His lids lowered as he inhaled, his gaze falling to her mouth. "That is apple?"

She nodded.

He blinked and gave his head a slight shake, turning his attention back to the road.

"Actually," she said, "the only reason I'm not running

away screaming is because it's all so interesting. I live with a two-thousand-year-old woman and an eight-hundred-year-old man. Did you know Lilith once tried to tempt Isaac Newton?"

"She told you that?" Colin glanced at her. "She may have been lying."

"Hugh said she wasn't. But even if she had been, it's still fascinating."

"And are you so certain Castleford tells you the truth?"

"I think so. Usually, if I ask a question he doesn't want to answer, he just says it's not for me to know." He didn't say it very often—and the majority of the times he had, it had been in relation to Colin and Chaos. "Except it doesn't sound so condescending when he says it. Is all that stuff about you in his book true? Have you read it?"

After he'd Fallen, Hugh had written a manuscript describing his life as a Guardian—a life he'd dedicated to saving Lilith. Savi had stumbled across the file on his computer and had assumed he'd been writing a fictional novel. She'd found out later he'd intended it for the library in Caelum, to be included with the Scrolls that detailed Guardian rules and history. But by then, Savi had already developed popular card and video games from its storyline.

"Yes. With a title such as *Lilith*, how could I not? But I am never mentioned."

"Not by name. But it's not all that hard to figure it out. The dates, the locations—they match up. You really lived a month only half-transformed?"

A puzzled frown pulled at the corners of his mouth. "I'm certain Derbyshire was not mentioned, Savitri. Nor were there specific dates."

"Oh!" She shook her head. "No, I don't mean the printed version—god, you read *that*?"

"Yes," he said. "It's quite terrible."

"It's not surprising: I ran his original Latin document through a language translator, then tried to spiff it all up before I had it printed for him."

He turned his head to stare at her.

"It was a present," she said, grinning. "I was young."

"It's *atrocious*." He passed his hand over his hair. "Oh,

good God. What does the Latin include that your version does not?"

"Not much. Something about your brother-in-law, and Hugh taking over a vow Ramsdell made to your sister, promising to watch over you."

"Anything of Michael's sword? Mirrors?"

"No. Nothing about Chaos, either."

His jaw tightened. He slowed for a red light and remained silent until he accelerated again. "I did survive a month half-transformed."

She blinked. Had he returned to her earlier question to avoid speaking of Chaos? "The nosferatu wouldn't have given you blood. Lilith said she tried to cut off his head while he attacked you—did it get into your mouth or something?"

"No. I bit him whilst trying to get away."

"How uncivilized."

"Exceedingly."

"What did you eat afterward?"

"Nothing, but for the broth Emily forced down my throat." His brows drew together. "And I believe I tried to eat raw meat from the larder, but I'm not certain."

"You don't remember?"

"No. I've only a partial recollection of those days."

Some things, she supposed, were a blessing to forget. "And Hugh and Lilith used the blood of the nosferatu who originally attacked you to complete the transformation?"

"That is correct."

"When did you find out you can withstand the sun?"

"The first morning I did not return to Beaumont Court before sunrise." He turned to look between the seats before switching lanes. "I'm surprised you do not know all of this already, my sweet Savitri. I'm well aware of how you located me last year. An illegal bit of computer wizardry."

She slid her tongue over her bottom lip to catch the last of the cinnamon and apple juice, and hoped the darkness would hide her blush from him. Probably not. Even if he didn't look at her, he could probably feel the heat and blood.

"It was only financial information—IRS and bank account records, a list of assets. Your address and phone number." It hadn't told her anything personal. Savi knew a lot *about* him, but she didn't know him.

And though she might have asked him in Caelum, she had been occupied—enthralled—by the impossible beauty of that realm.

Enthralled by Colin.

The streetlights washed over his features at regular intervals. His profile was as incredible as the rest of him. Even the rough shadow along his jaw enhanced his masculine perfection. She rubbed her tongue against the roof of her mouth; it suddenly seemed hot, tingly, as if she'd added too much cayenne to a dish.

He took a deep breath, and his fingers clenched the steering wheel. The movement shook her out of her silent inspection. God. It was so easy to fall into a friendly banter with him, but she knew too well how his mood could change without warning. He could go from passion to humor to cruelty in the span of a smile; she'd be an idiot to forget what he was, just because it felt like heaven to look at him.

And it was probably best to cover her stare with her curiosity. "Do you have to shave?" She bit her lip to contain her grin before she added, "Did you have a valet?"

"Rarely; I also have to cut my hair, as do most vampires. And yes, until 1945."

"What happened in 1945?"

"He died, and I learned to use a razor."

Without a mirror. Though she wanted to know what happened in Chaos, she wouldn't broach that subject. Even after seven months, it must still be too raw. And Colin's voice had taken on a rough edge; it hadn't been there before, not even when he'd used his blood on her wounds.

He reached out and pushed a button on the CD player. To silence her? She knew he could hear her over the music.

The Velvet Underground. Lou Reed and a soft, delicate melody. Her smile widened when he shut it off. He had a lovely baritone; did he sing when he was alone?

"Do my questions annoy you?"

He glanced at her, his surprise evident. "No. I'm far too vain to object; I am my favorite topic."

His easy admission startled a laugh from her, but it faded when his gaze sharpened. The warmth spread from her mouth, burned through her stomach and settled low in her abdomen. "What is it then?"

"We need to get out of the car," he said, and turned onto Eddy Street. Near Polidori's. "Your scent is . . . like a peach. Or a mango. And I'm starving." A muscle in his cheek flexed. "I don't always have control."

A shiver ran up her spine, but she couldn't name its cause. Not simply fear or lust; what was in between? "You said you'd eaten." Vampires—even Colin—didn't need more than one feeding a night.

"I did." Frustration tightened his voice. "Is it your soap?"

"No. It's probably in my skin. I must've eaten a hundred mangoes when I was in India, and two more just before I left. I have no control over myself, either, but I stopped short of taking a mango bath," she said, and waited for his smile. It came slowly. In the dim light, his teeth shone brilliantly white. "The mango *wallahs* sell them right on the street. Have you ever had one?"

"No." Another deep inhalation. "Tell me."

Tell me. Memory of the last time he'd issued that command flashed through her. She shifted in the seat, pressed her thighs together to ease the pulsing ache. "They're more intense, brighter in flavor than a peach, and the flesh is firm and smooth and slippery. And the juice . . . cold, sunwarm—it doesn't matter." She looked down at her hands, remembering how sticky they'd been. "There aren't any like them imported into the U.S.; you've got to be there, to know what a really, really good mango is like." Caelum on her tongue.

"Did you return with any?" His question was so low, she almost didn't hear it. He parked in a reserved space, killed the engine.

"No; it's too difficult to get through Customs. It's easier to kill a nosferatu on a plane than take a piece of fruit on one." She smiled wryly and glanced up. Her breath caught. He'd turned toward her; his face was expressionless but for the heat in his gaze. His eyes glittered with pale fire.

Her mouth was parched; she seemed to be burning from

the inside. She tried to moisten her tongue, to swallow. His hungry gaze followed the movement of her jaw and throat. "I need a drink," she said hoarsely.

His laugh was short, hard. He opened the door and cold air flooded in. "So do I."

CHAPTER 4

The nosferatu suffer from bloodlust, but they don't have to eat. That's how they hide undetected in caves for so long—there isn't a trail of corpses for the Guardians to follow. Vampires have to feed every day, though; and the bloodlust can make the urge to feed and the urge to have sex nearly indistinguishable. And the feeding feels incredible for whomever is being sucked on—that's what they tell me, anyway.

Savi to Taylor, 2007

Colin rested his hand against the small of her back as he guided her past a long line of clubbers. As an act of courtesy, it proved a masochistic one; beneath his palm, the gentle curve of her spine moved in rhythm with her steps, the beat of the music from inside. Matched the need throbbing within him.

He ground his teeth together, urged her forward a little more quickly. How could he be so desperate to feed? He'd taken enough for two days from the last blonde alone.

"It was popular before, but not like this," Savitri murmured.

Colin glanced at the queue; mostly human, but a few vampires waited, as well. A growl rose unbidden in his throat. He didn't want her here, he didn't want to be here—yet he'd been unable to refuse her request.

And she hadn't even flattered him.

His gaze dropped to her neck; her short hair left it deliciously exposed. He should mark her as his. Protect her from the vampires here and the others inside. Inhale her, drink her, sink into her—

He swallowed thickly and forced the territorial hunger aside. What he wanted to do to her could not be considered protection.

"It's morbid fascination," he finally replied.

She sighed, and her lashes swept down against her cheeks. The investigators—and the press—had linked Polidori's to last year's ritual murders; burning it had been determined a cult's symbolic way of beginning its quest for immortality.

All lies, of course; Colin had helped fabricate them. But the story had entertained the public for months, and many of the people standing outside had only come because of the club's connection with death. Her friends' deaths.

"And I spent a sordid amount of money on it," he added. "I can't fault them for recognizing my unparalleled taste and flocking here to revel in it."

Her lips curved into a smile, and she slanted a glance up at him. "Was it truly that much? Lilith claims you are the cheapest bastard she's ever known."

Pleased with himself for turning her thoughts from her grief, he said, "Agent Milton has a demon's tongue. I am not *cheap*, my sweet Savitri. I've an eternal retirement; I budget wisely."

Her throaty laughter pulled at already tight nerves along his skin. Her hip bumped against his leg as they rounded the corner to the entrance. Her fragrance wafted around her. In her heels, she stood only a few inches shorter than he. So easy just to bend and press his mouth against . . .

He dropped his hand from her waist, clenched it into a fist. This was bloody ridiculous. A fruity perfume, and he had as much control as an adolescent pulling himself off on his sheets.

A huge vampire guarded the entrance and ran the guest list; he towered over Colin by a bald head, outweighed him by half. His muscles bulged through the tight black T-shirt. An intimidating presence, and one most vampires respected; but then, they were often fooled by appearances. Colin had deliberately chosen him for his resemblance in size and baldness to the nosferatu—but though the vampire was strong, Colin could have torn him in two with little effort. It was one of the advantages of Colin's transformation with nosferatu blood instead of an exchange with another vampire.

And the taint Michael's sword had left in his blood had generated the other differences.

The bouncer's eyes widened—Colin usually didn't use the front entrance—and he quickly unhooked the velvet rope. "Mr. Ames-Beaumont."

The urge to dash inside, to find the nearest willing body and glut was almost overwhelming. "Mr. Varney, this is Miss Savitri Murray. She should be on the short list."

Her chin tilted up, her gaze leveled on Varney's features. It was difficult to tell human from vampire, but Castleford would have taught her to recognize the signs: the careful placement of the lips during speech, the slight perspiration in heated rooms or on warm nights, abnormal respiration and reflexes. "What's the short list?"

"Full access, miss, including Mr. Ames-Beaumont's personal suite. No charge." There was more, but Varney didn't mention that any vampire who tried to drink from someone on that list would receive a visit from Colin. It hadn't happened yet; there were very few people this side of the Atlantic to whom he'd give anything for free, and Lilith and Castleford were the only other names listed.

A vampire would have to be a blithering idiot to attack *them*.

"Except for tonight." Colin led her forward and descended the stairs. "You'll pay the cover and for your drinks." An auburn-haired beauty was going up; she glanced at him, then froze with her foot in the air and watched as he passed. "Do you know the Guardians' sign language?"

"No," Savi said, and looked back over her shoulder. "I hope she doesn't fall."

He suppressed his laughter with difficulty, and said in Hindi, "I'll walk with you to the bar; then I must leave you alone for a few minutes. Because you came in with me, you'll be a curiosity to the vampires inside. They may approach you. Don't ask them questions, don't talk to them."

"Why? Isn't the point of all this that I'm seen?"

"You'll be seen, sweet Savitri." But he didn't want them to have any more of her than that.

And hopefully, once he'd fed, his need for more would also fade.

❧

It was inelegant, perhaps even ill-mannered, but Savi eschewed the straw and gulped straight from the glass. Lime and salt, sour and sweet. And cold—she couldn't get enough of it.

Delayed reaction from the flight? Her breath fogged the inside of the tumbler. Heat from the mass of bodies?

Perhaps he'd been too stingy to pay for air conditioners.

She fished out a cube of ice, sucked it into her mouth. The bartender glanced at her. Another vampire. Colin had been right; they'd all watched as he'd taken her hand and led her through the club. As he'd dropped a quick kiss onto her forehead.

Like a little girl. A little sister. She'd known what it was: a display of protection. Because Hugh had saved Colin's sister, the vampire felt obligated to guard Hugh's adopted sister in return. She should have been grateful. Perhaps she would have, if she didn't feel so restless, as if she'd suddenly been caged.

It was a familiar feeling, but it usually didn't make her angry.

She crushed the ice between her teeth. Why was it so fucking hot in here?

She lifted her hand and gestured for another, asked for a water to accompany it. The wounds on her palm had almost completely healed; only a lingering stiffness remained. She examined the thin pink lines on her fingers. The blood sped healing—is that what allowed them immortality? Accelerated regeneration or cell replication, with no degradation over time?

But wouldn't their hair grow more quickly if it was replication? Did it simply keep existing cells in perfect repair, not speed the manufacture of new ones?

Why did it only heal humans when applied topically, or through a transfusion? And why was it safe? A transfusion would temporarily give a human some strength and healing ability, but it didn't last. Only through ingestion was there a danger—blessing?—of transformation.

Was it the *choice* to drink that provided the power, or the blood itself? Before Michael could transform a human to a

Guardian, the human had to agree to the change; she'd heard the same was true of a vampire—the transformation didn't take well if it wasn't voluntary. Could blood recognize choice and free will?

The blood*lust* supposedly did—except for the free will of the vampire it controlled.

She felt Colin before she saw him; he stood next to her, leaning gracefully against the bar. His expression was unreadable, his gaze hooded. Even in the dim lighting, she could see the slight flush on his skin.

She'd seen it before.

Lifting her glass, she took another long drink, licked the salt from her lips, and forced a bright smile. "The redhead on the stairs?"

His mouth tightened, but he gave a slow nod.

She arched a brow. "You must lose a lot of clients if those you feed from leave bleeding."

"She wasn't. And I don't often feed here; I prefer the hunt. Pursuit offers a challenge." He looked away from her toward the dance floor, his mouth pulled down in a grimace of distaste. "When it is readily available, it is merely scavenging."

Her chest squeezed painfully. She'd not only been available, she'd thrown herself at him. "So the aristocrat surveys the unwashed masses, and finds them lacking," she murmured.

And she was just a brown little girl.

"They have use during revolutions, but there is no rebellion here. Only a mess of conformity." His gaze met hers again. "But I do not care if they bathe, Savitri, as long as they bleed."

The glass was slick with condensation; she wiped her palm across her forehead, hoping to ease the heat with cold and wet. "I thought, because of—" She paused, switched to Hindi. He probably didn't want anyone to overhear that he couldn't create other vampires. Surely his impotency embarrassed someone like him, and she wouldn't prick his vanity again. "Because of your *incapability*, that you couldn't heal me. I was wrong."

He contained his emotions too well for her to interpret his response. "Yes. You also believed Castleford when he confirmed your assumption that I was gay."

It had been easier; a woman had little defense against a face like that—except to believe it couldn't be hers. But she'd been mistaken in that, too. Gloriously mistaken, until it had turned into something . . . painful.

"Did she tell you what you wanted to hear?"

A mocking smile. "She screamed it."

She nodded, drained her glass. "I'm going to go dance." Sweat out some of the heat boiling within her. Feel someone's touch on her skin.

Anyone's but his.

❧

She'd known better.

Before a few bullets had destroyed her family, Savi had been surrounded by stories—her mother had loved them. Both surgeons, her parents had limited time dedicated to Savi and her brother. But in those rare evenings when her mother had been home, fairy tales and fables had been standard bedtime fare.

The music drowned out the voices of the men dancing with her, but she could still hear her mother's voice clearly—one of the advantages of a memory like hers.

. . . and the girl came across a cobra curled up against the freezing night air. The cobra begged her to stop and carry him in her pocket until the sun rose in the morning, but she refused. "You will bite me," she said. But the cobra promised not to. "I will die here; if you save me, I will treat you as a friend." The girl was too soft-hearted to let him freeze, and so she picked him up and put him in her pocket. She'd taken not two steps before she felt his fangs against her breast. "Why?" she cried, her voice weak from the poison. "You said you would not!"

"It is my nature," the cobra replied, "and you knew what I was."

Cold hands clasped her hips, pulled her back to gyrate against him. Vampire, but not Colin's hands. His were warm. He could walk in the sun. He was beautiful and charming.

She'd thought if she offered her blood to him, she wouldn't be hurt by it.

She should have known better.

Frigid fingers drifted beneath her shirt, along the curve of her waist. It felt fantastic. Her skin was tight, burning, and his hand trailed over her stomach like a block of ice. His cold form rocked against her back. His erection. Perhaps he could cool her from inside, make her forget . . .

But no—that was one of the drawbacks of her memory. Her mother's screams, forever captured. Her brother's tortured, bubbling breaths. Her father's silence.

And Colin's fangs buried in her throat, desolation and horror tearing through her mind as her body shuddered beneath his.

He'd done it to teach her a lesson—and by god, she had learned. Her brain had gotten the message.

Her body had not.

She was on fire. Alcohol hadn't dulled it, water hadn't doused it. She hated being drunk; she couldn't think.

A shiver wracked her when his fingers slid higher. Her nipples drew tight beneath the silk.

"You're so hot," said the rough voice behind her.

Like a demon. Averaging 106.7 degrees Fahrenheit, 41.5 degrees Celsius, 314.65 degrees Kelvin. Or did he mean it in that you're-sexy-come-home-with-me way? Didn't he have a partner to share blood and a bed with? Perhaps he was one of those vampires whose partner had been killed by the nosferatu.

Vampires didn't drink from humans, not unless they intended to transform them. If that was what he offered, why not take him up on it? She was going to eventually, anyway.

He could turn her, and she would live forever.

Clammy lips touched the back of her neck. Cold, wet—like the nosferatu. *Oh, god.* This wasn't what she'd promised Nani. She ripped out of his grasp, staggered forward.

Colin caught her. He hadn't been there a moment before; she was certain of it. She'd seen him at his table, where he'd spent the whole of the night. Watching her.

She hadn't known he could move so quickly.

His arm circled her waist, his chest hard and warm against hers. He didn't look at her, but over her head. His jaw clenched in a tight line.

Behind her, the vampire babbled incoherently.

"He didn't do anything," Savi said quickly. This vampire didn't deserve to pay for her mistake, her stupidity, her drunkenness. But how to convince Colin?

She tried not to slur. "Your lips are beautiful."

He flinched, and lowered his gaze. "You bloody foolish chit. You think to manipulate me?" he gritted, but his eyes softened as he searched her features, as he inhaled her breath. "Christ. You're completely foxed."

"Deep in my cups," she agreed, nodding.

He blinked. After a long moment, a smile teased the corners of his mouth. "Sweet Savitri, what have you been reading?"

She needed to stop looking at him; surely he was worse for her brain than alcohol. But the firm curves of his upper lip were extraordinary—the dip in the center looked as wide as her forefinger. She reached up to test it.

"I had a phase about five years ago. I read about lords and ladies. Waltzes. Did you waltz?" The faint stubble was rough against her fingertip; a perfect fit.

Colin gripped her wrist, pulled it away, and slid his hand down to clasp his palm against hers. "Yes." His other hand settled over her hip. "Toss him out," he said to someone behind her. "Clear them all out."

And he swept her off her feet.

She didn't know how he did it; though past closing time, dancers still bumped and ground across the floor—yet he twirled her through them without touching a single person. She couldn't keep up or match his steps. He lowered his forearm to cradle her bottom, then he lifted her against him and glided.

"Oh my god." Lights and colors whirled around her.

"Focus on my beautiful lips, Savitri, lest you become dizzy."

"And cast up my accounts?"

"Yes," he said, laughing; how could she *not* look at his mouth when he did that? At his elongated canines, the sharp white line of his teeth. But it was safer than looking at his eyes and risking seeing the wholehearted, almost boyish delight that had so captivated her in Caelum.

The sound of his amusement rumbled through her, combined with the heavy beat of the music. He wore cologne, a light masculine fragrance with notes of orange and papaya and sandalwood. She buried her face in his neck, wrapped her thighs around his lean hips.

Oh my god. His cock was thick and hard beneath his trousers, nestled between her legs. Another perfect fit; she remembered all too well how perfect.

She could come just from this.

"It didn't work," he said in Hindi. He sounded almost apologetic.

She was burning, burning. Just like Polidori's. "What didn't?"

"The woman from the stairwell. Acting the ass at the bar, that you would put distance between us. It seems I can protect you from everyone but myself."

Her body went rigid; her eyes flew open. *I don't always have control.* He'd tried to regain it by feeding, but that had been hours ago. How thin was it now? Her heart pounded. "You were lying at the bar?"

"No. But a gentleman can tell the truth without being cruel, if he wishes it." He slowed next to his table, and eased down onto the sofa without letting her go. Her knees sank into the cushions. His arm across her lower back trapped her hips against his. "Do not mistake me for a kind man, Savitri."

She wouldn't. Not again.

"What are you going to do?" She pushed at his chest.

"Taste you." He cupped her jaw. His thumb smoothed across her cheek. "Only your mouth, and only if you agree."

Tension coiled through her stomach, arousal and fear. And heat. He was a fever inside her, a sickness. "What if I don't?"

"I'll carry you to my suite and do it there." The apology dropped from his tone. "I don't intend to take your blood, Savi. I simply want—*need*—to taste you." His chest rose and fell beneath her hand. "I think I will die if I do not."

She wouldn't believe that; only poets and horny teenagers did. But her gaze dropped to his lips. "Just a kiss?"

"Yes." With gentle pressure, he urged her nearer. "A sword lies behind the wall panel. The spring is two inches above the sofa, one foot in."

Did he think she would need it? But if he lost that much control, she'd have no possibility of defense.

She'd had a better chance against the nosferatu.

Her palms slid over his shoulders, up to curve around the back of his neck. Her fingers buried in the hair at his nape. So thick and soft.

"This must be because I'm drunk," she whispered as she lowered her mouth to his. "I know better."

❧

So did he.

Surely nothing good would come of this. He'd measured his desire against his sense for hours. In the end, he was simply too selfish a creature; no matter how heavy the consequences, his need outweighed them.

Her scent had tormented him. Distance hadn't helped. He'd watched her on the dance floor, as she sat at the bar and drank with an unquenchable thirst that seemed to equal his own, alternating between alcohol and water as if searching for anything to give her ease.

Her skin burned through the silk of her shirt; whatever she'd been searching for, she apparently hadn't found it.

Terrible and frightening had been the moment when he'd taken the woman he'd seen on the stairs, and realized his hunger had not abated—when he'd realized Savitri had caused it, and was likely the solution. But she was no different from any other woman: all without flavor but for their blood.

Her lips pressed tentatively against his, and his stomach hollowed in relief. He was hard, aching for her, but there was nothing magical in this. Just a kiss, something he'd experienced thousands of times with thousands of women.

Just her fragrance, tickling at a memory and creating an involuntary response. It must be.

Her mouth opened, and she swept her tongue between his lips.

And he *tasted* her. Sweet. Warm and mellow, and beneath it, a dark, rich essence.

Impossible.

Colin held himself still, disbelieving. Pleasure spilled through him, thick and heated. Not the same as bloodlust, but as powerful.

She drew his lower lip between her teeth. He wanted to beg

her to return to a deeper kiss, but didn't trust himself to speak, to move.

Don't frighten her. Don't let her stop.

He released her, dug his hands into the sofa cushions.

Her tongue sought his, stroking. A moan rose in his throat. Her slight weight was a delicious pressure against his rigid shaft, and she moved in time with her kiss.

How? Why? Chocolate, fries, apples and cinnamon, lime and salt—he could not taste them, nothing but that incredible sweet flavor, the heat of her mouth.

With each rock of her hips the ache of his cock became more exquisite, more unbearable. She suckled softly on his tongue. *Yes, Savi—don't stop. Don't—*

Bloody hell, he was going to spend. Right here, with this slip of a girl atop him. Astounded, Colin opened his eyes, met her velvet brown gaze.

She'd been watching him, gauging his response. Surprise and knowledge filled her psychic scent before she lowered her lids and began devouring his mouth, tasting and licking.

His heart raced. Her fingers tugged on his hair, and she sank deeper, deeper. She worked him over as easily as he had Fia, or any of the other women he'd fed from that evening . . . or in the past two centuries. He couldn't stop her—didn't *want* to stop her, but she couldn't do this to him, couldn't, not without

She bit his tongue; blood flowed into his mouth. His own, but it mixed with her flavor and flashed through him, a bolt of lightning arcing along his veins. He stiffened, panted into her lips.

She raised her head, her gaze narrowed on his face, triumph and pleasure chasing across her expression. Incredulous, he couldn't muster the slightest embarrassment, though it was impossible for her not to realize what was happening. Her sex pressed against him. She couldn't mistake the ecstasy that shook him. He could feel the heat of her, but the wet was his own.

Good God. She'd made him come in his pants.

And she'd done it with a single kiss.

His chest heaved, and he stared at her lips. Moist and swollen. He could smell her arousal beneath that ever-present peach scent; she'd be moist and swollen everywhere.

If someone didn't come and save her in the next few moments, she would be in his suite and in his bed. He'd taste every inch, just to see if it was only her mouth, or all of her.

He was going to eat her up.

"It must be the hellhound venom," she said, and sighed. The soft curves of her breasts pressed against the silk blouse, her nipples outlined by crimson.

And he wouldn't let her go. Not again. Vows and sisters and friends be damned.

"Or the nosferatu blood," she added, her voice thoughtful. She no longer slurred her words; had she sobered so quickly? She touched his lower lip.

Scarlet dotted her fingertip: his blood. Dread slipped through him; he caught her hand and frowned up at her.

"Did you swallow any?"

Another scent intruded on his senses; not physical, but psychic. Sickly sweet and rotting. Familiar. He shook it away. Impossible that it was here—it was only a memory, a hallucination brought on by his fear that she might have ingested his tainted blood.

"I think so," she said quietly. "It must be why I'm burning. Why I have been for hours."

Hours? Unease settled in his stomach. He slid his hand around her hip, under her shirt, and felt the skin on her back.

Hot. He'd expected that, from the exertion of dancing and the arousal between them. But there was no perspiration, none of the cooling slick sweat that should have accompanied it.

Dry. Feverish.

Her strange statement from a moment before struck him now, made him tense. "You swallowed venom?"

"I had to get it into his blood. I spit it." She blinked slowly. Her eyes were bright, glassy. "It doesn't harm humans or halflings."

"If they're *bitten*," he said through clenched teeth. Why hadn't Castleford told her of the dangers possible, that there was still so much unknown? "God knows what it does if you drink it. And the nosferatu blood? Did you ingest that, too?"

"It was spraying everywhere—in my mouth. Someone grabbed me when I was running, and I swallowed. It must have mixed with the venom a little. Not very much."

Beneath her fragrance, the psychic stink of rot grew stronger. He fought to control it; he'd been months without the flashbacks striking with such intensity. Why now? Could he not have one memory of her left untainted by Chaos?

"Why didn't you tell me before? How long have you been like this?"

"The car." She took rapid, shallow breaths. "The venom tasted like a peach, but I rinsed out my mouth on the plane."

He reached into his pocket for his phone. "You're supposed to be smart, Savitri."

"You fuck with my brain, vampire. And every time I've been with you I've been enthralled or drunk, so I can't think." Her body swayed before she jerked herself upright again.

"Christ." He pulled her tight against his chest and pushed the auto-dial for Lilith's cell. *Bloody fantastic job protecting her.* How could he not have noticed the fever? He'd only thought of his cock and his fangs and her mouth.

She'd twisted him up; he'd been out of his mind. That scent . . . from a fucking *dog*.

"You smell so good," she said against his neck, and her tongue swiped over his skin. He closed his throat against his groan of pleasure. She was delirious; even he wouldn't take advantage of her now.

A violent commotion came from the entrance of the club. Only a few vampires lingered inside, slowly gathering their things. Colin looked up as they stopped and turned toward the sound.

A sharp, male shriek of pain followed a deep shout of warning. Varney.

Colin opened his senses, searching for the source of the threat, and the putrid stink swept into his mind. He forced himself not to gag. Not to scream.

"Colin? Colin!"

Lilith's voice in his ear pulled him back from the edge. What the—

Savitri. He compelled the words from his frozen tongue. "Savi ingested hellhound venom and nosferatu blood. She's taken fever."

Colin closed the phone and dropped it, then slapped his hand against the wall. The panel sprang open.

Savi slid from his lap. Even in this state, she must have realized he needed to move.

"Stay here."

She nodded, and rubbed her face to rouse herself.

He selected two swords and rose to his feet. A dark form streaked across the dance floor, headed directly toward them.

Icy fear splintered in his gut, cut through the numbness.

A wyrmwolf. Scales and exposed flesh. Not as large as a hellhound, with only one head, but almost as deadly. Sweat broke over his skin. How could it be here? *It couldn't be here;* no Gate led from Earth to Chaos, no portal. The only anchor to that realm was in Colin's blood, and the only access through him.

Had he brought it back? Could he never escape it? Did he have to pay for one foolish mistake for eternity?

A vampire tried to stop the wyrmwolf, and lost his arm to a quick tear from its jaws.

Screams echoed through the club.

"Bloody fucking hell," Colin muttered, and ran to intercept it.

❧

Savi had never seen anything like the battle that followed— *couldn't* see most of it. Only a flash of swords, then two figures blurring as they moved. An instant in which they paused, caught in a violent tableau of blades and fangs.

She looked away once, toward those watching with her. The vampires' expressions were easy to interpret: horror and awe. They could see what was happening. Why didn't they help him?

But Colin didn't need it. He stopped suddenly, angling his left sword up like a batsman after smashing a cricket ball, his chest heaving and his face glistening with sweat.

The creature's head hit the wall and thudded to the floor.

The strength left her body at the same time, and she slipped down, laid her cheek against the sofa cushion. The heat burned through her, but she couldn't feel it anymore. Only tired, so tired.

Through half-closed eyes, she saw Colin return to her side, his gaze fierce upon her. Blood spread over one ivory sleeve, and from a slash on his thigh.

He lifted her from the sofa and began walking toward his suite. Her head swam.

"They have five seconds," he said softly.

Who? Before what? She couldn't make the effort to form the questions. Jet lag? A strange time for it, when she was flying, flying.

Colin's arms tightened around her, and he shuddered. "Castleford. Michael." His voice was flat. "And as usual, you've arrived too bloody late."

CHAPTER 5

I have determined that I shall have a holiday in Switzerland. A change of scenery shall do wonders for my digestion, though, but for P——, the company probably will not. They are exceedingly curious about vampires; but I have a personal dislike for "Poets," and the little acquaintance I have with one in particular will not induce me to divulge my secrets.

—*Colin to Ramsdell, 1816*

SEEKING alliance for 29/5'10", smart, handsome and successful software engineer in California. Pls respond with photo.

———————

AFFLUENT Hindu Punjabi parents seek very beautiful girl for their extremely handsome, 6ft, high achiever, educated, physician son. Photo & biodata must. Caste/religion no bar.

———————

HINDU Marathi parents seek an attractive, professional, vegetarian girl, with traditional values, for handsome son, USMD NYC. Please send biodata/recent photo.

Savi sighed and scooped more noodles from the take-out box. With her left hand, she drew a circle around the first ad. Nani would be horrified that Savi had even glanced at the matrimonials, but at least she would know Savi was trying to keep her promise. In any case, her grandmother had probably begun inquiries in the Indian communities in the Bay Area and with relatives in Mumbai. There would be plenty of potential grooms for Savi to meet.

And a software engineer would be okay; better than a doctor. She'd have more in common with a techie. She frowned and chewed. On the other hand, a doctor would be absent more often. Social obligations might be greater, though; when her parents hadn't been at work, they were usually at some function.

She glanced around the small, dark office with its glowing computer screens and felt a spark of hope. A techie might be gone just as often. She was never home, that was certain.

Of course, over the past eight months that absence had had little to do with her job and more to do with a vain vampire and his frequent visits to Hugh and Lilith. His presence hadn't been a factor in the month since her return from India, but she'd still kept as far from home as possible.

Running. She was such a coward.

She wouldn't run from this promise, though. *Pls respond with photo.* Perhaps she could digitally alter a picture, and when she met the prospective groom in person claim she'd lost most of her hair in a fire.

In a fire, saving a kitten.

"How long did you think you could avoid me?"

Savi's cardboard-box table shook as her foot slipped, and she whirled on her stool. Lilith stood in the doorway, Sir Pup at her heels. She must have come from home; she wore loose cargo pants, a T-shirt, and a fitted leather jacket.

Lilith's appearance was a bit more striking when she was at work. Not that she was ever less than stunning with a face like that.

Right now, a stunning and frighteningly triumphant I've-got-you smile sat on Lilith's lips.

Savi swallowed and managed, "I was hoping for at least another week. I should be out of here by then. You apparently got the info I sent about the nosferatu. How did you know it was me?" She glared at Sir Pup. The hellhound must have led Lilith to this office, followed Savi's scent.

He grinned at her, his tongue lolling from the side of his mouth.

"Considering everything else Hugh and I have discovered

in the last couple of weeks, it could only have been you."
Lilith's dark gaze skimmed over the room. Not much to see; a
few monitors, server racks, boxes. "What's taking you so
long? I'd have thought if you wanted to go, you could go."

"The connections in the new place. The current ones can't
handle the data transfer. And there's a security issue." Apparently here, too, but no security system would stop someone
like Lilith. Savi shrugged and studied the other woman's long
black hair. Too much curl.

Her eyes narrowing, Lilith said, "What is it?"

"I was thinking of making a wig." Savi gestured to a small
love seat, where she often took naps when the information she
needed was long in coming. "I imagine you're going to stay
and interrogate me. Pad thai?"

"I ate." Instead of sitting in the deep cushions, Lilith lowered herself onto the arm and pulled her right foot up to rest
on the seat. "It's been two weeks since you left the hospital;
Hugh and I have seen you a total of three times. He's worried."

Guilt tightened Savi's belly. She set the food on the table,
and tried to remember whom she was speaking with: Lilith,
a master of manipulation. Savi adored her, but knew Lilith
wouldn't hesitate to lie if it served her purpose. "You're here
for him? He knows what I do. How do you think he found
you and Colin so easily last May? He asked me to get your
info."

Sir Pup sniffed at the box of noodles; Savi dropped it to the
floor and let him go at it. He'd shifted into his public form, a
large Labrador with only one head. Did his other heads resent
it when only one got a treat?

"I found Hugh last May, standing over Ian Rafferty's
body," Lilith said. "Who wouldn't have been dead if not for
DemonSlayer."

Savi's lips parted on a painful gasp, and she fought the
tears that sprang to her eyes. "Jesus, Lilith. Why don't you just
fucking rip my lungs out?"

Regret slipped across Lilith's expression before her features hardened. "Because you always act without thinking of
the consequences. You had good intentions when you translated and printed Hugh's book, but you did it without asking

him, and without knowing the dangers of it. And you created the DemonSlayer card game based on the book, again without asking. At least you talked to him when you developed and licensed the video game, but that was a bit late. You're brilliant, Savi, but you do the stupidest things with it."

Savi clenched her hands to conceal their shaking, though there was no point in hiding; Lilith would see the gesture and know the reason behind it. Both she and Hugh always saw too much.

"Are you talking about the flight, the nosferatu? Because I was right, and you know it. We would have all been dead. Ten minutes later, Nani and I would have been at the bottom of the Atlantic. Michael and Selah were too late, and Hugh told me the nosferatu confirmed its plan had been to destroy us."

Savi didn't want to know how the nosferatu had been convinced to talk. There were places her curiosity didn't extend.

"No, I'm talking about this." Lilith waved her hand at the computers. "Sir Pup, can I have Savi's file?" A thin manila folder appeared on the cushion beside Lilith's boot. She picked it up. "There's very little in here."

Savi didn't reply, and Lilith sighed. "*Too* little. The ruse with Selah taking your approximate form and place in the airplane's bathroom last month worked—for the most part. We still had to go in and remove physical evidence, the passenger lists and airport video surveillance, change your flight date to the day before in the airline database and credit card records—"

"And your guy left his fingerprints all over the place," Savi said. No reason not to tell her; obviously Lilith had figured most of it out. "I had to go back in and clean them up."

"I know." Lilith tapped the file against her palm. "But that's not my point. Your data doesn't have any blocks, but there's nothing there. Not a single connection to Auntie, or to Hugh. And I wasn't the only one looking. It's not necessarily a problem, because it serves our purpose for the investigators to find what they *think* they're looking for—"

Savi's brow creased. "What does that mean?"

"It means that Special Investigations is too new and our responsibilities too undefined for anyone to be certain of us.

Most of those looking at the data are accepting appearances: that a terrorist who looks a hell of a lot like you duplicated your info and tried to bring down a flight, but failed and was caught in New York. And Selah's escape from maximum security two days later only confirms it for them: a powerful organization pulling strings. But the other half sees your lack of data and reaches the same conclusions I did: you're already working under an agency—probably Homeland Security. So they'll assume that the assassination on board was to stop the flight from going down, and everything else is a cover-up. There's enough conflicting evidence that they'll believe whatever they want to believe." Lilith pursed her lips. "All that really matters is that the public bought the capture and escape story, because it makes the DHS look like fucktards and the focus is away from SI."

Savi rubbed her forehead, laughing a little. It was all too convoluted for her taste; she concealed by making appearances very simple and straightforward. "So you know what I do here, or you don't? And what *is* your point?"

"Your juvie record is missing, but I know you have one. Hugh mentioned it once—that you'd created fake IDs for your friends when you were all still underage. Good IDs. That you got into the state Vital Records, Social Security, and DMV. But you were caught."

She met Lilith's gaze, and said evenly, "They offered me a job."

"Did you take it?"

"Yes."

"You're lying," Hugh said from behind her. After closing the door, he strode silently across the room and stood next to Lilith.

"That was unfair," Savi said, rising to her feet. "You shouldn't use superpowers against me."

Hugh laughed and shook his head. "I didn't need to read the truth to know it for a lie." Short, dark mahogany hair, a powerful form—beautiful, though he didn't take her breath away. He did Lilith's. When they were together, it was like being in a statically charged atmosphere.

He'd changed since Lilith had come back into his life;

though always intense, he had been tightly contained, focused on academia and books. Now he had a darker edge—the eight-hundred-year-old warrior who no longer denied his nature.

Lilith hadn't created that edge; she'd only torn away the layers that had hidden it. A strange couple: the woman who lied and the man who saw truth. Yet they were absolutely and completely devoted to each other.

Savi fought the urge to cover the matrimonials; concealment would draw their attention more quickly than openness. "So what is it?" she asked instead, and wrapped her arms around her middle. "You want to know what I do? It's pretty simple; I get a list of transactions—credit cards, bank accounts, plane tickets, phone records, property acquisitions, whatever—and I have to change them. I don't even know what they are from. Most of them are probably from ordinary citizens, to keep me from guessing."

And the others were the government's way of protecting its agents and covering their movements. A credit card purchase for a pair of sunglasses twenty minutes after a political assassination in the Middle East? She didn't want to know about it, she just transformed it into a baguette in Paris. Savi wasn't the only one in the network; she imagined there were many others across the country in dark little offices, doing exactly the same thing. Changing transactions that she'd changed, just to make the layers deeper.

"That isn't our concern, Savi," Hugh said. "You don't do it for the money; you have more than enough from your parents' trust and from DemonSlayer. And you aren't capable of holding a job like this."

Savi pressed her lips together before she said, "You think I'm unreliable?"

"No. But only because you don't commit to anything you can't follow through on. You wouldn't have accepted this job and stayed for so long except under duress. Your interests change too quickly."

Lilith smiled thinly. "And it really, really upsets me when people I care for serve against their will. Sir Pup, may I have Auntie's file?"

A much thicker folder appeared in Lilith's upturned palm.

Her heart pounding, Savi looked from Hugh's face to Lilith's. "What's the point of this? I can't lie to you. You're trapping me into something—if you'd just tell me the reason, this would be a lot easier. You don't have to do this to me. Not you two." Her voice thickened. "Of all people, not you two."

Lilith turned her face away for a moment, but Hugh didn't flinch. "Of all people, you should have come to us. We're doing it this way because you didn't." His gaze softened. "Auntie's resident alien status was revoked just after you turned eighteen. We can see that in her file. Also, that her applications for reinstatement were denied. Then she's given citizenship, though she never took the test or fulfilled the preliminary requirements. You did that? Or they did?"

"They did," Savi said tightly. "I'd have never left the rest incomplete."

"It was a different administration then; Homeland Security didn't even exist," Hugh said. "Why didn't you try to get out?"

"Because I brought it on myself with those fake IDs, and I *have* to consider these consequences. They might let me go; I don't know. For all I know it was a demon who forced the issue eight years ago because of my connection to you. We've learned enough about Lucifer's foray into different federal agencies to know that one of his demons might have had that power—it's probable they did. But I'm not going to risk it by asking them to let me go." She leveled a dark look at Lilith. "You understand that."

"Making a bargain with Lucifer is completely different than working covertly for the government," Lilith said.

Silence fell for a moment, then Hugh lowered his face into his hands and his shoulders began shaking. Unable to contain her own laughter, Savi sat down and bent forward, holding her sides.

"Lilith," he said finally, wiping his eyes. "That's a lie."

A smile pulled at her mouth, but she didn't glance away from Savi. "We'll get you out, if you want out."

Savi sighed. "It's not about me, but Nani. If she's deported, or even detained while I sort things out, it will be unbearably humiliating for her. She'll lose all *izzat*. And not just her honor, but the restaurant, everything she's accomplished here. Forty years ago she came with nothing but my mother, and worked like crazy to put her through medical school. Then she raised me when my other grandparents wouldn't have anything to do with a little brown girl. She took in Hugh." Pulling her hand through her short hair, she added, "There's embarrassment, and then there's humiliation. I won't subject her to the second. Won't even risk it."

Hugh crouched in front of her. "You know I would not, either. And last year, I would not have been in a position to help you, even if you had come to me. But I am now. Transfer to SI, and let us offer you our protection. Perhaps immediate escape isn't possible, but we can remove you from this, at least." He smiled. "And you'll be able to ask plenty of questions."

"I don't want to let you down," she said quietly. "It's true that I can't hold a job for a long time."

Lilith snorted with laughter. "Oh, you won't get bored. Identification for people who've been dead for decades, electronics to play with—garrotes to make. I'll use the hell out of someone like you." She shrugged. "And it'll give us time to make certain that if you want out, you can get out. I'll make inquiries, find out who we need to threaten—and if it *was* a demon. We won't trap you there if you eventually want to go."

The matrimonials seemed to stare up at her. "It might be soon."

"That's fine." Lilith slid down from her perch. "Are you making dinner tonight? It's been months since we've had your *pulao*. Hugh tries, but his doesn't compare."

Surprised by the change of subject, Savi blinked, then reluctantly smiled. She'd never had a chance against the two of them. "Yes."

Hugh walked past her to the door. Sir Pup followed him.

"Good. Colin will be coming after; he just got back from England." Lilith was watching her carefully. "You can finally thank him for helping to provide your alibi."

Her smile froze in place. "Great." She hadn't seen the vampire since the night at the club, a month ago. He'd flown out the next day, when she'd still been in the hospital, out of her mind with fever. Two weeks, it had burned through her, had her hanging on a thread between life and death.

And he'd left.

Sense told her he'd been under no obligation to stay. Experience reminded her he'd done the same before. Reason stated his response had been a result of the venom and nosferatu blood.

And the only conclusion to be drawn from the anticipation, dread, and hurt filling her in equal parts was that she must be a stupid, shallow lunatic.

"Savi," Hugh said from behind her. "There's something else."

She turned, then barely ducked the short-bladed knife streaking toward her. It sailed over her shoulder, and Lilith snatched it out of the air. Hugh lowered his hand.

"Jesus!" Her heart pounding, she looked between them. Her legs trembled. "What the fuck was that for? What if you'd hit me?"

"Hugh'd be tending to your shoulder right now," Lilith said. "But he isn't. Accelerated reflexes, enhanced speed. Not near that of a vampire, though. How strong are you?"

"I don't know," Savi replied stiffly. "I've been hoping it will go away, like the fever did."

"Until it does, you'll be training with me," Hugh said. His throat worked, then he cursed and slammed the door on his way through.

It was unlike Hugh to swear. He probably thought he'd failed her.

He hadn't.

"I can't," Savi said.

Lilith's gaze was not devoid of sympathy, but she shook her head. "You don't have a choice now."

Savi's teeth clenched. "How did you know? Did Michael tell you?"

"Michael? No, Hugh could see it within a minute of your coming home from the hospital. I don't know why you tried to hide it from us."

"I have to pretend I'm normal."

Lilith tapped her finger on the matrimonial classifieds. "We'll teach you how to *pretend*, but you won't be. Can you live with that? Can he?"

"Yes. And he doesn't have to know."

The dark sound of Lilith's laughter filled the small room. "I'm the last person to tell you not to lie. But can *you* be happy lying?"

Savi frowned. "It's marriage. It isn't only about happiness; security is important, too. Happiness is for later. Were your marriages any different?"

Still laughing, Lilith shook her head. "No. That's why I'm living in sin now," she said as she left.

Savi rubbed her forehead again and closed the door. She could be happy; she found it quite easily. Would the man she married be?

Probably not.

❧

Colin straightened his cuffs for the third time. A piece of lint disturbed the perfect line of his trouser leg, and he brushed it off.

Castleford's house rose up in front of him, a boxy, contemporary bit of architecture. Colin appreciated the clean lines of it, but preferred his Victorian. He'd parked in the driveway; his gaze rose to the lighted windows above the garage. Nothing to see from this angle, but he could hear Savi moving around inside.

He pulled at his collar and sighed. If he stayed in his car much longer, Hugh and Lilith might think he was nervous.

A door slammed, and Savi ran down the private stair from her flat. Was she so eager to meet him again? His body hummed with the pleasure of it.

But he didn't open the door; he needed to wait . . . and see.

She wore jeans, sneakers, and a thick cream sweater. She'd wound an azure scarf around her slim, beautiful neck.

Sir Pup squeezed through the pet door at the front of the house and shifted to a larger size. He bounded toward her, then tagged along beside her legs as she rounded the front of the Bentley and tapped on Colin's window.

He lowered the glass and inhaled.

Nothing. Her unique scent—wonderful, intoxicating in its way, but not the delicious, dangerous perfume.

The devastating sense of loss nearly undid him. His relief kept him upright.

She leaned down. The window framed her brightly smiling face like a portrait, and his breath caught. "I just wanted to say thanks for that night."

He cleaved his tongue from the roof of his mouth. "Of course, Savi. It was my pleasure."

Her smile never wavered. "Yeah. About that . . ."

"Think nothing of it," he said carelessly, and flashed his fangs in a rakish grin. "A temporary madness, but I am well recovered. As, apparently, are you."

"Apparently." She blinked; her eyes were a warm, rich chocolate. Her skin, cinnamon cream. "Did you have a nice holiday with your family?"

"Yes. Quite lovely."

"That's good. Anyway, thank you. I'm off for a stroll in the park; I ate too much. I'll see you later."

"Of course." He spoke to an empty window; she'd already moved on. And absent a mirror, he couldn't watch her leave without giving himself away.

He found Castleford and Lilith in a kitchen filled with Savitri's scent. And cinnamon and garlic, saffron and ginger . . . he had to stop this bloody foolishness.

Breathing through his mouth, he said, "It's gone."

Perched on a barstool, Lilith looked across the counter to Castleford for confirmation of truth; Colin didn't take insult. The tension eased from Hugh's form, then from Lilith's.

Lilith laughed, her relief evident. "Good. I'd hate to have to kill you. Particularly as you're so handsome."

"I'd hate to be killed," he replied easily and slid onto the stool beside her. "Particularly as exile to Beaumont Court proved as effective a deterrent as death. You sent the dog outside to protect her from me?"

Castleford's lips twitched as he transferred dishes from the granite counter to the sink. "Another deterrent, if needed. Perhaps you would have kissed Sir Pup."

"Forgive me if I fail to see the humor in that." Those few moments with Savi atop him, her mouth pressed to his, had been some of the sweetest of his life. Colin would not have them sullied.

Ice settled in Castleford's eyes, and he said, "It has taken me a month to see the humor in having to pry Savi away from you when you were at the edge of your control. Had we arrived but minutes later, what would have occurred?"

He'd have been inside her. Drinking from her. Tasting her. And he'd been so maddened by her scent and the stink of wyrmwolf blood—his own blood—he probably wouldn't have noticed if she was awake.

She mightn't have survived.

Lilith quickly said, "Don't answer that, Colin. I don't want to have to pick up pieces of you." Her gaze moved to Hugh. "Either of you. If the pheromone subsided with the fever, then it hardly matters."

"It matters," Colin growled.

Castleford stared at him for a moment, then turned to Lilith. "It always matters when you've hurt someone you mean to protect." He shoved his fists into his pockets. "She didn't know the consequences of drinking the venom, of mixing it with the blood. That was my failure."

As Colin agreed, he didn't respond.

Lilith obviously didn't ascribe Castleford the same blame. "You didn't know, either. Martyr." She muttered the word with exasperated affection, then glanced at Colin. "How long did your fever last when you were tainted by Michael's sword?"

He looked down at his hand. A silvery scar crossed his palm, a remnant of a blood-brother ritual he and Anthony Ramsdell had completed when they were boys. They couldn't have known the sword they'd used had once belonged to Michael, who had killed a Chaos dragon with it.

Nor could they have known that the dragon's blood had instilled its power in the metal of the sword, or anticipated that power transferring to their blood. Tainting it.

But nineteen years later, as a young vampire aware of his origins, Colin should have known better when he tried to perform a different—and apparently as harmless—ritual.

In such things, appearances were almost always deceiving.

"A week," he said.

"Did you have any extraordinary abilities before you were attacked by the nosferatu?" Lilith arched a brow. "Excepting your beauty, of course. Speed, strength?"

A smile pulled at his mouth. "No. None that I could discern."

"Did Ramsdell? Or your sister?"

"No." His throat tightened. "Aside from . . . the way they went."

Lilith's brow creased, and Colin looked away before she could ask.

A fruit bowl rested at the end of the bar, white porcelain against a backdrop of deep red. The crimson paint on the kitchen walls was the same hue as Lilith's demon-skin; had it been on purpose? Castleford had Fallen after he'd slain Lilith, then attempted to live as a normal man for sixteen years. Had he been drawn to the color from memory, even if the memory's influence had been a subconscious one? Had he wanted to surround himself with her in the room most necessary for life? The routine of eating, ingesting . . . it was as important to humans—even extraordinary ones—as to vampires.

Or had it only been aesthetics?

His fingers slid over the oranges, the apples, rearranging the composition. He draped the point of the grape pyramid over the lip of the bowl. The purple skins stretched tight beneath his fingertips, full and ripe.

Vanitas. Perfect now, but it would not be long before it succumbed to rot. Or digestion.

Colin drew his hand back, brought it to his face and inhaled. Citrus, sweet, clean. Like Savitri's skin, but scent was fleeting. She was best captured with raw sienna, tempered by titanium white and heated with a touch of burnt umber. Egyptian violet for the shadows.

Foolishness. "What of the wyrmwolf? How did it travel between realms?"

Castleford's mouth flattened. "We don't know." He glanced at Lilith, who nodded. "We may need you to go into the Room to look. We need to know what's going on in Chaos, and you're the only one who can tell us."

Sickness fell heavy in his gut, but Colin forced a lazy smile. "Must you capitalize everything when you speak? It is all so dramatic. Above, Below. Falls and Ascensions. Gifts. Rooms."

"I like dramatic," Lilith said. She smiled as well, but her gaze didn't move from his face. "He does it for me."

Colin lifted a brow. "I shall certainly give you a show in the Room." But he couldn't hold on to the mockery; his jaw clenched, and he pushed away from the counter and left the kitchen.

Mirrors. Nothing but mirrors in that room. Though he wouldn't physically be in Chaos, it was the nearest thing to it, and it was almost impossible to separate reality from the illusion.

He was shaking just remembering the previous times, dreading the next.

In the living room, he tried to steady himself with Caelum in front of him; the canvas was rough beneath his palm.

"Wait a few days, Colin," Castleford said. He and Lilith had followed the vampire, stood shoulder to shoulder. They didn't need a painting to cling to; they had each other. "There has not been another wyrmwolf. Perhaps we worry for naught. We simply want to make certain. We can wait."

"Even though waiting is a tool of the devil," Lilith said, and Colin laughed despite himself.

"Very well. This week." He took a deep breath. "And as we are speaking of devils, I could find no evidence of a rogue demon. The nosferatu's trail had faded beyond my ability to track it; what I did find was most concentrated near Belgrave Square in London."

"If it was Belgravia, then we can almost be certain it was a demon who supported the nosferatu in this," Castleford said. "He'd have the means to fund the nosferatu's tickets and provide the fake identification—then cover it up."

Lilith nodded her agreement, smiling darkly. "If he's connected to an embassy, someone's going to be pissed when we kill him."

And set off an international scandal she'd undoubtedly relish. "There have been residential openings in the area," Colin said. "He'd not necessarily be attached to a government."

"He would be if it provided him money and influence," Lilith said. "Goddammit. You can always count on a demon to be derivative and unoriginal; he's following Lucifer's example by trying to create an alliance with a nosferatu and using it as an assassin."

An alliance that would have benefited them both: the nosferatu killed *en masse*, which it loved; the rogue demon enjoyed the terror he created, his powers of deception.

"And he probably imagines himself superior to the nosferatu by making it serve him." Castleford released a heavy sigh, ran his hand through his hair. "The irony is that if we'd had Savi in those days immediately following the flight, she might have been able to dig him out. But the rogue is so far under now, she can't. She got the nosferatu, but the fever gave the demon time to escape."

Colin turned away from the painting. "I believe I heard you incorrectly. What has Savitri to do with this?"

A smile touched Castleford's lips; Colin couldn't determine if pride or concern sat in that expression. "About a week ago, I received an anonymous e-mail from someone within DHS. It traced the financial and identification info from the nosferatu's ticket and passport through about seven more layers than our technicians had been able to do. All dead ends, which our anonymous informant pointed out in the message. Also that such thorough concealment indicated something much more powerful lay behind it all."

"Savi," Lilith said. "So we stole her."

Colin looked back and forth between the two of them. "You are bringing her into SI? You are mad. Do you not endanger her enough simply by allowing her to live here?"

Lilith's eyes darkened. "Be careful, Colin."

"We intend to give her the knowledge she needs to protect herself." Castleford radiated tension and anger. He could have hidden it, but it served as a silent warning.

Colin didn't pay heed. "A month ago, I'd have had her spread out on my bed and my fangs in her throat, and there is little knowledge you could have given her that might have stopped me. What of the next vampire who tries? One who holds a grudge against SI . . . and sees a pretty little girl who's a bit too curious to be sensible, and who happens to be your sister. You'll make her a more appealing target than she already is. And it is not the first time your relationship to her has made her such."

Lilith's fingers clenched on Castleford's forearm. "It has been done, she is already linked to us; that will not change when she moves out," she said. "Should we send her to Caelum again . . . permanently? That isn't an option. We can't always hide her away to secure her safety."

Savi had not been safe in Caelum. His back rigid, Colin faced the painting again.

"And though we appreciate your concern, it is not your choice," Castleford said coldly. "It is hers."

Colin pressed his lips together to stop the invectives that leapt to his tongue. Hang all demons and Guardians and their respect for human free will.

"We can only make certain she knows as much as possible and has the best methods of protection before her wedding," Lilith said. "And that is what we'll do."

Her wedding? He would not trust himself to ask.

He traced the arching entrance to Caelum's central courtyard before dropping his hand to his side. A fountain lay behind that arch, though it was not visible from Michael's temple. He'd painted its impossibly flat pool before, the perfect arc of water, but not here. With a shrug, he finally said, "Very well. It hardly matters to me if you insist on acting the fools. And I must beg your pardon: I have yet to hunt. Have we finished?"

Colin didn't wait for their assent or for Castleford to call him on his lie; he left. The night air was cool against his face, heavy with moisture. A fog coming in.

The breeze carried a thread of scent. Sweet. He ground his teeth together and ignored it. Just memory, tormenting him.

He slid into the leather seat, leaned back against the headrest. Faint, but still there. Remnants from her presence in his car a month ago? It had to be, though he'd not detected it earlier that evening.

And it was odd that this memory had a direction. West, toward Lake Merced.

There would be hunting to be had there.

CHAPTER 6

The baseball arced over the tops of the trees, disappearing in the dark and fog. Two hundred yards, at least.

Sir Pup sprinted to fetch his ball, and Savi shook her head in disbelief. Though she wasn't a complete wimp, she'd long ago accepted she was less than athletically gifted. This was incredible. Even Barry Bonds couldn't have smashed a home run that far.

The hellhound barked in the distance, and she bit her lip in sudden alarm. Hopefully it hadn't hit someone on the head or destroyed a car window. But no, there he was, breaking free of the tree line and trotting across the grass.

Oh, shit—Colin was with him. She'd recognize that elegant stride anywhere. Dammit. As if it hadn't been difficult enough to pretend disinterest when she'd thanked him at his car. She'd spent most of the afternoon building her psychic shields to steel; assuming that she wouldn't see him again that evening, she hadn't maintained them.

Breathing slow and steady. Focus. And don't look at his face. Not right away.

She pasted on a smile and gazed at a point over his shoulder. She probably looked like an idiot—but she felt like one, so it was as well. Smart women ran when they saw a vampire approaching.

And if their hearts raced, it should be from fear.

The point over his shoulder rose higher and higher as he neared her. She lowered her gaze to the pocket of his jacket. Why did he wear it? He wouldn't become cold. Was it simply because it looked fantastic, as if it had been tailor-made to fit him?

It probably had been.

He stopped directly in front of her, less than an arm's length away. Too close. "You shouldn't be alone in the park after sunset, sweet Savitri." Though his words admonished her, his tone did not. It was low and warm. Seductive.

Her throat was dry. She swallowed and said, "Sir Pup is with me. I'm not being foolish."

"No, you are not. He's a fine protector. But you should not be alone." Colin trailed his forefinger from her ear to jawline, tipping her face up with gentle pressure.

A shiver ran over her skin. She stared at the cleft in his chin. Not too deep, just a lovely shadow.

"Do you know why I'm here?"

"To hunt?"

"No." She heard the smile in his voice. "I prefer not to chase after men and women on the jogging paths."

"It does seem creepy," she said. "Like a serial killer."

His fangs glistened in the fog-muted moonlight; his laughter was soft. "Yes, I imagine it does. I *was* off to hunt. But I was overcome by the most delicious fragrance." He slowly bent his head toward hers. A breath away from her mouth, he inhaled deeply. He didn't touch her lips, but she could feel the warmth from his. "It disappeared when I saw you across the lawn. Why do you think that is?"

"The breeze shifted?"

"I am downwind of you."

"Perhaps I'm not the source."

"Perhaps." He teased the corner of her mouth with a flick

of his tongue. She closed her eyes and concentrated on breathing, on standing. What was he doing to her? "Perhaps it is Sir Pup," he said.

"Yes," she whispered. "Yes, it must be."

"How would you test such a thing, Savitri? Send him away? Remove a variable?"

"I'm a variable," she said.

"But should you leave and Sir Pup stay, no one could protect you from the evil creatures stalking the night."

She had to smile. Such melodrama. "If he leaves, no one will protect me from you."

"Castleford believes you'll be able to protect yourself after you've had enough lessons." There was an edge of anger in his voice now, when it had only been soft.

"You doubt him? You doubt I will?" She finally looked up at him. "Or are you here to teach *him* a lesson?"

"No." He watched her with shadowed eyes. "I'm here because he's taught you well. Ask me why I can't suggest you sleep, as I did Auntie."

"I already know. My psychic shields."

"Then why did you ask before?"

Except for his hand against her chin he didn't touch her, yet his gaze held her immobile. Another vampire trick? Why had Hugh not warned her? Was it something only Colin could do?

"I didn't know if *you* could overcome them."

"I see." Sardonic amusement flirted with his lips as he tucked his fingers beneath her chenille scarf, slowly loosening it. Cool air wafted against her neck, sent prickles down her spine. "Because I once drank your blood, you thought I might have bound you to me. Like Dracula and Mina."

His lashes swept down as he dipped his head toward hers.

Her breath hitched. "Yes."

"No, Savitri. Only when I drink does your mind open to me." She began trembling as his mouth skimmed the side of her jaw. He spoke with his lips against her throat. "Invite me in."

"No." She gasped the word.

"I'll make it good for you this time." He dragged the inside of his bottom lip over her pulse. Hot. Wet. "Please invite me in."

She didn't trust the pleading note in his voice; she couldn't imagine him begging for anything. "No."

"Then lower your shields." He raised his head when she stiffened. "That is not a threat. Only that I ask the lesser pleasure if you deny the greater."

"I have no reason to give you either, or to trust you. Particularly as I don't know what you've done to me now."

As light and impenetrable as the fog, his gray eyes searched hers; then he tilted his head back, stared up at the sky. His laugh was pure frustration. "What *I* have done to *you*? What of what you are doing to me? I am risking one of the few friendships I've known by standing here. I've never run after a woman, yet the moment I realized what that scent was, I abandoned my hunt and came for you. Do you know what it is, Savitri? Do you know what you are doing to me?"

"It's psychic," she realized, shaking. "Not physical." It meant that the changes in her had gone deeper than she'd known. Would they fade?

Guardians who Fell retained some of their strength and speed, and aged slowly—though in all other ways they were human, with no psychic abilities. Once transformed, some things could not be undone—and the longer the transformation, the deeper the change. Would it be the same of a woman who accidentally ingested hellhound venom and nosferatu blood?

"Yes. I mistook it for peach through a trick of memory. I made the easiest and most sensible conclusion given what I perceived, likened it to a familiar scent—but it was wrong."

The Gestalt effect. Like in Caelum.

As if the same thought occurred to him, he tensed. "Do you deny me as punishment for Caelum? Is this a lesson?"

"No." She wrapped her arms around her chest. Small defense, but she still couldn't find the strength to move away from him. "I returned that favor in Polidori's."

He let go a shout of laughter. "With an orgasm? With the most bloody brilliant kiss I've ever received?"

She forced the rush of pleasure away. It had been good, but so had Caelum until he'd decided to give her a lesson. "You taught me to be wary, and it was what I most needed to learn. I taught you that you're no better than those you feed from, because that is what *you* most need to learn." His amusement faded, his gaze hardened to iron, but she forged on, "I don't deny you as punishment. I deny you because you taught me too well."

He stared at her, then lowered his head, his shoulders shaking. But there was little mirth in his voice as he said, "I am fortune's buggered fool."

"That's what Hugh told me, but he said you liked it." Sir Pup nudged her knee, and she was grateful for an excuse to look away from Colin's sudden grin.

The baseball dropped at her feet. She threw it with all the force she could muster. Perhaps she could take out all of this pent-up frustration in some kind of exercise; at least Colin's hold on her seemed to have faded. She could move now.

Sir Pup streaked away.

Colin had half-turned to allow her room to throw. His features were curiously blank when he glanced back at her. "What do you think I've done to you?"

"That thing with your eyes," she said. "Keeping me here, though I know I should leave."

"The thing with my—" He broke off. His gaze roamed over her face. Suddenly, his focus narrowed on her mouth, became sharp and predatory.

She took a step back.

"Oh, Savitri," he murmured. "You should have left when you had the opportunity."

"I couldn't."

"It was not my doing." He inhaled, and his lids half-lowered, as if in ecstasy. "*This* is physical. Your arousal."

Her eyes widened.

So did his, and he laughed with dark amusement. "You did not realize. But you know desire, Savitri. I was not the first."

Far from it. She looked down at her hands. They shook. Her breasts were heavy, her nipples tight and aching. Heat and moisture pooled between her legs. Her heart pounded.

It was her shields. She'd never been very good at listening to her body's cues; she could easily pass through a day without recognizing hunger or exhaustion—and when she held her psychic shields up it became worse.

Sir Pup returned with the ball. Colin quickly took it from

between the massive jaws, pivoted, and snapped his arm. The hellhound disappeared again.

"A variable removed," he said. "Shall we conduct an experiment, Savitri? Discover at what point your shields fail?"

"No." Her eyes held his. "I won't let them."

"But you feel it now." He brushed his thumb back and forth across his bottom lip. "I have the same difficulty at times; the bloodlust is so overwhelming I do not realize I'm hard until I'm inside her."

Her lips parted. She remembered all too well how that had felt: full, incredibly full. Surrounded by beauty, filled with it.

Now she seemed hollow, empty.

His smile faded, and the longing in his gaze reflected hers. "I know that, too. Your shields are strong, Savi, but your face is easy to read." His fingertips brushed her cheekbone, a simple caress. "Invite me in. I can't give you Caelum, but I can give you rapture. And we'll both have what we want."

She squeezed her eyes shut. "I don't trust you."

She waited breathlessly for his angry response, but he remained silent. His hand drifted down; his thumb strummed over her pulse. Oh, god. She couldn't hide its frantic beat. Did he think it was fear?

Unable to bear the tension, she looked up. "What are you doing?"

His gaze was cold, hungry. "Deciding if taking what I want is worth the losses it will incur."

Hugh and Lilith. "They'd kill you if you do it against my will."

"Yes. And so I must consider another option: earning your trust, so that you'll open to me."

Her mouth fell open in disbelief. "You want to be friends? At the same time announcing your ulterior motives? That your aim is not truly friendship, but to get into my head and my throat? Your methods are flawed, to say the least."

"I enjoy your company. Do you not mine?" He phrased it as a question, but his tone said she must.

And she did, too, much for sense. "When you aren't being a complete ass."

He laughed, and his eyes warmed. "I particularly enjoy that aspect of your company. We shall call it an experiment, to see if we can get along." He removed his hand and shrugged carelessly. "And as Lilith mentioned you are soon to be married, I cannot, in good conscience, tie you to my bed and conduct multiple experiments on you in order to achieve my goals."

Her breath caught. "But you could in bad conscience?"

"Exceedingly bad." He looked down at his wrists and pulled on his shirt cuffs, the white edges in stark contrast to the dark jacket sleeves. He had beautiful hands, his fingers long and graceful. Genetics, but the power in them was still a mystery to her, their appearance concealing unnatural strength.

And now hers did, too.

"I assume it is an arranged marriage. Are you engaged?"

Was he bored by such topics, only asking out of politeness? His tone and his primping suggested it. She forced herself to look away from his hands, up to his face, and caught the sharp gleam of interest before he blinked.

She didn't mistake the excited flutter in her stomach. Stupid, shallow lunatic. She should run. Friendship with him was madness. Dangerous.

But *would* it be dangerous? In Caelum, he had been under the influence of the realm's surreal beauty and the extraordinary emotions it had created. They both had been. Whatever his motives now, he seemed determined not to alienate Lilith and Hugh. And whatever he thought he might get from her, nothing would come of it. She had her promise to keep.

"No," she finally said. "I'm not engaged yet."

He smiled lazily. "Then may I kiss you until you are? Just to taste now and again."

She shook her head; not in denial, but to clear it.

"Do not fear, Savi; I'll wait until you trust me a bit more. I'll not take advantage of your confusion."

She was not confused. This was very simple: He was a vampire, intent on drinking her blood for his pleasure. Who would use her with little concern for the damage he could inflict. Her indecision wasn't because her head couldn't figure that out, but because the rest of her was brainless. And because her arousal and curiosity were far too strong.

She could ignore the first and make certain that she was

rarely alone with him—and perhaps friendship was a safe way to appease her curiosity. But was it worth the risk?

He offered his hand, accompanied it with a reassuring smile. "Shall I walk you home?"

Hesitantly, she placed her palm against his.

§

From the outside, the warehouse in Hunter's Point appeared as decrepit as the rest of the neighborhood. Rust stained the metal siding and the roof boasted a haphazard mix of materials, as if it had been hastily and cheaply repaired too many times.

Colin winced as one of his tires jarred into a pothole, and prayed the buckling asphalt in the parking lot wouldn't damage the Bentley's undercarriage. Such an expensive nuisance, mechanics and maintenance. If Colin didn't enjoy driving so much, he'd have hired a chauffeur years ago to take care of such things.

Castleford's and Lilith's motorcycles stood propped near the back entrance. Colin parked in the next space and deactivated the car alarm. It would not deter skilled thieves, and the warehouse had been soundproofed; the alarm could blare incessantly without anyone inside hearing it.

The entrance gave the first indication the warehouse was not all it appeared; Colin swiped his card and waited for the sound of the locks disengaging. The door had been constructed of reinforced steel, four inches thick.

Inside, a long undecorated corridor led him to the security desk. The white walls hid a myriad of sensors that read temperature and scanned for weapons. A defense system, too—venom-laced darts and gas canisters.

Jeeves sat behind a bulletproof glass shield and watched him approach.

A joke that Lilith aimed at him, Colin was certain. The Guardians undergoing training at the facility alternated shifts at the desk, but always took the same form: an elderly man, with the stiffest upper lip Colin had seen outside Windsor Castle. Castleford had claimed it was simply practice for the fledglings, disappearing into a role and maintaining a physical transformation—but Colin hadn't missed the humor in the other man's gaze when he'd given the explanation.

"Good afternoon, Jeeves. Do I pass?" Or not, as was better proof of his identity.

"I have been unable to attain a satisfactory reading, sir. Please enter a voice sample."

Colin rolled his eyes and moved to a panel on the wall. A demon could easily mimic his voice, but it was one of the few methods of identification they could use with him. "Colin Ames-Beaumont, vampire and master of the sartorial arts. Do you adore my waistcoat, Jeeves?"

"It is positively smashing, sir. Please submit to a retinal and handprint scan."

Colin's brows rose. "I never have before. Why now?"

"Agent Milton has instituted a new policy, sir."

He smiled, allowing the tips of his fangs to show. "What is the point, Jeeves?"

"Please submit, sir."

His jaw clenched, but he stepped forward, slapped his hand against the panel, and stared ahead.

"Thank you, sir."

A door to Colin's left slid open. He glanced back at the old man. "Did anything register, Rebecca?"

"No, sir. But if a demon had been impersonating you, he would have shown up on the sensors. We are no longer to rely upon your not appearing in the initial scans in the corridor. How did you know? Did my blocks fail?"

"No. You are simply the only one I had not yet instructed in the difference between a waistcoat and an Ermenegildo Zegna creation." He shook his head. "I don't know how you intend to kill demons without knowing something of fashion."

Jeeves's thin lips pursed in a gesture unmistakably female. "Miss Murray is in the tech room, sir."

"You are impertinent, Jeeves," he said, but smiled as he swept through the door.

Savitri. It had been almost a week since they'd made their agreement to try friendship—it was madness to attempt it, yet completely enjoyable. Even the ache and frustration of her denials and impenetrable shields had some pleasure attached: it made her inevitable succumbing all the more sweet.

And he was determined it would not be simply a psychic

yielding, but a physical one as well. Good God, psychic illusion or not, he'd tasted for the first time in two centuries. If, when she lowered her shields, he discovered that her psychic flavor still manifested a physical taste, Colin wouldn't relinquish it. Her wedding would be no obstacle; her husband could never give her what Colin could, and most of the arranged marriages he'd known had seen the couples going elsewhere once the heir and the spare had been produced.

He'd not even have to wait that long; there was no possibility she'd have a child other than her husband's if she was in Colin's bed.

He almost shivered in anticipation of it.

But his smile and anticipation quickly faded; unfortunately, it was not Savi he was there to see.

Colin forced his eyelids open and swallowed against the sudden vertigo. The mirror pressed hard and cold beneath his knees and palms—he could *feel* it, but his vision told him he was suspended in the air, hundreds of feet above rivers of blood and molten rock. The smell assaulted him—rot and sulphur and the sickly sweet odor of burning flesh.

Like the wyrmwolves' blood.

He fought against the nausea rising in his throat. God. He couldn't bear this, he couldn't—

Selah spoke, her tone warm and encouraging. Not afraid, as it had once been. "Colin, we need to see where they're going. How they're getting out. You must focus."

Selah. He reached out but couldn't find her hand. *Try again.* How many times had she tried to teleport them away and failed?

The ends of his fingers were stumps, but they didn't bleed because he'd barely any blood left. That was good; she couldn't leave with him because his blood was tainted. But when it was gone . . .

Feeding. Ripping and tearing. Strong enough to run if you feed—

Perspiration dripped into his eyes, blurring the scene below him. He wiped at it with his sleeve. He should have come in naked; his clothes stank.

He'd burn them. Like the bodies above him burned with the dragons' breath and the creatures below burned in the rivers of lava and everything burned—

A body fell through the air next to him. Colin felt the rush of air and heat, saw the flash of iridescent scales, and steeled himself. It couldn't touch him, but he didn't want to add his shrieks to those above. The dragon swooped down, caught the body in its enormous jaws, and downed it with a single bite. A small, young dragon; Colin could have spanned the distance between its eyes with his arms.

It flew away with a single beat of its membranous wings.

"Colin?"

"Dragon," he breathed in explanation, and glanced up.

Oh, good God. He shouldn't have. The rotting bodies. The nosferatu wriggling between them like pale worms. *Flying*, their hands scraping over the icy black ceiling in a manner almost familiar—

For an instant, astonishment overwhelmed horror. "They're writing. I can't see what—only that they are."

"The nosferatu?"

Colin felt the light psychic touch accompanying the question. Michael, with a request to look.

"Yes." Colin let him in, felt the quick frustration before the Doyen withdrew.

"You're too far from them," the Doyen said. "I cannot read it."

"The symbols?" Lilith asked.

"In all probability. They would remember those Lucifer used in the rituals last year."

Colin let his chin fall against his chest. No use looking up—only down. A shifting, sliding mass raced across the obsidian rocks below.

Wyrmwolves. Running together, in a pack of thousands. Tens of thousands. Ripping and tearing pieces from each other, then regenerating to feed and be fed from again. The reek of their flesh and blood and fur rose on waves of heat.

"They wouldn't know the meaning behind each," Castleford said. "Or which ones combined to form an effective spell. Lucifer didn't share that knowledge."

"No, but the ritual was designed to allow them access to the Gates—"

Shut up. Colin clenched his teeth, gagging against the stench. He closed his eyes, fought to hold on to reality. Mirrors. Not Chaos.

Don't leave me. Not here. Not alone.

Her voice faint beneath the screams, Lilith said flatly, "It's impossible."

And part of him left.

❧

"It's impossible," Savitri said. Her eyebrows lifted, as if daring him to defy her. "A tessellation made of circles?"

Colin studied the arch, its cylindrical marble blocks, the lack of a keystone. Though no mortar had been used, the pattern interlocked as tightly as if it had been made of straight edges. It shouldn't have been possible, and it should have fallen apart under its own weight—but it stood. Solidly, if her barefooted kick to the base had been any indication. "Apparently, sweet, it is possible."

"Hugh says that with Guardians and demons, appearances are almost always deceiving. Apparently the same is true of their homes." *Thick ebony lashes framed her dark eyes, made the curiosity and humor lighting them seem all the brighter. Strange that he could not read deeply behind them. She either had naturally strong psychic shields, as did many humans who repressed large portions of their natures, or Castleford had taught her to block.*

Given Castleford's fondness for lecturing, Colin decided it was the latter.

"Our brains aren't processing something correctly," she said, turning to examine the arch again.

He preferred it when she looked at him. He'd noted that she was most likely to whenever he said something incredibly vain or affected. As he also preferred to make such statements, it was no hardship to draw her gaze.

"Your brain may not be, young Savitri. You'd do well to forget all that Castleford has told you; I determined long ago that Guardian aphorisms are exceedingly tiresome, either certain to produce mental cavities with their cloyingly sweet

virtue, or destined to rot one's mind with boredom—particularly when one has heard them endlessly in one form or another for two centuries. Indeed, I stopped listening long ago, and you'll note my intellect is rather formidable."

"I've been taught to respect my elders, so I should let your blindness pass unremarked," she said, glancing over her shoulder and drawing her upper lip between her teeth. It appeared ridiculously soft and moist when she released it. "But since you are two hundred years old and likely deaf as well, it can't hurt to point out that your great age has obviously left you so mentally decrepit that you can't see what's in front of you. No wonder you pretended to be blind when we met; it was an outward manifestation of your inward deficiency."

He was certain he saw well enough, but he shouldn't have been looking. He batted his eyelashes together. "But don't you agree I have aged well?"

"Apparently," she said dryly. But her cheeks hollowed, as if she was biting the insides to keep from laughing.

Then she took his hand, pulling him beneath the archway, almost skipping in her eagerness. He walked lightly along beside her, no longer suppressing the smile that had threatened during the whole of their conversation. She'd continually surprised him from the moment of his arrival in Caelum; he'd quickly discovered she was an extraordinarily intelligent creature, if also hopelessly naïve and trusting. She'd not shown fear when he'd flashed his fangs, nor when he'd told her to run. Instead she'd stared at him with her wide, curious gaze and asked if he was strong enough to open the doors of Michael's temple.

Then she had offered him a sip of her blood in return for his feat.

Her questions had revealed she knew very well what a vampire was—even knew specifics about him that were different from others of his kind—yet she had risked being alone with him to experience the wonder of Caelum.

And he could think of no other companion he'd rather have shared it with. Not Lilith or Castleford—not even Ramsdell and Emily.

It was unsettling . . . but he could easily ascribe the foolishness of his reaction to Caelum.

He glanced down as her steps slowed and they entered a new courtyard. Her bare feet were silent on the creamy marble pavers. Now and again, her long, white linen skirt would flounce up, exposing her slim ankles and sleek calves, a flash of golden brown.

A white peasant shirt covered her arms and torso; the neckline sat at the points of her shoulders. Everything from her collarbones to the tips of her short hair lay open to his gaze.

Bloody hell, but it was such a pleasure to look; the sun brightened her skin, warmed the cinnamon tones until he thought he could smell the fragrance of her color beneath her natural, feminine scent.

He'd not taken the blood she'd offered, but as the hours passed in her company, his resistance began to wane. Not due to the bloodlust, which hadn't risen yet but certainly would soon . . . he simply wanted more of her.

All of her.

Foolishness. She was Castleford's sister, and he trusted Colin to look after her. After her grandmother, as well—and, indeed, both may have already passed into Colin's protection, if Castleford's insane plan to destroy the nosferatu with Colin's blood hadn't worked.

His tainted blood. *He clenched his teeth against the sudden wave of memory, but the rot filled his mind, the putrid scent of Chaos and blood and wyrmwolves.* Don't scream. Feed and you'll be strong enough to fight them. Strong enough to run.

Don't leave me here—

Savitri abruptly stopped, then staggered when he bumped into her, too distracted to catch himself. Automatically, he steadied her with his hands on her bare shoulders.

Reality in the form of her warm, smooth skin reasserted itself all too well.

The pulse beating at the base of her throat drew his gaze; his bloodlust ripened when its pace increased. He dropped his hands from her with a soft apology.

Good God, but she was light, fragile. She hadn't the least protection from him.

She'd be safer in Michael's temple, secluded there with her sleeping grandmother. He'd show her the symbols; she could lock him out.

"I just can't get over how beautiful it is," she whispered. She tilted her face up and spun in a slow circle. "It's unreal."

Colin looked as well, bringing his hand up to cover his eyes from the sun before he remembered that it wouldn't sting.

Sublime. The brilliant blue sky, pierced by pillars and spires of white. Huge onion domes and columned temples rose in perfect balance around them. It did not matter which prospect he beheld; it took his breath, his reason, and shattered every ideal of beauty he'd ever had.

And left him giddy with awe and delight. His chest ached, his eyes burned as if he were weeping—and yet it was laughter that spilled from him, left him so weak he had to lean over and brace his palms against his knees.

He couldn't make sense of any of it.

Don't leave me here alone.

Shaking his head, he straightened. Savitri sat on the ground beside him, her legs folded under her, her bottom resting in the curve of her heels. She stared at her hands; in the few hours they'd toured through Caelum, he'd come to recognize her attempt to regain her self-control.

She couldn't look much longer than he could without losing herself in it; that terrible, wonderful sense of shattering. Frightening, too—but she'd never shown her fear, though he'd heard her heart and lungs racing, had seen the trembling that had overtaken her.

What was wrong with her? His brows drew together, and he held out his hand to help her to her feet. "Does anything scare you?"

As if startled by the question, she blinked up into his face. Her fingers clenched over his for a brief second, and a half-smile shaped her lips. "Yes," she said. "When I think about it."

What the bloody hell did that mean? But the sparkle of water caught his attention, and he only said, "I shall have to make you think about it, then."

❧

"Think about what you're saying, Michael," Selah said, and Chaos roared in around him.

Blood filled Colin's mouth. His own this time. Thank God.

"The nosferatu have been feeding from creatures in Chaos for months now—maybe even from dragons. They're stronger, more powerful than before. If you go, can you fight them without your sword? Is it worth the risk to both of you on the slight chance they'll stumble upon a combination of symbols that opens a portal?"

"They're bloodsucking monkeys on fucking typewriters." The sharp rattle of glass accompanied Lilith's angry declaration. The dark mountain to Colin's left quaked—she'd hit the mirror. "The wyrmwolf was a fluke."

"He's back." Castleford's tone included a warning. To whom?

Colin shook his head, tried to clear it. Impossible. Not with the screams ringing in his ears. "Enough. Open the fucking door." He had to force the words out through clenched teeth. He closed his eyes, shut out the rot. Stopped breathing, to block out the odor.

But they still filled him.

❧

The décor in the observation area offended Colin's senses almost as badly as the Room did. Bland beige carpet, walls washed in a weak blue. Colors likely chosen to calm and soothe, but they only managed to declare the designer a tasteless idiot.

"Is the protection spell still active in this room?" Lilith looked to Michael for confirmation.

"Yes." The Doyen stood with his arms crossed over his massive chest, a tall, bronzed warrior with brutally short hair and an expression that could have been sculpted beneath Rodin's skilled hands. "We will not be overheard; you may speak freely."

Colin leaned back against the observation window; behind him, the Room was dark. "I've no intention of ever returning," he said. "And certainly not to see a horde of scribbling nosferatu."

"You may not have a choice," Michael said. "The danger is twofold: If they open a portal to Earth and return the stronger,

the death toll will be catastrophic. The vampires we are training cannot defeat nosferatu alone, and we have not enough
Guardians. More than wyrmwolves may slip through in their
wake; if they release a dragon—"

"Perhaps you can make yourself a new sword." Colin's
fists tightened in his pockets. "I'll not go back. If you simply
intend to look at the symbols, it only provides the nosferatu
confirmation of their ingenuity—unless you intend to fight
them? But if you are killed, who will teleport me out?"

"There would be no one," Castleford said softly. He
glanced at Michael. "I agree that the threat does not equal the
risk."

"I'm bloody thrilled that you agree with me, but it hardly
matters. I'll not return."

"There is the second danger," Michael said. "It can be no
mistake they make their attempt amongst the bodies above."

"You can't know that it will open into Hell," Lilith said.

"We've all thought it," Selah said, rising from the sofa.
Her wings opened wide; a quick shake ran through the feathers as she smoothed them. "Those souls who have reneged on
their bargains have their faces frozen in a field Below, and
they scream; in Chaos, bodies hang from the ceiling, and they
scream. And scream." Her blue eyes filled. "I don't know that
I wouldn't Fall rather than return, either."

"You wouldn't," Castleford said.

"I'd consider it. I only wouldn't because I have an easy
escape." Selah shook her head, and turned to face Michael.
"I can't teleport him out if you are defeated. If they break
through the ceiling into Hell, what is the danger? The Gates
are closed. If the nosferatu traveled through to Hell, they
couldn't escape—most likely, they'd be killed by the demons
there."

"Lucifer and Belial may even stop in their battles against
one another long enough to chase down the bloodsuckers."

"Yes," Michael said. "And the Morningstar would have access, once again, to Chaos. Nothing in the wager he lost prevents him from working to create a Gate from Chaos to Earth
before his five hundred years have passed. He has the knowledge, and he would bring the dragons with him."

"Let them come," Colin said tightly. "I'll not return."

Michael's eyes transformed; when he looked at Colin, it was with a blank, obsidian gaze. "You may not have a choice."

CHAPTER 7

*In the most absurd of circumstances, I find myself
struck by a curse. I pray that your next letter includes
intelligence from those blasted boring Scrolls of a way
to break it. I hang on by cravat and waistcoat; if not
for Winters, I'd be a terrible mess. I find it most dis-
tressing to look into a mirror and see . . . I've no idea
what I see. Only that it cannot be me.*

—Colin to Ramsdell, 1816

Savi wasn't surprised to find Hugh in his home office—nor
when she found him bench-pressing an enormous set of
weights instead of sitting at the desk.

"Can we talk?"

Hugh paused in the middle of a lift, looking down the
length of his body at her. Settling the bar in the cradle, he sat
up and wiped the perspiration from his face and chest with a
T-shirt.

The symbols scarring his pectorals were pale against his
tan. Savi wanted to cringe in sympathy just looking at them;
yet he'd willingly stood for it, sacrificing himself to save four
of his students—perhaps saving the city. The world.

If Savi hadn't been stowed away in Caelum, he likely
would have been rescuing her from Lucifer and the nosferatu.

And if her gratitude when he covered them was tinged by
guilt, it quickly disappeared when she realized that he'd put
on the sweaty shirt. "That's disgusting."

He shrugged, a smile tilting his lips. "There's less laundry
this way." His eyeglasses sat on his desk; he slid them on,
looked her over. "Talk about what?"

"My psychic blocks," she said, and moved farther into the room when he gestured for her to join him. "I know they're naturally high, but . . . you want me to take *that*?"

He had held out a large gray dumbbell. She glanced at the number on the end: seventy-five pounds. "That weighs almost as much as I do."

"If you drop it, I'll catch it before it smashes your foot."

Her bare toes suddenly felt small and vulnerable. "Okay." Hugh supported it as she gripped the handle with both hands, then slowly let it go. Heavy . . . but it didn't take much effort to keep it up. "Holy shit."

"Curl it." Hugh demonstrated by bending his elbows. "Do ten. They aren't naturally high, Savi."

"I asked Selah if she could read me. I wasn't consciously shielding, and she said she couldn't get very deep. And when I did concentrate, she couldn't get in at all." She hit ten, stopped. "I didn't have to concentrate very hard, either. It's been getting a lot easier."

Hugh gave her another weight, one for each hand. "Everything does with practice. Ten more."

Savi hadn't been practicing, but applying—whenever Colin had visited the house. "Or with hellhound venom and nosferatu blood."

Shaking his head, Hugh took the dumbbells. "No. You've been blocking since you were thirteen." He crouched and removed a few fifty-pound discs from each end of a long bar.

"Thirteen?"

Pausing, he glanced up at her, his forearm resting on his thigh. "You remember. Just think about it. Make the connection."

Her chest tightened. "That was the year I started running."

In response to no particular stimuli, Savi's heart would begin to race, she'd not be able to breathe . . . and when she recognized what was happening to her, she'd fall into a fugue state and run to the nearest small, dark space.

But not always a safe space. Usually closets and beneath beds, but Hugh had found her in the walk-in freezer at Auntie's twice; once Nani had located her in the trunk of a neighbor's car.

"And the year you stopped," Hugh said. With a sigh, he

rubbed the back of his neck. "It was a technique I used to prevent my physical response to Lilith."

Savi sank down on the floor beside him. The doctors had diagnosed her with post-traumatic stress disorder. "The drugs were working," she recalled. "But they made me . . ." Slow. Dumb.

"Aye."

She pressed her fingers to her forehead. "That was the stupid meditation thing you made me do for a couple of weeks with you—the counting and the yoga?"

"Yes." Behind his lenses, his blue gaze was direct . . . and filled with regret. "It should have taken you a year or two to adopt the shields—and you should have had to practice to maintain it. I didn't take into account your memory, and your ability to absorb information."

"So it pretty much separated my brain from my body? Didn't let me recognize what was going on?" She laughed into her hands, rocked forward. "Oh, god, that explains a lot. Do you know what I have to do when I'm in bed with someone?"

His cheeks heated. So did hers.

"Forget I said—"

"I can teach you to lower them so you might not have to—"

"It's not like it's *bad* when I'm . . . oh, god, I'm shutting up." She sealed her lips together, stared at him.

"I'm sorry, Savi. You can learn to have better control over your shields, but the unconscious level is likely permanent."

"Jesus, don't be sorry. It's better than a trunk, or not being able to think. And at least I know now there's a reason for it—instead of, you know, just being totally fucked up after watching a crazy asshole gun down my family." She released a long breath. "I still get them—the anxiety attacks."

"I know. I see them, now and again. More often since you've returned from Caelum. You handle them well."

She smiled wryly. "Not really. If I notice it, I freeze up and have to stop myself from going. If anything frightens me, the same thing happens."

"Better than blacking out and running." He stood, gave her the bar. She managed one lift before she had to put it down. "You were able to run when it mattered."

"On the plane? I guess. I thought it all out ahead of time; that probably helped. It wasn't an involuntary reaction."

"Perhaps. Four hundred and fifty pounds looks to be your limit. We'll test your speed at SI tomorrow."

She grinned, struck a bodybuilder's pose. "What's your limit?"

"About three times that. Lilith, six times. Before you ask, I've never tested Michael, though he's undoubtedly the strongest. Guardians' strength varies according to age, but most novices can carry five tons." His lips twitched when her mouth dropped open. "It's very, very rare that such a weight needs to be lifted or moved. And when fighting, the dynamics change completely; strength is important, but factors such as speed and skill play a significant part."

Lilith's strength was equivalent to normal vampires'. "What about nosferatu-born vampires?"

"Usually, about halfway between a nosferatu and a vampire."

Usually, because there was an exception. "And Colin's strength?"

He'd been able to open the massive marble doors in Michael's temple. She'd once estimated the weight of each slab: almost one hundred tons. All of it held up by the frame—but she hadn't been able to produce enough force to overcome inertia and swing them on the hinges.

Colin had, with little apparent effort.

Hugh shook his head. "I don't know. The few times I've seen him move faster than a stroll, I'd have put his speed in the range of a novice. He fought a nosferatu when we were attacked in his basement last year; he'd not quite the speed and strength, but equal the skill."

"Would he have lost?"

"Perhaps he would've eventually fallen if Selah hadn't teleported him out, but he held up well until then. Much better than I did," he said with a wry smile.

Savi looked at his neck; Michael had healed the nosferatu's bite. No evidence of it remained. "So, is there anything else you haven't told me?"

"Aye. But I've no intention of sharing it now."

As there was a lot she hadn't told him, either, she thought

they must be even. "I'm off to the kitchen. Do you know if he's coming tonight? I thought I'd give him another chance at DemonSlayer."

To Savi's surprise, the vampire had shown up every evening since their agreement, and refrained from making a complete ass of himself. They'd spent the previous night playing a video game; Colin had rolled up his sleeves and appeared to enjoy it—though he'd been shocked when his preternatural reflexes hadn't overcome her experience.

And though he had a wicked competitive streak and had tried to cheat several times, he'd taken his defeat gracefully. She hadn't expected it of him.

Of course, being a good loser hadn't prevented Colin from rolling his eyes toward the ceiling in exasperation when Hugh had pointed out that strength didn't always win over brains and training.

She glanced at him now, but instead of finding humor as she'd anticipated, Hugh wore a resigned expression. "I doubt he will."

"Oh. Why?"

"A personal matter; he may tell you if you ask him, but I won't." His gaze leveled on hers. "You're not avoiding him as you used to. Were memories of Caelum so painful?"

Uncomfortable, she shifted on her feet. He'd known? "Yes." She said the truth only because a lie was useless with him. "I thought I hid it."

"I've seen how you look at the painting," he said, and she relaxed slightly. He hadn't meant her encounter with Colin—but her answer was still true. "When I first became a Guardian, I looked at Caelum and thought: How could I ever want more than this?"

"It's overwhelming," she agreed, her throat tightening.

"Yes. In the beginning. After a while, it no longer had what I sought—but I can't deny its beauty. It's unfortunate you couldn't stay awhile, as Colin did. Have you asked Michael if you can go again?"

"Yes. I've asked Michael a lot of things; he says no to most of them."

Hugh's laughter was deep, and she smiled at the sound of

it. He hadn't always laughed; after he'd Fallen, and before Lilith had come back into his life, it had been rare.

And no wonder. How did someone voluntarily give up Caelum? She'd have given anything to stay . . . would give anything to return. "How did you bear it? When you Fell?"

"I didn't do so well."

"No, I guess not." Except with Nani and herself, he'd been like a man of ice. "You were a freak cold bastard."

"*That* wasn't just Caelum," he said softly, "but the result of many factors. I'd slain Lilith. I'd broken the Rules by trying to deny Anderson's free will when he shot you. And—" He broke off, shook his head. "It wasn't as simple as leaving Caelum."

No, Savi thought. It wasn't.

Colin not only arrived, but he came earlier than usual. Just after sunset, he settled himself onto a barstool in the kitchen. Unaccustomed to the subdued manner of his greeting, Savi washed and cut vegetables for the *pulao* in silence, hyper-aware that his gaze never left her as she moved from sink to counter.

"What is that?" His soft question after minutes of quiet startled her. "Cilantro?"

"Yes. For the chutney." She glanced up from the cutting board and narrowed her eyes at him. "A vampire, interested in herbs? Or are you sitting there in hopes that I'll cut my-self?"

How could she have forgotten from one day to the next how incredible his smile was? The slightest curve of his lips, and he was transformed from *beautiful* to *ridiculously, heart-breakingly beautiful.*

God. She kept her attention on her knife as she slaughtered a cucumber. Even if it was genuine, that smile was a means to an end: to get into her veins and beneath her psychic shields.

Why couldn't he have remained an ass?

"It used to be that you prepared the meal on Saturdays," Colin said, selecting a mango from the bowl at his elbow, holding it in his cupped palm. His thumb absently caressed the ripened skin. "You did last week, as well. If your change in occupation alters that schedule, I should very much like to know."

"No change," she said. "Except for this week. Why?"

He replaced the fruit and scented his fingers. "Castleford's house smells best on those evenings. I enjoy it. You'll not be here this Saturday?"

"No. I'm meeting a guy."

"A potential suitor?"

"Yes."

His lingering smile slowly widened. "Then I shall have to kiss you soon. What are your plans for tomorrow?"

"Not that." But her stomach fluttered as she rinsed off her knife. To give herself more time before returning to the counter, she selected another knife from the cutlery drawer, pulling it out from beneath one of Lilith's pistols. There wasn't a room in the house in which the former demon hadn't stashed multiple weapons. "After work, I'm helping Nani in the restaurant."

"Will she have to approve this suitor?"

"Yes. No." She paused. "It's ultimately my decision, but I won't marry anyone she doesn't like. She wants me to have security, and she needs to know that I won't be alone. And in her way of thinking, 'not alone' means a husband, kids. Not just friends and a half-angel adopted brother."

"So you'll not choose anyone who would make her uneasy."

"Right. There'd be no reason for me to marry if she just worried about my situation afterward." Savi grimaced. "Okay, who am I kidding? She will anyway. But it's a different type of worry."

"What of your father's family?"

"Dead," she said flatly.

His brows rose. "And good riddance to them?"

"Yes."

"You look upon *me* without that storm on your face. Do not keep me in suspense, Savitri. I adore tales of familial loathing, most likely because I've not personally experienced it; but I promise I shall hate yours viciously."

She stopped dicing, afraid she might cut off her thumb if he made her laugh. "It's pretty simple: my dad was an only child, his parents were from old money."-At his questioning look, she clarified, "My great-great-grandfather was a robber baron."

"That is not old money."

Savi pursed her lips before continuing, "Established money, then. My grandfather sat on boards, did the philanthropic thing. My dad was supposed to do the same; instead he went off to medical school, worked in the surgery, and married an immigrant."

"How irresponsible of him. Which was the most offensive of that vile list?"

"The immigrant. My mother was never welcomed, nor were my brother and I. And after they were killed, my grandparents wouldn't have anything to do with me."

His eyes narrowed, his head tilting to the side as he studied her. "Come now, Savitri—you cannot harbor that much vitriol for two people you'd nothing to do with."

She smiled slightly. "I don't think about them often; I only harbor it when I think of it. And I was probably better off for their lack of interest."

"I daresay." He picked up the mango again, smelled it before setting it back down. "Castleford once mentioned that your grandfather left you a significant inheritance. Guilty conscience?"

"I don't think it was out of guilt or duty."

"Fear of being discovered a virulent xenophobe?"

"Yes. Keeping up appearances. He always did it with money. Like when I was fourteen, Nani had had enough of his refusals to see me. So we flew to Boston, showed up at his office. She was convinced he was just grieving, and that all he'd have to do was look at me and I'd win him over. Remind him of my dad, or something. And it was pretty clear by then I'd be finishing high school early. I'd been accepted into Harvard without the pull of the family name, but I was too young to be on my own. She wouldn't have to move away from the restaurant if they would agree to take me in—or at least keep an eye on me. And she was proud of me, so she assumed they would be, too."

The memory left a bitter taste on her tongue. She popped a cube of cucumber into her mouth, took a second—and kept her voice light when she finally said, "I wore one of those cute little girly dresses. Nani even put on a nice conservative suit. Chanel. And we waited in the lobby for three hours, until his secretary came down with a ten-thousand-dollar check, and let us know that if we ever needed more, he'd send it here to San Francisco."

"Did you need it?"

"No. I had a lot from my parents, insurance—and Nani does well with the restaurant."

"Ah, don't tell me: You were self-righteous and tore up his check? Were virtuous and gave it to charity?"

Savi grinned. "Hardly. Nani blew it on a trip to India, and introduced me to some of her family. All very distant cousins, but they didn't treat us like shit."

His laughter was low, with an edge of surprise. "How I adore your *nani*. That is the perfect response."

"Yeah." It hadn't made up for the humiliation Nani had gone through, sitting like discarded trash in foreign clothing, but it had given a small measure of satisfaction. "Anyway, that was the last I saw of him. I didn't care—and we never spoke of them again until about three years ago, when family lawyers told me he was dead."

"And it *was* good riddance," he said, still laughing softly.

"Definitely." She pointed with her knife. "Pick out one of those mangoes . . . whichever smells the best to you."

He closed his eyes as he inhaled each one, and she let herself examine the angle of his cheekbones, the slight hollows beneath. Chic. Gorgeous.

Her gaze drifted down. His throat was tanned; how long would it take to fade? Eight months ago, he'd been startlingly pale.

"Savi. Do tell me what you are thinking."

Of how good his skin had felt on her tongue and between her teeth. She swallowed. "That you are the only guy I know who can pull off a velvet corduroy blazer with a Nehru collar without looking as if you are *trying* to pull it off."

"Perhaps," he said dryly, "because I am not a *guy*."

She couldn't keep her response to a grin; she chuckled softly, shaking her head. The mango he'd chosen was cool under her fingers, and she sliced it with deft strokes. "I was also thinking that I should stop being surprised when you, Hugh, and Lilith don't react to the idea of an arranged marriage the way I expect you to. The way most people do. Not just Americans—some Desis, too. Especially those my age."

"Condemning it as a barbaric practice?"

"Or at least old-fashioned."

"It may be that, but I prefer to save my expressions of horror for true barbarianism: polyester, reality television, and Castleford's wardrobe." He shrugged. "Old-fashioned and out-dated are not equivalent. I've known many successful arrangements of convenience, and many unsuccessful love matches. I've also known many to be the opposite. What do you care of the approval of others?"

"I don't. I'm just surprised."

"You shouldn't be. In my lifetime, arranged marriages have been commonplace far longer than they have been not."

"Yeah. But then, so were corsets and unequal gender rights."

"Every time you turn and journey to the faucet, I offer a prayer of gratitude for progress, liberation, and the designers who popularized hip-hugging denims." His gaze settled on her chest. "And baby tees."

She didn't glance down; if she was aroused, there was little she could do to stop it—but she could ignore it. "Here you go." The crescents of mango glistened a deep yellow-orange on the salad plate. "Eat it with your fingers; everything tastes better that way."

"Savitri, I cannot—"

"I know. I don't mean *taste* taste. This mango isn't the greatest, anyway—but it's got a nice scent. Half of flavor is the odor. I experimented once by holding my nose through an entire meal." She lied; it had only been through a couple of bites.

Colin arched a brow, but she could have sworn amusement lay beneath the doubt. He picked up a slice.

"The texture is almost perfect. So take a long sniff, and eat it."

He bit off the end with a decisive snap of his teeth. The hollows in his cheeks deepened, as if he was lightly sucking on it.

She licked her lips. "Smooth and juicy, right? Now imagine that smell in your mouth, and you're close."

His throat worked as he swallowed, and he set the remainder of the slice on the plate.

"Put it away, Savi," he said. "I'll not be held responsible for my actions if you do not. Your shields are up, but your physical scent is . . . and the flesh of the mango is almost precisely like—" His eyes closed. "No, you cannot know."

Oh, god. She hadn't intended to tease him. She swept the plate from the bar, stuck it in the refrigerator. "I know." Looking back over her shoulder, she found him staring at her. "I've always been curious. I just prefer what I can't see in a mirror."

Recovering himself with a visible shake, he said, "As do I."

He was serious. Savi caught her bottom lip between her teeth to stop her laughter. But he must have read it on her face when she returned to the counter; his own smile flashed.

"Pray tell me you have two of those." Colin nodded to the bottle of wine she'd retrieved from the fridge.

She blinked in surprise. "Do you drink it?"

"No. The alcohol has no effect, and the liquid no taste. But it does the most incredible damage to your psychic shields. I shall keep your glass filled."

He was right: either drunkenness or the fever had affected her blocks at Polidori's, it was unfortunate she couldn't test which one. Perhaps it had been a combination of both?

"I've sworn off alcohol for a while; this is for Hugh and Lilith. Will you bite this?"

His fingers enfolded hers and the jalapeno pepper she'd offered him, but he did not take it. "Why?"

"It's an experiment. There's flavor, and then there's heat— but both are chemical reactions, like alcohol on a body. So I'm curious to see if it's spicy to you, even if it doesn't taste like anything."

"If I comply, you must agree to allow me to drive you to Auntie's tomorrow."

"Okay."

"And to drive you home when you've finished."

"Okay."

"And to kiss me."

"If I feel like it."

He grinned. "You will. You do now." He released her hand, and she braced herself, took deliberate account of her body. Quick breathing, heavy awareness in her belly and breasts—

"Bloody hell!" Colin coughed, choked. His eyes were wide with shock—and they were streaming tears. In the next instant, he was around the bar, leaning over the sink.

"Not water! Bread. Or the yogurt."

She grabbed the tub of plain yogurt she had out, but he'd already unwrapped the foil from around the store-bought naan. He ripped off a piece of the flatbread.

His eyes narrowed dangerously as he chewed it.

"Sorry." She clapped her hands in front of her mouth, but couldn't stop her giggles. "Sorry."

He glanced down at the naan in his hand and froze, his features a mask of terror. "Is this garlic?"

"And onion . . . ohmygod." Her heart stilled. "I thought garlic didn't—" She *knew* it didn't. "You ass," she said, and this time her laughter rolled deep in her throat.

His fangs gleamed wickedly, and he tossed the bread near the stove. He'd taken his shoes off. His socks were silk, the same dark gray as his pants. Silently, he crossed the kitchen, until she backed up and he trapped her with his hands clamped on the countertop behind her hips.

She tilted her head to look up at him, her body still shaking with her laughter. "What are you doing?"

"Don't you want to observe the results of your experiment, sweet?"

"Oh. Yes." Slowly, she managed to get hold of herself. She scrutinized his face. No signs of reddening, and his eyes no longer watered. "Does your stomach hurt? Does your tongue still burn?"

"No." Deep grooves formed beside his mouth; he seemed to be suppressing his own amusement with some difficulty.

"You recover quickly."

"Yes. But I should have known better than to take such a careless risk." His gaze fell to her lips. "Where are Castleford and Lilith?"

Trying to steady her breathing, she glanced down at his hands clenched on the edge of the counter. His wrists were just outside the curve of her waist—an inch, and he'd be touching her.

The thought didn't keep her steady.

"Savitri?"

What had he asked? Hugh and Lilith. What had they been— "Oh," she said. Her throat tightened, and she tried to look away from him—but there was nowhere else to look. "They were in the living room a while ago. If you can't sense them, they must be in their bedroom or Hugh's office. Probably with the spell around it. Lilith was . . . upset."

He stilled, staring down at her. "As, apparently, are you. Did you quarrel?"

"No. I just listened." Though it had been difficult not to interrupt them with her questions. With her concerns. "They found out that Washington might deny SI's request to execute the nosferatu . . . Ariphale. His name is Ariphale," she repeated to herself.

"That does not make it more human," Colin said quietly.

"I know." She smiled up at him, but it quickly faltered. The idea that an entire race of creatures was inherently "evil" seemed ridiculous and stank of bigotry. Yet everything she'd seen and heard confirmed they were. She said with more conviction, "I *know* what they are. I attacked him on the plane would've killed him—because I knew. And it's the same, isn't it? I did it to protect myself and Nani; Lilith and Hugh want to execute him to protect SI and anyone else if he escaped. And it's inevitable that, eventually, he will. There's no doubt of his nature, no way to rehabilitate him. Yet the idea of his execution makes me uneasy."

Sensation skittered over her skin as Colin touched his fingers lightly against her waist before settling his hand beside her hip again. "How long has it been since you learned of the nosferatu? Of demons and vampires and Guardians? As smooth as your adjustment has been, eight months is not time enough to understand a world that has completely shifted its axis." Empathy filled his gaze, his tone. His compassion was undoubtedly manipulative, a method of gaining her trust—but did that mean the emotion had to be false? And why did she want so badly to believe it was authentic? "Do not chide yourself for your uneasiness, Savi. Those who easily accept things so different from what they've known are too easily led."

She gave a short, self-deprecating laugh. "I suppose it is only that I think of it as a judgment given without trial. Yet who are more its peers than the Guardians—and what's the alternative? That the nosferatu is released and Michael slays it when it attacks? That would be stupid."

"We would all prefer it that way, Savi. Few of us are so cold-blooded that we can kill a nosferatu or a demon without wishing it had been done in self-defense." He grinned suddenly. "But for me. I would stab one in the front *or* the back. It doesn't matter, so long as it's dead. But to unleash a nosferatu solely with the intention of killing it, and risking death or injury in the process? Stupid, indeed."

"I know." She laughed and shook her head again. "I keep saying that. Do you hate them?"

He didn't hesitate. "Yes."

"Don't you pity them? They couldn't have known what they brought upon themselves by abstaining in the First Battle—or that they'd be cursed."

"No. Their angelic intelligence must have been too great *not* to know the consequences. And so I save my pity for Anthony Ramsdell, his throat torn out on a battlefield. For my father and brother, and my brother's wife, whom a nosferatu set afire whilst they slept. For your friends."

"For the four hundred on the flight the week before mine," she murmured.

"Yes."

She held his gaze. "But also for what they had been, though it doesn't excuse their cruelty now. Even the most intelligent creatures are foolish, sometimes."

"And is there room in you for forgiveness of cruelty? Or are his offenses too great?" Colin asked softly.

She searched his eyes and didn't know if the need she saw there was genuine, but she couldn't halt her smile. "Are we speaking of the nosferatu?"

His answering smile was slow and wide, and her gaze fell to his lips. "Of course, my sweet Savitri," he said and leaned forward. His body pressed hard against hers; his mouth swept past her temple.

Her blood pounded. Her nipples tightened as textured velvet brushed over thin cotton.

His warmth disappeared.

She blinked, spun around—he'd returned to his seat on the opposite side of the bar. "What was that for?"

His brows rose, and he glanced down. A notepad and pen lay in front of him; they'd been beside the phone a moment before. "They were behind you," he said with patently fake innocence.

She rolled her eyes. "You intend to take messages?"

"No. I *had* intended to tell you stories, but the past week has convinced me I need to find another way to win you over. My two centuries of life cannot compete with their combined three millennia; I must take advantage of their absence as best I can. Isaac Newton," he said in disgust.

"So what are you doing instead?" She stood on her toes in an attempt to see.

He tilted the pad toward his chest. "Piquing your curiosity. You've never seen Lilith as a demon, have you?"

Her eyes widened. "No. I saw a fuzzy picture from a traffic camera, but she was mostly in human form. Just the wings."

"Have you yet seen any demon?" He looked briefly over the top of the page.

"Rael . . . Congressman Stafford came to SI once when I was there. But he wasn't in a demon form."

Colin paused. "Castleford allowed you contact with him?"

Was that anger in his voice? "No. I was asking Jeeves a few questions about the temperature sensors in the corridor when he came in. I just saw him; I didn't talk to him. And I've seen him on TV, of course." She sighed and placed a few dishes in the sink, ran the water to wash them. "I voted for him in the last election."

"He may have been the lesser of two evils, particularly as he was instrumental in funding Special Investigations," Colin said. "Though, as it is to his advantage to support SI in Washington, it is unfortunately *not* to the Guardians' advantage to slay him."

"And I have yet another demon to thank for a job."

"Has Lilith located the agent who recruited you?" He flipped the page over, and started on a new drawing.

"We know that he left his position in Homeland Security eight months ago. And he disappeared from any records after that—no financial transactions, no address, nothing. So it's likely he was a demon, and went Below before the Gates closed. Or rogue. Either way, he isn't around to carry out his threat to Nani."

"Will you leave SI then?"

"Probably as soon as I get married. Right now it's just too interesting." She bit her lip, shook the suds from her hands. He remained concentrated on his sketch. "You're killing me."

Colin laughed, a note of triumph in the deep tones. He slid the notepad across the countertop. "There you are, Savi. Lilith."

"Oh, my—this is incredible." He'd captured Lilith's face and posture perfectly, standing with her sword ready, her smile wicked. The ink drawing had simple lines, but contained extraordinary detail: the smooth curving horns near her temples; fangs that rivaled a nosferatu's in length; taloned, prehensile feet and large, batlike wings; the scrolling symbol etched between her breasts.

"I thought she wore boots—like she does when she's at work." He'd only included her corset and knee-length breeches.

"She did at times."

"And with red skin?"

"Yes."

"She's beautiful, but also . . ."

"Frightening?"

Savi met Colin's gaze. "Yes. Do all of the others look like this?"

"I don't know; Beelzebub took a human form when he came to my house. Lilith has told me Belial retained his angelic form, but she didn't elaborate on his appearance."

She nodded absently and turned the page to the second drawing. Her mouth fell open. "Ohmygod."

It was unmistakably Savi, though he'd drawn her in a Japanese manga style: impossibly long legs and oversized *chibi* eyes, her spiked hair defying the laws of gravity. He'd pictured her wearing a tiny skirt, leaning against the kitchen counter in a naïvely seductive pose.

Her laugh was astonished . . . horrified. "Is this how you see me? Like a schoolgirl?"

"No," he grinned unapologetically. "It's how I'd *like* to see you."

How could that be better? But it was. "How would you draw yourself?"

"In the same manner?" At her nod, he took back the pad. "You've quite a large collection in your flat; I glanced through several volumes last month."

"After you put Nani to sleep?"

"Before. She apologized for your choice of entertainment."

"She would."

He frowned, studying the page. "I'm most familiar with the animated style, and I don't practice—so it may not be correctly rendered."

"No, it's not," she said, though her mouth dried when he showed her the slender swordsman wearing a long duster, his chin tilted down and his forehead against the flat blade of his weapon, as if he were praying. "The clothes are right, but all of the beautiful heroes have long, flowing hair. And secretive, meaningful expressions. You've got a big smile." Like a villain.

"To expose my fangs. And brooding is so very tedious, don't you agree?"

"It's supposed to be sexy." God, smiling was sexy, too. She was sick, lusting after a drawing. Lusting after the model. "Or soulful." Colin wasn't that, at least. She glanced up at him. "Do you really like being a vampire?"

"Of course. I love nothing more."

Her chest tightened as she looked back down at the drawing. She'd have loved it, as well. She'd wished for it—but she should've known better than to wish. It never accomplished anything, except to bring disappointment when it didn't come true. Better to just live as hard as possible, and be grateful for what she had. But Colin . . .

"Wouldn't you rather be a Guardian?"

"Trade freedom and blood for endless service?" Colin stared at her in disbelief.

She shook her head. "No, I can see why you like the freedom. I would, too. What I mean is: Why doesn't it bother you that vampires are the third-class citizens of the—" Nether-world? Underworld? Caelum couldn't be considered either *nether* or *under*. "—Otherworld?"

"They're not. You're mistaken, Savi," he said. His mouth set in a firm line, and his eyes hardened.

"No, I don't think so. Have you ever heard the description of a vampire in the Scrolls? Hugh told me once. *The descendents of nosferatu, vampires are no threat except to humankind. If their bloodlust does not endanger human life, Guardians may allow them to live*. And that's pretty much it, aside from an in-struction of how to transform a human who has been drained by a vampire or nosferatu."

"Was that your brilliant translation from the Latin?"

She sucked in a sharp breath. "Yes. But I'm just saying that even though vampires were human once, neither Guardians nor demons have to honor a vampire's free will or their right to live. It doesn't matter if they're slain or not—even if the vampires *aren't* endangering humans, there's no consequence for killing one. And they're kept ignorant, even though the first vampires were made by Guardians. Like you were made by Guardians."

"I can hardly be lumped among the ignorant. You, how-ever, apparently can. You know all of fifteen vampires—are any considered unequal to Guardians except in strength?"

"No, because Hugh and Lilith brought them into SI with the purpose of teaching them. Training them. But as far as I can tell, they were the first not to see vampires as a nuisance, and to see that vampires could be useful now that there are so few Guardians." Was he really so blind? "Maybe you don't notice it because you're some kind of supervampire, and your brother-in-law and friends were Guardians and a halfling demon. It provides a nice ivory tower for you to lan-guish in."

His face darkened. "*I* live in an ivory tower? You've no bloody fucking idea of what I—" He broke off and half-rose in his chair, and Savi stumbled back from the counter.

Colin stilled. A muscle in his jaw worked. "Did I frighten you?"

"No. But it's an appropriate reaction when an angry vam-pire lunges my way."

A thin smile curved his mouth. "So it is." He stalked out of the room.

Savi stood dumbstruck in the center of the kitchen, her heart pounding, wondering if she should follow him. She didn't have to go far; she found him in the living room, staring up at the painting of Caelum. His hands were tucked into his pockets, his eyes shadowed beneath his brows.

"Will you invite me in tonight?" His voice was once again subdued, quiet.

He asked *now*? When she was upset and—oh, god, it shouldn't be this hard to refuse. She had a billion reasons; she could only remember one, and only because it was right in front of him.

"I did that once."

He nodded. The light washing over Caelum glinted off the gold of his hair. "Please offer my apologies to Castleford and Lilith when they emerge."

"You're leaving?" Dismay tightened her voice.

"You will apparently feed everyone tonight except me, so I must find someone more willing elsewhere." His lips brushed her forehead as he passed her. "Good night, Savitri."

Perhaps it was best that her throat ached unbearably; she couldn't call him back. But there was no reason for her chest to hurt so much when the door closed behind him.

🍂

Heavy, early-evening traffic prevented Colin from speeding through the streets. He veered into the left lane on Clarendon, then slammed the brakes and ground his teeth together when the bastard in front of him halted at a stoplight.

Sod this. The Bentley purred eagerly when he revved the engine. He waited for a lull in the cross-traffic, then tore past the bastard and screeched through the intersection, making a right turn onto Seventeenth. There would be plenty of humans in The Castro to choose from, whether tourists or residents, and the hunt would take his mind from the scene in Castleford's kitchen—though he doubted any could ease the hunger and frustration building inside him.

An ivory tower. Fucking ridiculous. *She* was the one holding herself on a pedestal, forcing him to beg for scraps, never letting him in. What did she want from him? Would she be satisfied if he went down on his knees and groveled for forgiveness?

Christ. If his need became much worse and if she withheld her flavor much longer, he probably would.

He drove through the center of the district and parked in the first available space. Brightly colored flags fluttered from streetlamp posts and store fronts. The night air was crisp and dry, and he stalked down the pavement, searching each face, touching each mind. So many choices, and all so appreciative of his beauty: the neatly dressed, bald male sitting alone in a deli who rose up from his seat by the window to keep Colin in sight as long as possible; the blond woman who turned and walked backward, gesturing wildly to her friends that they should *look*. Easy prey.

But Colin was searching for one that struck a familiar psychic note or possessed a fleeting resemblance to Savi—*anything* to ease the ache of his need for the wide-eyed, curious, stubborn woman. And it was the one who came out of a film rental shop that caught Colin's attention: small and dark, with skin like cinnamon. His hunger sharpened, and his nostrils flared as he tried to detect a scent. He hoped it would be sweet and clean.

Before Caelum, he had never needed a substitute—had never fixated on a living being. Savi might very well have called his behavior creepy; Colin would have agreed, if he'd ever managed to forget whoever he was with wasn't the one he wanted.

And if the community's vampires were still following him and analyzing his feeding patterns, they'd soon have more evidence of his latest obsession. He smiled grimly as he crossed the street toward the rental shop and performed a cursory scan of the surrounding area.

A vampire *was* near. His psychic scent burned with resentment, but was focused away from Colin—and the vampire gave no indication that he knew Colin was there. Not following him, then. A quick glance at the vampire confirmed it; two blocks away, the male sat at a café's sidewalk table, facing the opposite direction. Brown hair touched the vampire's shoulders, but Colin could easily see the hair above his ears had been cut short. Good God. The sod *could* see his reflection, and yet he'd retained a horrid, outdated—

A faint cry of pain and fear cut through the noise of the passing cars, the human conversations.

Colin frowned, turning toward the sound. None of the humans reacted; none had likely heard it. Only Colin—and the vampire, whose fists clenched at his sides. The cry had originated beyond the vampire, at least a couple of blocks farther down the street—and the vampire's psyche had not projected concern or surprise, but had flared hot with jealousy.

The mental probe Colin sent toward the sound was stronger than his initial scan, and he immediately sensed another presence—a female. Older than the first vampire, and better able to shield her mind.

Outside the rental shop, Colin's cinnamon-skinned prey paused, then stared at him. Bloody hell. Colin flashed a charming smile, but, to human eyes, he must have appeared to vanish an instant later. Colin didn't detect any indication that the male vampire had seen him move, either; perhaps the male had had a moment's glance in the wrong direction and missed Colin's dash down the street.

Just as well. Colin halted at the mouth of an alley—more of a small enclave between two buildings, backed by a brick wall—and in the darkness easily discerned the vampire, her long auburn hair and black dress. She stood over a raggedly-dressed figure lying twisted in the rear corner of the enclave.

The odor of human blood hung thick in the air—a large quantity of blood. The stench of new death slowly rose beneath it, and the fetid scent of a long-unwashed body.

Colin silently stepped from the pavement into the shadowed alley.

The vampire startled, her hand flying to her chest as she whirled around. Then her face relaxed into a smile that, two hundred years earlier and without an introduction, Colin would have thought presumptuous. She might have recognized him, but he did not know her. Did not wish to know her.

"You were right," she said, and Colin's gaze fell to her chest. Blood stained the bodice of her dress.

"I often am," Colin murmured as he moved past her and

crouched next to the corpse. "Pray tell me, however, what I have said that inspired *this*?"

She laughed, a studied trill from her starlet's lips. "That we ought not to be limited to our bloodsharing partners. That the humans ought to be ours for taking and feeding."

Her bloodlust was still strong within her; whatever she thought humans ought to be, she had not finished feeding from this one. Excitement coiled from her psychic scent, along with a swelling of pride, of power. And she deliberately projected reverence toward Colin, coupled with admiration. Was she attempting to flatter him?

With a tug on the threadbare military jacket, Colin rolled the body over. The man's throat had been torn open. The front of his trousers had been shredded, and his penis had not yet lost its tumescence. "I daresay he must have taken to you whilst you fed." He glanced up at her breasts, her face, and he stood. "Though I cannot comprehend why."

Her laughter trilled again, as if she'd assumed his statement was a jest, but her mouth quickly tightened into a grimace. "I thought his fear would prevent his lust," she said.

No. For some, a scare only increased their ardor. In the past two centuries, Colin had purposely frightened a few humans—but he never fed from them. He almost always chose a person that he found attractive in some manner, someone he wouldn't resent fucking; he'd never considered killing them to prevent the sex . . . though obviously this female had. And her psychic scent revealed that she'd enjoyed it.

"What of your partner?" Colin asked softly. "Will he have his turn next?"

"He does not want one. He only watches, so that no one happens upon me as I feed. But I will not have to concern myself with exposure in the future; I had not realized how easily humans are disposed of. No one will miss a beggar." She placed her hand on his arm, and her long nails slid down his corduroy sleeve. "My consort does not like that I sought blood elsewhere, but his attachment to me is much more powerful than mine to him." Her fingers circled his wrist, and her bloodlust burned hotter. "You *are* warm."

Her touch was cool; Colin did not think it unpleasant, except that it was hers. "I am," he said.

"The others who have fed from you have said that your blood is dark and powerful."

"Have they?" Brittle amusement curled his lips. He could not imagine with whom she had spoken; everyone who'd fed from him was dead. And if she'd had any sense, she might have seen the sharpness of his smile for what it was and been frightened.

But she was staring at his neck. "I am the eldest of them. The strongest. You and I could so easily rule the community together." Her eyes met his, her gaze hungry. "Tell me that you do not think so as well."

"I think," he said as he pulled his wrist from her grasp, "that I ought to retrieve a few items from my car." His weapons.

"No!" She caught his arm again. He stilled and looked down at her. And *now* terror threaded through her scent, but she did not recognize his anger; her gaze searched his face, and she blinked rapidly as if to clear her vision. "Don't go yet. We can get rid of the body later. Let me feed from you. Please." Her chest heaved. "Your face. I haven't seen you like this. You're so . . ." Her fear climbed and choked her words.

Yes, he was. "You do not want to feed from me." His swords were kinder than his blood was.

Kinder than Colin was.

"Yes." It come out like a hiss from a demon's tongue.

Revolting. "Very well," he said, and her expression reflected her surprise when he offered his bare wrist, already bleeding from the slice he'd made with his silver pen knife. She hadn't seen him roll up his sleeve, or cut himself, but she did not hesitate. Her mouth covered the wound.

Her pleasure flashed into his veins. Christ. Vampires' psychic strength increased when feeding, but her mind was no match for his. He reinforced his blocks, heard the noise of protest she made before the bloodlust gripped her. She held his wrist to her mouth and reached for his trousers with her free hand. He trapped it in his, kept her away from him.

She tried to writhe closer, drinking deep. Her bloodlust battered at his shields; he set his jaw and fought his hunger and arousal. Would that he could ignore his as easily as Savitri ignored hers—

No. Do not think of her now. If he did, he'd probably give in to the lust, fuck this vampire against the wall. Nor did he want to associate Savi with what would surely happen next. The burning—the reek.

The female's bloodlust broke and she lifted her head, gasping. "I have heard that . . . you have no desire, but—" She bent and licked the now-healed line on his wrist.

Colin stared at her. Nothing yet. Nothing. Perhaps after two centuries—

She stiffened, shuddered. Pain burst through her psychic scent. Her eyes opened wide. Her fingers warmed against Colin's skin, and he felt the flare of heat from her body.

Colin slapped his hand over her mouth before she began screaming.

❦

The Guardian dropped out of the sky like a falcon and slammed to the asphalt in a crouch, his wingspan stretching the width of the alley. Colin rolled his eyes. Show-offs, the lot of them—though Colin had not previously thought Drifter was.

The wings vanished as the Guardian rose to his feet; with his brown hair, a long brown coat, and coarse brown trousers, Drifter was a mountain of a man. A bloody *tall* mountain of a man.

Drifter's eyes narrowed as he looked at Colin leaning casually against the brick wall, and at a glance the Guardian took in the two figures at Colin's feet. "I reckoned Agent Milton lied to me when she said that you were in danger."

"She likely wanted to see how quickly you could move." No Guardian would have wanted to be assigned to cleanup.

Judging by the wry smile on Drifter's mouth, he'd come to the same conclusion. He sank to his heels and examined the bodies, the bottom of his duster bunching on the filthy asphalt. "That smell coming from this one?"

"Yes." Sulphur and burnt flesh, though no evidence of it showed on the female's pale skin.

With the tips of his fingers against her chin, Drifter turned the female's head, exposed her neck. "You didn't drain her?"

"No." And Colin had no intention of offering an explanation of how she could be dead with no injuries to show for it.

Drifter propped his elbows on his knees, his gaze traveling between the female and the dead man. "Did she have a consort?"

"Yes." Colin had returned to the street, but the moment the other vampire had seen Colin, his brief flare of recognition had been followed by realization and terror. He'd run, leaving a psychic trail of grief and fear in his wake. Colin had let him go. "He fled. There are many in the city who still need a partner," he said dismissively. "He'll find another."

"A woman like this, you figure he's mighty attached." The female and the human vanished into the Guardian's cache, and Drifter stood. "She may have been a murderer, but she was a fine-looking one."

"And even murderers need affection." Colin's smile was mocking.

"That we do," Drifter replied easily, and scratched his great anvil of a jaw. "Seems to me that you ought to have least found out who he was, explained the Rules, and warned him not to retaliate."

"Against me? Don't be absurd."

Drifter's brows rose. "Word around SI is you've been coming in every day, which you've never done before. And you've been visiting Miss Savi in the tech room regularly."

Colin straightened up from the wall. His voice hardened. "What is your point, McCabe?"

"Just that if *I* have heard where your interest lies, just passing through, it won't take long before others know it. Such as those who've been watching you."

The vampire community? Colin shook his head. "They wouldn't dare threaten her." And if they did, he'd kill each one of them.

"It may be you're right." Drifter shrugged and moved back to the center of the alley, forming his wings. "And this vampire I've got in my cache is a powerful indication nothing will come of that interest, anyway. It gives me quite the advantage."

"How is that?" Colin asked softly. If Drifter thought to capture Savi's affections for himself—

"I figure it'll only be another day or two before the

novices at SI start up a wager, placing bets on when you transform her. So when I write in 'Never,' I'll be guaranteed a win—though I reckon I'll have to wait an eternity to collect it." Drifter smiled; a wide-brimmed hat appeared over his hair, and he tipped it in a mock salute. His wings arched, and with a single beat lifted him straight into the air, high and quick; in the dark, no human would likely have noticed the movement or, if they had, been able to determine what it had been.

A violent gust of air followed in Drifter's wake, swirled the alley's odors around. Colin returned to the street, and looked for the one who had appealed to him before. Gone.

Blast. He ought to have just immediately contacted SI instead of confronting the female. It wasn't his responsibility to police the vampire community or to slay those who broke the Rules.

Colin plucked a rose from a vase on a sidewalk table as he passed it, crushing the bud in his hand, erasing the stink of the alley. Apprehension uncoiled in his stomach. Savi would undoubtedly learn of his killing the vampire. What would she think of it, when she was conflicted over the execution of a nosferatu?

He shook his head, a reluctant smile pulling at his lips. As absurd as her concern for the nosferatu was, it had been the first indication of dissent she'd shown against Castleford and Lilith, and it had surprised him. Colin had seen her siphon knowledge from them but never question their methods or the morality of their decisions. And although he usually found discussions of morality unbearably tiresome—humans and vampires tended to wax on and on about The Big Picture and Meaning—coming from Savi, it had been intriguing, startling.

Perhaps it shouldn't have been surprising. She'd attacked a nosferatu against Lilith's and—she'd thought—Castleford's request. And Colin knew she'd never shown any conflict or doubt before that evening because she was certain he'd use it against her. Colin *had* been waiting for such an opportunity, but he'd not thought that when she finally exposed a vulnerability, it would be regarding a sodding nosferatu. She'd let him in, but—

Oh, Christ. *She'd let him in.* Colin stopped, let the rose drop to the pavement. She'd finally trusted him again—and he'd lost his temper and frightened her.

What a bloody fucking mess he'd made of it.

CHAPTER 8

Demons and Guardians must abide by the Rules, which are really pretty simple: They can't deny a human's free will, and they can't kill humans. I suppose they could hurt a human, but only if the human wanted it.

—Savi to Taylor, 2007

The clash of swords and thuds of flesh against flesh filled the gymnasium at Special Investigations—vampires and fledgling Guardians, hacking and swinging at each other in practiced routines.

Colin spotted Savi at the back of the room, in desperate retreat from Castleford's flashing blade. His muscles tightened, but he forced himself to stay where he was. Castleford wouldn't hurt her, and she was covered in heavy, protective padding.

Colin winced as she tripped over her feet and landed hard on the floor. Awkward, clumsy. It would take years before she was proficient, even under Castleford's expert tutelage. He'd mentored countless Guardians over his eight centuries, but teaching the ungainly Savitri might prove his most difficult challenge.

They began again, and Castleford landed a sharp blow against the base of her blade, sending her sword flying. Savi hissed and shook her hand against the sting, and for an instant her shields fell.

Good God, but that fragrance was exquisite. Unable to help himself, Colin sucked in a deep breath. It was undoubtedly psychic, but somehow best experienced though scent—

and his reaction was physical, as well. He quickly sat on one of the benches lining the walls.

Her blocks rose into place, and he recovered enough to glance around, realizing that none of the other vampires—nor Guardians—had seemed to note her slip, let alone been overwhelmed by it.

Strange, but he didn't mind. He preferred to have it to himself.

He looked up as a familiar dark anger swept through the building, followed by the slam of a door. Lilith. The Pentagon must have denied her request to execute the nosferatu. Bloody fools.

"Clear out," Castleford said softly. "Or get to the side."

Colin caught Savitri's attention as she glanced toward the gym entrance. She met his gaze, and her wide-eyed curiosity narrowed into a smile of greeting. No anger? He searched for signs of irritation or wariness in her expression as she jogged over, and found none.

He barely suppressed the urge to shake his head. What was wrong with her? Did she forgive so easily—or did she care so little?

Neither alternative pleased him.

She slid onto the bench next to him just as Lilith burst through the doors, her sword in hand. Sir Pup was at her heels, but immediately veered toward Savi and Colin and flopped down at Savi's feet.

After scratching each of his noses, she began unbuckling the padding that protected the front of her thighs; she didn't look up as Hugh and Lilith met in the center of the gym, though the clash of their swords came fierce and loud.

Colin glanced toward the incredible display, then at Savi's mouth, set in a firm line. "Do you need assistance with the back?" He didn't wait for her nod, sliding his fingers beneath the buckle behind her shoulders. She didn't object when his hand lingered longer than necessary. He might have felt a bit of triumph, had she seemed to notice his touch. "You've seen them do this before."

She nodded and eased the padding away from her torso. Her dark T-shirt was damp with perspiration, her black hair glistening near her hairline. Colin fought to keep his inhalation inaudible.

Even with her shields up, she smelled incredible. Warm and sweet and tangy.

"In ten minutes they'll be laughing. But it's difficult to watch when they aren't." She rolled her shoulders. "Did you see me fall?"

Was that embarrassment flushing her skin? He skimmed his thumb over her cheek and smiled when he felt the warmth there . . . when she didn't flinch away. "Yes."

"My footwork sucks."

"Yes. As does your bladework."

She pulled her upper lip into her mouth, as if in contemplation, and leaned forward to watch the two combatants in the center of the room. "Hugh says that I overanalyze each movement, and it makes me slow and clumsy. That I think too much."

"You do." Far too much. "And you learn too well."

She gave a half smile at his rueful tone before she said, "Seeing them, I believe it. They don't have time to think, only react. Yet they're in absolute control." She spoke more to herself than to him, her gaze fixed on the battle as if memorizing and calculating everything before her.

Did she apply that focus and determination to her lovemaking? He'd had a taste of it, when she'd taught him his own lesson. And that had only been a kiss.

Heat rushed to his groin, and his fangs began to ache. In Caelum, she had been enthralled and acting almost purely on instinct. He'd been enthralled as well, and half out of his mind. Certainly no judge of pleasure. He'd had no judgment at all, but that which had proved poor.

Stifling a groan of frustration, he bent forward and rested his elbows on his knees. Willed away the arousal. He could wait. For now, he would be content to simply observe her reaction to Castleford and Lilith, until she found the questions she sought.

It did not take long.

"Does Lilith hold back? She is faster and stronger than he is." She glanced over at him, her gaze searching his as she waited for his answer. She had the most marvelous eyebrows—

almost without angle, but for a sudden arc above the outside corners of her eyes. In an underpainting, he could capture it with the flick of his wrist. Brush strokes, he took more care.

Now, they were slightly drawn together, her lips barely parted—an expression that in the last week he'd come to know meant *Tell me.*

Colin shook his head. "Castleford knows her weaknesses and exploits them to his advantage."

"If he wanted to win immediately, would he do the same?"

"No. He would utilize his strengths, not her weaknesses."

"Is Lilith utilizing her strengths or his weaknesses?"

"Weakness against weakness, or it would be over too quickly—and it demands more skill. I've seen them fight when it was in earnest; never did it last more than a few seconds." He lowered his voice so that she would have to move closer to hear him. "This is not a battle, Savitri. The pleasure here is not the victory, but what comes before."

"What is it?" She moistened her lips. "If not a battle?"

"Foreplay," he said, and awareness flared in her eyes before she blinked, hiding it. "Or a similar principle. The give-and-take, the dance toward a common goal."

Her teeth caught her bottom lip, as if she thought this over. "That isn't an apt analogy; one doesn't use a lover's weaknesses against them."

"*For* them, Savitri. Where is she most sensitive? What makes her shudder and gasp? What are those, if not vulnerabilities?" It took all of his control not to deepen his tone, to pretend as if the conversation were only of scientific interest. Did her breath come more quickly? "And is this not for her? To redirect her anger? So he meets his blade against hers; she is faster, but too low. She thrusts with greater strength but cants too far to the left. She is off balance, and he takes her."

Her gaze had not wavered from his, but now she raised her brows, humor evident in the tilt of her eyes. "We *are* speaking of Lilith?"

He grinned, unrepentant. "Of course."

"Of course." She tapped her finger against his knee, then rasped her nail over the slick denim. "I've never seen you in jeans. They look good." Her mouth curved slightly. "But everything does on you."

Did she think to manipulate him, as well? He would disarm her first, and let it be an impasse. "Wait until I turn around." She lowered her face into her cupped palm as if to catch her laughter. Her left hand was still near his leg; he brought it to his lips, pressing a quick kiss to the backs of her fingers. "Thank you. But I confess I only assume it is true. I can hardly look into a mirror and see."

As if his assumption was more hilarious than his certainty, she laughed the harder. Then she pulled her hand from his and leaned forward to collect the padding from the floor and bestow final pats to Sir Pup's heads. Her shirt rode up, exposing a strip of silky skin across the small of her back, the shallow corridor of her spine. His hands clenched in his lap.

"I'm heading for the shower; I don't need to wait for them to finish whacking at one another. Do you still intend to go to Auntie's with me?"

"Yes. No chaperones." Colin offered his most charming smile when she glanced back over her shoulder. "I'm all aquiver in anticipation of our kiss."

"I haven't yet agreed to it," she said dryly, sitting up. "Nani is there."

He lifted his brows. "I'm certain I shall kiss her, too."

❦

I will treat you as a friend, said the cobra.

Savi wiped the steam from the mirror—would a fogged mirror have the same effect on him?—and wondered if the little girl would have fared better with iron-lined pockets. Or would the snake have simply crawled to a better position before striking?

And what if the little girl liked it?

Shuddering, she closed her eyes and shook her head. Put that way, the question was too creepy to contemplate. And as much as she wanted to compare Colin to a scaly creature and herself to an innocent girl, they were neither.

"The new 'do looks great. Very Halle-Berry-coming-out-of-the-surf in *Die Another Day*."

Savi smiled slightly and looked up, meeting Fia's gaze in the glass. "Better than platinum-blond-wig Halle?"

The other woman grinned, her fangs protruding over her

bottom lip. "Much. Only—may I?" She raised her pale hands when Savi nodded and turned around. Her fingers were quick, pulling and tugging at individual strands. "I studied at a beauty school for a little while, before meeting Paul. You've got great cheekbones and face shape for this; not a lot of women can pull off something this short. Why are you laughing?" Fia's green eyes were sparkling—the easy confidence of a woman who knew the joke wasn't about her, and wanted to share in it.

"I think when I cut it a couple of years ago my intention was that I couldn't pull it off," Savi said.

"A breakup?"

"A rebellion."

Fia nodded, then pointed to the mirror. "Check it out."

It did look good; instead of the flat, shiny cap Savi had combed after her shower, Fia had added texture and softened the edges. Better than a hedgehog, but Nani would still think she looked too much the boy. "Thank you."

"Well, we can't all shape-shift like the Guardians," Fia said with a laugh. She glanced in the mirror and fluffed her shoulder-length brown hair, then grinned again. "You should have seen me a month ago, before Paul turned me and we came here. I was trying to do the whole black hair and leather look. Then I saw Lilith and realized I didn't have a chance of pulling it off half as well, and went back to natural."

"I think two thousand years as a demon gives anyone an edge."

"Yeah." Fia threw a quick, speculative glance at her. "You know the Beaumont—*Ames-Beaumont*—vampire pretty well."

Savi's smile froze in place. "A little."

"You were there the night at Polidori's when he fought that thing—the wyrmwolf."

Savi couldn't hide her surprise, and Fia shrugged. "I was there, too, with Paul. Hell, we were almost always there. And until we saw you, we thought Lilith was his . . ." She shook her head. "Anyway, there are others in the community who are thinking that he's half demon or something because of that. He was so fast—and he can go out in the sun."

"I don't know," Savi lied.

Fia sighed. "You don't want to tell me."

"I can't tell you." If demons learned of Colin's anchor to Chaos, he'd be endangered by it. Lucifer would have done anything to regain access to that realm; a rogue demon on Earth might try to do the same.

Disappointment creased her brow, but Fia shrugged again. "It's okay if you can't. We were just trying to understand why he wouldn't want to lead the vampire community; he's the strongest figure. SI is great, but too secretive, and a lot of vampires outside are becoming distrustful of it. A little afraid, too."

Savi walked over to her locker, began pulling her clothes from it. "You should tell Lilith."

"I will; I was just hoping to get it out of you first. She intimidates me," Fia said as she sat down on the bench.

"All of us."

"So you aren't his consort?"

"Colin's?" She choked on her laughter, and yanked a powder-blue tank over her head. "No."

"We saw what you did to him at Polidori's, when you kissed him." Embarrassment tinged Fia's voice. "The same thing he did to me. No other vampire has that power."

"Oh." Her face flamed. Probably better not to mention the hellhound venom; if Lilith and Hugh hadn't explained to anyone at SI why Savi had above-human strength, then she wouldn't. No wonder vampires were suspicious and thought SI too secretive—they were. But perhaps with good reason, given how little even Michael knew about such things. "I bit his tongue."

It wasn't a lie, but Fia would assume that Colin had simply been physically aroused, and the blood pushed him over. And it was less embarrassing than admitting it had nothing to do with Savi, but rather the psychic effects of ingesting hellhound venom.

"Oh." Fia sighed. "I'd really hoped that someone had gotten the better of him. It's not fair that he can look like that *and* have that kind of power."

Savi grinned and shook her head. She'd tried, but apparently the only person she'd gotten the better of had been herself.

What would happen if she allowed him in? What price would she pay? Whatever Fia had experienced, it obviously wasn't the same as Savi had in Caelum.

Savi pulled on her jeans, then shrugged into her white cotton shirt and left it unbuttoned. "Was it that good? What he did to you?"

Fia's gaze unfocused. "Yes. I think. Afterward, I was completely blown away and shaky, but trying to pretend I wasn't. But when he was feeding from me—" Her brows drew together, and she shook her head. "I don't really remember. Maybe it was *too* good; now it feels absolutely unreal."

So were demons and Guardians and vampires. Given that reality had shifted so drastically in the last year, Savi had no idea what that meant.

When Savi pushed through the locker room door, Colin was leaning against the opposite wall with his hands tucked into his pockets, an easy smile on his lips, and a predatory gleam in his eyes. "It was that good, Savi."

She couldn't conceal the flush that rose over her neck, but she didn't need to feign her laughter. "You just lost all of the progress you made this week. You could've at least pretended you didn't eavesdrop." And she shouldn't have assumed he'd remained in the gym waiting for her.

He placed his palm over his chest. "You wound me, accusing me of such." His smile faded. "You should indulge your curiosity."

She looked away, tried to steady her heartbeat.

He gave a short, self-satisfied laugh. "Your line *used* to be: 'I did that once.' "

Her breath caught painfully, and she glanced back at him. "That bordered on 'complete ass.' "

He stilled. "So it did. I shall try not to triumph over my small victories, sweet Savitri."

Surely it'd be like trying to deny himself blood—but at least he didn't falsely apologize for it. "Not aloud, anyway."

The corners of his eyes crinkled with amusement. "Yes."

But if Colin still triumphed as they neared the exit, Savi

was certain it left him the instant Michael teleported into the corridor ahead of them and folded his giant black wings against his back.

She read the sudden tension around Colin's mouth and eyes; he'd been smiling over Jeeves's overly formal farewell, but now his lips were stiffly curved, as if he held the smile through force of will.

The Doyen nodded in response to Savi's greeting, but his eerie obsidian gaze remained on Colin. There was no differentiation between whites and irises and pupils—just a deep black. They weren't always so inhuman; why adopt that look now?

"You are not going in tonight?"

A muscle worked in Colin's jaw before he said, "Tomorrow. After sunrise."

Though almost impossible to tell, Savi thought Michael's gaze shifted to her before returning to the vampire. His hand rose, and his fingers moved in the sign language the Guardians had adopted for silent communication. Colin had apparently learned it in the past eight months; Savi had not.

Colin made a tight gesture of assent, then added sardonically, "I've delayed my daysleep this week, intending that it will come upon me quickly after I leave tomorrow. If you take me, please wait until I am fully asleep. And remove my head first; I'm certain curators at The British Museum would like to pickle it for posterity."

Michael remained silent for a moment, then sighed and disappeared.

Savi blinked and listened for a pop of air rushing to fill the Doyen-sized vacuum; but as always, there was none. Nothing worked as it should with these Guardians. She glanced at Colin and found him watching her with a raised brow.

"I'm trying not to," she said, and pressed her lips together.

If his laughter was a bit strained, she barely noticed—not when he took her hand in his and tucked it into his elbow, holding it clasped there as they continued outside. He wasn't as massive as Michael or Hugh, but there was no mistaking the lean strength of his muscles under her fingers—the result of an active lifestyle when he'd been a human, not magic. "You may ask. But allow us to reach the privacy of the car first."

The scent of his cologne clung to his jacket—and she

thought she detected a deeper, warmer scent beneath. Male skin. Had her senses been enhanced along with her strength? She hadn't noticed any difference before now. "May I ask others on the way?"

"Such as?" He guided her around a hole in the asphalt.

"What did an aristocrat's son do that gave him a laborer's hardness?" She squeezed his taut forearm.

"Primarily, I beat my valet for tying my cravats in an unsatisfactory manner," he said, and her bubbling laughter evaporated against the heat in his gaze. "You should not ask about my hardness, Savitri."

"I don't mean to be a tease," she said softly.

"I know. It is your prejudice against the upper classes speaking, not your desire to bed me. Alas."

She opened her mouth and closed it again. He'd said it lightly, as a statement rather than an accusation; she wasn't certain how to respond. He stopped beside the Bentley, and she withdrew her hand and crossed her arms over her chest.

"The truth is, my valet was worth a thousand men. I'd have beaten my father before I spoke harshly to Winters, for fear that he'd abandon me for a more amiable employer," he said as he unlocked the passenger door. "The answer you seek is: riding and driving my horses. Fencing. Pursuing other pleasures, usually of the female variety."

Savi nodded absently, arrested by his lack of reflection in the car's tinted windows. She had one; her cream coat mirrored in the darkened glass—why didn't his clothes? And though half of him was between her and the window, none of her seemed to be blocked or missing. How could light pass *through* him?

The key in his hand didn't show up, either—nothing he held or wore did, apparently. "Can you see my reflection in the window? Does it look like I'm alone?"

His voice hardened. "Yes."

She peered intently at the image. Her coat ended midthigh; it belted at the waist, though she hadn't bothered to button or tie it closed. It should have fallen straight past her hips, but it slanted in toward her left leg. "You aren't completely absent; I can see you in the way your thigh against the bottom of my coat keeps it from hanging vertically."

He drew in a sharp breath, and stepped aside. In the window, the fabric swayed as if from a breeze. She was watching the reflection, and couldn't see his expression when he reached out and lifted the end of her dangling belt.

"Oh my god," she laughed, enchanted. Instead of vanishing as the keys had, the belt floated upward; it dropped back to her side when he released it. If he lifted her, it'd probably look as if she were floating, too. "And apparently, only things that are yours are affected. Like placing items in a hammerspace—the disappearance is contingent upon possession."

She turned her head to glance at his profile; he stared at the window, his gaze tracing whatever he saw reflected from that angle.

"Hang Michael and his bloody mirrors," he said quietly. "I'm going to kiss you senseless once we are in the car."

Liquid heat slid down her spine, and she had to swallow past the sudden dryness in her throat. "What he said must've upset you very badly."

He turned from the window. The halogen security lights washed his hair to pale gold, highlighted each plane and angle of his face. She couldn't look away.

"Yes. And I will tell you about it, after I have your mouth. But it must be your choice, Savitri; I'll neither open the door, nor assist you inside. I'll not even ask that you lower your shields." He smiled without humor. "Unless you need to call for help, as a scream will not reach through the soundproofing."

"Will I need help?" Her skin tingled in anticipation; she ran her hands up and down the sleeves of her coat, trying to ease the gooseflesh that shivered over her arms.

He shook his head.

"Why?"

Without answering her, he walked around the front of the car. She stared at him over the top; he held her gaze before swinging the door open and settling behind the steering wheel.

Oh god. Why did he have to do it this way? Her choice. Undeniably her choice. No vampire tricks—she couldn't even see him, and blame it on his beautiful face.

It was just a kiss. Between friends.

She lowered her forehead to the metal roof, hoping to cool the fever that raged through her. He must see her standing there, her torso outlined against the window. The handle was smooth and cold beneath her fingers; she didn't remember taking hold of it.

Think, Savi.

They weren't friends. His interest and pursuit would only last as long as she didn't give him what he wanted. Would it wane after that? Shouldn't she give in, so it would?

Didn't she want to give in?

And why not? Then she wouldn't be standing outside a run-down secret warehouse, her body trembling in anticipation of a simple *kiss*.

She lifted the handle. She didn't look at Colin as she slid into the soft leather seat and tossed her bag to the floorboard. The dome light closed with the door.

"You think too much," he said.

"I can't help it." Any of it. This was madness.

"I know."

Why didn't he do it? She sucked in a deep breath, tried to control the beating of her heart.

Impossible. Even demons and Guardians couldn't control that.

Ah, hell. She shifted, planted her knee in her seat. He'd turned toward her. The center console was in the way, but she leaned over it as his hands rose to cup her face, as his mouth lifted to hers.

His fingers were warm, and his lips firm and soft. How could they be both? God, she didn't know, but she wanted to explore them until she found a satisfactory explanation. It might take forever. She fisted her hands on his lapels and pulled him closer, then used his chest as support when his tongue slid past hers and her strength left her.

Gently, he traced the shape of her mouth, the curves of her lips, the edges of her teeth as if memorizing the texture and design.

No, no—he could have the kiss but not *her*. She tried to wrest back control, licked his fangs with delicate flicks of her tongue, but he only growled low in his throat and took over again.

Oh, god. *Think, Savi.* But she couldn't; he tasted like mint and he smelled so good, his skin and hair like heated satin and thick silk beneath her fingers. When had she moved them from his chest to his nape? She had no memory of it.

And now she straddled him, the steering wheel tight against her spine. He groaned into her mouth and fumbled with one hand and the pressure eased as the seat fell back.

"Colin," she gasped as his lips left her, but he was pushing aside her coat and lifting her tank and then her breast was deep in his mouth, his fangs pressing into the softness surrounding her nipple. Her back arched. His tongue circled and stroked, and she panted and ground her hips against him—she couldn't get to his cock; there wasn't enough space to find the angle to rub against him, though she was tight and wet and aching.

In the next second he pulled her down, flat against him, her face buried in his neck. "Bloody hell." He said it from between clenched teeth, but she heard the amusement lurking behind the frustration.

"What is it?" Lilith and Hugh coming for their motorcycles? She began laughing silently, uncontrollably. It had been years since she'd made out in a car—usually parked a block away from Nani's house and praying her grandmother wouldn't happen upon them.

He took a deep breath, and her entire body lifted with his chest. His shaft rose hard beneath her abdomen. She shivered, and her laughter died.

His hand came up between them and covered her bare breast, still wet from his mouth. "I almost bit you. Your nipple like a berry against my tongue, and I'd have bit and drank and—" He stopped, as if his words were a temptation in themselves.

She didn't move, tried to process what it meant. She couldn't—there were too many thoughts, too many emotions, too many sensations.

"I should get up," she finally whispered.

His fingers briefly tightened on her waist before he nodded his agreement.

Earlier, she'd slid over the console as if need had oiled her way; now, she bumped and lurched awkwardly to her own seat. She tugged her tank into place. A glance confirmed that he was as elegantly composed as ever—if she disregarded the glittering heat in his eyes.

She was certain she'd held her shields. He could've smashed through them with a single draw of her blood, but he hadn't.

She licked her lips; his flavor lingered on her tongue. "Are you still waiting for an invitation?"

"Yes. The bloodlust, however, is a bit of a bounder. It cares nothing of etiquette, or being the gentleman. And as you were willing, so it would be. I'd not be able to resist it." He touched his forefinger to the dash. Three glistening drops remained on the veneer when he drew back; she leaned forward and saw the symbols etched beneath the blood. "In the gym, you lowered your shields in response to pain. I imagine a sharp bite would produce the same effect. If I'd simply wanted past your psychic blocks, I would have hurt you without taking your blood, made it seem a part of loveplay."

Her heart caught in her throat as she stared at him. Did she have any weaknesses that he hadn't filed away for reference? "Why didn't you?"

"I was tempted," he admitted, and his grin flashed. "You should be wary, Savi: I may take such a question as the invitation I long for."

It didn't feel like a warning—it felt like a tease, a promise. She couldn't seem to catch her breath, and she turned toward her window, concentrated on finding an even rhythm.

He hadn't truly answered her, but he didn't need to; he'd had the opportunity to take what he wanted, but hadn't. He was determined to offer her pleasure in exchange for her blood and psychic scent. She could trust him not to hurt her . . . unless she asked for it.

Her breath fogged the glass. Condensation crept around the edges of the windows. He slid the key in the ignition; the engine purred. That she could hear it at all must mean the spell surrounded the whole of the car's exterior, not just the interior. The heaters blasted, but he didn't wait until the windows cleared before pulling from the space.

She couldn't see. Feeling slightly claustrophobic, she wiped off the steam in front of her as they passed through the gates. Two pale faces stared back at her from inside a black

SUV parked across the street. More vampires, probably, but they'd driven by too quickly for her to be certain.

"Tell me what you think Michael asked me, Savi."

She looked over at him. "Why do you want *me* to tell *you*?"

"You must know even that?" When she nodded, he said with a touch of mockery, "I want to know how much you've learned about me before I offer you further information. To feed my ego."

She studied his face, watched the grooves form beside his mouth. No evidence suggested that he cared what others thought of him; if he had, surely he'd have taken the role of vampire leader Fia had spoken of. Did he care what anyone thought? If so, that number of people must be very few. And while he obviously enjoyed compliments or anything that gratified his vanity, he certainly didn't seek approval.

More likely, he wanted to guide her questions by first discovering what she didn't know, and then leading her away from anything he didn't want to answer without appearing to deny her curiosity.

"Okay. Where do you want me to start?" How much did he think she knew?

He shot her a disbelieving glance, then his mouth slid into a wide, laughing smile. She bit her lip against her own smile when she realized she'd questioned him anyway.

"The roads are crowded yet; it will be a long drive to Auntie's." He turned and looked out between the seats. "And perhaps longer than typical," he added softly.

"The vampires in the Navigator?"

"They've been observing my feeding patterns. I haven't noted them since my return to the States, but apparently they've decided to continue the practice." He touched the back of her hand. "Do not worry; I'll not lead them to the restaurant."

She sighed and picked up her bag from the floor. "Yet another reason to marry quickly and leave all this behind: protecting Nani."

"Yes." The warmth of his fingers left her skin, and he shifted gears and shot through an intersection beneath a red light. "Tell me about myself, Savitri."

She looked down at the infrared detector she'd pulled from

her bag. "You don't appear in reflective surfaces, like polished metals or still water or windows, but in mirrors, you see and hear Chaos. And you're anchored to that realm by your blood, because of Michael's sword and the changes it made in you when you were human. And maybe because the nosferatu whose blood Hugh and Lilith used to transform you had been killed with the sword, perhaps doubling the effect. Am I right so far?"

At his nod, she continued, "Last year, Lilith and Hugh used your blood to send a group of nosferatu to Chaos. Hugh tricked them into drinking it during a ritual, and they gained an anchor to Chaos so that Michael could teleport them there. There's no escape from that realm, no Gates. And only Michael and Selah can teleport, so there's no possibility they'd get out. They hoped the nosferatu would be killed and eaten by the dragons and smaller creatures in that realm. But we know they haven't all been eaten; if anything, the ones who live grow stronger."

"Yes." His voice was flat.

"But Michael lost his sword, which was *his* anchor to Chaos. He can't go there." A terrible thought occurred to her. "Has he tried to use your blood—body parts—as an anchor?"

"Yes." He stared straight ahead.

Oh, god. Horrified, she said, "But it didn't work?"

"No. Go on, Savitri."

She *really* didn't want to consider that, so she said, "So I think that Michael is using your ability to see Chaos to keep an eye on the nosferatu—and the wyrmwolf's attack last month suggests that some kind of portal has opened. You immediately left for England, however, so Michael couldn't keep watch over it. But now that you're back, he wants you to use a mirror until they figure out what's happening, and if the nosferatu in Chaos have something to do with it." She took a deep breath and powered on the detector, checking its settings to keep her hands busy. "And I know that while I languished with boredom in Michael's temple in Caelum, you were trapped in Chaos for almost a week, starving and almost mad. So I think seeing it now, even through the safety of a mirror, must be . . . unpleasant."

Terrifying. The lesson he'd taught her in Caelum had given her a very good idea of how terrifying.

His fingers clenched on the steering wheel. "Castleford told you I could be teleported to Chaos? That I was *mad*?"

"No. He wouldn't divulge such a confidence, even if I'd asked. Nor did Lilith," she said before he could ask. "I guessed. Are they still back there?"

After another glance over his shoulder, he took an on-ramp toward the city center. Probably letting the vampires think they were headed to Polidori's. "Yes. Forgive me for doubting you, Savi—but that's a rather spectacular bit of deduction."

She tested the wide stylus against her legs; on the small handheld screen, her thighs appeared orange and yellow. "Not so spectacular. Lilith can't be teleported anywhere because her anchor to Hell is too strong; if either Michael or Selah tried to take her from SI to our house, they'd end up Below. And if they did, even Michael couldn't teleport her out—she has to go through a Gate."

With the press of a few buttons, she changed the display mode. The screen blanked, and a moment later read: **Human .2 meters**. She suppressed the little thrill that went through her; it was still a prototype, and hardly worth celebrating.

She continued, "Selah teleported Hugh to my apartment the night Beelzebub and the nosferatu set fire to your house. Hugh told Selah to return for you in your basement before fetching a Healer for him, and she teleported away. Did she find you?" Savi was certain Selah had; Hugh had inadvertently told her as much the previous day.

"Yes."

"But she didn't come back. Hugh had been her mentor, and the injuries were bad. Really bad. If she could have, she'd have come back. And neither you nor she came to the hospital in the days following, before Michael took me to Caelum. I saw Selah in Caelum three days afterward; she was really shaken up. And when you came to Caelum, it was Michael who brought you . . . though, given that they were preparing to go against the nosferatu within hours, Selah would have been a more sensible choice to leave Earth at that time, even for a few moments. Unless she *couldn't* bring you. So I think your anchor took you both to Chaos, but she couldn't get you out. Until, eventually, she left you alone and went to find Michael.

And he's the one who brought you back."

"I should have let you question me," he said. She looked over at him; his tension and stillness belied the rueful humor in his tone.

Her throat tightened. There had been more. His hands, which had been immaculately manicured only a week before Caelum, had been reddened at the tips of his fingers, the nails half-torn away—as if he'd tried to claw his way out of something. Michael couldn't have healed that; self-inflicted and human-caused wounds were beyond his power to repair. And Colin should have healed more quickly on his own, unless hunger had taken its toll and slowed the process. "I'm sorry."

He cast her a puzzled glance before maneuvering around a truck. "For what do you apologize?"

"Dredging it up. I don't always know when to stop."

"Must I remind you that I requested your recitation?"

"I could've just asked, 'What did Michael want from you?' And you could have said, 'He wants me to make a dreadful observation in a mirror, my sweet Savitri.'"

A smile touched his lips. "Your accent is dreadful. What is that gadget?"

"Just something I've been playing with—I pulled apart a pair of infrared goggles and a handheld game, made some adjustments to the display function. It's for newbies, or humans who can't quickly tell if someone is a human, a demon, or a vampire. I can see the differences after looking for a while, but this would take a temperature reading and tell me right away. And there aren't any human agents at SI now, but eventually there will be. Without psychic abilities, they'll need something like this. Only better—not a bunch of junk."

"There are humans: Castleford, Lilith . . . you."

"They can't really be called human—and neither am I, not anymore. I wouldn't be in this car with you if I were normal, would I?"

"You weren't normal before you ingested the venom, sweet; if you had been, I'd not have spent more than five minutes in your company."

Wrapped in such flattery, his confirmation shouldn't have stung as much as it did, but at least he didn't lie and pretend it was her, and not what he could get from her.

"Anyway, I wanted to see if it could read through the spell to the vampires behind us." She frowned down at the screen as she swept the stylus toward Colin, then switched to the IR display. Just a light green blob—no shape at all. "Except it doesn't seem to be working now."

"It probably is. Try the vampires," Colin said.

She half-rose and turned to peer through the window behind them, saw the black Navigator as it passed beneath a streetlight. "Why do you still have an accent? You've lived in the States for a century."

Bright red filled the display: the SUV's engine. The device was too primitive to separate the vampires' data from the motor's, but apparently it could detect heat from outside the spell's protective shield.

"Do you think it an affectation?" He sounded amused.

"Maybe." She settled back into her seat. "It probably makes it easier for you to hunt. You just say something poetic and they swoon."

He gave a heartfelt sigh, and said, " 'I die! I faint! I fail! / Let thy love in kisses rain / On my lips and eyelids pale. / My cheek is cold and white, alas! / My heart beats loud and fast;— / Oh! Press it to thine own again, / Where it will break at last.' " He lifted his hand from his chest and arched a brow. " 'The Indian Serenade,' yet you are not swooning."

Only because she had something to support her. "Shelley has always struck me as overly dramatic and sentimental," she managed.

"My sweet Savitri—do *not* tell me you are a cynic. I'll not believe it. A skeptic, but not a cynic."

"No, I've seen too much evidence to the contrary. Hugh and Lilith. My parents. Selah and Lucas. My best friend just married a man she'd met once before her wedding, and in her last e-mail she declared herself madly in love with him." She shrugged. "I just think the odds of finding the perfect person are very low, particularly when you've got only sixty years to do it in. So most people either settle for security and fond companionship, or divorce when it doesn't work out and keep on looking. Are you?"

"I have also seen too much evidence to the contrary." He

smiled slightly. "And the odds have not increased over two hundred years, despite the reams of poetry I've recited."

"Perhaps your odds would increase if you wrote your own."

"I believe it would utterly destroy them. And I've no desire to become a starving poet. I'm content placing my failure at Shelley's feet; I blame the poem for your resistance, not my recitation of it."

She met his eyes and bit the inside of her cheek to hold back her laughter when she saw the mirth reflected there. "You knew him, didn't you? Shelley? Hugh once mentioned that you'd known John Polidori, and that you were near Lake Geneva the same year as he and Byron. So you must have encountered the Shelleys."

She didn't miss the sudden darkening of his gaze before he nodded. "Yes. His wife had some sense, but Shelley was a bloody fool—though I suppose I was no less, at the time." He paused, and a pleased expression lit his features. "Did you read his work for his connection to me, sweet Savitri?"

"Hugh was a literature professor for years, and 1816 is a rather famous summer in the literary world. Ghost stories and competitions and all that. I also had a phase when I was a teenager and read tons of Romantic poetry. I don't forget anything easily." She worried her lip with her teeth, then added quickly, "But I'll admit that I reread *Frankenstein* and *The Vampyre* after learning you were there. We've gone on a tangent: a century?"

If he triumphed, he hid it well. "Auntie has lived here almost half that, and she still carries an accent."

"But her first language is different, and when she's not hosting at the restaurant she's talking to her friends in Hindi or Marathi. You speak English." Was it possible that he didn't talk to many people in San Francisco? Perhaps he only came into frequent contact with Hugh and Lilith—and more recently, those at SI.

"That is true. I confess I prefer to speak English rather than American."

She rolled her eyes, smiling. Or maybe he was reclusive because he preferred his own rarefied company to the plebs'.

"You are such a snob. You probably have *Masterpiece Theater* on all the time at your house. Do you call it a 'telly'?"

His shoulders shook. "No."

"At least there's that, as televisions weren't in development until the 1920s. If you did, it'd be proof of your affectation. You still say 'bloody' a lot, though."

"Given my lifestyle, it's frequently appropriate."

Her laughter was cut short by a gasp as he whipped into an alley, plowed through a chain-link fence, scraped past a Dumpster, and accelerated onto a street, now headed in the opposite direction.

Savi unclenched her fingers from his upper thigh and her door pull, and ran her palms down her jeans to wipe away the sudden perspiration. "Well," she said shakily. "That's one thing the symbols are good for: preventing scratches in your paint."

"I'd have warned you, but I rather like where your hand went." He reached down beside his foot and fished for the IR detector that had flown from her grip.

The vampires didn't follow them through; she watched for them until Colin drove down another side street and her heart eased into a normal rhythm. "Gadgets, car chases, a suave British gentleman. I'm officially a Bond girl. I shall call myself Curry Delicious from this day forth."

He didn't laugh; instead, he ran a slow perusal of her form. "The decorator and I performed the final walk-through of my house today. I have a new theater in the basement, and a collection of Bond DVDs. You should make use of me, Miss Delicious."

Her breath caught. "My Bond phase ended two years ago."

"My film library is ridiculously large. What is your newest obsession?"

"A repeated one: horror noir anime. Why so extensive?"

"I've little else to do during the day. My daysleep only comes upon me every five or six days, and I prefer to paint in the predawn hours."

"You can go out in the sun; you could leave your house."

"Yes, but it's extremely uncomfortable."

Her brow furrowed in confusion. "In Caelum, you were out for hours." For the first time she noticed she could think of

Caelum without that familiar tightening in her throat, the dread of memory. Only a sense of wonder and loss.

His tone echoed the same. "In Caelum, it was not painful."

She averted her eyes and studied the IR display with more attention than it deserved. The green blob wasn't completely formless, she realized—it was the leather of his seat, absorbing his body heat.

"Do you appear on any display? Film, digital cameras, video?"

"No," he said softly.

Two hundred years, with nothing to confirm his existence but the gaze of others, his determination not to lose himself. *Look at me.* How many times had he asked her—begged her—to do that in Caelum? But she hadn't . . . couldn't.

He obviously didn't feel sorry for himself; so why did she suddenly feel like crying?

She stared out the window, and asked nothing more the rest of the way.

CHAPTER 9

It is not that the Rules exist, or that I must abide by them; my anger originates from the insulting and outrageous notion that he thought it necessary to remind me of them.

—Colin to Ramsdell, 1816

Auntie's sat between a beauty salon and a laundry, its colorful awning stretching over the sidewalk. It was a restaurant without pretension; though the menu boasted of authentic Bombay cuisine, an outline of the Taj Mahal surrounded the restaurant name. The décor was a mix of old Hollywood and new Bollywood, unapologetically invoking a stereotypical, homogenized vision of India. There was nothing subtle about it, and it catered to anyone who wanted spicy fare and an atmosphere that screamed foreign, exotic, and unreal.

And it smelled incredible—Savitri, saturated. The few times he'd accompanied Lilith and Castleford, Colin had left starving, salivating, his hunts more desperate, the bloodlust deep.

He dared not attempt several hours inside without soothing it first.

Music pounded from the Bentley's speakers; he'd turned it on to cover the silence that had fallen between them—the lull had been awkward for him, but apparently not for Savitri. He'd hoped she would interrogate him on his latest obsession with British punk, but she'd only closed her eyes and leaned back against the headrest.

She looked at him when he lowered the volume, then frowned as he pulled over in front of the restaurant and double-parked beside a green sedan. "You aren't coming in? No kiss for Nani?"

He watched her features carefully as he said, "I need to feed."

Her lips parted. "I assumed you'd already . . ." She smiled brightly, then gathered her bag from the floorboard. "It's probably best if you go anyway; she'll just try to force you to eat." She blinked. "Eat *food*. Well, I'll see you later then. Nani will give me a ride home after we close, so don't worry about that."

That inane babbling. That ridiculously sunny smile. She'd worn the same expression outside Castleford's house while thanking him for the night at the club. The smile that meant she'd thrown her shields up full-force.

"I'll return when I've finished," he assured her.

"Why?" Her smile wavered before it fixed to her lips again. She swung open the door and stepped out. "Oh. Of course. Happy hunting, Colin."

Bloody fucking hell. "Savi—" The door didn't slam; its design prevented such inelegant noise, no matter the force with which it closed. And she couldn't have heard him. He clenched his jaw and wiped away the congealed drops on the dash.

The bell above the restaurant door jingled as she disappeared inside.

Why? Her question, and one she'd quickly answered for herself. He'd hoped his mention of feeding would pique her curiosity, stir her arousal. But he'd only succeeded in reminding her why he'd begun this slow chase and seduction, reducing the desire and budding friendship between them to fangs, blood, and his pursuit of her scent.

A horn blared behind him. He suppressed a crude gesture and slid back into traffic. When had she forgotten his motives, that remembering them had engendered such a reaction? Certainly not on the ride over. So what new fear had he inadvertently raised?

Unless it was not fear, but jealousy—and she'd reinforced her shields to prevent him from sensing it.

Oh, sweet Savitri. He was grinning as he found a space in a parking lot two blocks away. The more he considered the notion, the more it made sense and the better it pleased him. An emotional entanglement might initially frighten her, but if he cultivated it along with her physical attraction, she'd be more likely to overcome any scruples she might have had in straying from her future husband.

Poor sod. No matter how suitable he proved to be, he was going to lose Savi before he'd met her.

Colin tucked his hands into his pockets and wandered from the parking lot to the courtyard of an apartment complex. He leaned his shoulder against a wooden trellis and waited; someone should happen by before too long. A more fascinating hunt waited back at Auntie's—tonight, he'd let his prey come to him.

A tired, feminine sigh alerted him to the woman's presence before he saw her through the beveled-glass security door. She was dressed to go out in a flirty pink dress and heels, but she'd topped it with a worn beige coat. The bloodlust rose up within him, and he stroked his tongue against his fangs, soothing the hungry ache.

Short dark hair.

He shifted impatiently when she paused in the lobby to check her mailbox; disturbed by his movement, the air swirled and the odor of rot wafted around him. *Feed*. Warily, he tested the scent—winter cuttings, mulch.

Just a false association. He forced the memory away, recalled himself to the woman as she neared his location.

She couldn't overlook him; beside the concrete walk, landscaping lights flooded the trellis and surrounding greenery. He'd deliberately selected a well-illuminated spot. Her fingers tightened on her purse strap and she gave him the half-hearted, quick glance so common from a woman alone at night.

She stopped. Disbelief emanated from her psychic scent. Her pulse pounded, and she turned to him with her eyes wide. Silently, without expression, he let her stare; she'd make the decision now—to speak with him or not.

"I know you," she said.

He was not surprised. Inevitably, this happened—he was too old for it not to, now and again. "When did you know me?"

As if his soft question had been a command, her gaze unfocused. "Twenty-three years ago. I . . . dreamed of you. You came to me one night and I invited you up—" Her voice failed, and her cheeks filled with color. Blood, just under her skin. "It was a good dream."

He couldn't keep the bitter smile from his lips. A night of extraordinary pleasure from a stranger, and he always became a drunken hallucination or a dream. Yet she remembered him better than most; he must have remained in her bed throughout the night instead of immediately forcing her to sleep.

"And you're still so beautiful." A wistful note lilted in her voice, but she glanced down at her hands, not at Colin. His gaze followed hers. Age had not settled deeply on her fingers, but he could see the slight loosening of the skin, the veins more prominent than a young woman's would have been. "Will you come up again?"

He placed her hand in the crook of his arm. "Yes."

Walking drew his attention to the stiffness of his cock. He'd not noted it over the bloodlust, but now it annoyed him—how vulgar it was for one's prick to lead the way to dinner when its destination should be to bed. He loved the blood, he loved sex, but the mindless rutting that often accompanied the bloodlust could not even be considered fucking.

Not that they were of a mind to complain once he began feeding.

That did not mean, however, that he had to be an animal up to that moment. He'd have little choice if the bloodlust demanded the rut—and if she willed it. But until he lost that choice, he refused to devolve into barbarity or to rely upon the rapture for his pleasure and hers.

He looked down at his companion as they stepped into the lift. A mirror screamed at him from inside the tiny cube; his focus narrowed to a swath of pink silk. "I pity the gentleman for whom you meant that astonishingly lovely dress. Did he see you in it before he cancelled? He must not have."

"No." She blinked and shook her head as if to clear it. "How—?"

Her skin shivered beneath his fingertips as they followed the U of her neckline from shoulder to the upper swell of her breast. "One does not cover beauty with drab." Smiling, he tugged on the collar of her well-worn mackintosh. "This is the coat of a woman who has no fear that her lover will arrive early." After a glance at her left hand, he amended, "Or her husband."

"Barely. We're reconciling, but his standing me up tonight reminds me why we split." Self-consciously, she checked her reflection—and didn't notice Colin wasn't there. The lift doors opened, and he pulled her quickly through.

She hesitated in front of her flat. He took the keys from her, and once inside, there was no hesitation in her kiss. Colin kept his eyes open, surveyed the room. The edge of a mirror frame was visible in the hall; he'd not take her to the bedroom, then.

It hardly mattered; the front door worked well enough. Her mouth moved beneath his—experienced, aroused, but not hungry for him.

Savitri had been starving for his touch, her lips and tongue eagerly seeking his, her body a sweet weight, the scent and sound of her passion all the flavor he needed.

Until the bloodlust.

He edged the pink silk down over her breast, licked and suckled; she was lovely, but there was no flavor here, just the need to bite, to feed, to take the blood inside his mouth and fuck.

I don't want you tonight. Only your blood.

But his hands lifted her against the door. He closed his eyes. Savi had wanted him. He'd not needed to pierce her shields to sense her desire. Ten minutes of seduction, and she would have willingly been his. One taste of rapture, and she'd not want to relinquish it. If he'd had her here, in the car, standing or lying . . . it would have been of her free will.

Why the bloody fucking hell was he taking a substitute?

Fear crashed through him—not his. He looked at her. She stood frozen, her body taut. Her lips trembled. Her eyes filled with tears.

"You're so beautiful."

He didn't need to hear it from this one.

Only your blood. He covered her eyes and turned her face away from him, pushing her cheek flat against the door panel and exposing her neck. He struck deep; liquid life pulsed into his mouth. His left hand tore at pretty pink silk and under-clothing.

Until it flowed into him, with the electric slide of her blood over his tongue: *I don't want you.*

His cock ached with need, but the bloodlust immediately retreated, regathered and shot upward, until there were only fangs and feeding. She shuddered against him, cried a name that wasn't his. He smoothed her skirt down over her thighs.

And he drank.

ॐ

"Oh, *naatin*, he is very handsome."

Savi grinned at the note of pleasure in Nani's voice. Her grandmother leaned forward in the chair, squinting at the computer screen to read the text beneath the picture. The restaurant's office was small, and Savi barely had room to maneuver around the desk to scroll down the e-mail to find his stats.

"Manohar Suraj. He only has a master's, but it's a terminal degree in his field." And better than anything she had to offer, Savi added silently. But it was probably best not to break Nani's good mood by reminding her of her granddaughter's shortcomings. "He's a software engineer and he lives in Stonestown. He recently bought a condo there."

"You've spoken with him?"

"Just e-mail. But I'm meeting with him tomorrow; we're going to that little coffee shop off Wawona."

A small expression of distress furrowed Nani's brow. "This is not how it is usually done, *naatin*. I should speak with his family."

"This is better than you talking with his parents and then having to withdraw later if we don't like each other. Let us see if we are compatible, and if we aren't, it'll save you any embarrassment."

Nani gave a little headshake of assent. "What of his family? It cannot be good that they placed an advertisement; they must have no connections at all."

Savi had gone around that—found out who had paid for the matrimonial and then contacted Manu directly. "His father is at Cisco Systems. You might be able to ask Mr. Sivakumar if he knows him." It would go a long way toward easing Nani's fears if someone she knew could vouch for the family, and the son. "You should call Mrs. Sivakumar tomorrow."

Again that headshake. "Did you send a picture?"

Savi nodded, trying not to laugh. "He wasn't horrified. He still agreed to meet me."

"It looks better today, *naatin*. But still—"

"I know. I'll grow it out. My braid will be as long as yours before the wedding."

"Hopefully you marry before then," Nani said, smiling. "Your mother cut her hair when she first started university, and it took eight years to reach this length again."

Savi couldn't remember her mother without a *chotee*. Her father had often tugged on it, laughing. And when she'd brushed it out, it had fallen down her back like a waterfall of ebony satin.

Her only memory of her mother's short hair had come from pictures.

Savi's chest tightened, and she wrapped her arms around Nani's shoulders. Neither she nor Nani were given to displays of affection, but there was no surprise or rejection in her grandmother's form.

It was brief; Nani patted her arm and pulled back. "Do not make me cry, *naatin*. Have you eaten?"

The ache beneath Savi's heart faded, replaced by amusement. Her grandmother would stuff her full, as if food would heal all of her ills, ease any grief. "Not yet, but I'll get something in a moment—there's not much here to do. Ranjit has been keeping it up well." Though Savi had once been her grandmother's sole help with the books, during their vacation to India and her subsequent fever, another employee had maintained them . . . and continued to do so. As Nani seemed comfortable with the arrangement, Savi hadn't done more than act as fill-in when he took time off. Like tonight.

"Yes."

"Do you need help out front?" As if on cue, the bell rang merrily, and voices carried into the back. Auntie's did not have a large dinner clientele, but it managed a brisk take-out business in the evenings. "Is Geetha the only one out there?"

Nani stood up. "We're slow now. Eat first, and then you can take phone orders."

"Okay. Did any of the DemonSlayer players show up last week?"

"No, *naatin*. Perhaps it's best? That was a terrible business, what happened to them."

Savi nodded. "You're probably right."

With a headshake that said, *Of course I am*, Nani left the office in a rustle of magenta silk and clinking bangles. Savi sighed and sank into the chair her grandmother had vacated.

As much as it'd hurt, Lilith had spoken true: had Savi never translated Hugh's book, and printed it at a vanity press as a present to him, and then developed a card game based on the story, the gamers who'd once gathered at Auntie's every Friday night would never have been targeted. Lucifer and the nosferatu were to blame for their deaths, but Savi was responsible for creating the circumstances that had brought Demon-Slayer and its players to Lucifer's attention. Two dead, plus one of Hugh's fellow professors—and four more taken and frightened beyond belief before Hugh and Lilith had rescued them.

No wonder they no longer came to play—reality had taken the fun out of it. And they still didn't know all of the reality; Lilith had managed to twist the truth so that the nosferatu became a cult of wannabe vampires. Insane, dedicated to extreme body modification, but human—and inspired to action by Hugh's book and DemonSlayer.

Just as Polidori's popularity had soared, so had Demon-Slayer's sales.

She glanced up at Manu's picture. That was one thing she had to offer: a hell of a lot of money. None of the victims' families had wanted it—they'd called it tainted . . . cursed. And though Savi would have once laughed off such an idea, perhaps it could be cursed. She was afraid to use it; her lesson had been learned. An anonymous donation to an orphanage in India? It would probably be destroyed in an earthquake.

"Eat something, *naatin*," Nani commanded. Savi glanced over in time to see her sweep past the door, heading for the kitchens with an order ticket in hand. "Take something out to Mr. Ames-Beaumont, as well. He cannot only want tea."

Colin *had* returned. She blinked, trying to decide how she should feel about it. Her body didn't wait for her mind to decide; it seemed to hum in anticipation. Even with her shields up, she could no longer ignore the effect he had on her.

Slowly, she turned back to the computer and moved the mouse pointer to close the e-mail window. Before she could click, a warm hand covered hers and a low voice purred in her ear, "What is this, *naatin?*"

Colin. His chest against her upper back, his jaw against her temple as he looked over her shoulder. His middle finger slid alongside her forefinger, and he used the mouse wheel to scroll down through the e-mail.

"A prospective groom?"

She closed the window with a keyboard command and fought an overwhelming urge to run. "Yes."

"You hold your breath. Your heart races. Did his picture cause this sudden excitement?"

"Yes," she lied.

"He will not do at all, sweet Savitri. He is far too handsome." His voice seemed to rumble through her, prickling beneath her skin.

"I've always liked a pretty face."

He laughed softly. "Is that so?"

His teeth scraped her throat.

And then she was alone in the office again, her grandmother singing lightly as she carried a dish to the dining room.

Oh god. The air left her lungs in a shuddering rush, and she gulped in more. She scooted forward in the seat, tried to use the movement to ease the sudden, unbearable ache that pulsed low and heavy. Hot and liquid.

It didn't work.

"Naatin?"

"I'm coming," she said, and bit her lip. "I'll be right there." *Let me dry hump this chair first.*

What had that been? Sometime between her leaving his car and now, his "let's be friends" had apparently lost its allure. Or he grew impatient with her, his obsession for a taste outweighing his intention to wait for an invitation—to wait for her to make a choice.

Both options were sobering . . . and ridiculously painful.

She liked being with him, but it was all too quickly becoming something deeper, something *complicated*. His attractiveness and her arousal were simple. Their easy banter was simple. Knowing what he wanted from her made it simple. Her experience on Caelum had been simple.

The shuddery ache she was feeling now was not; the whole had become more than the sum of its parts—and she had to keep it simple. She couldn't let it go any further. After she met with Manu and started on that path, she couldn't turn back.

She didn't want to leave part of herself bleeding behind her. If this continued, she would.

Unless she gave Colin what he needed tonight; the object attained, the hunt would be over. And she would gain pleasure from it, as well—her curiosity fulfilled.

A perfectly simple solution.

＄

Savi automatically looked for Colin at the table where she'd first seen him eight months ago. He'd been wearing sunglasses, pretending to be blind so he could bring Sir Pup into the restaurant.

But she didn't see him there—didn't see him anywhere.

Very few diners sat at the tables. Colin would have stood out even if the restaurant had been crowded. Savi frowned, then noticed the table near the front window with a single teacup steaming on its surface—though no Colin. Geetha stood at the front counter, giving a woman in a pink dress and a gorgeous black shawl a take-out order.

Savi smiled and said a quick hello; Roberta was a regular, though she appeared rather dazed at the moment. When she left, Savi pointed toward the window.

"Is that Colin's table? British, white?"

Geetha grinned. "Handsome? Yes."

Nani brought another take-out bag to the counter and clicked her tongue. "Did you call Mrs. Karlen? Did she come for her order?"

"Yes. She said she fell asleep."

"She makes too long a day, that one. And her divorce! So much stress. Is that all you are eating, *naatin*?" Nani shook her head at Savi's soup bowl and disappeared into the kitchen again.

Savi met Geetha's laughing gaze, and sighed. "I'll be by the window if the phones get too crazy."

It didn't surprise her that Colin was at his table when she turned around. His fingers curled around the teacup, his thumbs absently tracing the rim.

Her bowl clinked against the sheet of glass protecting the crimson silk tablecloth. She kept her tone light. "You drank from one of our customers?"

"Hiding beneath the table was its own reprimand," he said easily. He looked at her soup and drew in a long breath. "What is that?"

"Mulligatawny." She pushed her spoon into the thick soup. "Lentils, vegetables. Tamarind and coconut milk. Lots of spice. Not true Indian cuisine, but popular, so we make a meatless version of it." She lifted her gaze to his. "The British are responsible for its creation, actually."

"Our colonies did produce many a spectacular concoction." His teeth flashed briefly. Though he laughed and smiled openly in private company, he was careful not to expose his fangs in public. It was a shame, she decided; his mouth was incredible. Remembering how the sharp edges of his teeth had skimmed over her neck, she repressed a delicious shiver.

She studied it for a bit longer, until the headlights of a passing car illuminated him with bright light. Her gaze dropped to the table, and she slid her napkin across the glass.

"You have lipstick. Here." She pressed her finger against the corner of her bottom lip, and watched her spoon swirl in the bowl.

She glanced up to find him staring down at the streak of color against the white linen. "Pink is not a flattering shade on me."

She couldn't help but smile at such a rueful observation. "No." And she prevented any further conversation by taking a bite of the soup, letting its heat fill her mouth.

She had to force herself to swallow past the ache in her throat.

He kissed them. She'd known, but the implications of it hadn't truly occurred to her before—of course he would kiss them. Hadn't he told her that physical lust rode behind the bloodlust?

I do not realize I'm hard until I'm inside her.

No wonder Roberta had seemed so dazed.

The napkin crumpled in his hand, and he threw it to the table. "I didn't fuck her."

Startled by the anger beneath the statement, she met his gaze again. "I didn't say that."

"You assumed it."

Her brow furrowed. "You have to take blood; you're a vampire. Sex goes along with it." She waved her hand at his cup. "Like tea and sugar. You can have one without the other, but it isn't as good. Is it?"

"I don't know," he said tightly. "I can't bloody taste it."

She pressed her lips between her teeth and played with her soup.

"Don't laugh." But his voice shook, and he passed his hand over his face as if to hold back his own laughter.

When she looked back up, she found him staring at her with an expression that could have been amazement—or pain. "I want you, Savi. Your blood, your body. I would do anything to have you. Tell me what I need to do."

Her spoon rattled against the rim of the bowl. She carefully set it down and said, "I'll come home with you tonight."

He was at her side in an instant, pulling her to her feet.

"Wait," she laughed. "I have to stay and help. We close at ten."

A soft groan of despair escaped him, but he sat down. Peripherally, she saw Nani come out of the kitchen and began eating the mulligatawny as quickly as possible.

Colin's eyes gleamed. "Shall I tell her?"

"No," she choked, torn between horror and amusement. "I'll tell her you ate one of the regulars."

He laughed, his elbow propped on the table and his fist curled loosely in front of his mouth. She paused with the spoon halfway to her lips, struck by how boyish he looked in that moment. He'd been only twenty-two at his transformation, but his features usually gave the impression of ageless youth; he could have been a man of eighteen or forty. His laugh took away that untouched facet of his appearance without reducing his beauty.

When it faded, he leaned back in his chair and smiled

lazily. "There's no evidence. I was nothing but a dream to her."

A dream? That was similar to what Fia had called it: unreal. "That's what you make them think?"

"I don't *make* them. It's how they remember it."

"How do you know, if you leave them directly afterward?"

"I have been living in San Francisco for a long time, Savi."

One hundred years multiplied by an average of one a night . . . "Oh, my. And some twice? Was Roberta?"

An indefinable tension passed over his features before he nodded.

"And I thought *I* had gotten around," she said.

His lids lowered. "Does it trouble you?"

"That I'm a slut? No."

The corners of his mouth turned down, flattening the curve of his bottom lip. "That is not what I meant. I would hardly hold your romantic nature and your desire to increase your odds against you."

She stared at him. Is that what he thought—and was he correct? She loved the physical pleasure she found in bed, but she'd never analyzed her reasons for seeking it with so many people, afraid of what she'd discover. And she wouldn't begin now. "And yet you wonder if I'd hold *your* nature against you. As if you should starve yourself."

"I don't have sex with every one."

"Neither do I."

"Only one or two a week."

Oh, god. "Okay." It didn't come out as strongly as she intended.

A muscle in his jaw flexed. "It's always consensual. And I don't take advantage of—"

"It's fine, Colin." Her cheeks hurt from the width of her smile. "Really. Even if you wanted to—and there's no reason you should—you couldn't stop."

And he couldn't; he *had* to feed. The number truly didn't matter, either; it was the knowledge that a few days from now, maybe tomorrow, he'd be with someone else. And then someone else.

The dull pain in her chest had returned. Thankfully one

night of sex—even spectacular sex—wouldn't whet the pain from dull to sharp.

Perhaps it could be a dream for her, too. Unreal. Her smile softened as she looked up at him again and caught him studying her face with dark intensity. As if reassured by her response, he relaxed.

She took a sip of water, then said, "It's probably a good thing that most vampires aren't like you. Can you imagine even twenty in a city like this, trying to feed from a different person every night? Within a decade, ten percent of the population would have been sucked on. And a community of a hundred vampires? No way to keep that secret, even if everyone had your ability to make them forget."

"Yes, it is fortunate," he said. "But there would be no community if they were like me."

"Because you can't reproduce? Or because you're reclusive?"

He shook his head, and the tips of his fangs showed in a smile before he hid them. "Choose one."

Which question? The second didn't signify, she realized; even reclusive vampires needed to eat, community or no. "Have you ever tried to reproduce?"

"Yes."

"What happened?"

"They died." A bleak expression sat upon his features for a moment. "Not this one, Savi. I'm sorry. Another time."

She wouldn't have many other times with him, but she nodded. "Why don't you take a consort? Do you love the hunt that much?"

"Savitri, my sweet, you double up your questions as if they were naughty schoolboys in a dormitory bunk."

She laughed despite herself. "The consort?"

"I can't share my blood," he said. He lifted his shoulder in a careless, elegant shrug. "It's tainted."

"You used it to heal—" She broke off as she understood; he meant he couldn't let another vampire drink it. Like ingesting the hellhound venom . . . it was impossible to know what the consequences would be. "I'm tainted, too," she said, feeling sick to her stomach. "You can't take my blood."

Colin was shaking his head. "You're still human."

"How do you know it won't have an effect on you? How many hellhound-venom-and-nosferatu-blood-tainted women have you had?"

His lips quirked. "Savi, consider my blood and Anthony Ramsdell's blood—though Michael's sword is fatal to the nosferatu, our human blood didn't carry any of its power. The nosferatu drank from us without consequence. The sword's taint only manifested with our transformations: his to Guardian, mine to vampire."

"And your sister? She was human, but didn't it allow her to resist Lilith?"

"Some psychic resistance," he admitted. "But as you are well aware, that is natural to humans; it only strengthened what she already possessed."

As Savi had been strengthened? "Could she throw a baseball into the next county? You weren't changed by it when you were human, as I am changed," she pointed out. "And there is a significant difference between a demon dog and Michael's sword."

"Not particularly significant. Lucifer bred the hellwolves from wyrmwolves; a hellhound is, in essence, a creature of Chaos—just as the dragon whose blood altered Michael's sword was of Chaos." His mouth thinned with bitter humor. "I do not have to fear you might anchor me to that realm."

She rubbed her forehead with her fingertips, then lowered her hand back to the table. "I don't know."

He reached forward and clasped her hand in his. His thumb slid over her knuckles, dipped into the valleys between. Her cupped palm reflected against the crimson-lined glass; Colin's did not.

All too quickly, he drew back. "I'd not drink from you unless I was certain of this, Savi. If it has any effect—and I sincerely doubt it will—perhaps I'll begin to emit an odor somewhat like a peach."

She smiled, but she couldn't laugh, not when she still wondered: "Why not a human consort then? Or humans, since one couldn't support you with her blood."

"A harem? And should I keep them in separate houses

as I would a stable of mistresses, one for each day of the week?"

"Too expensive?"

"Indeed. And returning the next week to find she has all but forgotten the pleasure I gave her is hardly flattering."

"You've done it before," she realized.

"Yes. It did not suit."

"So a human is out. But you could drink from another vampire, and she could get hers elsewhere."

"My personal blood depot, with its accompanying sexual access?" He arched a brow, his mouth softening with amusement. "Even I am not so callous, nor so selfish, as to treat a woman as that. Not for more than one day, that is."

Savi grimaced. "I suppose that would not work for very long; she'd feel used and resentful, eventually. Or I would I know I could not spread myself between two men that way, particularly if one just wanted my blood. But there must be a vampire who would like that. Everyone has her little sexual kink."

Noting his sudden stillness, she reviewed their conversation.

"Ah, you just realized that you lied. You probably thought I didn't know, but you *did* use a Guardian as your personal blood depot. The nosferatu were around and you couldn't hunt, so when Lilith caught Selah you kept her for a few days. Selah told me you had her chained to your bed, and that, except for your frequent drinking, you were the perfect gentleman—"

"Stop, Savi."

She flushed. "Sorry. That not-knowing-when-to-quit problem."

"Not that; I enjoy your interest in me." His eyes searched hers, his brows drawn together. "But I don't *just* want your blood."

"I know," she said. Had he misunderstood what she'd offered? Better to make it absolutely clear. "I'm not coming over to be your snack. You can have my blood, yes—and I'll drop my shields. But I expect sex in return. Hard and fast is best. And a few times, if possible."

His gaze darkened; his voice was low and rough. "It will be. More than a few. I'll not let you sleep the whole of the night."

"That will be good," she whispered, her throat suddenly dry. She just hoped it would be *enough*.

CHAPTER 10

The only alternative food source for vampires is animal blood, but it isn't really an alternative except temporarily, unless the vampire wants to be a celibate idiot. And the longer a vampire feeds from an animal source—or even human blood from a blood bank—the worse the effect.

—Savi to Taylor, 2007

Colin resented every moment Savitri sat perched on the barstool behind the front counter. Her questions shouldn't be limited to how customers preferred their dishes and what their names were. Why did she and Auntie continue in this business? They could each afford to live well without it.

How aggravating that she should serve anyone, voluntarily or not.

She trapped the phone between her jaw and shoulder as she wrote down yet another order. And he resented the twenty feet separating them all the more when she slid her fingers beneath the white shirt collar at her nape, massaging caramel skin that he couldn't see or feel—only imagine.

He swallowed and forced himself to turn and look out the window before the bloodlust rose. He'd have her in a few hours; there was no need to torture himself in the interim.

Though he could hardly believe she still intended to leave with him. The interlude in the office had accomplished what he'd intended, and the conversation had started well enough—but he'd lost control of it over a bit of lipstick. The gratifying jealousy in her gaze had become something wounded, and he'd lost his sense.

He'd never before felt the need to explain his sexual history . . . and what a sodding mess he'd made of it. He'd exposed something that must appear dirty and sordid to a human, even as he'd been attempting to convince her of the opposite.

Only one or two a week. Christ. Her mind was too quick—she'd probably calculated the numbers before he'd realized what his defensive statement had meant: in two centuries, he'd taken blood from seventy thousand humans, and had sex with twenty thousand.

Little wonder he'd always preferred art to arithmetic.

He didn't know how he'd recovered from such a bungle or what had kept her from bolting, but he wouldn't question his good fortune.

His teacup and table reflected in the window, and he watched the spoon circle as he stirred it with his invisible hand. Remembering the delight on Savi's face as he'd lifted her belt beside the car, he pressed his lips together to stop his laughter. The illusion had never amused him before—but he'd never seen himself in that movement, only that he was missing.

Such a simple thing, yet she'd had to point it out to him. What else did she see that he could not?

He glanced back at her, and his body tightened in immediate arousal. She'd turned in her seat and rested her arm across the back, her slim torso in a graceful curve. She studied him with her upper lip caught between her teeth, her lower pushed out.

She was considering something—and whatever it was made her heartbeat and breathing quicken until it was all he could hear beneath the music of the sitar, the murmur of voices from the other tables, the noise from the kitchen.

She didn't look away when he met her gaze; instead she arched one of her exquisite eyebrows in a clear query: *Why are you laughing?*

Good God, she could ask a specific question with nothing more than a quirk of her brow. He shifted in his seat, gave a small shake of his head.

He was suddenly quite certain he adored her.

Her mouth opened, and she touched the tip of her tongue to

her upper lip, slightly swollen and rosy from her bite. Her left brow rose. *Tell me.*

And now a demand. What would she do if he didn't?

Colin leaned forward, rested his elbow on the table, and cupped his chin in his palm to hide his grin. He lost sight of her when Geetha passed between them, heading for the kitchens, leaving Savi alone at the counter. Then he slowly turned and looked through the window again.

"I want to see your mouth," Savi murmured.

Need tore through him, made him as lightheaded as if he'd been feeding. The passing headlights blurred into long, brilliant streams before snapping into sharp focus.

Her voice was low and a touch playful. "I want it all over me. Your lips, your tongue . . . your teeth."

Christ. He fought the urge to look at her, fearing she'd stop.

"Hugh taught me to lower my shields today. I'll drop them if you—"

Colin slapped both palms flat against the table. The teacup and spoon rattled together.

If the few other patrons startled at the sound, he didn't know. He only heard her soft, throaty laughter. When it faded, she whispered, "Will you have control?"

A fine tremor shook his fingers. He nodded.

"Look at me," she said. "I want to see what it does to you."

Could she not see what her *voice* did to him? She must know. How extraordinary that she didn't recognize her body's sexual response much of the time, but could deliberately work him into aching hardness with a kiss . . . or a few words spoken across a room.

"Hurry. Nani and Geetha come." As if to emphasize her urgency, the phone rang.

He turned his head and stifled his groan of pure visual pleasure.

She'd twisted a little farther in her chair; the edges of her white shirt had pulled back. The soft blue cotton she wore beneath clung to her small breasts, outlined her nipples. His tongue dried, felt thick and heavy in his mouth. The low neckline left her collarbones and throat bare. He forced his gaze up over the expanse of smooth skin, past her soft lips. They glistened as if she'd licked them.

He would drink from them, too.

She was looking sidelong in annoyance at the phone. Then she raised her gaze to his.

He couldn't stop the low, harsh growl that escaped him as the scent filled the room, overpowering every physical odor. There was no possibility that she heard it, but her lashes lowered as if in her own pleasure, and she watched him through that heavy-lidded gaze.

She lifted the phone to her ear, never looking away from him. "Auntie's."

Bloody hell, even that was torture. *Say something more, Savi. Ask a question.*

"Okay. How hot would you like that?" Her mouth curved slightly.

He drew in a deep breath, filled himself with the essence of her. Not just the sweet scent; her arousal added a new, irresistible note, cinnamon and spice. Had he said he'd have control? It was quickly becoming a lie. His hands fisted on the table.

Her brows drew together, and concern layered a different flavor. *Too much?* She mouthed the words, then said into the receiver, "No, we close in half an hour. You should have time."

Half an hour. He'd have her against the wall before then. His jaw clenched in denial, but he nodded.

It eased to a light fragrance, no stronger than the breeze from an orchard on a sunny day. Then she broke her hold over him, glancing away to speak with Auntie.

Colin closed his eyes and simply breathed for several minutes. So easy to bask in this.

Until another psychic scent intruded. His lip curled in irritation, and he looked through the window in time to see the black Navigator drive past the restaurant, two vampires inside. Bloody nuisances.

Uneasiness slid through him. He'd told Savi he wouldn't lead them here, and he was certain he'd evaded them. His car was parked two blocks away, off the street. Nor could they have seen Savi in his car and guessed their destination— Savi's exit from the warehouse had been blocked from their view, and the Bentley's tinted windows would have prevented their seeing inside. Colin knew her psychic shields hadn't fallen, revealing her identity; and his own psychic blocks were too strong to reveal his location.

Particularly to such young, inexperienced vampires as those he sensed within the vehicle.

He held on to their minds as they drove on, slipped quietly into the emotions of the weaker one. Not much within him above the level of his shields; hardly more than a sheep. Just a sense of duty, combined with disillusionment and anger. An ill-tempered sheep.

And, despite the vehicle, completely different from the two vampires he'd sensed earlier.

He shouldn't have used the symbols to shield the Bentley so quickly after kissing Savi. He'd known the vampires waited outside the warehouse but had only given them a cursory scan. Still, they'd had a maturity neither of these possessed.

The Navigator passed again, and Colin gave a hard mental push—it would alert them to his presence, but also serve as a warning.

Surprise flared from their scents, then a careful probe from the weaker one. Bloody stupid of him. Without experience to guide it, reaching out like that opened one's own shields. Colin seized hold of it, tasted.

And found a dark, powerful presence hovering foremost in the vampire's thoughts. Behind that, Savitri.

They were looking for Savi?

The weakling struggled; in Colin's moment of shock and anger, the vampire managed to rip away and throw his shields up. The Navigator accelerated out of sight a moment later.

He tossed a glance at Savi; she was chatting with Geetha, oblivious to the exchange that had just taken place. Good. He drew in a deep breath. Her psychic scent remained the same. Sweet, a hint of arousal.

Very good. He'd take care of this, and she wouldn't have to fear anything. Nothing should mar their first night together. Just once, it would go right between them.

Denim pulled tight across his groin as he reached into his pocket for his phone. He was no longer achingly erect, but her fragrance left him half-hard, as if ready to leap to attention for her. Simple physical lust.

He rather liked the sensation.

Castleford answered with a succinct "Yes, Colin?" and waited.

Colin raised his face toward the heavens in exasperation. The barbaric medieval knight, Castleford never observed the niceties of polite conversation. "I need Sir Pup to escort Auntie home this evening and watch over her home until dawn."

If the vampires had any notion of trying to get to Savi through her grandmother, the hellhound would quickly dissuade them.

Castleford's voice sharpened. "What's happened?"

There were benefits to his bluntness, Colin decided as he relayed the psychic exchange and the presence of the first pair that had followed them. It meant that he wasted no time. "It's possible they are curious about her, as there have been rumors that she is my consort," he concluded. "And I'm not certain if there were two vehicles, or if they traded observation duties. I have the plate number of the later one."

"But not the first?"

Colin stifled his sigh. "*They* are stalking *me*," he said. "I'd not intended to return the interest." Though the interest he'd sensed from these had a different flavor—darker, resentful. And Colin had not been the powerful figure foremost in their minds.

"Did Savi see the first car?"

Castleford's question prevented him from pursuing the disturbing direction his thoughts were taking. Remembering how she'd turned around to test her little gadget, Colin said, "Yes, but only for a moment."

"Ask her."

Colin's mouth set in a thin line; he didn't want to alert her to their concern on only the slim chance that she'd caught a number or two from the plate. If she thought Auntie was in danger, she wouldn't leave with him that evening. But Castleford's tone was implacable—if Colin refused to ask her, the other man would likely call the restaurant and speak to her directly.

He caught Savi's attention, and felt her curiosity as she slid off her chair. Ungainly in the gym, here she moved with graceful ease. Her eyes were bright as she approached him, her smile playful.

He didn't want to see it fade. He held his hand over the mouthpiece as he said, "Do you recall anything particular about the Navigator that followed us?"

A tiny crease appeared between her brows. She rocked back and forth on her heels as she studied him. "Particular, how?"

"Did your device record a picture of it?"

"No, but that would be an interesting feature to add. Particular, how?" she repeated. "What are you looking for?"

"Do you remember any identifying marks? The plate number?" The question was sharp; he hoped to dissuade her from digging deeper. If she asked him why, quirked one of those eyebrows, he could hardly resist her.

Her shields rose, and her expression drained of emotion. Her tone flattened. "Yes. Is that Hugh?" She nodded toward the phone. "I'll talk to him."

Not bloody likely. Already she'd withdrawn; he wouldn't risk Castleford doing more damage. "I'll ring you back," Colin said and snapped the phone closed before the other man could respond. "Tell me."

"Fine." She touched her fingertips against her forehead, closing her eyes. She looked through him when she opened them again, and her hand fell to her side. "The license is four-A-V-X-seven-eight-five, California plates. Black Lincoln Navigator. Chrome grill. No dings or flaws that I can see. The passenger is blond white male, early forties. Too dark and far away to see eye color. Hair length, short. Gray blazer, blue tie, white shirt. Driver has brown hair, mullet, thirties, white male. Black or navy jacket, red tie, white shirt." She blinked and focused on him again. "That's a sixty-thousand-dollar SUV. It shouldn't be difficult to track him down even if the name on the registration is bogus. That kind of money stands out in a community where a vampire's lucky to hold a job at a twenty-four-hour convenience store."

He couldn't answer. Astonished, he stared up at her. Demons had complete recall, but they'd been angels once, their minds different from humans' and halflings'. And in two centuries, though he'd heard of such, he'd never met a human with the ability. Nor any Guardians or vampires; transformation drastically improved memory, but couldn't make it perfect.

If it did, Colin wouldn't have possessed a gallery of self-portraits.

In sudden realization, he drew in a sharp breath; she would never forget his face. Never let him fade into a dream.

"Don't look at me like that." Her lips firmed, her hands clenched. "It makes me feel like a monkey. 'Savi, what a neat trick. Do it again. Tell me what you had for lunch on November third, 1989.' "

Bitterness filled her voice; little wonder, if that was the type of response she usually got. What a fucking ridiculous question. "My sweet Savitri, I'm simply astounded by the revelation that I'm being chased by a vampire sporting the horror of a mullet." The same manner of hairstyle worn by the partner of the female Colin had slain. Bloody hell.

The tightness around her mouth eased. "Do you remember it all?"

Colin belatedly recalled the phone in his hand. Castleford probably grew impatient. "Yes. Four-A-V-X-seven-eight-five?" Different vehicles.

"Yes. Tell him I'll do a search on it tomorrow. Unless you need the info tonight?"

He shook his head, forced himself to speak evenly. "It'll wait." As long as Auntie was safe, the rest could be pursued after he'd had Savi, and bound her to him with pleasure.

Even more important that he did so now.

"You've rebuilt your shields. Have you reconsidered your decision to leave with me?"

"No." Her dark gaze searched his for a moment, and the uncertainty there prevented his relief from overwhelming him. "I wasn't trying to be nosy when I asked you why you wanted me to look. I have to focus on a few details or there's too much to see. You wouldn't want to be in my head when I'm narrowing down to that point—and the strongest emotion I use as my connection to the memory lingers for a few minutes. That's why I'm blocking now; I'll let them down again when it goes away."

His brows rose, and amusement curled his lips. "You can

let them down now. There's nothing in you that can shock me, my sweet Savitri. There's very little I haven't experienced."

"I know. I imagine you know what this feels like all too well." She wrapped her arms around her middle; her fingers were trembling. How long had they been so? He'd only been attending to her facial expressions.

His throat closed with sudden dread. His teeth clenched together in denial, but he knew what she'd say next.

"My memory in the car centers around you. To get there, it's like walking along the threads of a web, from one memory of you to another." She released a shaky breath. "And my strongest link to you is what you gave to me in Caelum."

Terror. Despair. His chest constricted; a painful, leaden weight settled in his gut.

She'd never forget that, either.

She'd apparently picked up a dramatic flair from Lilith, but what she really needed to learn was when to stop.

At the front counter, Savi bit her lip and cast another glance at Colin. He stared unblinkingly out the window, his jaw set. He'd only looked up once, just after she'd lowered her shields.

He'd turned to her with a disbelieving arch of his brow, and then resumed his brooding.

"You're acting just like Hugh," she said softly.

His head jerked around, and his offended stare pinned her to her seat. For two men who had vows of protection and loyalty between them, there also ran a mutual antagonism. Entertaining at times, and useful.

Her eyes narrowed. "It's true. He used to mope around, 'Woe is me! I've done something terrible to the woman I want to screw!' It's stupid."

"Are you talking to yourself, *naatin*?"

Savi's mouth snapped closed, and she flushed. Colin turned to look out the window again, but his hand came up to cover his lips.

Nani's exacting gaze traveled over the front counter, and she straightened and arranged items to her satisfaction.

"I was just thinking that Mr. Ames-Beaumont has waited long enough to take me home. It's all closed here up front." Savi waved toward the dining room, the chairs she'd turned upside down on the tabletops, the swept floors.

Her grandmother's lips pursed, but she nodded. "You shouldn't take advantage of him this way, Savitri. I would have driven you home."

"It's out of your way. He's going to see Lilith and Hugh anyway, and I thought I'd find out if he knows of anyone suitable at Ramsdell Pharmaceuticals. There should be lots of doctors and researchers." Her cheeks were hot; thankfully Nani was still checking to make certain everything was in its place.

It wasn't the first time she'd lied to her grandmother about her activities—and it was better Nani didn't know—but it was the first time someone had witnessed her doing it.

How humiliating that Colin would see that she had to explain her decisions and gain approval. He surely couldn't know that according to Nani and her friends, no matter a woman's age, she wouldn't be considered responsible or her decisions given any credence until she was married and had produced a few children. Or grandchildren.

And Savi's continuing fascination with things Nani considered childish—video games, manga and anime, electronics—certainly hadn't helped any. Nor had her ever-changing interests.

A woman was steady, dependable. Savi was not.

Nani put her hands on her hips. "You didn't feed him anything, *naatin*. If he's to help find you a husband, you could at least have given him something to eat."

Savi didn't dare glance his way for fear she'd begin giggling uncontrollably. "I'll make sure he eats after we leave."

Nani waggled her head from side to side in assent and walked toward Colin's table. Savi left him to defend himself, slipping into the office to collect her coat and bag before returning to the front.

She stopped, and the swinging door bumped into the back of her shoulder. Colin danced around the tables with Nani in his arms, and he sang along with the Bollywood tune playing lightly through the speakers. Her sash trailed behind her, a brilliant flash of magenta.

Nani's face was suffused with delight, though she obviously tried to suppress it. Reluctant, breathless laughter punctuated her protest. "No, *beta*—you will make an old woman lose all sense."

Colin winked at Savi over Nani's head, and then twirled. He moved effortlessly, gracefully; it was pure pleasure just to watch him. "Only if you cease calling yourself old; it makes me feel an ancient. Compared to me, you are but a blushing maiden." He began singing again.

Savi leaned against the doorjamb, her knees weak, her heart pounding.

They danced past the kitchen door as the song came to an end. Colin paused, bent, and gently dipped Nani back over his arm. He dropped a loud kiss to her flushed cheek.

"*Beta!* You must stop this silliness!"

Colin unrepentantly pressed his lips to her other cheek. Then with a flourish, he set her back on her feet. "Do you think me a wicked scoundrel, Auntie?"

Nani dipped her chin as if to hide her enjoyment, and kept her hands busy rearranging her clothes, her hair. "Yes," she finally said.

"Savitri likes me, even if I am a scoundrel." Colin's eyes gleamed as he turned and met Savi's gaze. "But only because I'll give her a ride."

"It is very kind of you to do so," Nani said.

Savi choked and started toward the exit before she burst into laughter. "We should go. Bye, Nani!" The bell over the door rang as she slipped through. She leaned back against the plate-glass window as she waited for Colin to follow; he was probably more polite in his good-byes than she'd been.

He strolled out a moment later, his hands tucked into his pockets, his grin wide. His golden hair had been mussed by the dance, or he'd run his hands through it, but it still managed to look perfectly, artistically unkempt.

"You're terrible," she said. Her breath puffed in the cold air.

"And what of you, teasing me? 'I'll make sure he eats after

we leave, Nani,'" he mimicked. Despite his amused tone, his gaze sizzled through her, lithium and water. He took her hand in his. "Come along, sweet. I'm hungry."

Oh, god, she was too. Awareness burned from their linked hands to her body. Her nipples were sensitive and aching beneath her shirt, and desire pulsed low and heavy and wet. His stride lengthened as he turned down the alley beside the salon, pulling her through to the back lot. The slap of her flip-flops against her soles seemed incredibly loud in the darkness.

The streetlight glinted against his watch, and she looked down, catching her breath. His shirt cuff edged high on his wrist, exposing its lean, strong lines. He led her across an intersection, and the tendon in his inner wrist flexed; it should have looked soft, not powerful.

"How much farther?" She wasn't going to last more than a second when he finally touched her.

He threw her a heavy-lidded glance over his shoulder and led her into another narrow alley, cutting between the back of an apartment complex and the side of a convenience store. "To my car? Or my bed?"

Just the word from his lips made her crave smooth sheets and naked skin. But that could be for later, as could leisure. "Do we need a bed the first time?"

His steps faltered. "No."

His mouth muffled her cry of surprise; he'd pressed her up against the shop's cold stucco wall before she'd registered his movement. His tongue dipped between her lips as he lifted her and wedged his hips into the tight cradle of her thighs.

Oh god. Too much denim, too many clothes keeping her from that rigid, thick length. She rocked against him desperately and dropped her shields, hoping to urge him faster.

A shudder wracked his body, reverberated through hers. His lips closed over her tongue, and he began sucking on it with slow, excruciating tenderness.

"In me," she gasped when he stiffened against her, raised his lips from hers. He'd come just from her kiss before—and a bit of blood. She wanted to go over with him this time.

"Wait, Savi . . . wait." He was breathing hard, his chest

pushing against her breasts with the rough rhythm of it. "I'm—" He broke off and shook his head, as if to clear it.

She tugged on his shoulders, tried to pull his mouth to hers again. "The bloodlust? Don't stop because of that . . . it's kind of the point tonight, isn't it?"

He inhaled deeply, turned his head to look down the alley. The tension in his body heightened.

"What is it?" she whispered.

"Wyrmwolf," he said quietly, but he sounded uncertain. After a frozen moment, he relaxed and glanced down at her. "I don't sense it now. Likely a false association with the taste of you—from the night at Polidori's."

"You can *taste* me?" She stared up at him; shadows hid most of his expression, but with his enhanced vision he would not mistake the arousal on hers. "When you said that before . . . I didn't realize you meant it literally."

"I did."

"Just my mouth? Or everything?"

His lids lowered. "That's what I intend to discover, my sweet Savitri." He bent his head, and she instinctively arched her neck toward him as his tongue ran up the length of her throat. Her core seemed to melt, hot as liquid copper. "Yes," he breathed as he reached her jaw. "Your skin, a light flavor. Your lips, like sweet nectar." His hands pulled her hips tightly against him, and her inner muscles fluttered and grasped for fulfillment—but she remained empty. So empty. "What shall we find here, I wonder? I may decide to drink from you in every possible way when I taste you here."

She should have been frightened or disgusted, she realized dimly. But the thought of his fangs piercing her so intimately pushed her beyond reason—as did the knowledge that she was the only one he could taste. Two, three days from now, when he had another . . . she would not give him what Savi had.

And she should have been ashamed of the depth of her triumph. It was impossible to hide it from him; her emotions were wide open for him to read.

He laughed softly and nipped at her bottom lip. "It's not so easy, is it? But I'll not think you an ass for it."

Chagrined, she raised her shields. Better to keep them up until she controlled her stupid—

His head snapped back, his eyes wide. His skin drew taut over his cheekbones.

"How quickly can you run now, Savi?"

CHAPTER II

The holiday in Brighton should be an amusing diversion; I may decide to bring back to Beaumont Court an ocean landscape, and depict myself as the beautiful hapless victim of a siren, bashed upon the rocks. By the by, P—— has requested I transform him. I think I shall do it; aside from the ridiculous story he published, I have little reason to refuse.

—Colin to Ramsdell, 1821

Colin's softly voiced question frightened her more than the deep growl echoing down the alleyway. She unwrapped her legs from around his hips, set her feet on the ground. Remembering the speed with which he'd moved at Polidori's, she said, "Not fast enough."

He nodded tightly as he turned his head, his gaze locking on whatever he saw there. She knew what it must be, but was too afraid to look.

A wyrmwolf.

"Do you have anything in your reticule? A knife, a gun? A garrote?" Colin's body still pressed hers into the wall; protection instead of passion now.

"No weapons. I'm sorry."

A feral snarl ripped through the air, shivered down her spine. Why did it wait? Was it uncertain, confused by the two of them there?

Though he didn't look at her, his lips tilted in a quick smile. "Don't apologize, sweet. Just brace yourself, and hold on. It's a short distance to my car, but it'll chase us." He pushed a pair of keys into her palm, then slowly bent and slid his forearm behind her knees. "If I fall, get inside and use the symbols."

Her heart thundered, a protest rose in her throat, but she didn't let it out. She wound her arm around the back of his neck and tucked her chin down.

Even with that precaution, the rotation and acceleration whipped her head against his shoulder, made the world swim sickeningly around her.

She forced herself to stay conscious, though she couldn't breathe, though her chest felt weighted by a boulder. G-forces? The rear end of the Bentley rushed toward them with startling speed. Oh, god, how would he stop in time?

He didn't. They were suddenly airborne, and the world spun again as Colin twisted, lifted her arm from his neck, and curled himself around her. She had a brief glimpse of the wyrmwolf directly behind them, its jaws wide open and slavering.

They crashed through the wide rear window; Colin took the brunt of the impact on his back, but it still slammed through her. Lights exploded behind her eyelids. She barely felt it when he tossed her over the headrests and she landed in the front seats. She bit back the gasp of pain as her stomach jarred into the console.

She had no air for it, anyway.

Growls filled the car, Colin's and the wyrmwolf's. Tiny cubes of glass lay on the seat beside her; with shaking fingers, she picked one up and sliced the edge across her palm in a jagged line.

She held her hand over the symbols on the dashboard, and turned to look, waiting.

The wyrmwolf's head and shoulders were through the shattered window; Colin was ripping at the backseat, while trying to hold it off with his other hand. He didn't make a sound when it clamped its jaws around his wrist, but used his trapped arm to batter the thing's head against broken glass and metal trim. The roof dented with the force of it.

It whimpered and let go; Colin pivoted on the seat and slammed his foot against the side of its jaw. It fell back, outside the car.

Savi activated the symbols.

The wyrmwolf smashed soundlessly into the back window as if the glass had been intact. The Bentley rocked beneath the impact, but the spell held.

Colin clawed at the seat back, leather and stuffing flying to the side. Trying to get to the trunk, she realized. He must have weapons inside. She could see the small leather loop that would allow him to pull the seat forward, and give him access—didn't he know it was there?

"Colin—"

"Don't talk!" he commanded hoarsely. The seatback tore from its fastenings with the rip of fabric and screech of metal. "Don't fucking move, and don't lower your shields."

She bit her lip and nodded. Her palm burned, and she cupped it tightly over her knee to staunch the wound—but he must smell it. Shudders wracked her body, welling up from deep within.

Her blood, his blood. The pain of the wyrmwolf's attack. He had to be at the edge of his control.

She could hardly believe he had *any* control.

He leaned forward and withdrew two swords from the trunk before straightening up. He kneeled for a moment, his back rigid, his breathing harsh.

"Are you hurt?" he finally asked.

The wyrmwolf's grisly muzzle and glowing red eyes appeared in the window beside her face. She swallowed her scream, and whispered, "No." Not critically.

The car shook. But the wyrmwolf outside the window hadn't—

"There are two," she realized in horror.

"Yes," he said grimly. "It's on the roof, waiting." He turned his head, looked at her over his shoulder, his profile drawn in stark relief against the darkness of the empty window beyond. "I can't stay in here, Savi. You're bleeding."

She forced the words past the ache in her throat. "You would have fed from me tonight anyway."

His eyes closed. The blades rattled together before he separated them; he held them to his sides, one in each hand. "I don't know that I could stop, or make it pleasurable. I'm not at my best at this moment." He dragged in a deep breath. "Auntie will shortly be leaving the restaurant."

Oh, god. He'd danced with Nani, kissed her. If the wyrm-wolves were attracted to his scent, they might abandon the protected car for easier prey only two blocks distant.

His face wavered in front of her. "Colin—"

"Don't cry, sweet; I've every intention of trouncing them soundly." He sighed. "Though I must confess I didn't expect to make my heroic exit through the boot."

She covered her face with her uninjured hand. How could she laugh at such a time? "At least your exit will be a beautiful one," she said, looking through her fingers. "Your assumption was correct; you are spectacular from this angle."

His teeth flashed in a grin. "Consider yourself kissed senseless. I daren't do it in reality."

He paused, held her gaze for a long second. Then he was gone in a blur of movement; the trunk lid swung up and thud-ded shut.

The wyrmwolf at her window disappeared.

Savi scrambled into the destroyed backseat, peering into the trunk cavity. There had to be something. She was useless with a sword, far too slow, but with a gun or a crossbow she could remain at a distance and offer him some help.

Blood spattered silently across the passenger side window. *Let it be theirs. Please let it be theirs.* She groped wildly, blindly around the trunk's interior.

Nothing. The car rattled, as if an earthquake shook the ground beneath. She rose up on her knees, her breath coming in desperate pants as she stared into the darkened parking lot. *Think, Savi.* But everything took too long, or would put her in a position that might divert his attention and endanger him.

A short, hysterical laugh fell from her lips. As if he could be in any more danger than he was.

Colin suddenly landed on the trunk, splayed on his back. He instantly flipped upright, and his feet danced across the gleaming surface before he leapt down. A wyrmwolf's underbelly—scales and glistening flesh—flashed into her view as it followed him. Only one . . . where was the other? Had he killed it?

Her fingers clenched into fists. She really fucking hoped so, and she wished she could have seen it happen.

At the far end of the lot, another four-legged beast streaked across the pavement, its canine form lit briefly by a security light.

Savi started forward in terror, ready to jump through the back window and alert Colin, but there was no need—halfway across the parking lot, it shifted into a familiar, horrifying form: a hellhound in its demonic state. As tall as Colin at its shoulder, three heads, and eyes that shone with hellfire.

Sir Pup.

Colin's blades caught the moonlight as he slashed at the wyrmwolf. It launched itself at Colin's head; he ducked, and Sir Pup caught the wyrmwolf mid-air. The middle pair of the hellhound's jaws clamped over the wyrmwolf's midsection, the others on its hindquarters and head.

Sir Pup made a single, jerking motion, and the wyrmwolf ripped into three pieces. He tilted back his heads and gulped them down.

Savi clapped her hand over her mouth, and was suddenly grateful for the symbols that disallowed sound to accompany sight.

Until Colin looked up at the sky, and the expression on his face told her he was laughing—she'd have loved to hear that. After a moment, he waved toward the car with one of his swords, and Sir Pup hopped eagerly in place, like a dog waiting for the toss of a Frisbee.

Telling him where to find the other wyrmwolf, she supposed. And indeed, Sir Pup ran toward the car, paused briefly with his forelegs braced on the trunk to look at her, and clambered up. He dragged a carcass to the ground beside the car and began tearing at it.

Oh, no. "Wait!" Savi cried, but of course they couldn't hear her. She slid into the front seat, pushed open the door on the opposite side. "Wait, don't eat it!"

Colin stood near the trunk, watching the hellhound. "A little late, sweet."

"Oh. Dammit. We might have been able to use traces of soil from its feet to determine where it came from."

"Its head is here." He nudged a lump on the ground with his foot, then glanced down at his shoe and grimaced. "Perhaps it ate a few things on the way, and you can pick bits of them from its teeth."

She tried to cover her disgust with a smile; she could smell the odor of its blood now—rotten, sulphuric. "I can scour the missing pet notices. 'Your cat, Fluffy, is missing? Yes, we've found his collar caught in a wyrmwolf's jaws. Do you have a portal to the Chaos realm in your basement?' "

Her smile failed as his jaw hardened, and he turned his face farther away from her. *Stop, Savi. Don't mention Chaos again.*

His sleeve was torn from the attack in the car, and a stain spread over his abdomen near the top of the inverted V formed by the unbuttoned bottom half of his jacket. She'd have gone to him to examine it more closely and would have tried to bandage it if not for the forbidding expression on his face.

"You were bitten."

"And I'm not likely to forget it." He tossed his swords through the shattered back window, and they clanged together as they landed on the seat. "You're still bleeding."

She tucked her hand beneath her opposite arm. Blood soaked the denim over her knee—cold and wet, sticking to her skin. "Sir Pup will protect me."

"And who will protect *me* from Sir Pup?" There was no amusement in his tone. "You shouldn't have come out."

Her stomach twisted painfully. "I'm sorry. I didn't think." She'd just trusted that all was well after she'd seen him laugh, that he'd regained control. And acted impulsively, to stop Sir Pup from devouring evidence.

"Ah, yes." A sardonic smile thinned his lips. "*You didn't think.* I thought I taught you well; yet despite your playing the wronged little girl for eight months, and your insistence that you know better now, you haven't learned a bloody thing."

The color drained from her face, left her features stiff. Her wide smile almost cracked her cheeks. "Excuse me."

The car door was open; she only had to reach in and slip her cell phone from her bag. She couldn't look at Colin, and perhaps it was foolish to turn her back on him, but she did. She dialed the number for the taxi service from memory and walked to the front of the car as it rang.

Her legs shook with the need to run, but she forced herself to sit down on the concrete parking stop. She leaned her shoulder against the bumper, and began counting the tiny, pentagonal holes in the radiator grill.

She was at fifteen when the disinterested voice of the dispatcher answered. For a moment Savi couldn't recall her location, but it only took a second for it to pop into her head.

Sixty-five holes when she hung up. Fifteen minutes until the taxi would arrive. She could make it to two thousand holes by then.

Colin's cold laughter floated over the night air. "I must confess I'm shocked you didn't ring Castleford. Your knight in armor, come to defend your honor and save you from the evil vampire. Would he have been pleased he didn't have to pry you away from me this time? Or disappointed he didn't have a reason to exile me for another month? Or, God forbid, a reason to remove my head from my shoulders?"

That was why Colin had left for England? Because he'd been a danger to her?

One hundred and seventy. *Don't think, Savi.*

But it was impossible. She knew what he was doing; perhaps she should have been glad of it. He'd coated truth with cruelty at Polidori's, too—as his fucked-up method of protecting her from himself, and of putting distance between them.

But it didn't make sense. What kind of bastard protected someone by hurting them?

"Perhaps I should give him a reason," Colin rasped into her ear. His knees rose alongside her waist, his chest hard against her back. He must be sitting on his heels directly behind her, like a hawk over its prey. Her teeth dug into her lip as his hands slid around to cup her breasts. "Why deny myself? You run now, when you should have run a week ago. You claimed you'd learned and yet you agreed to try friendship, then denied our mutual satisfaction like a tease. Did you think to hold off until I panted after you?" She shuddered when his fangs scraped the soft skin below her ear. His erection was thick against her bottom, his breathing harsh. "I felt your jealousy, little Savi. Did you intend to string me along until I was so mad for you that I'd beg and promise to forsake every other woman for a taste of you? Perhaps I should give you a repeat performance; you'll certainly learn then. *It can be just like Caelum.*"

A selfish bastard. A thoughtless one.

"Sir Pup," she said, and flattened her palm, holding it out. "I need a knife."

In his Labrador form once more, Sir Pup looked around the front of the car and whined softly. A long-bladed dagger appeared in her hand.

Bless demon dogs and their limitless, invisible hammer-space.

Colin's laughter rumbled against her neck. "Do you think to fight me, sweet Savitri?" His long fingers sought her nipples, caught the taut buds in a pinch. Then he smoothed his thumbs over the stinging peaks.

She had to close her eyes against the pleasure that speared through her; she must be completely sick for him to affect her now. "Sir Pup, will you go make certain Nani is okay, and follow her home? But don't let her see you." When the hellhound hesitated, she looked up at him and repeated, "Go."

He disappeared. A moment later, the rapid click of his claws against the pavement faded in the distance.

Behind her, around her, Colin's lean body tightened. "I will disarm you without effort. Call him back." An edge of desperation sharpened his voice.

"I'm removing a variable," she said, and flipped the hilt of the dagger around in her hand. "One of your strengths. You use his presence to help maintain your control, or you wouldn't have dared try to approach me and scare me like this."

"Are you scared, Savi?" If he sought a mocking tone, he failed. Instead, he sounded anxious, as if *he* was suddenly afraid.

"I should be. Mostly I'm just pissed," she said—and dropped her shields.

In his instant of paralyzed surprise, she pushed off with her legs and caught him off-balance.

She was more powerful than she'd realized; they flew back and skidded across the asphalt until his shoulders wedged against the front tire of the car in the adjoining space. She took no time to triumph in that small victory; before he could react, she twisted and slapped her bleeding palm over his mouth and nose.

He froze. Above her hand, his eyes widened. His pupils dilated, leaving a thin ring of pale gray.

Her breath came in short pants. She straddled his abdomen, the ground hard and cold beneath her knees. His fingers clawed at the asphalt, then clenched and stilled.

Keeping himself from touching her. If he could manage that much control, she'd be safe. And if not, Sir Pup would still hear her scream.

His chest was motionless, as if he was trying not to inhale the scent of her blood. His lips were sealed together beneath her hand, and she could feel the tightness in his jaw, the effort it took for him not to open his mouth. That suited her; he didn't need to breathe except to speak, and she just wanted him to shut up.

She leaned forward until her hand separated them from a parody of a kiss. "You did teach me well. Strength against weakness makes for a short battle. Your weakness is my scent and blood; they are apparently my strengths." The dagger clattered to the ground as she opened her right fist. "I didn't even need this."

Not that she would've used it; it had only served as a distraction. Nor could she hang on to her anger any better than she did the knife. She'd never been able to.

She didn't fight the deep, overwhelming exhaustion that took its place. "I think we can call the friendship experiment a complete failure," she said, drawing back until she was sitting almost upright, her arm stretched out in front of her. Her sleeve was streaked with blood. "I've just proven that, even under the worst circumstances, you have enough control not to rape me or drain me to death—but you obviously don't give a shit about the rest of me."

His brows drew together, and his gaze searched her features. In her peripheral vision, she saw his hands flex.

"You don't even realize, do you?" A short, tired laugh escaped her, and she shook her head before looking at him again. The wheel formed a dark nimbus behind his golden hair. "I thought, at the restaurant, you were feeling sorry for what you'd done to me in Caelum. But now I think you must've simply been feeling sorry for yourself. Perhaps concerned I'd change my mind about tonight; no wonder you danced with Nani when you found out otherwise."

Something flickered in his eyes. It looked a bit like guilty comprehension, but the first thing she'd learned about him was that appearances were deceiving.

"And I can just imagine what went through your mind a couple of minutes ago: *I'm* doing this for her own good; this is hurting *me*, not her. *I* won't get to fuck her now because she'll hate me for this. *I'm* sacrificing tasting her to save her from me. *I'm* risking my friendship with Hugh and Lilith, and *my* pretty head."

Her voice broke, and she dragged in a ragged breath. She swiped at her cheeks, pressed her forefinger and thumb against her eyelids to stop the burning.

"Do you understand?" she said hoarsely. "You're not frightening me when you say these things—*you're hurting me.*"

Colin flinched beneath her, and a rough sound of denial came from deep in his throat, vibrated against her palm.

She couldn't stop. "And there are many things for which I deserve to pay, but your selfishness is not one of them. What Michael's sword did to you is not one of them. What happened to you in Chaos is not one of them."

She lowered her hand from her face, but she couldn't see him through her remaining tears. Her shoulders hunched, and her palm slipped away from his mouth. A blurry red streak remained. "You could've just asked me to get back into the car, but you chose to exercise your frustration and to hurt me instead. And you didn't even know you were doing it—or you didn't care. I'm not sure which is worse."

Her gaze fell to her lap, his chest. She stared at them blindly, waiting for his response before recalling herself. She'd effectively gagged and bound him. He wouldn't risk speaking or moving, not with her blood covering his lips, not with her shields down.

A folded silk handkerchief poked up from his breast pocket. Of course he had one. She wadded it and brought it to his mouth, then paused; the green hue of the material protruding between her fingers matched perfectly the pinstripe in his shirt collar.

It was so *Colin*—and it shouldn't have made her feel like smiling. Not now. She bit the inside of her cheek to prevent it.

Colin watched her, his expression tormented as she gently wiped his skin, as she traced the seam of his lips to collect the blood pooled there. Stretching a clean section of the handkerchief over her forefinger, she dipped the silk between them, skimmed it along his inner bottom lip.

He had such a beautiful mouth. Wide and masculine, the curves strong and firm, yet his lips possessed the most intriguing softness . . .

She averted her gaze, stuffed the bloodied silk back into his pocket. Her knees protested when she stood. She crossed her arms over her middle as she walked back to the Bentley and sat down on the edge of the hood. Her neck was stiff, her stomach sore.

It would all feel worse in the morning.

Colin rose slowly to his feet, as if he didn't want to frighten her. Didn't he realize yet that he couldn't? But he approached her with the same care, pausing once to reach down for the dagger and then carrying it by the blade. A nonthreatening gesture.

He stopped in front of her, an arm's length away. A smile hovered over his mouth, though not wide enough to show his fangs. "It was a bloody brilliant defensive maneuver."

Admiration filled his voice, and it sounded genuine. Flustered, Savi lowered her head and rubbed at the back of her neck. She'd not known what to expect from him, but that response hadn't been it.

Her brows drew together. That was odd—he held the tip of the blade between his forefinger and thumb, and was lightly drumming the broadside of the dagger's hilt against his thigh. She'd never seen him given to nervous, fidgety displays; perhaps he was as uncertain of her response as she had been of his.

"I thought it an offensive one, actually. I hate violence," she said finally, and looked up at him. The quirk of his lips told her he was likely remembering her penchant for James Bond and horror movies—or DemonSlayer—and she amended with a reluctant smile, "*Real* violence. Though I'm also practical, and admit it has its uses against nosferatu."

"And vampires," he said softly, but not without amusement.

"Yes. Now I have only to attack a demon and my trilogy of violence against otherworldly beings will be complete."

The corners of his eyes crinkled. "Or you could bring it to an end at the sequel. Third installments are usually the least satisfying."

Her laugh sounded strained to her own ears, and she pinched the bridge of her nose to ease the ache forming behind her forehead. "And yet another reason to marry, I suppose. To avoid the need for a third."

"Yes." His voice flattened, and he tossed the knife carelessly onto the hood next to her hip.

She glanced down at its gleaming blade, then lifted her brows in query as she raised her gaze to his again.

The humor had fled from his expression. He tucked his hands into his pockets and stared down at her, his eyes bleak. His throat worked above his collar, as if he had to force words to his tongue—or attempted to swallow them.

"Forgive me, Savi."

She lowered her hand to her lap. "Okay."

He shook his head, as if he thought she only meant to appease him with her easy capitulation. Sincerity deepened his voice. "I did not intend to hurt you."

"I know, Colin. And it's fine." She said it barely above a whisper, and through an effort of will she called up a wide smile, a stronger tone. "I can't carry anger or a grudge; you'll see upon our next meeting, it'll be as if nothing has happened at all. That's my other big failing, you know: not just a lack of fear or not thinking, but forgiving far too easily." Remembrance made her throat tighten. "Even for those who probably don't deserve it."

A muscle in his jaw hardened. Self-derision darkened his eyes.

"Not you," she said, realizing how he must have interpreted her statement. "The man who killed my brother and my parents."

He blinked. "That *is* a failing."

She gave a half-hearted smile. "I told you." Her gaze dropped to his stomach. The bloodstain hadn't spread, but the skin showing through the tear in his shirt looked raw. She patted the hood next to her. "You should sit. You're in as terrible a shape as I am."

He didn't, but he leaned his hip against the side, still facing her. "You said you weren't injured."

"Not really; a bit of whiplash, a couple of bruises here and there. Michael or Dru can fix me up tomorrow." The two Guardians could heal everything but the cut across her palm— she'd inflicted it on herself. "I've had worse. This is nothing."

Colin's gaze traveled the length of her, as if determining the truth of her statement—or thinking of that which had been worse. "How is it that a man can murder an eleven-year-old boy, a man, and his wife for the sum of twenty-three dollars and two gold watches—and but for the interference of a Guardian, would have attempted to silence a little girl, as well—yet you forgive him for it? What an extraordinary creature you are."

He said the last with a smile, but there was an edge of disbelief and disapproval in his tone. She knew he probably likened it to the nosferatu killing his family; a heartless, evil act, committed by a person of the same nature.

And as she'd reproached herself for it more than once, she couldn't blame him. "You know of it—from Hugh?" At his nod, she looked down at her hands. She had to swallow before she explained, "I didn't want to. I hate what he did, and I wanted so badly to hate *him*. James Anderson. His name was . . ." She closed her eyes. "And I probably would have, if I'd never found out what happened to him afterward."

Colin made a scoffing sound. "Shooting himself in the head?"

"Yes," she said quietly. "He did it the same night, only an hour after. So I think there must've been something terribly deranged, something terribly wrong with him . . . even more than whatever drove him to rob us and shoot Mom and Dad and Ras." She had to pause before she could continue, and still tears clogged her voice. "I mean, you have to be pretty fucked up to do something like that. But then to kill yourself afterward? And the cops said it wasn't drugs or anything. So there was remorse, or guilt, or something—he couldn't have been so cold-blooded. Maybe he was mentally sick, and when he realized what he'd done . . ." She trailed off. Colin had gone rigid beside her, his hand clenching at his thigh. She glanced up at him, saw the shock on his features before he concealed it. "What is it?"

He smiled quickly, tightly, and shook his head. "Nothing, sweet."

Her eyes narrowed. "What?"

He averted his face, and his fingers played with the dagger at her hip before he said, "I've simply had a moment of clarity." He turned his head to arch a brow at her, and his smile widened until his fangs glistened in the darkness. "Aside from my spectacular appearance—on both ends—I love nothing so much as a moment of clarity."

"Please share it." Her lips pursed against a laugh when he shook his head again. His humor had a dark edge to it, but it was infectious. And much preferable to dwelling in the past. "We have enough time. It's still five minutes until my taxi arrives."

"Five minutes is never *enough* time." He ran his thumb down the length of her jawline, and laughed softly when her breath caught.

Savi flushed, but didn't bother to deny her response. She had no reason to be ashamed of it, and he would've known a denial for a lie. And as she wouldn't pursue it after that night, it didn't matter what she gave away in the next few minutes.

Regret tightened her throat. What a disastrous end to a promising evening.

He'd been watching her silently, but now curiosity formed a ridge between his brows. "And so that is why you've forgiven me for Caelum? You've discovered I was suffering from flashbacks, and couldn't discern my memories of Chaos from reality. That I had been starved and terrified beyond reason for the better part of a week. That I resented being shuttled off for my protection, and manipulated by Castleford and Lilith into leaving them to fight the nosferatu by themselves. You've analyzed the events surrounding my arrival there, and made excuses for my behavior."

She hadn't known most of that. He hadn't wanted to go to Caelum? And he'd had moments of hallucination? She tried to fit it into her memories of their time in Caelum, and couldn't.

But she finally recovered herself enough to say, "As I have done again this evening—made excuses for you. The blood, the wyrmwolves' attack."

His lids lowered, only a pale arc showing beneath his lashes. "Yes. But tonight's offense against you was unintentional. Caelum was not. I knew exactly what I was doing when I sent you a part of Chaos."

A tight band squeezed at her lungs, and she only managed a pathetic, "Oh."

He added quietly, "But I didn't realize that you'd remember it as anything more than a vague—if rather unpleasant—dream."

She stared up at him, her lips parting in surprise. No. She couldn't have forgotten. It couldn't have been a dream . . . or a nightmare.

Oh, god. Her eyes widened. And how close had she come to fooling herself that it might be a dream, and that she could experience it like every other woman did? That she could forget?

That would have been disastrous.

He slid his fingers from her jaw, around the curve of her ear, as if tucking away a stray piece of hair. "I regret that assumption as well, and what it has left in you." She shivered as his fingertips skimmed the length of her throat. "I would give you its opposite, when we again have the opportunity. Something better to add to your web of memories."

She shook her head. "It's okay."

His lips thinned. "Savi—" His teeth clenched, and he bit off the rest. His hand dropped away from her neck. "You cannot forgive *everything* so easily," he said with a touch of exasperation.

She smiled weakly. "You'd be surprised. I don't like to obsess over the past, particularly offenses and misfortune."

"No, and I am glad of it, for it does nothing but create the most tiresome sort of brooding maniac." His eyes gleamed with sudden humor; behind him, twin headlights cut through the parking lot. The taxi. "Like Castleford."

She pushed to her feet, laughing reluctantly. "Yes."

Colin shot a quick glance over his shoulder, then strode past her to collect her bag from the front seat of the car. She didn't argue when he escorted her with his hand upon the small of her back, nor when he leaned down to give the driver her address.

And, she noted with a quick grin, a few twenty-dollar bills; it was far more than the fare would be. His courtesy—or his guilt—must have overwhelmed his budgetary scruples.

She lifted the handle of the back door, but his hand on the top of the door frame stopped it from opening.

"Kiss me good night, Savi." His gaze rested on her lips. His eyes glittered with suppressed hunger. "I saved your life."

Her heart pounded and she weighed and calculated, asked herself a million questions before deciding it was one regret she didn't want to own.

He sighed. "You think too—"

Her mouth covered his, and she swallowed the stupid words he'd been preparing to say. No one could think too much. But they could feel too much, and that frightened her more than he ever could.

But she didn't want to think now. Not when he no longer tasted like mint, but tea and tamarind—why tamarind? From her mouth, during their earlier kiss? God, and he wouldn't even know how she lingered on his tongue.

His hands settled at the sides of her waist. Somehow he managed to keep his fangs from cutting her lips—though with the greedy abandon with which she fed from his mouth, she wouldn't have been surprised had she paid in blood. And if she had, she'd no doubt he'd have given her back a taste of heaven.

But she'd had that before, and couldn't risk losing it again.

She turned her head away, pulled free of his arms. Her chest ached, and for a moment she thought she'd never breathe again. But she focused and forced the air into her lungs—and the urge to flee faded.

He'd only chase her; that's what a hunter did.

She opened the door, dared a final glance at him. He stood watching her, his hands tucked in his pockets and a broad smile on his lips that seemed out of proportion to a kiss.

And she should have known better, but she had to ask. "What is it?"

"You'll think me an ass, my sweet Savitri, but I wish

Castleford *had* come to rescue you. I'd have triumphed, seeing his countenance when his little sister kissed me as if her life depended on it." Her mouth dropped open, but before she could respond, his humor vanished and he said, "But not as much as I do, knowing that you're falling in love with me."

CHAPTER 12

Demons and Guardians have the ability to shape-shift into any human form; a hellhound can shape-shift into any canine form. The bats and the wolves are all wishful thinking, popularized by vampires and a few misinformed humans.

—*Savi to Taylor, 2007*

❧

Since when did a custom Bentley take a year to produce? It was ridiculous to wait so long; but as much as he hated to sacrifice style for speed, Colin found himself buying a new Jaguar straight off the lot. Then, too exhausted to haggle over the price—and too conscious of the early morning sun streaming through the dealership's floor-to-ceiling windows—he allowed the pretentious sales manager to ream his pocketbook.

But felt marginally better when, after receiving the keys, paperwork, and a pint of blood, he left the sod quivering on the floor behind his desk in the throes of a powerful orgasm. Nothing reminded a man of his price—or his place—as much as coming in his pants, be they thrift store cast-offs or the salesman's four-hundred-dollar Dolce & Gabbana trousers.

Savi had been right in that.

Colin paused to rip off the side and rearview mirrors; a body shop could clean up the mess later. He tore out of the car lot just as the assistant-to-the-sod's startled laughter pealed out, loud enough for Colin to hear her through those damnable huge windows and the steel-and-fiberglass shell of his nicely endowed XK.

Rage Against the Machine fit his mood and would keep

him awake; he slipped in the CD from the pile he'd transferred from the wreck of the older car, and let it screech through him until he reached Hunter's Point.

Three blocks away from the warehouse, a motorcycle cut in front of him, the rider's long black hair streaming behind her. Leather jeans and jacket. Lilith. Colin's lips pulled back in a grin. She couldn't have known it was him in this car, but within a second she'd find out.

He shifted, and shot around her. The visor on her helmet was up, and he saw the brief widening of her eyes before she slapped it down and rocketed ahead.

God, he loved a good race. And the car cornered brilliantly; he didn't have to decelerate as much as she did around a turn. The engine roared as he downshifted and careened into the parking lot. He spun the wheel and slid boot-first into his parking space a second ahead of her.

Laughing and bracing himself against the sun, he got out, then reflexively caught the helmet she pitched at his head.

"You're a terrible sport, Agent Milton." He tossed it back to her, then shaded his stinging eyes with his left hand.

She snarled something in a language he didn't know and glared at him. "You were supposed to be here before dawn. Get inside, you gorgeous fuckwit."

"Your flattery is sweet music, my dear. I comply." He walked with her toward the entrance, grateful when they passed into the shadow cast by the warehouse's bulk. "Where's Castleford? You've become disgustingly inseparable."

"Savi's riding with him, and she's still sore. He had to go slower than normal." Lilith swiped her card through the lock, then turned to look at him when he opened the door for her. "You really fucked her over," she said darkly. "She was crying all night."

For an instant, unbearable pain ripped through him, tore at his heart and lungs with venomous teeth. Then he recalled the easy smile Savi had given him before sinking into the taxi's backseat, her laughing reply.

Feel free to triumph all you want, Colin. It's just a phase.

"You're lying," he said with certainty. Yet the tightness in his chest didn't immediately subside, even when Lilith gave him a demure smile.

"Of course I am." But she glanced pointedly at the door. Colin lifted his hand, saw the impression his fingers had left in the handle. "But isn't *that* interesting?"

She swept into the corridor; he trailed after her, waited until Jeeves had verified her identity before remarking, "You're a bitch, Agent Milton."

"You love me." She shrugged out of her jacket, revealing her black leather corset. He grimaced, and her eyes narrowed. "What?"

"The trousers are fine, but the top is horrid. I'll order you something less—" He searched for the right word. It wasn't *tacky* . . . exactly. She carried it better than any other woman possibly could, but it was still intolerable. "—hackneyed. Though just as striking." Giving demons and vampires a particular image proved useful to her, but it didn't have to be so uninspired.

"Will you pay for it? Your tastes are more expensive than mine."

"No. Don't be absurd." He turned away from her to stare into the wall panel; after a moment, Jeeves nodded at them. "Castleford can afford it."

"He likes this."

"For the whole of the two hundred years I knew him as a Guardian, he wore the most revolting brown robe I've ever seen. His likes and dislikes are hardly worth consideration. He'd probably think it smashing if you wore a nun's habit."

She grinned at him, as if pleased by the idea—or she was considering dressing as a nun for Castleford. Christ, how soft she'd become. A year ago, she'd have stabbed Colin for mentioning Castleford's name.

She'd still stab him, given the proper encouragement, but he supposed he was fortunate he didn't have to be quite as careful around her. "Why has Castleford not told Savitri he forced his Gift on James Anderson?"

Or perhaps he did. Lilith whirled and pressed her dagger against his throat. He stared at her, taken aback, but unconcerned. Though as quick and strong as a vampire, she posed no real physical threat; this was simply an expression of her displeasure—and her protective instincts. Not for Savi—only concern for Castleford could've produced this aggression against *him*.

"You don't tell her," she hissed between her teeth. "If he hasn't, it's for a reason. But whatever the reason, it's between them."

His eyes narrowed speculatively. Could Savi forgive Castleford's deliberate execution of a human? A human she'd convinced herself had been mentally incapacitated?

If Colin ever needed a wedge between Savi and Castleford, Lilith's response suggested this might be a useful one. She, too, must assume that Castleford feared Savi's reaction—and Lilith wouldn't allow him to be hurt by it. "It merely surprised me to discover he'd not told her the truth of it," he lied.

"And why do you care?" Stepping away, Lilith slid her dagger back into its sheath.

"I don't." He smiled lazily. "You give me too much credit; I've simply little else to do."

But he couldn't completely deceive her. "So that's why you've been around so much the past week? You're bored?" Lilith asked as soon as they were through the security door. "Or is it the pheromone again?"

The suggestion was too insulting to be borne too insulting to him and to Savitri. But he was also too tired to shrug it away. "Fuck off, Lilith."

Her mouth thinned with anger, but she was silent the rest of the way to the Room.

♪

This couldn't be right.

Savi placed the printout by her mousepad and stared at it, her mind racing. Around her, the comfortable clacking of keys and a low electronic hum sounded as Jake and Drifter spoke in low voices, Drifter watching and offering suggestions as Jake used the computer to investigate a demon's activity.

CPUs, servers, monitors, and reams of paper—altogether, the office wasn't much different from her previous one, just a bit brighter.

She leaned forward to check the looping signature at the

bottom of the purchase order again, but she hadn't been mistaken: Colin Ames-Beaumont.

The PO had been signed and dated three weeks ago, in Los Angeles. Fifteen Lincoln Navigators, acquired through Norbridge Medical Supply—a subsidiary of Ramsdell Pharmaceuticals. A veritable fleet, but hardly suitable for transporting crutches and wheelchairs.

But Colin had been in the U.K. three weeks ago. And he didn't personally manage his assets; she couldn't imagine him concerning himself with something as mundane as a business's vehicle purchases.

Nor could she imagine him voluntarily traveling to Los Angeles.

Obviously there'd been some kind of identity theft; but the vampires' involvement and the sheer balls it would take to impersonate Colin and forge the purchase order indicated it wasn't a matter of someone stealing bills from Colin's mailbox to cash a few checks or run a credit card scam.

She bit her lip, debating. It'd be easiest to go get him; he was somewhere in the building. With his help, she could weed more quickly through legitimate accounts and purchases to find any false ones.

Except . . .

You're falling in love with me.

She groaned a little, rubbed her hands over her face. How could he have so easily seen what she hadn't recognized in herself? Had she been stuck in an inert emotional position for so long that it took a force like Colin to push her out of it? Once it gathered momentum, could she stop it? She'd known her feelings for him ran deeper than she wanted them to, but she hadn't thought she'd reached such a critical point.

And how embarrassing to admit to herself that she probably hadn't recognized it because she'd never come to that point before. She didn't lack for sexual experience, but was she so emotionally naïve? She hadn't thought so. Certainly, her attachments never lasted, and usually never delved beyond the physical combined with a light friendship. But she wasn't ignorant that deeper feelings could exist; she'd hoped it would eventually happen.

But she'd never thought it would happen with a vampire.

How unsuitable could one person be? Colin surely topped that list.

And as well as they got along, as certain as she was that he appreciated her company and had developed an affection for her—and undoubtedly wanted her—she knew that he'd use her feelings to his advantage. He'd been too pleased in the realization for her to reach any other conclusion. And her instinctive, defensive reply, laughing it off as a phase, would only be seen as a positive to him; he would think they could have a fling without her being seriously hurt.

She was certain he wouldn't deliberately hurt her—his reaction the previous night had been evidence enough of that. But deliberation and action were often completely different things.

Her gaze fell on the paper again. How tempting it was to hide here in this little room and deny herself contact with him in order to protect her heart. Any information she found could be forwarded through Lilith and Hugh.

How tempting. And how much like running.

Before she could change her mind, she swiveled in her chair and stood. Jake—a Guardian for forty years, but who looked no older than twenty with his military haircut and chiseled face—paused in his typing and glanced at her.

Drifter had had his hand braced against the computer desk as he'd read the computer screen; when he straightened up, she had to fight the instant sensation that, next to him, she was a little girl.

"Can you tell if the vampire Ames-Beaumont is still here?"

Jake scratched absently at his chest; he was wearing a Grateful Dead T-shirt. Had he made it himself, materializing it with his Guardian powers, or had he purchased it?

Why could they materialize clothes, but not weapons? And hadn't they ever heard of the Law of Conservation of Matter? And even if it transformed from energy, where and how did the transformation take place?

"He's here," Jake said finally, and for the first time she noted the tension around his eyes and mouth.

"Where?" Her stomach sank as she recalled the conversation from the previous evening. But hadn't Colin told Michael he'd go in before dawn? "The mirrors?"

Jake and Drifter exchanged a glance; Drifter shook his

head and said, "We know the location in the building, Miss Savi, but we don't know what's in there. And they've sealed and locked it with the spell, so they likely wouldn't hear even if you pounded on the door."

"Can you unlock it?" she asked. He could open any lock with his Gift, whether mechanical or electronic.

"No, miss," Drifter said. "My Gift doesn't work on the spell. I can let you know when they've removed it from around the room."

She nodded numbly and turned back to her chair. "Thank you."

Jake stopped her. "Savi . . . he isn't always himself when he comes out. We've all noticed it; we respect his privacy, but it's hard to miss a psychic backlash that dark. You might want to wait until later to see him."

"Thanks, but I think I still need to know."

Jake's reluctant assent hung in the air between them, and it was several moments before she heard him typing again. She sat, stared blankly at her monitor.

Then she roused herself, flexed her fingers. A quick, hard trip through her memory gave her an image of his account listings and assets, which had appeared on a similar computer screen eight months before. Hugh had only asked for Colin's address and telephone number; now Savi was glad she'd been nosy and poked a bit further.

It wouldn't be perfect—Colin had bought Polidori's and renovated his house, which would show as a huge spike in financial activity—but it would give her a place to start.

What other transactions had been taking place in his name? And how far back did they go?

§

"Colin, love, open your beautiful eyes and tell us what you see."

Lilith's voice was soft now, and he barely heard it over the screams. When had he closed his eyes? Had he lost consciousness?

"Colin," Selah said. "You've got to come back."

Come back from where? He was so tired. When would *she* come back? She'd promised not to leave him, but she did.

No, he'd told her to go. To find Michael. And she had, but not before the wyrmwolves had found him—

"Colin! Goddammit, you fucking pantywaist, sit yourself up on your beautiful ass and look!"

Christ, but she had the devil's own tongue. "Sod off, Lilith," he said hoarsely, and her relieved laughter pushed the screams away. A pleasant memory surfaced in their place.

The night before, Savi had called it spectacular. Though tears had brightened her eyes, she'd been laughing, and the delicious scent of her blood had filled—

No. Don't make her part of this.

He gave his head a hard shake, and the screams poured back in.

"Colin, what are the nosferatu doing?" Michael's melodic voice was impossible to ignore.

He didn't want to look up, but he did. The shrieking filled his brain, but he didn't allow himself to see the dangling bodies, only the pale creatures that flew between them. "Still writing."

"Is it intact?"

"Yes." Colin dropped his chin to his chest, closed his eyes again. On his hands and knees like a fucking dog, but it was better than falling.

"And the wyrmwolves?" Castleford asked quietly. "Can you see them?"

Colin lifted his head, slid his knee forward, then his hands. The ground below sped by with dizzying speed. An inch here, miles in Chaos.

Or he was just so tired he couldn't tell the difference between speed and sickness.

There. A writhing mass. A pack moving across a plain of solid black stone, at the base of a towering mountain. It had been that mountain in which he and Selah had found the caves, where they'd clawed their way to safety.

Safety, for a time.

"They're still congregated near the mountain. All of them, moving together." Almost aimlessly, it seemed—but they hadn't formed such a large pack when he and Selah had run from them. Or flown, rather—Selah carrying him until they reached the mountain. In the caves, her wings had been useless.

Don't leave me here alone.

The screams built and built, and his lips trembled with the effort of keeping them in. He shook his head, fought a wave of exhaustion and vertigo.

"That's enough for now, Colin," Michael said quietly.

Colin stared blindly at the mountain. Somewhere behind that black pile of stone, a sheet of tinted glass, they all stared back.

Damn them all.

❧

Savi ran up the steps to the second level of the warehouse; Drifter's footsteps fell heavily behind her on each metal riser. Though she'd only asked the Guardian for directions, he'd insisted on leading her there.

But he wasn't in as much of a hurry as she was.

She hadn't needed to bring the sheaf of papers she held in her hand; every detail buried itself in her memory. But Colin would want to see. As would the others.

On the landing, Drifter drew even with her. Ready to provide protection from Colin, she assumed. Perhaps because Hugh had been Drifter's mentor—now he felt obligated to protect her, even though she'd insisted she didn't need it. Always the little sister.

She forced her resentment away. "Are Colin's shields still down?"

"No, Miss Savi. He's raised them again; it was just those few moments."

Colin would hate that. Even if it was only a few moments, he'd hate knowing that whatever the mirrors did to him, each of the Guardians and vampires in the vicinity—even the imprisoned nosferatu—would feel it, too.

Not out of concern for them, but that it allowed them more of himself than Colin wanted to give.

The layout upstairs was less utilitarian than the first floor, and the rear portion was used for tiny dormitory-style living quarters and common rooms. Drifter guided her to the northwest corner via a narrow, unlit corridor. The solid wooden door at the end hadn't been marked with anything as obvious as a NO ADMITTANCE sign, but everything about the approach stated it clearly.

Drifter stepped in front of her, and she heard the click of the dead bolt. He opened the door and silently signaled to Michael. She looked beneath his arm, taking a brief second to see into the room, to prepare herself. But it wasn't a scene of terror— more like a waiting room. Calming blue paint, soft lighting, and an overstuffed sofa that Sir Pup had taken up with his enormous form. The only unusual feature was the large, darkened window that took up most of one wall of the room. . . .

Not a window, a two-way mirror. Like the observation glass in a police interrogation room.

Colin stood in front of it, leaning against the pane as if he needed it to prop him up, his eyes closed. Exhaustion and despair sat in the line of his body, the slump of his shoulders. His face was taut and pale, his mouth compressed into a thin line. Beneath the flat front of his trouser pockets, she could see the outlines of his fists.

Tired and furious.

Selah was beside him, speaking quietly. She paused as Savi entered the room, as did Hugh, Michael, and Lilith. Judging by their stiff postures, the anger on Lilith's face, they'd been arguing.

She barely heard Drifter leave and the door close behind him.

Hugh's expression softened into concern. "What is it, Savi?"

Savi glanced back at Colin; he'd opened his eyes. Her gaze briefly locked with his, then his lids lowered into a predatory stare.

He eased away from the glass.

Savi's heart climbed into her throat, seemed to pound the blood into her head at a dizzying pace.

"Oh, fuck," Lilith breathed.

Savi silently echoed the curse. She'd been so careful; her shields were up, impenetrable. No scent could have leaked through to tease him, yet there was no mistaking the rapacious hunger that pulled his lips back over his fangs, that darkened his features.

Stay there, Colin.

"Savi," Hugh said, his voice studiously even, "can this wait until later?"

Colin's lashes flickered as he stole a glance at the three standing by the sofa. Selah moved in front of him, but wasn't tall enough to hide Savi from his sight.

He met her gaze again. "Are you afraid, my sweet Savitri?"

"No," she said, shaking her head. "Not *of* you."

She only added the last for Hugh's benefit; she didn't know if his ability to see truth would differentiate between specific fears. She was afraid, but not that Colin would attack her.

He was deliberately provoking them. Why? And did he think they wouldn't realize it? Hugh could read truth as easily as he could read words on a page; one verbal slip on Colin's part and Hugh would know. And Michael . . . who knew what Michael could see.

She turned to Hugh. "It can't wait. I need to talk to him before he goes home."

"They won't allow you near me," Colin said, leaning back and bracing his shoulders against the glass again. He didn't appear predatory now; instead he looked and sounded as if this were all a tedious bore. "Lilith and Castleford fear my reaction, for I'm nothing more than a dog on a bitch's scent. And Michael worries as well, though with more compelling reason: he knows what I did to you in Caelum."

Her heart stopped. He was *punishing* them. Why? For the mirrors—or for their lack of trust in him? Or something else?

"Michael, get him out of here," Lilith said. Her gaze moved warily between Savi and Colin. "He doesn't know what he's doing. Let him sleep it off."

"Before I say something I regret?" Colin said silkily. "I daresay Castleford would regret it more than I would."

Hugh's jaw unclenched, and he turned his head to stare at Savi. His blue eyes were glacial. "What happened in Caelum?"

She'd never heard such a tone from him before—cold and deadly. Even knowing it was in him, she'd never seen it brought to the surface. A killing edge, one that called for execution, if the offenses were terrible enough.

She was going to be sick. If he'd still had his Gift to force truth, she was certain she'd be spilling out a simple confession: *We had sex; I offered him my blood; he took it, and taught me a lesson. Michael only knows because he healed the puncture wounds before Nani saw me.*

But it hadn't been that simple.

Swallowing hard, she said, "Nothing that wasn't of my free will. I allowed . . . opened myself to . . . *welcomed* everything we did together. It was all of my free will."

It wasn't really an answer, but it was the only thing she could think of that wouldn't result in bloodshed. The Rules stipulated that Guardians and demons had to honor a human's free will; though Lilith and Hugh no longer had to, they followed the Rules almost to the same degree. And but for life, Hugh held free will above nearly every other ideal—had Fallen to regain his.

And Savi watched helplessly as Hugh's anger shifted, turned back on himself. Now he likely blamed himself for not warning her.

As if she'd have listened. It was stupid.

She opened her mouth to tell him so, but Lilith caught her eye and gave a quick shake of her head. The tightness around Savi's lungs eased. Lilith had known Hugh for eight hundred years; she'd work him out of his guilt.

Why did Colin have to push it that far? Dammit. But if Savi couldn't ease Hugh's mind about the past, then she could at least in the present.

She took a deep breath before looking at Colin again. He stared disinterestedly back at her. "I'm going to walk over there and show you this," she said, gesturing with the papers. "Are you going to hurt me?"

A sharp smile curved his mouth, then froze as he flicked a glance over at Hugh and Lilith. A muscle in his jaw flexed.

He couldn't lie. He could posture and threaten silently, but the moment he spoke a lie, Hugh would know it. As it was, his hesitation had already given him away.

"Bloody hell," he relented, and his voice was thick with exhaustion. He sagged a little more against the glass. "Even if I weren't so tired I'd fall down if I tried to chase you, I couldn't hurt you."

Selah turned her head. Though Savi didn't glance that way herself, she assumed the Guardian was looking to Hugh or Michael to confirm Colin's statement. A moment later, Selah stepped from in front of the vampire and the tension in the room all but disappeared.

Colin's gaze remained on Savi as she approached him. His eyes narrowed slightly with amusement. "You've become as manipulative as the rest of us."

"It's not manipulation, but an increasing sense of self-preservation," Savi said. "You can triumph; I learned it from you."

"Be certain I shall triumph wholeheartedly and in the most fashionable way . . . when I'm up to it. Until then, please allow that I'm an old man who can barely stand."

"Then brace yourself, *dadu*." From the top of the sheaf, she pulled out the photo she'd downloaded from the DMV database. "Look familiar? The original is in color; this is just black and white because of the printer. It's a perfect likeness."

Colin blinked. "That's not me," he said with certainty.

"Of course not. I found your old photo—it was a picture of a painting?" She waited for his nod before continuing, "I had to zoom in pretty close to tell. Whoever forged the ID for you did an excellent job. But this one is a real photo, and a real license; it was taken two weeks ago in a Los Angeles DMV. A replacement for stolen ID, or so this person claimed."

His brows drew together, but there was no surprise in his tone when he asked, "A demon?"

Savi nodded. Only demons and Guardians could shape-shift, but there was little danger of a Guardian trying to impersonate him.

"Fuck," Lilith said. Savi glanced over at her; Lilith was still on the other side of the room, though now she sat on the sofa arm. Hugh sat on the cushion next to her; Michael and Selah remained standing. "What's the damage?"

Swallowing, Savi turned back to Colin. "So far, seventeen million siphoned from your established accounts into newly opened bank accounts. Credit cards to a P.O. Box, and the physical address given is always Norbridge Medical. The Navigators? Fifteen of them through Norbridge."

The corners of Colin's mouth turned down, and the cords of his neck stood out as if he'd had to quickly suppress a violent reaction. "He's using the vampires to watch me? And my acquaintances?"

Behind her she heard Lilith and Hugh talking with

Michael, their voices tight with quiet alarm, but she ignored them.

"Apparently," Savi said. "What do you want me to do about the money? I can freeze the accounts, transfer it back."

"Fuck the—" Colin closed his eyes, pressed his mouth shut. "It's nothing. Pin money. And he'll know we're aware of his activity if you stop the accounts. Where is he now?"

"Here. Transactions began showing up in San Francisco last week. Some of them must be yours, but not all of them. I need you to tell me which ones are legitimate, and I might be able to get a better fix on his location and activities. I've got a list here; the ones I'm certain are bogus I've separated here." She showed him a section flagged with a sticky. "The legitimate ones are clipped together here—and these are the ones I have questions about."

He stared down at the papers for what seemed an endless moment, then looked back up at her. Fatigue and apology had drawn his skin tight. "I can't do it now, sweet."

"I know. It'll wait until after you wake up." She hesitated, then added, "Colin, he must've seen you, been around you at some point within the past month or two. Maybe in your house. He couldn't have created such a perfect replica based on description, and there are no photos anywhere to give him reference. Even his hairstyle is like yours is now."

Hugh said, "Perhaps your self portraits?"

Colin gave a small shake of his head. "Those that survived have been crated since the fire. I've only had them taken from storage in the past week."

"And he's always painted his hair in an early-nineteenth-century style," Lilith added. "He loves that image of himself—probably because it's the last one he saw."

Colin threw Lilith an amused glance before closing his eyes again. "Bloody hell. I should have realized. Those blasted vampires that followed us, and the female in the alley—" He cut himself off, shook his head again. "Careless," he muttered and his chin dipped forward to his chest.

Savi automatically laid her hand against his cheek to steady him. Faint stubble rasped against her skin as he turned his head, pressed his lips into her palm.

Her throat ached at the vulnerability exposed by the simple caress—his and hers.

Inertia. Momentum. Perhaps it was already too late.

"Colin," she said quietly. "Go home. Come over to Hugh's tonight, and we'll go through these then."

She felt his smile against her hand. "This is much more pleasant than what awaits me in my daysleep, Savitri. I'll take a minute more, even if I humiliate myself by toppling over."

She bit her lip. Vampires had lucid dreams during their daysleep, but she'd only heard them described as pleasant. The dreams drew from the last strong emotion during waking—which, for vampires, was usually the drinking of blood. Or sex.

But she couldn't stop herself. "Chaos?"

He raised his head, and her throat closed at the bleakness there. "Yes."

Perhaps she could give him something else. She slid her hand around the back of his neck and tugged. "Kiss me good night," she said, and allowed a smile to curve her lips. "I'm saving your fortune."

Disbelief replaced the despair. He glanced over her shoulder, then back to search her features, as if to determine if she was serious. "Savi—"

She wouldn't let herself think of what they'd see. "How far can you sense me, if my shields are completely down, and I'm projecting? A couple of miles? Will you feel it while you sleep?"

His eyes widened, and he raised his hands to her face. His fingers trembled as he smoothed his thumbs along her eyebrows, then lowered his hands to cup her jaw. "I think so. Yes. God, if there is any mercy in the world for the cursed, then it will be yes."

She had to rise up on her toes to meet his lips; he dropped one arm to her waist and lifted her against him. Exhausted, but strong enough to hold her.

Her shields fell away, and he sighed into her mouth, a soft, grateful exhalation. Though she could feel the need in him, he kissed her lightly, with a quick sweep of his tongue between her lips that would be imperceptible to their audience.

Not wanting to embarrass her with a more sexual display?

Or an unwillingness to have more than this without privacy between them? He hadn't taken such care at Polidori's—was it the difference in his regard for those who shared the room, or a difference in his regard for her?

It didn't matter; it was care, and it slipped into her and wrapped itself around her heart.

He broke the kiss gently. Then, watching her with an expression of surprise, as if she'd done something beyond his understanding, he set her feet on the floor.

But she couldn't stop falling.

"Michael," Lilith said, and her voice was strained, as if she was trying not to burst into laughter, "I think it's best that you take him now."

"We'll send along Sir Pup in a few minutes, Colin," Hugh added. "He can watch for the demon as you sleep."

Never tearing his astonished gaze from Savi's, Colin nodded his agreement.

He disappeared a moment later. Savi stared at her reflection in the dark glass, then saw Hugh in the background, his face buried in his hands. His shoulders were shaking. Lilith wasn't holding hers in anymore. Even Sir Pup was grinning.

Her cheeks burned, but she forced herself to turn and look at them.

Lilith flashed her teeth in a wicked grin. "I never thought I'd see the day when Colin didn't protest Sir Pup coming to his house."

"Or kissing a woman as if his life depended on it." Hugh finally lifted his head, and wiped at his eyes. He sobered quickly. "But then, maybe it does."

"Maybe it does." Lilith's gaze narrowed. "Are you going to tell us what happened in Caelum?"

"No," Savi said. But she wouldn't have a chance against both of them if they pressed for answers. She turned to Selah, whose face was impassive but for the amusement sparkling from her blue eyes. "Please take pity on a poor human, and teleport me the hell out of here." When the Guardian hesitated and looked to Hugh, she added, "You'd be thwarting Lilith. Didn't she beat you up and chain you to Colin's bed last year? Consider this a form of payback."

Selah vanished, then instantly reappeared by Savi's side.

She held out her hand, an impish smile widening her cupid's-bow mouth. Savi took it gratefully. "Home, please."

"You manipulative little slut!" Lilith gasped in mock outrage. They teleported away to the sound of Hugh's laughter.

Not manipulation. Self-preservation.

CHAPTER 13

*Disaster has struck my poor friend. I do not know if
I am to blame; I only know that he is dead.*

—Colin to Ramsdell, 1821

❧

Once the world righted itself again, Colin regretted he hadn't been more specific in his destination. When he'd projected an image of his bed to give Michael an anchor, he'd assumed Michael would take him to Polidori's.

But he was in his newly refinished Haight-Ashbury home—in his bedroom—and the Doyen's attention had been arrested by the paintings hanging against every available inch of wall space at one end of the suite.

The enormous third-floor room with its vaulted ceilings was almost empty of furniture—only a wide, tufted chaise longue was centered in the gallery. His bed dominated the other end, its heavy, chocolate-brown velvet curtains tied back in welcome. The turrets flanking the northern end of the house served as his dressing room and shower; each circular room was open to the main suite, and subtly decorated.

The paintings served as the focal point of the room, but Colin had never intended the focus to be anyone's but his.

Not that it mattered. Everything he'd had to hide had been laid bare with a simple question: *Are you going to hurt me?*

God, no. Never again.

Savi's psychic scent surrounded him—oh so light and elusive, but it prevented the darker, rotting odor from intruding. Reality over memory. She gave him this, when she should have punished him for revealing anything of Caelum to Castleford and Lilith.

What was wrong with her, that she forgave so easily?

Colin pulled off his jacket and pushed off his shoes, then sank down onto the chaise lounge. He couldn't remain upright. Didn't want to make the effort to get to the bed. Probably couldn't stay awake until Michael finished his perusal.

"It's an incredible likeness." The Doyen's quiet observation came through Colin's haze of sleep, and he looked up. Michael stood before a portrait of Emily and Ramsdell, his bronze hands clasped behind his back as if he were a visitor in a museum. His profile could have been a statue's, but a smile softened his lips. "It is unfortunate he could not remain in Caelum; he would have made a fine Guardian."

Colin roused himself enough to respond, "Perhaps, but he and my sister wouldn't call his decision unfortunate."

"Yes." Michael regarded Colin briefly. "Her countenance is remarkably like yours."

Colin studied Emily's face, her expression enraptured as she stared down at Ramsdell, and swallowed past the ache in his throat. "Yes."

Savi had looked at him like that. Once.

The Doyen took a turn through the turret room and continued until he faced the piece that served as the nexus of the gallery. "To be truthful," Michael said after a moment, "I did not realize you were strong enough to open the doors. Any other nosferatu-born vampire could not have. You were both fortunate in the outcome; Caelum does not always show itself kindly to those unprepared to see it."

The broad line of his back obscured the bottom middle of the painting from Colin's view, but he did not need to see it to know what the Doyen's body hid from him.

Savi, standing on the lip of the fountain. The sun shining through her wet clothes, limning her form in golden light. Her gaze bright and warm, inviting.

She'd been utterly enthralled, and the most beautiful creature he'd ever seen.

He closed his eyes.

"You must take more care that this demon does not discover your link to Chaos," Michael said from a great distance.

"But do not fear that I will ask you to return to that realm, unless it is absolutely necessary."

With his last bit of sense, Colin grasped at Savi's psychic scent, pulled it in tight, and thrust the Doyen's words away.

He'd die before he'd go back.

❧

This time, Colin was the one who pulled her forward. A fountain sat centered in the courtyard: a marble obelisk ringed by a waist-high wall of stone. Water sheeted from around the top of the pillar in a perfect, unbroken arc, falling silently to the pool below.

"My brother-in-law told me of the sea surrounding Caelum, but he did not mention this. Listen," he said, drawing to a halt a few yards from it.

Savitri held her breath, her lips slightly parted. "I can't hear it."

"Nor can I. Ramsdell said he'd dive into the sea and wouldn't create a splash. That it remained smooth as glass. I'd assumed he was boasting of his excellent form."

Again that giddy panic rose within him, but he pushed it down. But for the noises they made and the faint sounds of Auntie sleeping in Michael's temple, Caelum could have been a tomb. Nothing lived or grew there—only Guardians, and they'd left to fight an impossible battle against Lucifer and the nosferatu.

And no Guardians would live to return, unless they sent the nosferatu to Chaos, where the screams and the dragons and the wyrmwolves . . .

No.

Savitri let go his hand, walked toward the fountain.

No. He fought it back.

The screams faded.

She laid her palms flat atop the wall, leaned forward to look down into the pool. Lifting herself, she straddled the wide edge, her legs dangling on either side. Her skirt slid up to her knees. "It's just like a mirror," she said. "Come see."

A short laugh escaped him. "No. I will forgo that particular pleasure." He did not want to see himself absent in a reflection of Caelum, of all places. Nor, heaven forbid, have it act as a real mirror.

"Oh. I'm sorry." She turned back to him, her bottom lip caught between her teeth.

He lifted his shoulder in a careless shrug, and tucked his hands into the pockets of his trousers. His rough fingernails snagged the finely knit wool.

Her head tilted, and she subjected him to a scrutiny as thorough as she'd given all of the impossible forms they'd run across. Interest so intense it pinned him in place, burned through him.

Unable to bear the heat of it, he dropped his gaze to her throat. The bloodlust nipped at his tongue. His mouth was parched, his thirst sudden and powerful.

"You look as though you belong here," she said quietly.

He stepped toward her and didn't try to hide his fangs when he smiled. "Are you telling me that I'm beautiful?"

Her lashes fanned against her cheeks as she looked down at her hands. After a moment, she raised her gaze to his again. "There is that, but you are also incredibly white. You could have been formed from the same marble." She ran the tips of her fingers along the edge of the wall.

Arrested by the contrast of her skin against stone, Colin paused. His gaze followed the long, smooth sweep of her hand.

Savitri was the only bit of color, the only bit of life in the beautiful, sterile tableau.

He could be beautiful without appearing lifeless and pale. He preferred color; in the past century, he simply hadn't wanted the pain that came along with gaining it.

But here . . . he lifted his face to the sun, gauged its strength. His hands slipped from his pockets, rose to his collar. The shirt buttons irritated his raw fingertips.

She turned her head and reached down to dip her hand into the pool.

No, Savitri. Look at me.

Her fingers glistened when she lifted them again, and the water she poured from her cupped palm fell soundlessly. She shook her head in disbelief, then wiped her wet hand on her skirt.

"I pass the test, and remain Savi," she murmured, then blushed slightly when he lifted a brow. How extraordinary. Savitri had a fanciful streak hiding beneath the curiosity and logic.

She quickly added, "There's something written at the base of the obelisk, but it's too small for me to read from here. Can you read it?"

To his surprise, he could only discern the tiniest etching, not make out individual letters. "No. My eyesight is phenomenal, but that must have been written by your Elves. Or faeries."

He peeled away his shirt, let it drop to the ground.

"Are there Elves and faeries? Michael has a magic sword, so I can't rule out rings, Hobbits, and dark mountains." Her voice deepened. Her gaze moved over his chest, and she licked her lips, swallowed before she spoke. "What are you doing?"

"I intend to bathe in the sun," he said.

"Oh," she said breathlessly. Then her mouth pulled into a frown, her eyes narrowing. "You can tan?"

"Yes. Quite easily, though another vampire would be a fool to try." He raised his eyebrows in an imitation of her expression. "I shall be gilded within an hour or two. You know that I'm resistant to the sun, why are you surprised by the tan?"

She pursed her lips and glanced up at the sky. "It just completely overturns the theory I'd been forming about vampire immortality. I didn't think your cells changed—that you remained exactly as you were in life. But you must produce melanin."

"The changes that take place are all superficial; features and form don't alter—thank God. I like my features as they are." At her quick smile, he added, "Good God, Savitri, to be this pale in life, I'd have to have been the most simpering, lily-livered dandy ever to grace London." He placed the back of his hand against his forehead and sighed dramatically, bending his knees as if in a swoon. "I confess I may have been a bit of a dandy, but I never simpered."

She tilted her head back and laughed; the perfection in the curve of her throat made a joke of the fountain's arc of water. The deep, rich sound should have echoed in the *courtyard of stone, but Caelum seemed to swallow it, take it for itself.*

Colin could not fault it for that.

He slid his tongue across the tips of his fangs to soothe the ache building in them, then softly said, "You complained earlier of not bathing these four days; perhaps you should take advantage of this opportunity."

Her laughter faded. "I do stink."

Her sweet, feminine odor may have been stronger than she liked, but there was nothing offensive about it, and very much about it he found appealing.

Colin was all too familiar with stink, with burning, rotting odors, terrible . . . No.

He held her gaze and didn't attempt to hide the heat in his. "No, Savitri. I simply want you out of your clothes."

Her lips parted. "Oh, god, it's too much," she breathed, and rolled over into the water.

Her shriek pierced the air.

Colin fell to his knees as if he'd been struck from behind, fisting his hands against his eyes. "Freezing." He heard Savitri's laughing cry beneath the screams of the frozen faces and the howls of the ravenous wyrmwolves. He held on to the sound, forced himself to lower his palms from his face and see—not Chaos, but Caelum.

Heaven. He looked up, at the spires and the impossibly sublime arrangement, and welcomed the awe and fear. Let it tear through him, leave him senseless.

Until Savitri's laugh surrounded him again. Colin crawled forward, gripped the fountain wall, and pulled himself up. He didn't look down into the water, but across; Savitri had swum to the center and was examining the base of the obelisk.

His fingers trembled. He concentrated on the beating of her heart, the pulse of her blood, and let hunger push the lingering weakness and terror away.

If he had to lose himself, he preferred to do it within her.

"It translates from the Latin: 'Deeper than you think.'" *She threw him an amused glance. Drops slid from her shining cap of hair, down her cheeks and brow, fell from her delicately pointed chin. "I can't touch bottom, though I could have sworn it wasn't deeper than three feet. Appearances are*

deceiving—and despite all appearances, Michael must have a sense of humor."

"Oh, I doubt that very much," Colin murmured, unable to manage a stronger tone. Need rode hard on his tongue, swelled his shaft almost painfully erect.

He had to taste her. Had to have her.

"Come here, Savitri."

Her eyes darkened, and she pushed against the obelisk with her feet. She arrowed through the umbrella of falling water; it splashed against her cheeks and hair, her hips, but fell unbroken around her. Her movement created not the slightest wave in the pool, as if the water were thick, heavy.

He stepped back as she came near the edge; he couldn't look away from her, but it was better to remain at an angle that would not expose him, would not declare him absent.

She gripped the low marble wall. For a moment, she seemed all coltish long legs and awkward elbows and knees. Then she braced her foot against the edge of the wall and rose in a flowing, elegant motion, a cascade of water slipping silently away.

Oh, sweet heaven.

His chest tightened. His breath stopped.

She stood with her legs apart, and the sun outlined every curve, framing her exquisite composition with golden light. Water rendered the white linen transparent, hiding nothing from his hungry perusal—every color and shape, his to see. Her small breasts and taut nipples; the slender line of her waist; her slim hips and the shadow of her sex.

She stared down at him, and the warmth and arousal and awe in her eyes left him aching with need that had nothing to do with blood or lust.

How perfectly her expression reflected everything within him.

Her throat worked, her lips parted, and the movement gave life to the scene, made it flawless.

"We're enthralled," she whispered. "Like a Guardian going back to Earth for the first time. Only it's the opposite for us. Completely overtaken by sight when other forms of sensory input are effectively absent."

"I know." It didn't matter.

"And we aren't thinking clearly. I've never been this . . ." She trailed off, her gaze falling to the front of his trousers as he pulled his belt from the loops. The tug of material stretched over his cock was like a brief, teasing caress. "I don't know what to call it," she finished hoarsely.

"Overcome?" Astonished. Entranced. Lost.

"It's exponentially greater than that." Her eyes closed as he stepped forward and gathered the hem of her skirt in his hands. The linen was wet; her skin was cold.

She shivered as he ran his palms up the length of her legs, drawing the soaked cloth ever higher.

Look at me.

He wrapped his hands around her lower thighs, to support her, to keep her open for him. Leaning forward, he covered her sex with the heat of his mouth, pressed his tongue against linen and the sensitive flesh beneath.

Disappointment speared through him, exposing a wish he hadn't realized he'd made. He couldn't taste her. Why had he been foolish enough to hope he could?

He'd known better.

He inhaled instead, and the scent of her arousal filled his mouth, his lungs. It was flavor; it would have to be enough.

"Colin—" She broke off on a soft, breathy moan. Her legs shook, and she sank down onto her heels until her eyes were level with his. He held her knees wide, the skirt bunched atop her thighs.

She rested her palms on his forearms, balancing her perch. A teasing smile pulled at his lips.

"Savitri," he said. "Your hands are as cold as a vampire's."

She blinked, her eyelashes matted into thick spikes. Her gaze fell to his mouth. "I don't have fangs, but—"

Rocking forward, she drew her lips close to his . . . then dipped her head beneath his chin and bit his throat.

Oh, good God. His body stiffened in unbearable erotic pleasure. Biting him. No one had ever, only—

No, no.

A sharp, sweet pain brought him back: her teeth, fastened on his neck. A long, high-pitched keening rose from her chest, resonated through him.

Tight, slick heat sheathed his cock.

When had he . . . bloody fucking hell, where had he been? Colin froze, trying to regain control. His breath came in desperate pants.

She unclenched her teeth, swiped her tongue wetly over the stinging skin. Her thighs flexed as she lifted her hips, and she pressed a kiss to his neck, sucked lightly before her mouth released him.

"Savitri . . ." Bloodlust raged through him—and fear; he began shaking with both.

Run, Savitri.

Too late. Her head fell back, a blatant invitation. Impossible to resist, impossible to let go now. She slid down over his shaft with a trembling moan.

Her eyelids fluttered shut.

No. "Don't close your eyes." He stroked into her, a demand. "Tell me. Tell me what you see."

See me here. Keep me here.

"So . . . beautiful . . ."

Triumph shot through him. "Yes." He laughed raggedly and thrust again, dropped quick, biting kisses to her collarbone, her shoulder. "Tell me."

"Perfect. Don't know—" The breath ripped from her as his teeth closed over her nipple, tightly drawn beneath her shirt. Her hands gripped his biceps for support. "—what to call it. So blue."

Realization struck. The sky. She was staring up at the sky. Overcome, but not by him. Caelum.

"Cerulean," he supplied thickly.

"Cerulean," she echoed, her voice filled with wonder.

Straightening, he cupped her nape and brought her face to his, then used both hands to hold her hips motionless at the edge of the wall. He thrust deep and withdrew. "Look at me. Tell me."

Her lids were half-lowered, her gaze soft and unfocused. The racing of her heart pounded loud in his ears. Her chest heaved, and she tried to move forward, wrapping her legs around his waist and pulling. When he gave her no inch, she emitted a frustrated, panicked laugh and fell back, lying on the wide fountain wall.

He didn't look away in time, and her body no longer blocked the pool from his sight. Not there. The reflection of her arms, her hands held on to nothing.

Slipping . . . slipping. "Look at me," he pleaded. She had to feel him inside her, touching her. "Tell me."

"I can't—it's too much." Her back bowed, and she drew a sobbing breath. "It can't be real."

Despair clogged his throat. Always a dream. I'm here. He pushed in deep, hard, and she cried out.

Screaming and tearing. Blood, need to feed, then he can protect himself, protect Savitri—

Savitri.

Her teeth clamped on his shoulder. Safe, shaking beneath him, her warm flesh clenching around him in an unbearably sweet caress.

He hadn't seen her go over. He would—his fangs ached with need. She'd come again, and this physical release would be a pale substitute for what he'd give her.

She let go of him with a shuddering sigh, easing back. Her gaze roamed over his features, her eyes bright.

"I don't want to wake up," she said softly.

Bitterness swelled through him. "You'll awaken. And you'll forget." He ran his thumb down the length of her neck, felt her pulse beneath the thin layer of skin.

Her lips curved slightly, and she turned her chin to the side in welcome. "No, I won't."

Good God, if only that could be true. He lowered his head, kissed the corner of her jaw. She shivered when he scraped his fangs over her vein, and he paused. "Are you frightened?"

"No," she said without hesitation.

He smiled. "You should be. I should teach you a lesson in self-preservation, about vampires and their dark needs. You should not offer yourself so easily to one."

"Go ahead," she said, trembling with her laughter. "Teach me. Hugh says I've always been too trusting for my own good. But I hardly think immortality and incredible sex are things to fear." She rocked her hips against him, and he groaned against her throat. His cock was still buried deep within her, still hard and aching, though the bloodlust had temporarily over-

whelmed the physical desire. "Next time I'll ask you to turn me, and I'll explore those dark needs myself."

He raised his head to look at her, traced his finger over her cheek. "I've not the ability to transform you, Savitri." And he was surprised by the regret that accompanied the admission.

"I'll settle for great sex then," she said. "If you'll just get on with teaching me that lesson."

Delightful girl. Castleford was an idiot if he thought he could keep Colin away from her after this. A kiss to her neck, to soothe the fears she must *have, despite her words. The tips of his fangs pierced her skin; a sharp prick, but as soon as the blood flowed, he could breach her psyche, send her the rapture of it.*

Yes, too trusting . . . too fearless. Her blood filled his mouth. Pleasure spilled through him, and he gathered it, prepared to give her the same.

Chaos roared up from beneath. Feed. *Ripping and tearing and running.* Feed. *He choked, stiffened. No. He reached for the ecstasy, found despair and terror.*

"Colin?" Her voice, vibrating against his lips. Fearless. "It's okay. I want this."

And she wouldn't remember, he realized numbly. It wouldn't matter. It would only be a dream. For him, too—for one moment not being alone in this. Sharing beauty and perfection, and the depths of Hell. Savitri, she wasn't afraid. Never afraid. And she'd wake up. Despite her wish, she'd wake up.

He hadn't wanted to awaken, either.

Chaos rose and rose . . . he opened his psychic shields and let it out. He sipped. Tasted.

She was sweet. So very sweet. Her mind lay ordered and calm, with a single dark corner that she'd covered and pushed away as if she'd been expecting guests. He skated around it gratefully, tried to go deeper—and slammed into a thick, dense spiral, sticky with curiosity and striated with brilliant emotion . . .

What the hell was that?

Startled, he pulled away, then gasped as the bloodlust broke and the orgasm tore through him in pulsing streams.

Pain joined it, agony that began in his testicles and radiated out—his chest, his neck, clawing at his cheeks.

Savitri. His eyes flew open as her knee rammed into him again. Her fingers swiped at his face. He instinctively jerked his head back; her nails scraped his chin instead of blinding him.

Her eyes were vacant with horror, tears leaking from the corners. Scarlet trickled from the wounds on her neck.

Oh, good God. What had he done?

On the verge of panic, he bent his head to her throat again. Heal her, put her to sleep. *She'll forget.*

With a strangled scream, she slammed her foot into his chest. He didn't move, but she did, sliding back across the slick marble and tumbling into the pool. She went under, and he lurched forward, her name tearing from his lips.

He could still taste her blood.

She surfaced, slapping at the mirrored water and taking deep, gulping breaths. Cupping her hand over the punctures, she swiveled to face him. Wariness tightened her features. Her lips were trembling, her eyes dark, shimmering wells.

"Savitri . . ." His throat closed. What could he say? And her shields were too high for him to put her to sleep. He held out his hand, gave a charming smile. "Allow me to assist you."

"You've helped me enough. Lesson learned," she said, her voice harsh. A denial rose to his lips, but it died when his gaze fell to her fingers, clasped against her throat; she was shaking, shivering with cold. And fear. She shut her eyes. "If you'll excuse me, I feel the desperate need to bathe."

Without looking at him, she turned and swam toward the center of the fountain. She laid her cheek against the base of the obelisk, presenting her back to him.

He couldn't breathe. His stomach burned, the acrid flavor of shame stiffened his tongue. Her shirt clung to her shoulder blades; each vertebra in her spine was clearly outlined by the thin linen. *Bloody hell, but she was so slender, frail. Defenseless.*

The sickly odor of rot filling him, overwhelming her sweet psychic scent.

But he didn't dare remain with her, not when he couldn't protect her from himself. Better she feared him, would stay away from him.

He couldn't trust himself to do the same.

Slowly, he backed away. He could watch from a distance, make certain she left the frigid pool. He'd not hit her vein; she'd bleed a little, but it wouldn't be life-threatening. And when she fell asleep that evening, she'd wake up with only the vaguest remembrance . . .

Running. The frantic whines of the wyrmwolf. Too bloody tired to fight it.

Colin shook his head, trying to rid himself of the dangerous memory. The putrid scent faded, moving off to the southwest. The sun began to burn, and he glanced up at the crimson sky.

The grass was warm beneath his bare feet.

Wake up.

§

Colin opened his eyes and immediately squinted against the sun. He stood outside, on a lawn—the UCSF campus. A mile from his home.

His heart was pounding; perspiration poured from his brow. Dazzling, intense sunlight danced like fire across his exposed skin. Bewildered, he looked down. Sir Pup tugged at his trouser leg, a questioning edge to his high-pitched whines.

Odd . . . he'd dreamt the sound had been coming from a—

Oh, Christ. He broke into a sprint before it fully registered. Sir Pup cantered along beside him.

A wyrmwolf . . . heading southwest.

"Savi," he said hoarsely. "It's after Savi. *Run.*"

Sir Pup streaked ahead. There was no contest between a vampire and a hellhound.

Even a vampire like Colin. Already at Sunset, he leapt across the wide avenue, soared over the speeding cars. Not fast enough. He was going to be the loser in a futile race; the wyrmwolf was too far ahead.

His feet hit pavement again as terror flared through her

psychic scent. No. God *please* no. He stumbled; it took everything in him to stay upright.

Then her fragrance vanished, and it didn't matter anymore. He fell.

CHAPTER 14

Demons can simulate sex, but they don't experience arousal or orgasm. Halflings—the Guardians, vampires—were originally human, and have a human's physical responses. Nosferatu . . . I don't know about nosferatu. And the idea of nosferatu sex is kind of disgusting, isn't it?

—Savi to Taylor, 2007

After witnessing her family's murders, Savi had thought it would be on par with a feat of Hercules for her to shoot a living thing—but unloading ten rounds into the wyrmwolf's head and chest took no more effort than calculating a tip.

Enhanced speed had certainly helped; Savi wouldn't have been able to track the wyrmwolf's movements without it. Nor would she have had time to retrieve the gun and silencer from her towel drawer after spotting it through her kitchen window. The few extra moments she'd gained had allowed her to get as far from her front door as possible, crouch down behind her sofa, and wait for it to break through.

Then, remembering how confused the wyrmwolf in the alley had been when she'd raised her shields, she'd done it again.

Because hard upon the realization that a wyrmwolf was outside the window had been the knowledge that none of them had been after Colin. The first had come when she'd been out of her mind with fever; the second attack when she'd been out of her mind with lust; and this one when she'd been in her mind—but with it completely open.

They were apparently attracted to her psychic scent, so

she'd hidden it. The semiautomatic pistol and ten lead bullets had done the rest. Thank god Lilith had placed her weapons all over the house. Savi planned to kiss her senseless—as soon as she could stand. Her knees were no more solid than water.

She had to get up soon, though. The thing lay in the middle of her living room . . . but it wasn't dead. Rarely did bullets fatally damage a halfling, demon, or nosferatu—only cutting off the head, bisecting the heart, or draining the body of blood killed them.

It seemed the same was true of wyrmwolves. No wonder Colin had used his swords to fight them.

Her legs shook as she rose to her feet. How fast would it heal? She could see the holes in its fur and skull slowly closing. It whimpered and twitched.

At most, only minutes before it could attack her again—and it was suffering now.

Her vision blurred, but she kept the gun trained on its forehead as she skirted the living room. Her sword was in the umbrella stand by the front door—knocked over when the wyrmwolf had burst through the wooden door frame.

A clatter of claws on the outside stairwell had her heart leaping into her throat. Only five rounds left—but her shields were up. Perhaps it wouldn't get an immediate fix on her location in the room, giving her time to make the best shot.

A familiar bark sent relief crashing through her, and she finished her circle of the wyrmwolf as Sir Pup appeared on her porch, his black fur glossy in the winter sunlight.

"You can't eat it this time," she said before he could get any ideas. Before *she* could get any ideas that would be too close to running, too close to avoiding responsibility.

She tried to wedge the door closed, but it remained open a couple of inches. Shivering, she abandoned it and retrieved her sword. Her silky crimson top with its spaghetti straps and her jeans had been sufficient for inside, but now she felt ridiculously bare. And cold—colder than the sixty-degree day warranted.

The handle of her sword was icy in her palm. It shouldn't be this hard. Only one stroke, to an unmoving object.

She'd have preferred self-defense. Apparently violence of

that type came easily to her; she likely had Colin to thank for it. She was going to kiss him senseless, too—as soon as she could find the courage to cut off the wyrmwolf's head.

What if it healed enough to strike at her like a supposedly dead creature in a horror film, and she would be too close to get away? But to use the sword, she had to be near it. Within a foot or two. And she couldn't hold the gun on it and swing the sword at the same time; she wouldn't have enough strength to make it merciful if she used one hand.

Her fingers trembled. Both the gun and sword wavered. Oh, god, she was overthinking it, and taking too much time, and it would heal completely and kill her before—

A band of steel snagged around her waist, turned her, and yanked her up against a solid male chest. She buried her face in the warm curve between his shoulder and neck, squeezed her eyes closed. Cologne—citrus and sandalwood.

Colin. She didn't question why or how. It was enough that he was there.

"Let me do it, Savi." His voice was rough, gritty. Nothing like his usual smooth baritone.

She tried to pull back to see him, but he held her fast, his hands splayed across the small of her back and between her shoulder blades. "Quickly, Colin. It's in pain."

His arms tightened. "Then I shall wait a moment longer."

She shouldn't laugh. "Please."

His fingers slid down the length of her forearm, and he loosened her sword from her grip. "Don't look, Savi."

She wouldn't anyway. God, she was such a wimp. The sword whistled through the air; though she faced away from it, she flinched and covered her eyes.

Taking another cowardly moment, she stepped forward and placed the gun on a table piled high with the guts of several CPUs. "Can Sir Pup put it in his hammerspace—his cache—to take to SI for analysis?" The pocket of space would keep it preserved until he reached the lab.

His voice was still rough, but darkly amused now. "Stow it away, Pup." The hellhound gave a disappointed whine, until Colin added, "There will be a bloody mess for you to lick up—but be certain not to clean any of mine the same way."

Of his—? Oh, god, he meant *bloody* literally.

She turned, and her heart dropped to her knees. Her watery, useless knees. She sank to the floor, saw the red footprints leading from the door. His red, burned skin. The red, raw scrapes on the side of his face and on his knees through the tears in his trousers.

"What did you do?"

He watched her with hooded eyes. "It will heal before I wake up again."

He was in his undershirt. His feet were bare . . . bleeding.

"You came out of your daysleep? Did you *run* here? During the *day*?" Her chest felt hollow. Her heart was in her legs, somewhere. All she knew was that it was missing.

He nodded tightly, and his jaw clenched. The tendons in his neck stood out as he turned his face away from her. "I need to use your bed. Unless you prefer I sleep at Castleford's?"

"No." She could barely get the denial past her throat. "Use mine."

He walked toward her bedroom, his back stiff. He hesitated at the threshold. "Are there any mirrors?"

"No. Only in the bathroom." She'd taken the rest out.

"Don't lower your shields, Savi."

"I know," she said, but he was already through the doorway. He'd probably heard her, though.

She lowered her face to her knees and silently began to cry.

❦

It didn't have to mean anything. She knew better than anyone how uncontrollable it could be, the urge to run. Caused by an involuntary physical response, not free will. He probably hadn't known he was doing it—if he had, he'd have taken the precaution of a sword and a covering.

And shoes.

A long sliver of glass had embedded in the heel of his left foot. Savi carefully probed into the gash with a pair of tweezers, slid the shard out. It clinked into the pan she'd set on the floor, joining the other pieces of glass and metal and gravel—and blood.

She'd had to reopen several wounds to clean them out;

Colin hadn't moved during the long process, just as he'd remained still when she'd smeared aloe over his skin, tended to the abrasions on his face and knees.

How he must hate knowing she'd seen him this way.

And perhaps she should have left him alone—but if he could feel her psychic scent during his daysleep, then he must the sunburn and injuries as well.

She pressed a clean towel against the last cut and waited for it to stop bleeding—it never took long. His body repaired itself with amazing speed. Already, the burns had faded to pink; his skin had taken a bronze cast in some of the less-affected areas. She looked up over his feet, down the length of him.

He lay sprawled across the honey-gold sheets on his stomach, his feet hanging over the edge, his face turned into her pillow and his mouth half-open, his blond hair sticking up in random disarray.

Only his fangs kept him from appearing too boyish. She'd had an instant when, spreading the gel over his cheeks and lips, she'd wondered if he'd unknowingly attack her in his sleep. But she'd been able to maneuver him from side to side without a change in his deep, regular breathing.

She'd not been similarly unaffected.

With a sigh, she removed the pan from the wooden flooring beneath his feet, slid a bowl of warm soapy water in its place. God, but she was sick, playing doctor and searching for signs of intimacy when he'd made it perfectly clear he didn't want her to see him.

But there was intimacy in this, if an unintentional one, and it was widening the hollow ache in her chest, leaving an unbearable pain in its place.

She began washing his feet.

Soap instead of milk, but it felt the same. A vow, a welcome. If her parents had been alive, they'd have washed the feet of her groom, showing their acceptance of him into the family. Perhaps Nani would do it; they'd never spoken of how traditional her wedding would be. Finding the groom came first.

But it hardly mattered who it would be now.

One sharp blow—that was all she needed. Not to stop her suffering but to make herself face reality, and one simple truth: she had a choice between her heart breaking once, marrying a suitable boy; or continuing on like this and having it broken every time Colin was with someone else.

Even if he tried, he couldn't be faithful to a human. It was a physical impossibility; the bloodlust didn't care, and one human couldn't supply all of his blood without endangering herself. He had to go elsewhere to feed—and his body would go elsewhere, too.

And that was assuming he'd try. He might have run through the city by instinct, not choice.

Her bedside phone rang, and the water sloshed in the bowl as she startled, leaping forward to answer it before it could disturb him.

As if her clambering across the mattress wouldn't. She sat on the edge of the bed, answering it breathlessly, then froze as Colin rolled over and his arm came around her hips.

"*Naatin?* Were you running?"

His chest pressed against her bottom and lower back. His eyes were closed; his lashes lay in thick, dark crescents across his cheeks, his chin tucked beside her hip.

"No." She glanced at the clock: one thirty. What did she usually do on Saturday afternoons? "Just cleaning a few things around the house."

Colin's lips curved into a tiny smile. They'd been chapped less than half an hour before. Now they were soft, smooth, as if the aloe had soaked into them. She clenched her fist to keep from tracing their shape. To keep from burying her fingers in his golden hair and kissing him while he was half-conscious.

"You should put away your clutter, *naatin*. You may have guests next weekend, if your meeting with that boy tonight is satisfactory. I spoke with Lakshmi Sivakumar today."

"Oh?" She rubbed her eyelids with her forefinger and thumb, then dropped her hand to her lap, stared at the cut across her palm. "Did she know the family?"

"Oh, yes. A very good family. From what his parents described of him, you won't have any objections to the boy."

Her stomach knotted. "You talked to them already?"

"That's how it should be done, *naatin*. But I won't protest if you decide to meet with him alone, and decide for yourself. He's to be your husband; it is your choice."

"Okay," she said. Then, because her voice sounded dull and Nani might think she was ungrateful, Savi forced a lighter note and added, "This is really good news then. It was a good idea to talk to Mrs. Sivakumar. And Manu's parents."

A burgundy Persian rug lay on the wooden floor next to the bed. Savi began counting the saffron buds in the pattern as Nani related the conversation in an animated tone, including a list of Manu's accomplishments and connections within the community. It was several minutes before she hung up the phone.

Savi hadn't forgotten she was supposed to meet Manu that night, but it hadn't been important before . . . hadn't mattered if it went well. She'd considered calling and canceling—too much had happened in the past day to meet a prospective spouse with any equanimity—and had given herself until three o'clock that afternoon to make that decision.

Nani's call erased any choice. She couldn't stand him up now.

A soft, rhythmic pressure at her thigh made her look down again. Colin rubbed his jaw lightly against the side of her leg, like a cat nuzzling in. The denim of her jeans had to be rough on his skin.

His arm tensed when she tried to pull away.

He rolled again, took her with him. She laughed in surprise as her back hit the mattress, but he continued turning her until she lay on her side, spooned in front of him. His breath brushed hot and moist across her neck.

His left forearm wrapped around her midriff, his hand cupping the curve of her waist. The other angled up from beneath her rib cage, between her breasts, his hand resting on her shoulder. His fingers slid beneath her shoulder strap, as if he didn't want any material—even silk—between his touch and her skin.

His body was a solid sheet of heat behind her. His knee insinuated between hers, and she bit her lip to stifle her moan as he raised his thigh until it lodged firm against her sex.

Oh god. He was half-asleep, recovering—and she was

sick, thinking what she was now. About how it would be so easy to ride against that tautly muscled thigh . . . hell, maybe vampires went into rigor mortis in their daysleep, and she could just unzip his—

"Thank you," he said drowsily into her ear.

For being *this close* to molesting him? "What for?"

"My feet. The lotion."

"Oh. I didn't know you felt it."

His right hand drifted down until his fingertips brushed against the hollow of her throat. "I wasn't fully asleep when you began. You didn't need to. The glass would have worked itself out as I slept."

She thought of the wounds she'd opened, and her stomach tightened. "I'm sorry. I didn't know."

She heard the smile in his sleep-deepened voice. "Don't apologize, sweet. It's more comfortable this way . . . and I'm pleased by your attention. I thought you'd less pity for my pain than you did the wyrmwolf's."

Surely he was kidding. "You would've preferred I cut off your head for a bit of sunburn?" she asked lightly, though her chest began to ache again. Perhaps her reaction had seemed heartless—too overcome by the realization of what he'd done, she'd questioned him instead of helping him.

His silent laugh rumbled against her back, loosened the vise around her lungs. "More than a bit, I wager."

"It wasn't so terrible." His laughter intensified, shaking against her, and she admitted, "Okay, so you looked like a demon who'd been jumped by a gang of Guardians. Not that it mattered; you couldn't look bad if you tried."

"I'll certainly never try." A series of light kisses fluttered over her shoulder, followed by a sigh. "Ah, Savi, I'd take care of you in return, but I'm so tired a harem of succubae couldn't get a rise out of me."

Embarrassment flushed her cheeks. She should have realized she couldn't hide her arousal from him whether she humped his leg or refrained. "I need to get up and clean, anyway."

"All of your clutter?" A teasing note entered his voice, and her embarrassment deepened.

His left palm slid up to rest flat over her stomach. His thumb dipped into the indentation of her navel.

"Yes." It came out as a squeak.

"Surely you can't need all of it." His hand moved lower, his fingers working beneath the waistband of her jeans. The buttons of her fly popped open, one by one.

Oh god. "Probably not. But I hate to throw anything away." She couldn't help herself; she rocked against his leg, trying to ease the throbbing, liquid tension.

"Ah, sweet—that's so good. Use me. Take what you need." She needed more than this.

"What of your lovers?" he said. He softly nipped at her nape, and she had to concentrate to recall herself to their conversation. "You've had several, but they do not clutter your bed now. You must've thrown them away."

"No." His hand rested at the elastic of her panties now, as if he was waiting. She didn't want to do this herself. She gripped his wrist, urging him on. Not an invitation, a request, a plea. "They let me go."

Colin dragged his fingers through her soft curls, then tugged. Fire streaked through her, and a gasping moan fell from her lips. He circled her clit, then delved deeper.

He stilled, groaned. "Good God, Savi—I could bathe in this. They were all blithering, sodding idiots. How could they let you go?"

"I'm not attentive to them. I'm just there for the sex." She ground desperately against him, trying to get him inside her—and then cried out when he complied, his long fingers pushing and parting. Truth spilled from her as easily as her moisture into his hand. "And I'm too impatient in bed. I only want to get to the good part—the fucking."

"That's absurd, sweet." He lifted his thigh, widening her legs. His hand moved leisurely, each stroke torturously slow, in and out. "No man would object to that."

"It's the pain thing," she breathed, watching. Unbearably erotic, though there wasn't much to see—just the V of her fly, his hand disappearing into her black satin panties, a strip of skin across her abdomen. "It either freaks them out after the first couple of times or if there's blood, or they want to take it further, into S&M, and that's not what I need."

She had to look away from the picture they made—it was too much. Her hands rose to her breasts, and she lifted their light weight through her shirt. God, but she wished she didn't have to do this . . .

"What pain thing? What do you need?" Then, as if he'd just glanced down over her shoulder, he rasped, "Oh, Christ—let me see you touch yourself, love."

The shoulder straps snapped as he tore the silk bodice away from her skin.

She gave another startled laugh and cupped her breasts again, this time to cover them. "Are you sure you're too tired?"

"It's a bloody miracle I can do this much. What pain thing?" His hand ceased its luscious motion through her wet folds.

She turned her face into the pillow. "I told you in Caelum. At the fountain, during . . ."

He was suddenly so silent, so still, she realized, "You don't remember."

"Did I hurt you?" It ripped from him in that gritty voice.

"No! I just wasn't ready because the water had been so cold, and I'd bitten you and you were inside me so fast and I was . . . surprised at how big you were, and you asked if I was hurt, so I told you." And now she recalled the dazed expression in his eyes, as if he hadn't been completely aware of what was taking place. She'd thought it was part of the enthrallment, but—"You were hallucinating *then*?"

She tried to turn to look at him, but he didn't let her move.

"What did you tell me?"

Her eyes squeezed shut. "That I can't come without a little bit of pain, anyway." He didn't immediately respond, and she explained, "I have to use it to get my head into my body, get past my shields, to really feel what's going on. Like closing a circuit; it jolts me in there."

His thumb took up a lazy rhythm over her clit. "And that is what took place in the gym, when you dropped your shields in response to Castleford's strike?"

Yes, she thought, but couldn't say it. Her lungs lost their air when he pinched the slick bundle of nerves. Her back arched, thrusting her taut nipples against her palms.

"What did I do after you told me, Savi?"

"You told me to bite you again and then—ah, God . . . *please*." His fingers slipped into her, then withdrew to circle wetly around her clitoris, teasing, teasing.

"And then . . . ? What did I do?"

Another thrust inside, and she began shaking, her foot sliding back and forth over the sheets in an uncontrollable need to *move*.

"You fucked me." She gasped. "So hard. And I came so hard." Desperate, she twisted her nipples between her thumbs and forefingers, but he caught her hands in his right and drew them forward and up, holding her wrists in front of her forehead.

He pushed another finger deep, stretching the delicate flesh, rubbing thickly against smooth inner muscle. "Are you thinking of it now? How I felt inside you?"

His cock, pounding into her with a force that bordered on painful but was too good to hurt. His skin firm against her tongue, trapped between her teeth. "Yes. *Please*, Colin. Don't make me do it myself."

"How would you do it, sweet? I've got your hands."

She twisted forward at her waist and bit the skin just below her elbow; not hard, just to demonstrate. And she had no time to process his reaction—a sharply drawn breath, a whispered "bloody hell"—before he let go of her wrists and used his thigh and both hands to thrust and pinch and send her hurtling into orgasm.

She cried out against her arm, shuddered as the world broke into pieces, breathed his name as she tried to reorder it again. Dimly, she felt a tug at her waistband as he refastened her jeans, then his strong, soothing touch across her chest as he wrapped his forearm around her again, but his other hand was at her back, tracing a line between . . .

Her scars. She tried to remember if he'd seen them before, and realized he hadn't. Better to have prepared him.

"I should kiss Castleford for saving you." The exhaustion and roughness had returned to his voice. "Then kill him for allowing it to happen."

She smiled, too satisfied to move anything but her lips. "They just look terrible because they're exit wounds," she said, and glanced down at the puckered scar over her breast, its mate high on her abdomen. "Not so bad in front. And the marks from the surgeries have almost completely faded." Only thin, silvery lines remained.

"You should have run."

"From a gun?"

"From the wyrmwolf. Locked yourself in here. You have the symbols ready on the door."

A precaution used in almost every room. "If I had, it might have gone after a neighbor. Or taken Hugh and Lilith by surprise when they came home."

"They can't be taken by surprise. And you're too fragile to be fighting." She felt him shake his head, as if to keep himself awake. "A gun wouldn't have protected you if there had been two. You have to run."

He was right; she'd been lucky. But it wasn't that simple. "It's difficult for me to run."

"Why?" The question was heavy with fatigue. He laid his cheek against her neck, and his breathing slowed. "It doesn't matter. I'll give you the protection you need. I'll give you everything you need."

Her heart constricted. "You will?"

Why did those two words make her sound like such a needy little girl?

He made a sound of assent, a hum against her throat. "The sod you plan to marry won't be able, if he's like the others. When you find he can't, come back to me."

She stared down at his arm crossed over her naked chest, her throat tight. That's what he'd meant?

"For sex? After I've married him?" The hollow ache opened up again, worse for having been filled for a brief, stupid moment. She'd had sex. She'd always had sex—often good sex. "I don't need an orgasm, Colin; I need something that will last. I won't cheat on him. Even with the others, even if it was of short duration, I was faithful. Could you be?"

She immediately regretted asking, hated the pain that it exposed and the wish behind it . . . and he was silent for so long that she began to think—*hope*—he'd fallen asleep.

And when his softly spoken answer finally came, it was the sharp blow she'd needed. But it was hardly merciful.

"If I could, Savi, it would be with you."

A simple "no" would have been easier to take.

CHAPTER 15

*You may be correct; he was melancholy and hesitant—
and he had taken a concoction designed to ease the
pain from the initial attempt. Perhaps that interfered
with the transformation? I shall rest easy, then: I am
obviously not responsible.*

—*Colin to Ramsdell, 1821*

❧

Colin woke slowly, and the heavy weight upon his chest was
not wholly unexpected. He'd fallen asleep with Savi lying still
and silent in his arms, then dreamt he drowned in a sea of
warm salt water, unable to draw a breath—unusual, but not in-
explicable, as in deep daysleep vampires did not breathe at all.
No, the torment had come from sensing her pain yet being unable to move or offer comfort.

Bloody hell . . . there'd been none to offer. And God knew,
he could have used some, too. The weight on his chest grew
heavier.

Where was she? He couldn't feel her in the room, nor did
his psychic probe detect her in the apartment. Even with her
shields high, he'd have sensed her—but there was only the
familiar presence of Castleford and Lilith . . .

Lilith. Oh, Christ.

"Get off," he said, opening his eyes.

Lilith grinned down at him from her perch on the center of
his chest, her dark eyes and her teeth gleaming. She rested
lightly on the balls of her bare feet, her leather-clad knees out-
spread and her hands against his collarbones, as if she could
hold him down. "That's so much better than 'Fuck off, Lilith'
and 'Sod off, Lilith.'"

Colin glanced heavenward, but relief was not to be found on the ceiling. "Good God, this is my worst nightmare come true: I've woken up with you in my bed."

"*Savi's* bed. And it gets even better, bloodsucker," Lilith said. "Hugh's here to watch. He likes to see me work."

A single look confirmed it; Castleford stood by the door, leaning against the wall with his arms across his chest, regarding them with an unreadable expression.

"As you are still wearing that corset, he's probably the only one who likes to see you work."

Her grin widened. "Savitri liked it, as well. She kissed me, she liked it so much." Her feet slipped to his sides; she straddled him and leaned down, her mouth just above his lips.

He inhaled—and God, yes, almost imperceptible, but there: Savi's sweet, tangy physical scent.

"Jealous? She really appreciated my guns, gave me a nice hard smack . . . but apparently she didn't appreciate your little pistol as much, because she left to go meet her suitor." Her mouth flattened. "You know how she likes her men; she might be in another bed with him right now."

Colin's gut clenched, agony tearing through his chest. Christ, but Lilith knew how to stab a man where he was most vulnerable, and in a location Colin had done everything he could to hide from himself.

But slicing him open, leaving him raw and exposed was not enough for her demon tongue. "You're so pretty, she was probably flattered that you panted after her. But a smart girl like that wouldn't take long to realize you've more interest in your pleasure than hers, and that you'll only sniff around until you get what you want."

"Lilith, you're on the verge of damaging a bloody fine friendship," he said tightly.

"As are you." Her eyes narrowed. "Why are you so tanned?"

He flashed his fangs in a snarl. "Won't you tell me how beautiful it is on me? Perhaps you can manipulate me into a confession about Caelum. That's what this is about, isn't it?"

"No," Castleford said quietly. "It's about making certain Savi wasn't crying over a demon. It's Colin, Lilith."

Startled, Colin's gaze moved back and forth between them.

Then anger took the place of surprise. "Next time, shove me in front of a fucking mirror."

He sat up, and Lilith leapt lightly to the floor. He pulled a hand through his hair, threw the sheet back.

"When was she crying? And how the bloody hell could you confuse me for a demon? He copied my *face*. You may not have psychic abilities, but you've two hundred years' acquaintance and a sodding hellhound!" Walking around the side of the bed, he faced them and said softly, dangerously, "And why was she crying?"

Castleford slid his hands into his pockets. His gaze skimmed Colin's length, pausing briefly at his knees. "Sir Pup went with her, and if you were a demon and only pretending the daysleep, we didn't want to alert you to our suspicions. That is also why we didn't bring in a mirror, take a picture, or examine you physically. She said your skin was still hot—that, combined with the difference between the way you two parted at SI this morning and the way we found her, the fact that you should have been across town in your daysleep, and that Savi is very, very wealthy—an excellent target for a demon, particularly if the vampire he's impersonating is already connected to her—gave us concern."

"Of course, now it's obvious that when she spoke of your skin, she meant a burn . . . Cerberus's balls, Colin, what the hell were you thinking? Why didn't you call SI and have Selah or Michael teleport over here?"

A hoarse bark of laughter escaped him. "I didn't think. I sensed the wyrmwolf and . . . ran." And had been certain that he'd been too late. Even his experience in Chaos hadn't equaled the terror and dread that had accompanied him the rest of the way here.

How easy it had been when he'd seen her alive, the sword wavering in her hands, to decide to be anything she needed, do anything she wanted. Followed by the triumph of knowing he could fulfill her needs as no one else could, and the certainty that once she realized it, she'd not seek out anyone else.

And then to discover the one thing she wanted most was something he couldn't give her. *I need something that will last.*

A phase didn't. Why would his confirmation of his incapability make her cry, if she knew her feelings would be short-lived? He swallowed thickly. "How did you find her?"

"Like this." Lilith hopped up on the bed, folded her legs beneath her and sat on her heels. She laid her hands in her lap and gazed at them morosely for a moment. "She'd been wiping up blood from the floor." She raised a brow at him. "Yours? We wondered why Sir Pup hadn't taken care of it."

"Yes." It was all he could manage. She'd been on her hands and knees cleaning up after him?

Never again.

"And then she did this." With a flourish, Lilith pretended to swipe tears from her eyes and cheeks, then pasted a huge, sunny smile on her lips in a perfect imitation of Savi's guarded expression.

Castleford lowered his head into his hand and began laughing. Colin could not.

"And then she said, 'Oh, great, you guys are here! I was just finishing up, then I've got to go meet this guy at the café, and I'm taking Sir Pup with me, because the wyrmwolves are after my psychic scent. Oh, and I shot one and I'm kissing you for putting your guns all over my house, and Colin cut off the thing's head and he's sleeping in my room, but his skin is still a little red and hot. Oh, and could you go to Auntie's to watch after Nani until I come back here and we all talk to Colin about those transactions, and we'll send Sir Pup to look after Nani for the rest of the night? Thanks!' "

Castleford lifted his head, his eyes bright blue with amusement. "Actually, it took about half an hour, during which Sir Pup carried the wyrmwolf's corpse to the lab and returned with your car—else we would have determined your identity with him. But that neatly sums up all we learned from our inquiry."

"And then she left," Lilith said.

"What time?" Colin started toward the bedroom door. It was almost six now. The sun had set shortly after five, and wyrmwolves weren't the sole danger after night had fallen. "She only has Sir Pup?"

"She left in a taxi at three." Lilith's mouth curved into a mocking smile. "You're going to stalk her?"

"Yes, but I prefer to call it the protection that you two have been too lax to provide her. Why so bloody early? She doesn't meet with the sod until eight. I'd have woken by then and offered her a ride."

He walked into the living room and stopped as quickly as if he'd slammed into a wall. He turned, looked through the door to her office. Oh, Christ. The desks and tabletops, clear of electronics. The boxes of wiring and components, gone. The racks of DVDs, video games, and graphic novels, pared away to a few volumes. The DemonSlayer posters taken down. And despite the colorful silk paintings, pillows, and furniture that decorated the flat . . . it was sterile, lifeless, as if she'd taken everything that had ever been of interest to her and thrown it away. Gutted herself.

If this was what she turned herself into to please her suitor, Colin would murder the fucking sod. *This* was what she wanted to last? Stripped down into a clichéd representation of a suitable woman?

"It's remarkable how much cleaning one can do with a hellhound and his cache," Castleford observed from behind him. "Lilith does the same thing on her night for dishes, and they reappear when it's my evening."

Not discarded then. Concealed. Yet so much worse: to be close to everything she needed to reflect her, to know where it was but be unable to *have* it . . .

He'd known that ache too well since Caelum. Now she was slipping away from him again. And this time, taking everything with her.

"Your clothes are by the door," Lilith said. "The courier delivered them about fifteen minutes ago."

His brows drew together as he crossed the room toward the door connecting to Castleford's house; he immediately recognized the elegant packaging and discreet logo from his preferred clothing store. Oh, sweet Savitri. His throat thickened with an unnamable emotion. Lowering himself to his heels, he slid his fingers beneath the tape on the largest package.

A card sat on top, with a message scrawled in nearly illegible handwriting. *For saving me—three times. And because ripped pants are so 1990s. I hope they all fit; they had your measurements on file but these are off the rack. There wasn't time to do alterations. The receipt's in here if you want to return them.*

She hadn't signed her name, but had drawn a big smiley face. Guarded, even on a note. And prepared for rejection.

They let me go.

An ivory cashmere sweater. A pair of charcoal trousers. A jacket. A shirt, gray with green pinstripes. Trousers identical to those he wore now. All replacements for items ruined fighting the wyrmwolves.

But she'd included more—things he'd need to leave her house without borrowing from Castleford or going without: handmade shoes, silk socks and handkerchiefs, underclothes. Cologne.

And a finely knit sweater in cerulean blue. No use for it, nor was it a replacement. It was the only item she hadn't seen him wear before. A personal gift—and he could easily imagine her stopping, her attention arrested by the color, touching it . . . and choosing it on impulse at the last minute.

It had to have been at the last moment; if she'd taken time to reflect on how much it revealed, she'd have put it back.

I'm not attentive to them.

Was this attention, or simply what she'd learned about him from casual observation? It didn't matter. It would be wasted on any other man. And if she would only offer it to one, if it had to be a suitor so that she could fulfill her promise to Auntie . . . then it would be him.

He *needed* this. He'd secure her attention for himself if he had to move heaven and earth to do it.

And there was no way in hell he would let her go.

❧

Colin's hair was damp when he went down the stairs to Castleford's. He glanced at the painting of Caelum, then followed the sound of cursing and found Lilith in the hallway near the garage, shrugging into her jacket and snapping her cell phone closed. The rest of her leather ensemble had been exchanged for loose cotton cargo pants and a T-shirt. Castleford entered from the kitchen moments after, his helmet dangling from his fingers.

"That bitch Taylor is avoiding me," Lilith announced, sliding a gun into a holster at the small of her back. Her long black hair concealed the slight bulge it left in the line of her jacket.

A pair of grooves bracketed Castleford's mouth, but he refrained from commenting.

Colin shook his head in disbelief. "Your diplomatic skills are atrocious, Agent Milton." The last time he'd seen Lilith and Detective Taylor in the same room together, Lilith had been using Sir Pup to frighten the woman and her partner speechless. "I'll speak with her before you completely destroy all relations with the San Francisco police; it primarily concerns me, anyway."

He ignored their surprise and tugged on the cuffs of the blue sweater, made certain they lay perfectly over his wrists.

He raised a brow at their continued silence. "I've a vested interest in routing this demon; it's not an altruistic offer."

"And a vested interest in Savi," Lilith said flatly. "As he's been using the vampires to watch her, you have even more reason."

"Yes." He met Castleford's eyes. "I find I cannot keep my promise to stay away from her. And as I cannot remain in good faith to you, I release you from the vow of protection you gave to me two centuries ago." His jaw clenched, and he swallowed before adding, "But I would appreciate your help in securing her safety and felicity."

Castleford's expression gave no evidence of his thoughts. "What do you imagine could secure such for her?"

"I need a long-term food source that I won't fuck," Colin said bluntly. "You've had access to Caelum's library, have read all of the Scrolls, might have knowledge of a—"

He broke off as pity darkened Castleford's face.

Colin glanced at Lilith, saw the same in her eyes. Panic began to claw at his chest, and he forced it away. This wasn't the only option. There was Michael, and if nothing else, a demon might bargain with him.

Chaos would be an irresistible temptation.

"There isn't one, Colin." Castleford's knuckles whitened as his grip on his helmet tightened. "She's in love with you? She told you this?"

"No." Bloody hell, but he wished he could lie to Castleford as easily as Savi had to him. "She said it was nothing. Just a phase. It isn't true."

It couldn't be.

Castleford gave a short nod. "Even if it was a lie, it was a choice she made. Respect her will and let her go."

"Everyone lets her go," Colin growled, fisting his hands to keep from launching himself in an attack. "I'll not be like them."

Halting in the doorway to the garage, Castleford looked over his shoulder, ice in his blue gaze. "She doesn't commit to anything she can't follow through on. Don't use her feelings to force her into a commitment. You'll be little better than a demon, and I'll treat you as such."

Lilith snorted with laughter, though her dark eyes held no humor. "Treat him as you do me? Please do. I've been waiting to see that kiss between you two for a year." She turned to Colin. "Why the fuck are you at his throat?"

Good God, but Lilith was intolerable at times—and worse when she was right. Castleford was not being unreasonable, nor was he responding in any way Colin hadn't expected. Yet he'd immediately reacted as if the other man had considered him a triviality to be dismissed.

Chagrined, he said, "I came to inform you that I intend to court her. I'm not asking permission, I simply don't want to wake up with you in my bed again." He stole a glance at Castleford. "I'd not force her into anything. I will, however, charm, seduce, and if necessary, prostrate myself at her feet."

Castleford closed his eyes, leaned against the door frame. "Court her?" he echoed in a curiously strained voice.

"Why, yes," Colin said with a lazy grin, recognizing the other man's suppressed laughter. "I do believe that is what they call it when a man decides to win a woman's affections."

"Typically, when a vampire does it, it is called 'wedded to the night,'" Lilith said dryly. "Or 'eternally bound by blood and darkness.' Very dramatic and frightening."

Colin's light mood vanished. It wouldn't be eternal, but he would take any time Savi had to offer him. And he wouldn't let thoughts of the future, his eventual loss, destroy his new-found hope.

It would last . . . but it couldn't be forever.

"Dramatic, perhaps," he said quietly. "But my vampirism doesn't frighten her." She only objected to the uncontrollable lust that went along with it—but he would find a way to overcome it, or bypass it.

Castleford tapped his helmet against the side of his thigh. "Nothing's likely to frighten her anymore."

Lilith gave a mock shudder. "It does me. It's revolting."

Sighing, Castleford straightened up from the door frame. "We shouldn't delay any longer before going to Auntie's. If this is something Savi wants, too, I'll make an effort to reexamine the Scrolls and speak with Michael. But I'm fairly certain in this, Colin: There's nothing." He ran a hand through his short hair, then met Colin's gaze again. "*This* I'm asking as her brother: For her sake, don't make promises you can't keep. For now, if she allows your attention, then court her—but don't speak of the future unless you are certain of a solution."

Lilith stepped forward and lifted her fingers to Colin's collar, adjusting the neckline of the black undershirt layered beneath. "The easiest way to destroy a human's soul is with false hope, whether fed by truth or lies," she said quietly.

Astonished, Colin didn't move. But for Castleford and Sir Pup, Lilith rarely touched anyone with care. And though they'd established a close friendship in the past decade, he could count the number of times she'd done so to him: a distracted pat to his cheek when she'd been deciding whether to help Castleford despite her bargain with Lucifer, a careful examination of Colin's hands when he'd returned from Chaos, and now.

How many women had he been with? He hadn't mattered to them, nor they to him. He'd been grateful for each one, but very few had touched him.

He could count them as well. Too effortlessly for two centuries of living: Emily, Lilith, Selah, and Savi. One his sister, two his friends.

He wanted so much more from Savi.

"Don't serve the needs of those Below, Colin, no matter how deep the desire." She dropped her hand back to her side and arched a dark eyebrow. "It's much more rewarding to be wicked while serving ourselves."

The heavy weight settled on his chest again. In his determination to have Savi, he'd have told her anything, promised her everything. And he wouldn't have considered how damaging it would have been if he failed; he would have only thought of pleasing her in the present.

He'd have realized it too late.

When had he become so careless? Yet he'd been so from the moment he'd been teleported to Caelum, and with the woman whom he should have been taking the most care. Had his desire for her overwhelmed his sense so much—or was it the selfishness she'd accused him of?

His lungs too tight for speech, Colin simply nodded, then followed them out into the garage.

Their motorcycles flanked his car, and he watched as they strapped swords and other gear onto the bikes. In Sir Pup's absence, they had to carry their own weapons. Normal behavior for them—and for Colin, though he preferred to stow them in the car boot . . . but for Savi, who abhorred violence, what had the past eight months been like?

Why hadn't she moved into her own house? She could afford it, and she'd have avoided the risks living with Lilith and Hugh posed.

Yet she'd remained, and shot a wyrmwolf as steadily as if she'd been training with a gun for years. She should have been terrified . . .

She *had* been terrified. He'd felt it in the seconds before she'd raised her shields. And though she was smart enough to know better, though Castleford had obviously prepared the symbols for her protection, she hadn't fled.

His brow furrowed as he realized where his thoughts were leading, the conclusion he began to draw between her need for pain and her mental distance from her physical responses. "Why isn't anything likely to frighten her? And when it does, why is it difficult for her to run?"

Bent over the motorcycle, Castleford stilled for a moment, then thrust a sword into a scabbard; the bike skidded forward with the force of it. "Because I fucked up," he said.

Lilith's head jerked around, and Colin thought the surprise on her face likely reflected his; Castleford seldom swore, and only when his anger was self-directed.

"And I taught her something she learned too well."

There was a name for a man who sat in a parked car outside a café, watching through a window while the woman he obsessed over spoke with another man. Lilith would have called him a stalker. Savi might have said he was creepy.

Colin preferred besotted.

God, but she looked incredible. The window framed her perfectly; she sat at a tall cocktail table, her heels hooked on the rung of her chair. Supple boots hugged her calves, and the hem of her skirt allowed a tantalizing glimpse of smooth caramel at her knee.

He intended to kiss that spot, then taste every hidden bit of skin. Peel away the creamy wool sweater. Slide his hands up the exquisite length of her legs, hold her close.

And safe. She wouldn't have to run again.

A light rain began to fall, spattering against the windshield and side window. Colin eyed the sky in accusation. No moonlight spilled through the heavy gray mass above. A cloud cover would have been bloody brilliant midday; too late for it to be of any use to him now.

Lying on the sidewalk in front of the café, Sir Pup raised his head from his forepaws and looked toward the Jaguar. His jaws opened wide, his lips pulled back. The hellhound was laughing at him.

Colin grinned, showed his own fangs. "At least I'll not be soaked, pup."

A burst of laughter came faintly through the car window, and Colin's gaze shifted to the suitor. His eyes narrowed. The sod was handsome, and obviously had brains enough to appreciate her humor—but if the bastard didn't fall on his knees and worship her as she deserved, or at least propose within a minute or two, Colin would kill him.

A tall, barrel-round man walked in front of the Jaguar, crossed the street toward the café with a quick glance into the car. Detective Preston.

The tap on the passenger window didn't surprise Colin, but Detective Taylor's appearance did. The once impeccably pressed woman was a hell of a mess. Instead of the sleek bob, her short auburn hair rioted around her head in thick, uneven curls; her countenance was drawn and tired, her skin pale but for the dark circles around her eyes. Already slender, petite, she must have lost half a stone in the past eight months.

Colin unlocked the door; Taylor slipped inside, wiping the rain from her face. The strong odor of cigarettes and coffee clung to her wrinkled jacket.

She turned to look at him. Her eyes closed, and she breathed, "Dammit."

He could only summon half a smile. "Detective. I know appearances are often deceiving, but—"

Her mouth tightened. "Don't say anything. I hear it enough from Joe."

Colin widened his smile, designed it to charm. Lifting her hand, he brought it to his lips before she could pull away or protest. "Detective Preston often remarks upon how beautiful I am? I shall have to thank him."

"He went in to grab us something to eat while I talked to you," she said absently, her gaze arrested on his mouth. Her fingers curled on his, and she blinked. "Jesus. Stop that. No vampire mojo."

His brows rose, and he said evenly, "As I need your assistance in locating a demon, it would hardly benefit either of us if I used mojo. This is my natural allure."

A breathy laugh escaped her, and she pulled her hand from his. "Thank God. Or whatever." A wry expression flitted over her face; then her gaze flattened, and she observed him with cool professionalism. "Agent Milton gave very few details in her voice mail. And as she has made it clear that all vampire and demon activity doesn't fall within our jurisdiction, I'm not certain what you want from us."

It was not just Lilith's lack of diplomacy; the need to conceal all otherworldly activity had forced her to use federal powers to take over any cases involving it before the local authorities could determine the truth about the abnormal nature of the crimes.

It was a means to a necessary end, but it didn't allow for smooth relations when they were needed. And the few who knew the truth—such as Taylor and Preston—were treated in an overbearing manner that they likely read as a not-so-subtle insult, suggesting a lack of trust or faith in their skills.

Frustration had Colin briefly clenching his teeth before he said, "Quite frankly, I'm not interested in the squabble over jurisdiction; I'll leave that to you and Agent Milton. *I* need your help. You have access to information at a different level than I do through SI."

She regarded him without expression; she could have been Castleford's double. Colin fought the instant irritation that accompanied the realization. "The street level," she said.

"Yes."

Taylor was silent for a moment, then she looked past him and gestured with a lift of her chin. "Is that Savi?" Her eyes narrowed. "And the dog . . . the hellhound?"

His lips firmed. "Yes. I didn't realize you were acquainted with Miss Murray." Not well enough to use her nickname.

"Not much face-to-face after the Feds grabbed the investigation last year. Primarily by e-mail after that. She has a lot of questions." She glanced at Colin again, her gaze speculative. "And quite a few answers; she's more willing to share information than others are. Information that allows me to better perform my job, and protect my partner and myself—recognizing demons and Guardians, vampire strengths and weaknesses. All very, very useful."

He bit back his smile; Taylor had apparently learned about the power of bargaining, as well. "I can supplement her answers."

Taylor nodded. "I thought so. What do you need from us?"

Colin quickly described the identity theft, the vampires who'd been following him. "Miss Murray can track any recorded activity—police reports if the Navigators are involved, financial transactions—but it doesn't give us an accurate representation of their movements."

She flipped through the folder he'd given her. "You just want me to keep my eyes open, then. And listen around, see if anyone's talking about these guys."

"Yes. You don't want to engage or approach them," he said. "This isn't typical behavior for a vampire community. If a demon is directing them, they may disregard the Rules."

She looked up at him. "You mean he might have them kill. Kill humans."

"Yes."

Letting go a long breath, she nodded again and said, "How will I know him from you?"

It hadn't occurred to Colin. He was unaccustomed to being mistaken for anyone else. He stared at her blankly before remembering, "Miss Murray has been working on a gadget. I'll request that one be sent to you."

"We can't ask her now?" Taylor looked through the window again.

He hesitated; then he heard Savi's laughter, the echoing rumble from the suitor. "No." Taylor might not respond kindly to his draining the sod dry. Savi likely wouldn't, either.

Her eyebrows drew together, but she nodded. "There's Joe anyway."

She gripped the door handle, pulled it open.

"Detective Taylor."

She paused, glanced back at him.

"I know you are not on the best of terms, but Milton and Castleford have answers, if you seek them. More answers than Miss Murray and I do."

Taylor sighed. "I saw an angel drop Castleford out of thin air into the middle of Savi's apartment. His throat had been torn out. I saw kids who'd been ripped apart by something neither Heaven nor Hell wanted. Then I saw what Lucifer did to that dog . . . right in front of us, after the poor thing had saved our lives." She gestured toward Sir Pup; her fingers shook. "Considering that both Milton and Castleford chose to be human, I don't think the answers they have to give are what I want to hear."

He smiled without humor. "I've had a similar experience of late."

CHAPTER 16

Anyone who enters into a bargain or a wager with a demon can get out of it, until the demon fulfills his part. If either party dies with the bargain incomplete, then the human or demon—whichever still owes something to the other—is sent to Hell, and their soul frozen in eternal torment. A pretty bad deal, imho.

—Savi to Taylor, 2007

❧

She could have been happy with him.

Manu Suraj was exactly the type of man she'd have chosen for herself—that Nani might have chosen, as well. So attractive—and with his dark hair and eyes, his unpretentious eyeglasses and clothing, intelligence, and fantastic laugh—the type of man she'd always been with in the past.

He should have been perfect. He probably was. The problem lay with Savi; she shouldn't have allowed herself to fall for someone completely unsuitable.

As long as she didn't fall any deeper, she'd be okay. Or she hoped. Was there an event horizon or a point of no return for such things? Would a person traveling through an event horizon know it? But she could still pull herself out.

She *could*.

"You don't live with your *nani*?" Manu sipped from his cup, his gaze steady on hers.

Shaking her head, she said, "No. I couldn't do it anymore." Her lips curved in remembrance. "One day, I'd rented *Bend It Like Beckham*, thinking that it would be a nice change from the Bollywood movies she always brought home. And something I could watch without falling asleep halfway through a dance number."

Manu began laughing softly, and Savi was certain he could see where she was heading before she finished her explanation. Perfect.

"So, we got to the part in the car . . . you remember that?" At his nod, she grinned and continued, "They weren't even naked, but she made me cover my eyes—and I decided that living on my own might be a nice change. God, if I'd rented *Monsoon Wedding* I'd probably be living in another state right now."

She looked down into her cup, swirled the tea at the bottom. It hadn't been that simple, but it had been a different point of no return. Though one of her own making. "I think she enjoys living alone, though. Her friends come over quite a bit—and it's the first time that she hasn't had to take care of someone in . . ." Savi blinked in realization. "Well, her entire life. But she still nags, of course."

" '*Beta,* did you eat today, or was it only junk?' "

"Your parents, too?" She glanced at him in sincere sympathy, though her smile tempered it with humor. "College, food . . . riding the bus. She's certain I'll be killed on it."

"Yes. God forbid I walk outside without a jacket and three layers, even during the summer." He regarded her closely. "If you don't mind my asking, how is it that you don't have your degree? Your *nani* seems as if she'd push you, just as my parents did."

"Oh." She glanced down at her hands, then at the window. It was difficult to see much outside; their reflections hid the darkness beyond. Movement near her feet on the opposite side of the glass caught her eye: Sir Pup. She smiled down at him. "She did, I just . . . I just kind of didn't follow through. I have my bachelor's, but . . ." She lifted her shoulder. "Not the same as a master's or doctorate."

"What was it in?"

His tone had changed from simple curiosity to something more; this was not just about her personality, discovering if they would get along—this was the interview.

"Premed. I went to Berkeley when I was fifteen, then to

Stanford after getting the bachelor's. I was in my second year in the medical program when—" When a demon had used Savi's stupid mistake with the IDs to threaten Nani's status. "—when I transferred to SF State so I could help at Auntie's—Nani's restaurant—and I switched to electrical engineering. Then I got frustrated with that, so I went to mechanical. Then into a liberal arts program, because I hadn't done that before. History and literature, but the papers drove me nuts. Same with physics—I like the reading and the research, and the theory, but there wasn't a future in it for me. I don't have any ambition to publish or teach. And getting stuck for years in one line of theory—or one project—while doing research and development didn't appeal, either."

Manu's eyebrows drew together, his fingers clenching on the cup.

Stop, Savi.

She couldn't. "Then to programming and information systems, which was rather redundant by that point. I thought about going back to medical school, but my credits had expired and I didn't want to redo everything I already knew. And I considered CalTech, but I didn't want to move away from Nani. So I went into graphic design, but I wasn't very good at it. So I dropped out of that program, too. And then finally dropped school altogether, and worked on a few other projects."

He leaned back in his chair a little. "What are you doing now?"

She swallowed. "I just started a new job. Updating a law enforcement personnel database. It's mostly data entry."

Biting her lip, she watched his reaction. Confusion, withdrawal. She should have lied.

His gaze dropped to his cup before he met hers again. "I looked up your name after you contacted me. Online."

She tried to smile. "I did you, too."

He nodded, pressed his lips together. "Are you the same Savitri Murray that developed the DemonSlayer game? Your name is on the credits for the card game, but I thought it must be someone else until you mentioned Auntie's, and your projects . . . I just put it together with that stuff on the news from last year." His brow furrowed. "Do you actually believe in all that?"

All that. Her smile widened. She was probably blinding him with it. "Vampires and demons and guardian angels?"

His expression lightened, as if the words, when spoken aloud, declared their own absurdity. "Yeah. Sorry."

Her knuckles were white with tension. Lilith's voice suddenly echoed in her head: *Can you be happy lying?*

But marriage wasn't about that. Not *just* that. And it didn't matter; she wasn't going to be happy either way. She should lie. Concealing the truth wouldn't hurt him. She should—

"Yes," she blurted. *Stop, Savi.* But she didn't. "I do."

The right words, but the wrong time to say them.

And he was so perfect, so *nice*; he steered the conversation back to innocuous topics, the kind they'd started with—though he likely thought her insane at best, and an idiot at worst. Not much different from what she'd called herself many times since Caelum.

Since Colin.

It was ten minutes before Manu paused, and said earnestly, "Savi, we get along well, so I really enjoyed meeting you. But for marriage . . ." He took a deep breath, studied her with an apologetic curve to his mouth. "I just don't think we'd suit."

Not unexpected, yet it was still difficult to hear. She gave a short, soundless laugh, dipping her head in acknowledgment. "No," she agreed. She rubbed the back of her neck, glanced up at him. "We probably wouldn't."

"But it was great meeting you," Manu repeated as he slid from his chair. "It's gotten late, though, and I should . . ." He hesitated, waved toward the door with his hand. "Do you need a ride?"

She shook her head. There was no reason to make this any more awkward than it was.

It seemed less pathetic to watch him leave than to hide her face in her hands. At least until he moved past the wide windows and could no longer see her; then she could privately berate herself for her stupidity. Though she couldn't imagine Manu telling too many people the truth behind his reason for rejecting her, how long would it be before word had spread through the Desi community, spoken in loud whispers over dal and roti, sandwiched between comparisons of MCAT scores and wedding costs, until all of Nani's acquaintances thought that her granddaughter danced naked in the moonlight and worshipped demons?

They would blame it on America, and TV. And the number of suitable men willing to meet her would quickly decline.

She'd completely screwed herself over—and she wasn't certain if she'd done it deliberately. And if she had, if it was for her sake . . . or for his.

With a sigh, she turned to the window again. Sir Pup had his head raised, looking at something across the street. She narrowed her eyes, trying to focus through the reflection—but it was too bright inside, too dark out. Until a passing vehicle's headlights illuminated—

Colin. Standing beside his new car with his jaw set and his gaze locked on Manu. Oblivious to the vampire's attention, he walked quickly down the sidewalk, his shoulders hunched against the rain.

Savi blinked in surprise, and Colin was on this side of the street, his long stride easily matching Manu's rapid steps.

Her chair scraped against the tile floor as she jumped to her feet, pressed her palms against the cool windowpane. "Don't do anything," she said desperately, loudly, staring through the glass. The couple at a nearby table turned to look at her—but she'd just admitted to a potential suitor that she believed in vampires. Talking to herself was nothing.

Colin turned and flashed a playful grin over his shoulder. His eyebrows tilted in mock innocence. *Me?*

She saw his lips move, and Manu halted. His mouth dropped open as he looked up into Colin's face.

Oh, god. It worked on heterosexual men, too.

"Sir Pup, stop him."

The hellhound yawned and lowered his head to his paws.

Relief slipped through her. If Colin had been intent on hurting Manu, Sir Pup wouldn't have allowed it. Or would have at least showed signs of nervousness.

And Colin was . . . her lips parted, and her throat dried. Both men stood in profile to her, and the intensity of Colin's gaze as he spoke to Manu sent heat tearing through her—and she wasn't even the focus of it.

Then Colin smiled, and his fangs gleamed. Manu stiffened, took a step back, nodding frantically.

Apparently satisfied with that response, Colin turned on his heel, walked toward the café entrance. Savi took her seat again, tried to smooth her ragged nerves. Silence fell over the patrons facing the door when he strode through, and deepened as others looked up to see the cause of the sudden hush; then it was broken as, behind the counter, a barista dropped a dish.

Despite the noise, despite the attention, Colin's gaze didn't stray from her. He stopped next to her table, but made no move to take the seat opposite.

"No wonder you're reclusive, if this is what happens when you go somewhere," she said, and her gaze drifted down to his throat, his chest. He'd worn the blue sweater. "It fits."

He performed a slow spin, his arms held wide in blatant invitation to look and enjoy. She did. "Beautifully," he agreed when he faced her again. "Everything does. You've excellent taste."

Rolling her eyes, she took a sip from her cup and attempted to appear unaffected. "Not mine. I just remembered where you'd made the majority of your clothes purchases." And there had been a lot of them in his financial records; his wardrobe must have been completely destroyed in the fire.

But then, previous years' records indicated he replaced his wardrobe regularly.

"Yours. I could eat you in those boots." He smiled lazily, as if the sudden increase in her heartbeat and the catch in her breath pleased him. "I may yet. Come and sit with me, Savi."

He lifted her cup, threaded the fingers of his left hand through hers, and tugged.

She blinked in sudden understanding; a mirror sat above the bar. The café was shaped like an L, with sofas and comfortable, upholstered chairs in the short leg—and it angled outside of the mirror's reflection.

"Or this is why you're reclusive," she said as he led her to an unoccupied love seat. "Mirrors everywhere. And cameras."

"Yes." He brought the cup to his lips, inhaled. His eyes closed. "What is this?"

How could he sniff tea and make it an exercise in sensuality? "Chai. Tea, milk, vanilla, sugar, and cinnamon. A little ginger." Food, everyday ingredients. Something she knew intimately; listing them shouldn't have this effect on her, make her want to pour it over herself and let him inhale her, too.

Colin set it on the low table in front of the love seat, drew her down beside him. Resting his arm along the back, he turned toward her.

His pale gaze held her immobile. "Don't move," he said softly.

She couldn't anyway. His warm hand tilted her chin up; he leaned forward, his mouth hovering above hers, and breathed in.

Exactly as she'd wanted. But she wanted more.

"Cinnamon. Vanilla." His thumb traced the curve of her bottom lip. "What I would not give for a taste. I am mad for you, Savitri." *Did you intend to string me along until I was so mad for you that I'd beg and promise to forsake every other woman for a taste of you?*

She hadn't. But she didn't need to think about what he could give; she'd already thought it over—dreamed it, wished it—too much, and it came easily. So easily.

"A month," she said against his mouth. "I want a month."

His brows drew together. Pulling away, he echoed, "A month?"

She couldn't interpret the sudden hardness in his eyes, the clench of his jaw. She looked at her hands fisted in her lap. She could do this. There was nothing left to lose, anyway. And if he said no, why not pile one rejection on top of another?

"A month. Just me. I'll give you as much blood as I can; I've been looking at donation and testing sites to see how much is safe. And I'll look for any drugs that will keep me from becoming too anemic, and boost my blood production. And if you supplement with animal . . . I know you can't for long, not more than a month or two."

Probably not two; he'd had to rely on animal blood the year before, and it took time to rebuild immunity against it. Years, for most vampires, but he was stronger than most.

"I don't want you to get to the point that its degenerative effects begin to slow you down, or make you sick, especially not with a demon impersonating you. And if it's only a month you'll be at full strength again within a couple of days of regular feeding—"

"Stop, Savi."

She bit her lip, held her breath.

"Look at me."

She was too afraid. "Tell me first."

His silence stretched her lungs tight, knotted her stomach.

"On the condition that you move into my house for the duration," he finally said. "I want you readily available to me."

She exhaled, and a relieved smile curved her lips as she met his eyes. "Won't that be like scavenging?"

"*And* on the condition that you never remember anything I said to you when I was being an ass."

"There won't be many conversations to recall, then."

"No." He brought her hand to his lips, watching her over the kiss he pressed to her fingers. The tip of his tongue swept into the sensitive juncture between her middle and ring fingers, streaked a wet line of heat from her hand to her sex.

"Let's go," she breathed, and tried to pull her hand from his, get to her feet. She might as well have tried to escape a singularity. Yes, she'd likely already crossed that critical point. Nothing to do now but let it take her.

"Your impatience is flattering, but I'm too aggrieved to give in so easily; you have completely disrupted my plan to seduce you into my bed tonight. I'd thought of witty observations, romantic lyrics designed to sweep you off your feet. Yet all my scheming has gone to waste."

He smiled against her hand when she laughed, but he made no effort to move.

"One more condition: If you'll make a list, I'll procure any medications you require through Ramsdell—but if the drugs have side effects, don't use them." His eyes narrowed thoughtfully, and his voice carried a thread of something that sounded like wonder . . . or hope. "And it's possible that with your new strength, you'll not need them."

She shook her head and turned her palm over. He glanced down at the jagged cut, just beginning to scab over; then back up, his brow lifted in query.

"It's not healing at an accelerated rate. I doubt my blood

production has increased. In vampires and Guardians, the two seem to go together."

His lashes lowered as he examined the wound again. "I could heal it for you with my blood—as I did before."

She curled her fingers, covered her palm. "No. Some scars are better to carry. This one will remind me to be careful of my shields, so that I don't endanger those around me by attracting wyrmwolves."

"You cannot forget."

"No, but I don't always think." She tried not to laugh at his affronted stare. "You were being an ass then—but you were right."

"If I was right, then I suppose it is acceptable to mention it." His hand lifted from the back of the love seat, and he tweaked a short strand of hair near her temple. "We shall have a matching pair, Savitri."

She glanced down as he spread his fingers, turned his palm up. The overhead lights shone on the ridge of the clean, straight scar. His hand, so strong and elegant.

She clenched her thighs together, remembering how easily he had brought her pleasure that afternoon. Thinking of how desperately she wanted it again. She had to swallow before she said, "It's comforting to know that you have *one* flaw."

He gave a short, deep laugh, exposing his fangs before he dipped his chin and hid them. He slanted her an upward glance, his eyes bright with amusement. "I hate to cause you discomfort, my sweet Savitri, but this is not a flaw."

She arched an eyebrow. "No? It's brought *you* much discomfort. Don't you resent the sword's effects? You don't enjoy the . . . the—" Unwilling to say "Chaos" aloud, she settled for, "—what you see in the mirror."

"No." He leaned back, his elbow propped against the back of the sofa, and he rested his chin on his loosely curled fist as he studied her. "But it is a price worth paying."

"For not immediately burning in the sun? Extra strength? Giving an orgasm with a sip?"

His lips quirked. "You make my argument for me." Then he sobered, and said, "Ramsdell and Emily were also tainted; it is not for myself I am grateful, but for them. What it gave them."

She quickly reviewed everything she knew of the couple. "But I thought there hadn't been any lingering—" Her lips rounded as she realized, "Oh, my god. I hadn't really calculated the date before, their age. He'd been a Guardian, so it didn't strike me as unusual, but she . . . and on the same night?"

"Yes." His throat worked, and a sheen rose in his eyes before he turned his head in profile. "I didn't expect it for several more years. Perhaps another quarter century. They never appeared much older than fifty, though they were over twice that and ridiculously healthy." He expelled a long breath, smiled slightly as if in memory. "I heard them in their room. She said she was a bit tired, and he said that perhaps it was time to see what came next."

Oh, god. She could hardly speak past the lump in her throat. "Colin—" Her hands shook as she touched his shoulders, his jaw.

"I found them in their bed, wrapped in each other's arms, as if that was exactly what they'd done—turned to each other, and left to see what came next. If their faces were any indication, whatever they found together was perfect. Beautiful." His eyes locked with hers, and the moisture pooled there seemed to flood hers. "It gave them that, Savitri. A bit of Hell is nothing."

She couldn't respond; only look at him, touch him. Her fingers traced his brow, the angular beauty of his cheekbones.

He sighed, caught her wrists. "Oh, sweet, don't cry. I can't bear it."

"Then don't tell me stories like that. I'm such a sucker for happy endings. It's my mother's fault," she whispered, and leaned forward to bury her face in his neck. She'd have given anything for her family to have had something like that, instead of violence and fear. "Do you miss them?"

"Every bloody day." His arms tightened around her, and his voice was rough in her ear. "No more crying. I shall have to punish you if you stain my sweater with your tears. It has quickly become my favorite."

She choked on her laughter. When she pulled back, he had a handkerchief ready, and she gratefully mopped her face with it. She glanced around them; everyone on the other seats and sofas was looking intently at something else.

"Shit," she breathed, her cheeks flushing. "Is there any other way I can make a spectacle of myself tonight?"

"I could push up your skirt and take you here," he said, shrugging lightly, but the intensity of his gaze when it lowered to her legs belied the casual gesture and tone. She looked, too; she'd turned toward him, and the linen had slid up to expose a few inches of skin above her boots.

He brushed his fingertips across the sensitive inside of her lower thigh; her body reacted to the touch as if had been a kiss to her mouth, a slow lick through moisture and heat.

"I could drink from you. Make you scream as you come."

"That would do it," she said, her voice not much higher than a moan. Though she was tempted to adjust it the opposite direction, she tugged her hem down over her knees, smoothed the line of it. If he touched her again, she just might not be able to help herself. "Is that what you threatened Manu with?"

"My sweet Savitri." A smile teased his lips. "That was full on ten minutes. Was it terribly torturous?"

"Not *terribly*."

His gray eyes gleamed with sudden pleasure. "I shall assume that my presence erased all concern for him from your thoughts, stifling your curiosity."

"Or I didn't want confirmation that you'd been eavesdropping again. There are moments of stupidity I'd rather suffer with as few witnesses as possible."

"You speak of your shocking admission that you believe in ghouls and goblins?" He caught the tip of his tongue between his teeth, as if to hold back laughter. "Do not fear, sweet. I said it might behoove him to forget you admitted to such, and that if an explanation for his rejection must be given, he should say your beauty and intelligence overwhelmed him. Upon the realization he could never be a match for you, he sacrificed you so you could be with someone you would love. And that he will live in agonies for the rest of his life for cocking up his one opportunity with the woman of his dreams."

Her stomach dropped. To hide her dismay, she averted her face and collected her teacup from the table, drank down the last of the lukewarm contents.

"Are you displeased with me?"

She pressed her lips together, shook her head. "With myself." Setting her cup down, she forced herself to look at him, met his questioning gaze. And she admitted it to herself, as much as she did him, "I did it on purpose, knowing what the result would be. And I have no idea how I've gotten to such a point that I tell the truth to people that don't matter to me so that I can fuck up any chance of finding a husband in this community, yet I lie to Nani, who does matter, and whom my confession would have embarrassed the most. And I should be glad that you saved me from myself. But mostly I just want to leave here and spend the night in your bed, and not think about how I'm going to lie to Nani again when I do the complete opposite of what I promised her: stay at your house for a month, instead of meet with suitable men."

Though Colin had watched her steadily throughout, his expression unreadable, at the last his brows rose and he said, "I'm eminently suitable. Handsome and rich. A Cambridge graduate, though I confess I was far too interested in feminine studies to accumulate honors. You could claim to be trying me out."

Closing her eyes against her laughter, she pinched the bridge of her nose and tried to rid herself of the ache behind her forehead. "I just need to tell her."

"Yes."

She exhaled, nodded. Looked back up at him. Had she ever thought his eyes were cold? Perhaps a warm, sunlit winter. "What aren't you telling me? Last night, I announced my intention to go home with you and you almost dragged me out of my chair to your bed. Why are we still here?"

A wry smile tilted the corners of his mouth. "I did not want to frighten you."

The shiver that ran up her neck wasn't at all pleasant, but cold, clammy. "Should we be frightened?"

His hands enfolded one of hers, brought it down to his upper thigh. A hard, steel length lay beneath the fine wool of his trousers. "Not precisely what I'd like you to touch in that location, but it's there if you want it."

A gun. Either loaded with tranquilizer darts made with hellhound venom, or bullets laced with the same. The bullets would hurt a vampire, slow one down—perhaps even temporarily disable it—but the venom wouldn't have an effect on one.

Only on a demon or nosferatu.

Her fingers trembled as they slid higher, found the edge of his pocket. She wouldn't have anything to fear from a demon, but Colin would. His speed and strength would easily overcome any other vampire, even if he didn't have a weapon—but a gun and the venom would be necessary for him to even the odds with a demon.

"When?"

"Directly after we sat down. The pup sent it to me."

Good dog. And for him to sense it before Colin had, he must have scented it physically instead of psychically; was the demon trying to conceal itself to surprise Colin? Or just observing him? "Would it dare attack you here?"

"I hope not; I'd hate to pay for damages done to the place." His boyish grin accompanied the statement, but his gaze was humorless as it centered over her shoulder. "Take it out, Savi. If it comes to that, the pup will send me more. Or do the job himself."

She began to turn her head, but he caught her chin, met her eyes.

"If it comes to that, and you can't run . . . grab the pup and hold on to him, and he'll run for you." He leaned forward when her lips parted in surprise, and dropped a quick kiss against them. "And I'm making it a condition: if you want a month, I have to know you'll protect yourself first."

"If I were interested in protecting myself, I wouldn't stay with you for a month." She returned his kiss before he could reply, using her body to shield her hand's movement from the other patrons. She didn't want the weapon, would rather it be available to Colin; the demon could move more quickly than she could hope to aim. But if it reassured Colin to know that she had some protection, she'd take it.

No silencer. Dammit. She slid it beneath her thigh, thumbed off the safety, and kept her forefinger against the trigger guard.

Sir Pup flopped to the floor next to her feet, laid his head on her boots.

"Hugh told you? About the fugues?"

"Yes. No worries, Savitri. You're safe here for now." He rested his hand on her knee, squeezed it comfortingly. "Good God, but I'm a handsome devil."

Savi burst into laughter, and it eased the nervous tension that had overtaken her. Whether Colin had done it for that purpose, or just to annoy the demon who sat down in the chair opposite the love seat, she didn't know. How wonderfully insulting, for a human to laugh at a demon's approach instead of fearing it, yet couching the statement in flattery.

And the demon was a perfect replica, though his smile had a hard cast to it, his gray eyes without the lively humor she'd come to adore in Colin's. He'd altered his hair since the DMV photo had been taken, smoothing the rumpled golden strands into a neat cut.

The change wasn't unexpected; demons' egos disallowed them from disappearing completely into another persona. The physical features remained the same, but minute adjustments in mannerism and style reflected the demon inside.

She worried her bottom lip with her teeth as she studied him. Something else was different, though she couldn't determine exactly what it was.

The demon met her gaze, then glanced down at Sir Pup. For an instant, uneasiness flickered across his face. But the public venue gave them no more advantage than it did him, and his expression changed to mockery.

"Given the legend that you have created for yourself amongst the vampire communities here and in London, I had wondered what sort of vampire I would find. But it is a pathetic, neutered one, using a hellhound for protection and bargaining with a human for blood. I wonder that I should even bother to kill you; you would do well to end it yourself."

The demon must've heard Colin speaking, yet he didn't try to emulate the vampire perfectly. He used a clipped, almost ridiculously posh accent; for the first time, given the comparison, Savi could hear his century in the U.S. in Colin's voice.

But if the demon intended to make Colin feel inferior, he must not have studied the vampire very well.

Colin erased every bit of American inflection as he said,

"Already one is bored. Is originality impossible amongst demonkind? With such a face, you ought to be fascinating, brilliantly innovative; instead, you rely on ye olde demon routine and exhibit the inimitability of a BBC news anchor. One finds oneself utterly disappointed."

Savi couldn't discern much difference between demon and vampire, but from the subtle tightening of the demon's face, Colin had outclassed him.

Savi took it as her cue. Many demons didn't handle insult well, and they were more likely to talk when angry or defensive. "Lilith would've had you jumping from a bridge at this point, and she was only a halfling."

"Not a bridge. That passed out of fashion years ago." Colin shuddered facetiously, then raked his gaze over the demon's form, the pinstriped three-piece suit and red tie, the fat diamond pinkie ring. Apparently satisfied he'd made his point, he eased back into his hybrid accent. "With that in mind, I should lend you access to my closet. I can hardly allow you to go about impersonating me dressed as an oversexed gangster. Neutered, indeed. People will begin to think me all mouth and trousers."

Though his eyes briefly flared red, the demon's lips tilted in amusement. "You do well to enjoy yourself now. You have not much longer to live."

"That is unfortunate. Though time is relative when one is immortal; 'not much longer' can mean so many things: a day, a year, a century," Colin said easily. "Pray do not keep me in suspense, and tell me which it will be."

"I believe your suspense will not come from anticipation of your demise, but of hers."

Savi's eyes widened, and Colin's fingers tightened on her knee.

"Then I shall have sixty years, at the very least." His lazy tone didn't change, but steel lay beneath it now.

"I rather doubt it." The demon's gaze shifted to her. "Your continued existence is a thorn in my side, Savitri Murray. I intend to pluck you out."

"A human?" Colin mocked him openly. "You concern yourself with a human?"

"Who has inconvenienced me to an intolerable degree. I am

not above revenge." He smiled to himself. "I'm far below it."

But what could have— "The nosferatu on the plane," Savi realized.

"Yes. It promised to be such a rewarding alliance. You cannot imagine how limiting it is to be bound by the Rules. We cannot kill humans, we cannot go against their free will. One would have thought closing Hell's Gates would have given us a reprieve, but alas, no."

"But the nosferatu had been a convenient way around that," she said.

"And now vampires are," Colin said. "Also less bother, as we do not pose a threat to you as the nosferatu might have done."

Most vampires wouldn't, but Colin probably could; was he downplaying his strength? His difference?

The demon leaned forward, placed his elbows on his knees. His voice lowered conspiratorially. "Oh, but you cannot imagine my pleasure in coming into this community, searching for the woman who caused me such distress, and finding that she was connected to a vampire such as yourself. The vampire who had caused such a stir in the London community when he came searching for *me*. The vampire whom those in San Francisco looked to for leadership, but who denied them—and left them in disarray. The vampire who could keep me in the lifestyle I prefer, with little effort on my part. It's a very convenient setup; all it wanted was my initiative. I attain the wealth I need and the sycophants I desire." He steepled his fingers, pointed at Savi. "And they are all too willing to carry out a minimal task to prove their fealty—the one task I cannot perform."

Asking the vampires to kill her. Savi glanced quickly at Colin's face. Anger whitened his lips, drew his skin tight over his cheeks and brow.

"Why are they waiting?" she wondered aloud. There had been plenty of opportunities to take her out—and for the demon to attempt an attack on Colin, as well. She narrowed her eyes. "And why are you warning us?"

"He cannot help himself, sweet," Colin said, his mouth curling into a thin smile. "He's a living cliché; there is no one to congratulate him but himself, and his villainous monologue allows him the pathetic comfort of self-aggrandizement."

Savi nodded. "Next he'll be killing his henchmen."

"Laugh between yourselves, if you must; it only increases *my* pleasure. This disgusting relationship you have developed is ripe with entertainment value." The demon gestured between the two of them. "How gratifying his fear will be, anticipating the moment he fails to protect you. His anguish when he sees your lifeless body. I'll likely kill him while I dance over it. And your terror, knowing the painful end that is near. For me, the wait is almost as satisfying as the act."

Sir Pup sat up when the demon rose to his feet; Savi placed her hand on the scruff of his neck.

"So begin your month; you will not see the end of it. The next full moon will rise over your graves." Staring down at the hellhound, the demon flared his eyes again, then turned back to Savi with a wide grin. "And you need not worry about explaining your whorish behavior to your sweet grandmother. My new allies are delivering a message to her . . . right about now."

Colin's arm around her waist stopped her from launching herself at him. She struggled silently, and the demon laughed, a low and contemptuous rumble.

"Vampires," he said, shaking his head. "Much more effective than the INS. And you've only yourself to blame, Savitri Murray. You hid your connection well—I wouldn't have known of her if you hadn't had such an irresponsible youth. Perhaps a bridge *is* in order, no matter how passé. Or the gun you have would do the trick." He pointed to his temple, cocked his thumb. "Bang."

He disappeared; perhaps Colin had seen him leave, but it had been too quick for Savi.

"Let's go, let's go—" Her voice broke. Colin swept her up and carried her through the café. They were at his car within a moment's time.

"Call Castleford. Warn them." The tires squealed as he pulled into the street, then he was using his phone as well, asking for Detective Taylor.

She got Hugh's voice mail. Tried Lilith's. No answer.

Red and blue lights flashed behind them.

"They had better fucking keep up," Colin growled, and

shifted. The engine wound from a purr to a roar. He looked over at her, and his mouth tightened. "I'll get you there, Savi."

She nodded numbly, though she knew there was only so much he could do. The distance wasn't far, but it wasn't about speed; it was about momentum, and something she'd started long ago. And about being too late to stop it.

CHAPTER 17

I will accede to his request, though I am convinced that, of that party in Switzerland, his wife was the sole being who emerged with a bit of sense. God love intelligent women—though she was far too kind to her monster: she did not make him the originator of his curse. And she was far too kind to her doctor, for not forcing him to bear it.

—Colin to Ramsdell, 1822

"Ohmygod, ohmygod." Savi didn't recognize the low, panicked chant as hers when the restaurant came into view. The front windows were shattered, and one missing completely. No lights shone from inside; it was impossible to see if anyone was moving around. Small, dark holes peppered the front door and stucco façade.

Bullet holes?

She pulled on the handle before Colin screeched to a halt. The scent of burnt rubber assaulted her nose; her ears rang with the approaching sirens and the bystanders' questioning cries. Colin was instantly at her door, took her hand, tucked her into his right side. The length of his sword flashed on his left.

"She's alive, Savi," he said, but his tone warned her that all wasn't well.

They didn't bother with the front door; her boots crunched the glass as she jumped through the window, as her eyes adjusted to the dark.

A large, masculine form was bending over a prone figure. "Hugh?" She ran to his side, fell to her knees. He was holding

Nani. Blood streaked the side of her neck, her stomach. "Oh, god."

"I need you to hold it, Savi. I've got to see to the others." Hugh gestured to the wadded sash he'd pressed to Nani's side. The shoulder of his white T-shirt was crimson. "The blood on her neck is mine; I didn't get her down quickly enough. But Dru is on her way."

A Guardian—a Healer. Nani only had to make it until she arrived. Nodding frantically, Savi took over, applying pressure. Too hard. Nani moaned a little, stirred. Her eyelashes fluttered.

"No, Nani . . . don't wake up. I know it hurts," she said quietly, pushed back a loose strand of hair from Nani's perspiring forehead. Colin crouched beside her. "Can you make her sleep?"

Outside, the scream of the sirens grew louder, then cut off with the squeal of brakes.

Colin leaned down, spoke into Nani's ear. Her body relaxed, though her breath was still shallow, her pulse thready.

"Colin," Hugh said, looking up from a flesh wound on Geetha's arm. "Lilith went after them."

Savi glanced between them. He meant he wanted Colin to go offer Lilith backup, if she needed it.

Anticipation, merciless and hard, flashed over Colin's features. "Do you want any alive?"

Hugh had turned back to Geetha, but the coldness in his voice could've answered for him. "One. For questioning."

Colin nodded and gently caressed Savi's cheek with the tips of his fingers. He no longer had his sword; he must have hidden it when the police arrived.

"I've notified Taylor and Preston, love," he said, his pale gaze holding hers. "They'll be here shortly. They'll have an idea of what truly happened, but Lilith will spin it to anyone else as a gang hit. It'll go over."

She drew in a shuddering breath, wiped at her eyes with her forearm. "Okay. I'll tell Hugh about the demon, too." If Hugh stayed after he'd been healed and spoke with the detectives; he was likely anxious to go help Lilith. "You'd better hurry if you want her to leave *one* alive."

A part of her hoped that he wouldn't.

His lips quirked slightly, but his face darkened. He hesitated, then he stood with a muttered "bloody hell" and disappeared.

Savi looked up as a pair of red tennis shoes came into her view; Dru stood above her, smiling as she squatted beside them, her long white lab coat flaring around her.

"Don't worry, Savitri darling; I'll have her fixed up in a jiffy. She'll only feel a little pinch." She winked as Savi stared at her without expression. "Just a bit of medical humor."

God, but Savi hated Hollywood doctors.

❦

It took little effort to locate Lilith; Colin followed the shrieks of pain, the scent of leaking fuel. Four blocks from Auntie's, he found the Navigator rolled over on its side in a weed-choked lot, the windshield broken out. At the end of the lot, near the rear of a brick building, a vampire lay facedown on the asphalt.

Lilith was on top of him, her knee jammed into his back, her fist locked in his hair and her sword against his throat.

She looked up at Colin's approach, and her angry snarl widened into a wicked smile. "Are you hungry?"

"Starving." Colin's gaze narrowed on the vampire's weapon, lying next to his side. An automatic rifle. Icy rage worked itself from his stomach to his veins. "Were there others?"

"Two." She yanked on the vampire's scalp, and her eyes gleamed when he yowled. "Sir Pup is giving chase."

"I want them," he said softly.

Lilith stared at him for a long moment, then yelled an instruction into the air for the hellhound to return the vampires alive. "If it isn't too late," she added with a lift of her brows. "Hugh?"

"Healed."

Her throat worked. "Good." She bent toward the vampire's ear. "For you. You wouldn't believe the tortures I'd have designed for you. I've had the best instructors."

The vampire coughed, spit. His nose was bloodied, his forehead raw and spotted with flecks of mud; she'd likely slammed his face into the ground. "Fuck you," he managed, and Lilith sighed.

"Allow me," Colin said. He laid his sword on the ground and crouched in front of them. Studied the clothes, the face. Pale skin, though it retained some natural olive pigmentation. His eyes were closed, but judging by the dark hair, Colin would wager they were brown. The vampire couldn't have been older than twenty when he'd been transformed, and probably in the past year or two. Not more than a boy. "Look at me."

Dull brown eyes, not the rich bittersweet chocolate of Savitri's. The vampire gasped, and emitted a low, panicked moan. His mouth slackened, revealing his fangs, his tongue.

"Fuck me," Lilith breathed. "Your beauty can be terrifying sometimes, Colin."

"Yes."

He felt her stare a moment longer before she turned her head.

She didn't allow the vampire the same mercy.

Colin reached out, ran the backs of his fingers down the vampire's cool, rainwet cheek. "Tell me your name."

"Denver." The boy shuddered. "Denver Jennings."

"Denver." Colin rolled it seductively off his tongue. There was no chance the boy was older than his estimate with a name like that. By the way Lilith's form stiffened, she realized it, as well. "Where is your partner, Denver? One of those who escaped?"

If fear didn't convince the boy to talk, the threat of losing his partner might.

"No," the boy panted. "She was an elder. The nosferatu killed her last year; I was only with her for a month. These are my friends. He asked me to turn them." Fat tears rolled down his cheeks, but he hadn't yet blinked or looked away from Colin's face. "*You* aren't him."

Colin smiled, clasped his hands loosely in front of him, his elbows on his knees. "No. I'm not him. Why would you follow a demon?"

Denver shook his head, the movement abbreviated by Lilith's tight hold. "A vampire. Like us, only stronger. We'd all heard of him. He's been here for a long time. And he feeds us; those who don't have anyone else. And the bloodlust doesn't make us . . . make us—"

"No. A demon." Colin raised his head, met Lilith's eyes. Dismay was written across her face. Only too obvious what had happened: the demon had taken advantage of those vampires without a partner. Those who faced expulsion from the community for breaking its rules, and who were likely too young and ignorant of any other options available to them.

But there were other, more important Rules to follow.

"You tried to murder humans, Denver. My consort's grandmother. Her brother."

"Tainted humans. He said their blood will kill us, and we made a bargain." His tears fell faster. "And the others are vampire slayers."

"A little old lady?" Lilith growled the words. "You're fucking joking."

Denver broke into harsh sobs. Colin studied his terrified face, pushed away the pity. "Pull him up, Lilith. I want a sip."

The clatter of claws announced Sir Pup's return; two vampires dangled from his enormous jaws. Alive, though unconscious. Colin would deal with them next.

Denver looked at the hellhound, and a squeal of fear lent a pathetic note to his cries. Colin lifted his hand to the boy's neck, flicked his fingers against his racing pulse.

The boy fell silent, torn between terror and desire. Behind him, Lilith grimaced and turned her head.

"I'm not going to kill you," Colin said, then smiled coldly. "Unless you struggle and bloody my sweater."

Lilith backed away with an expression of wry gratitude. After such a warning and the horrifying specter of the hellhound, the boy wasn't going to move.

"I do intend to teach you a lesson. I'll show you what awaits anything that makes a bargain with a demon. And when I've finished, I'll put you into Agent Milton's tender care." His smile faded. "You and your friends will be extremely helpful, and answer any questions we have, won't you?"

Lilith's eyebrows knitted. "Colin—"

"It'll be punishment enough, Lilith," he said, his voice hard. He returned his attention to Denver and repeated, "Won't you?"

Denver nodded, took a deep breath as if to prepare himself.

Preparation was impossible. Colin tilted his head and sank his fangs into the boy's neck. Blood, thick and young and heady. He forced away the pleasure of it.

And called up Chaos.

❧

The gentle murmur of voices alerted Colin to Castleford's arrival. Sitting on his heels, his elbows braced against his knees, Colin lifted his head and watched blearily as Lilith wrapped her arms around the other man's neck. Castleford hugged her tight. He'd replaced his bloodied shirt with some hideous tunic a Guardian had likely created for him.

And Lilith melted softly against him.

Colin hadn't vomited in almost two hundred years—not since the drinking binge that had followed news of Anthony Ramsdell's death on a Spanish battlefield—but he thought he might at that moment.

He rested the back of his head against the brick wall behind him and let the cold stone support its pounding weight. What a bloody ridiculous mistake channeling memories of Chaos had been, though he couldn't completely blame his headache on that realm. If he ever again had to punish a trio of idiots, he'd remember to seal their mouths shut first. Denver had screamed shrilly into his ear, as had the third boy.

But they'd learned their lesson well—and if they remained awake long enough, wouldn't forget its effects . . . even if they didn't remember the actual feeding.

Nor would they forget Sir Pup carrying them through the city to SI's holding cells; Lilith had only told the hellhound to avoid being seen, not to be gentle with them. It was no more than they deserved.

Savitri's tearstained face rose in his mind, her trembling hands as she'd held her grandmother.

Chaos had been much less than they'd deserved.

Colin rose to his feet, ignored the ringing in his ears, the throbbing behind his forehead. "Who's protecting Savi?"

Without relinquishing his hold on Lilith, Castleford turned toward him. "Drifter. Michael. Dru. Auntie has regained consciousness; Taylor was speaking with them when I left."

Relief eased the tension from his muscles, the lingering ache in his head. Releasing a long breath, Colin closed his eyes and nodded. "Thank you. Did Savi have an opportunity to tell you about the demon? His threat to her?"

"Yes. Though she elaborated better on his threat to you."

Surprise etched a line between Lilith's brows. "She saw him?"

Unwilling to stay away from Savi much longer, Colin began walking back toward the restaurant. Lilith and Castleford fell into step beside him, listened as he detailed the meeting in the café.

Lilith groaned when he finished. "Describe him to me again?"

Colin indicated his length with a sweep of his hand. "Though much less appealing, I assure you."

"I'm this close to gutting you," she said.

Castleford grinned, and drew her to his opposite side as if to prevent her from carrying out her threat. "Savi said he seemed a cross between a 1920s gangster and a 1970s mobster. His posture, his clothes. Given the manner in which they hit Auntie's, it could be Dalkiel. Or Rugziel."

Lilith shook her head. "Rugziel is dead—1975, a New York subway." Castleford glanced at her, his brows lifted. She shrugged and added, "He was one of Belial's. Lucifer didn't care if I killed him." She leaned forward a little to look at Colin again. "If it's Dalkiel, we would expect tactics similar to this—finding muscle in the disenfranchised part of a population, running up their fear to make them do things they normally wouldn't. But also trying to manipulate the stronger, established community by promising 'a new era,' shit like that."

"And if he doesn't act as you expect?" Colin said quietly, and halted in the middle of the sidewalk. Auntie's was a block away now, and he could clearly hear the activity surrounding it: the rote questions of the police officers and the answers given from bystanders; Savi's query to her grandmother, ascertaining her comfort; Taylor's impatience with Michael. Rain pattered softly against the awning overhead. "You didn't anticipate a demon coming after Savitri, though you knew the nosferatu had been allied with one."

"We also didn't anticipate having a vampire community leaderless for so long, nor so many willing to act as a demon's assassins." Castleford slid his hands into his pockets, regarded him evenly. "What do you suggest we do?"

Bloody hell. There was no mistaking the censure in Castleford's tone. Was he trying to lecture Colin into the role? "I suggest you find Dalkiel, and do what you do best: play the executioner."

Lilith's fingers clenched at her sides. "Until another comes to take his place? Brilliant, Colin. Absolutely fucking brilliant."

He returned her stare, affected a bored tone. "I'm a second son, Agent Milton. I drink. I fuck. I remain useless. It is not just my birthright, it is my preference."

Lilith tilted her head and studied him with shadowed eyes. "You're a vampire, Colin. What gave you the impression that your free will is of any concern to us when human lives are at stake? Savi's life."

"And your brother is dead. As is his heir, and his heir. As is your sister, and all of her children." Hugh didn't flinch as he delivered the statement; the executioner at his most merciless, words his weapons. "It has been many years since I've concerned myself with the laws of primogeniture, but I believe that leaves you in a position to acquire a bit of responsibility."

Manipulative bastards, the both of them; this wasn't what they believed, but digging at what he did. And they would corner him into it, but Savi was his only concern—the only responsibility that mattered to him.

"Yes, but how can I protect her and assume a position of leadership? You ask the impossible." But if he could make the role assist him in defending her against the demon . . .

Bloody fucking hell. Hadn't he made the decision when he'd taken responsibility for the boys' punishments? When he'd spoken with Detective Taylor? When he'd slain the woman in the alley?

"I want Fia, and her partner, Paul. And any other vampires you can spare."

Triumph flared in Lilith's eyes. Good God, little wonder it had annoyed Savi so badly when he'd shown his. "They'll continue their training, I hope."

"Yes." Colin glanced between them. "But I—and they— won't answer to you."

Castleford shrugged and began walking again. "Then don't do anything for which you'll be made answerable."

Colin waited until his irritation faded before heading out into the rain after them. Christ. He wasn't above irritating them in turn. "You do realize, my dear agents, that I'm the least suitable vampire for the role? Indeed, the only reason you've coerced me into this is because I'm much like Dalkiel: I have physical power, and don't follow tradition overmuch."

"Like him, yes, but with better ends." Castleford glanced over his shoulder. "Also because you don't like to serve, and you understand that's what leadership of this type would be. When they are ready, and you have a suitable replacement, you can leave them. The demon would never voluntarily relinquish his power. I think you'll suit."

"Most vampire communities require partnerships and bloodsharing for its members, including the head," Colin pointed out. "San Francisco is no exception."

Lilith rolled her eyes. "You're a freak. Just do your great and terrible beauty thing and convince them to love you."

Castleford raised a brow. "What thing?"

"I don't know. Except for Belial, I've never seen anything like it. Have you?"

Belial—the rebel demon who'd refused to give up his angelic form. Colin grinned, pleased by the comparison. Lilith had once told him Belial's beauty hurt to look upon, so brightly did it shine.

"No," Castleford said slowly. "Can you do it now?"

Shaking his head, Colin admitted, "I know it happens— rarely—but I don't control it. And I confess I'm glad of its infrequence; I'd rather admiration when women look at me than terror."

"It was psychic in nature. My shields were already in

place, but I had to reinforce them and actively hold the blocks to stop its effect." Lilith considered him for a moment. "And the other?"

Chaos. Colin quickly signed the word with his hand. *The emotional experience of it.*

She drew in a sharp breath. "You punished them with it?"

Colin's mouth pulled into a thin line. "You pity them for something they'll hardly remember, yet you would have allowed Sir Pup to kill them and not given a second thought. And you send me into the fucking Room, knowing I'll experience the same thing."

"It's not pity, it's surprise," Castleford said. "Have you done it before?"

He could choose not to answer, but that would be as damning as a lie. "This was the second time," he admitted, and watched as comprehension frosted the other man's gaze.

Lilith frowned. "When was the first?" *Could it have been the cause of the tear between the realms last month?* she finished by signing.

"No," Castleford said flatly. "It was Savi. When they were in Caelum."

Her eyes flickered with unease before she grinned. "Is a testosterone-laden fight to the death about to ensue?"

Colin smoothed his hand over his chest and soft woven silk. "I don't want to ruin this." Bad enough the rain had dampened it.

But better than her tears of grief, had Auntie's injury been worse.

"And as Savi told me she plans to spend the next month with you, I imagine your punishment has not yet concluded." Castleford turned away. "I'm satisfied."

Lilith sighed. "Then can you two kiss? Please?"

"Do you truly want me to? Think about the consequences, Lilith. Your two thousand years can't compare to what I have to give him," Colin said.

She sighed again as Castleford's deep laughter rumbled through the moist night air. "But you're both so pretty."

"Perhaps he is marginally attractive, but I've someone more suitable in mind to kiss."

"Your 'consort'? You may as well have declared her your wife." Lilith arched her brows. "Does Auntie know?"

He grinned unrepentantly. He'd only used the term to frighten the boy, to intimate a closer relationship between Savi and himself, but he found himself growing attached to the idea.

And if he openly acknowledged Savi as his consort, it would offer its own protection. Vampires who followed Dalkiel out of a desire for leadership and adherence to tradition might balk at killing a companion; protecting partnerships was as intrinsic a value in a community as bloodsharing within a partnership.

"Agent Milton, my dear, even Savi doesn't yet know."

"No false hope that way?"

He sobered quickly. "Yes."

But for his.

❧

For once, Savi didn't feel the need to question the hows and whys of a Guardian's power; she gratefully accepted the new sari Dru created for Nani, and carried it into the restaurant's office.

The police swarmed outside and in the main dining room; the office was a sorely needed retreat, even if it would only be of short duration.

Nani was readjusting her skirt to hide the ragged bullet hole in the material above her hip; Dru had removed the blood from her skin and clothes, but the hole was clear evidence she'd been hit. To Savi's surprise, Detective Taylor had been the one to suggest covering it—remarking that the other officers would notice such a detail, even if they couldn't explain its existence.

"Dru sent this for you."

"This conceals it." Nani's bangles jingled as she tucked in the edge at her waist. She glanced up at Savi's face, clicked her tongue. "I've no intention of stripping naked with half of the city in the next room, and Guardians who might teleport in at any moment."

All in Hindi, but for "Guardians" and "teleport." The

incongruity of it pulled a smile from her, and Savi dipped her head and nodded. She'd never heard her grandmother directly acknowledge them before, in any language. Caelum had always been "that place"; Guardians, demons, and nosferatu, "such as them."

Did she even know vampires existed? Know what manner of being had shot her? And why?

Sudden guilt rose, and her vision blurred. "Oh, Nani," she whispered, "I'm so sorry." She hardly recognized her own voice, it was so thick with tears. But her grandmother would not want her to give in to them.

And she'd cried enough in the past twenty-four hours. Surely it was time to stop. Swallowing hard, Savi turned and set the sari on the desk, fought down the shame. The demon had put this in motion, not she.

But it *had* been set into motion—with her grandmother placed in the middle. Savi would get her out, one way or another.

Nani sighed. "*Naatin*, you look just as your mother did when she told me she was going to marry an American."

"This may be worse." Crossing her arms over her chest, Savi clasped her upper arms and rubbed slowly. Warming herself, gathering her thoughts. "I met with Manu Suraj."

"That is worse?"

"He rejected me. I told him I believed in the DemonSlayer stuff."

Nani pursed her lips and shrugged. "This is what comes of searching for a groom through advertisements. The next one will be more reasonable."

Savi's heartbeat raced beneath her crossed arms. "I don't think I can keep my promise to you, Nani."

Dark eyes met hers, filled with sudden worry; Nani sank into the desk chair. "Savitri, you are not always consistent, but I have never known you not to keep your word. What has happened?"

What hadn't happened? But it was best to start when she'd made her promise; everything before then didn't apply in the same way. "On the plane, when I attacked that nosferatu—you remember how I had blood on me when I came back?" At her grandmother's nod, she continued. The fever, the changes in her strength. The wyrmwolves. The demon and his plan for revenge. "That's why the vampires shot at the restaurant tonight. I don't think it would be fair to marry someone when I bring so many problems into it, endanger them just by living."

Nani had listened quietly, her face paling and her mouth slightly parted as if in shock. But now she leaned forward, her gaze fierce as she gripped Savi's hands in her own.

"What protection have you?"

"Hugh is teaching me to protect myself."

Nani's eyes closed, as if in gratitude. "He's a good boy. A strong one. It is good that you live near him; he can care for you."

"Yes," Savi agreed thickly. "But I'm going to be staying with Mr. Ames-Beaumont for a while."

Nani withdrew her hands and sat back, studying her silently.

A flush heated Savi's cheeks. "He's the only one who can sense the wyrmwolves' approach. He's almost as strong as a Guardian. He can protect me better than any other."

Her eyebrows lifting in disbelief, Nani said, "Savitri. Now you look exactly as your mother did when she tried to convince me that she was marrying your father because he had a good family."

Savi snorted with laughter before she caught herself; her dad's family had only been *good* in the most superficial of ways. When her amusement faded, she said earnestly, "He'll take care of me. I'm most concerned about you. I want you to go back to Mumbai for a little while."

"No—"

"Yes," Savi said firmly. "Look at what happened tonight; the demon is trying to hurt me by hurting you. I need to know you're safe, and away from here until this is resolved. Not more than a couple of weeks. And I'll take care of the restaurant's repairs while you're gone. Maybe do some updates in the kitchen."

Her grandmother's mouth tightened, and Savi could see she was getting ready to protest again, when a knock sounded at the door.

She turned as Colin opened it, stepped through. His golden hair had been flattened by the rain and his clothes wrinkled, yet he managed to exude a careless elegance. It had to be some obscure vampire ability—but she knew the sudden happiness and relief that swept through her upon seeing him had little to do with superpowers. It was just him.

Colin looked between them with a boyish grin that he didn't attempt to conceal. He casually brought his thumb to his mouth and pressed it to one of his fangs, then used the blood to activate the symbols scratched into the door frame.

Savi hid her shock; it was as clear a declaration of his nature to Nani as her long-winded description had been of the changes in hers.

His gaze settled on her grandmother, and he asked in Hindi, "You are well?"

"Yes, *beta*." Her grandmother did not seem similarly surprised; instead, she scrutinized him as carefully as she would the front counter at closing time, the food preparation surfaces in the kitchens.

"You must forgive me for eavesdropping—" His grin widened as he darted a glance at Savi. "—but I would offer an alternative. Particularly as, if they know the language, any demon or vampire listening would have heard your granddaughter's suggestion that you flee to India."

With an embarrassed laugh, Savi said, "You see, he's already protecting me from my impulsive nature. I either think too much or not at all, and often do both at the same time."

Nani gave an amused headshake of agreement, but her gaze remained on Colin. "What do you suggest?"

"Beaumont Court. Selah or Michael could teleport you, and there would be no record of travel; we could make it appear you took a flight to Bombay, as Savi suggested. I will send someone along to act as guard—a Guardian, if one can be spared, or a partnership of vampires from those Castleford has been training."

"It is your family home? Would I inconvenience them?"

Colin smiled. "Of course not."

Savi's stomach knotted. It was the perfect solution, but it

meant Nani would be staying with the Earl of Norbridge. An aristocratic family. "They would welcome her?"

For an instant, his eyes darkened to stormy gray, his jaw clenched as if in anger. "Yes, Savitri." His words were almost as clipped as when he'd spoken to the demon. "We no longer require untitled foreign guests to sleep in the stables."

Her throat tightened in dismay. "I didn't mean it that way."

"There are few other meanings to be taken." His voice softened when he looked at Nani. "I promise you would be treated the same as they would me. Probably better; they'll feed you."

Nani's lips pursed for just a moment. "Savitri? Will this alternative suit?"

Her grandmother had solicited her opinion. Savi knew she should have been feeling triumphant, but when she met Colin's flat stare, she only wished it would warm. "Yes. Thank you."

"Very well, *beta*."

He gave a short nod. "I'll make the arrangements. You can go tonight; already it is early morning there. Continue to speak of it as if you are leaving for Bombay. I'll return in a few minutes to drive you home so you may collect your things." With a swipe of his hand, he erased the blood from the symbols and left.

Savi released a shaky breath, sat on the edge of the desk. "Goddammit."

"Savitri, do not use such language," her grandmother admonished. "Why would you insult him so, question his hospitality? You can't think he is the same as Jonathan Murray."

"No. God, no." Her grandfather; she could not think of two men more dissimilar. She glanced at the older woman, remembered her lack of surprise when Colin had bloodied his thumb. "You knew he was a vampire."

"I am old, *naatin*, not blind. Are you in love with him?"

Her chest hurt too much to answer. Savi simply nodded. "There is no future in it," she managed after a moment.

"Oh, Savitri." Nani leaned forward, patted her hand. "That is what I told your mother when she said she wanted to marry your father. And you know the conclusion to that."

Nani's smile was somewhat watery, but Savi's was, too. "Yes. I know." They'd had fifteen blissfully happy years.

And Savi was going to do everything she could to squeeze the same into a month.

CHAPTER 18

A vampire's psychic powers aren't as evolved as a Guardian's, demon's, or nosferatu's. Nosferatu-born vampires are somewhere in between—and all of the bloodsuckers are more psychically powerful when they are actually drinking the blood.

—*Savi to Taylor, 2007*

Colin's quiet tension didn't ease; not on the journey to Nani's and during the flurried activity of packing, not after Savi's teary-eyed good-byes before Selah whisked Nani away. They'd returned to his car in silence, and in the first few minutes it stretched awkwardly between them until Savi was certain she'd scream from it.

Instead she fell asleep.

A change in the car's speed woke her as he turned into his neighborhood. Tall, elegant Victorian houses lined the avenue bordering the western side of Buena Vista Park, decorated ladies standing shoulder to shoulder. A wrought-iron gate guarded the drive; it slowly squeaked open when he pushed a code into a remote.

She bent forward to look up through the windshield, and her mouth dropped open. "Oh my god, it's the fairy-tale house. I've seen it in photos, like on 'the best of San Francisco' sites and whatever. I had no idea it was yours." She'd known his address, but she'd never made the connection between the two— and she was certain the name of the owner had never been listed with the pictures. "How did the fire not make the news?"

"The exterior was not badly damaged. There was little to film, and I immediately began to rebuild. Lilith did the rest."

Lilith must have concealed any connection to the fire and to Colin during the investigation into the ritual murders the previous year. Savi grinned, too enchanted by the house to feel slighted by his brusque tone—and the realization that he'd probably been the reason for her unexpected nap.

A high fence and leafy trees hid most of the house from view of the street: an enormous Queen Anne, with rounded towers at each corner, gables, a steeply pitched roof, bay windows, and a second-floor balcony. The moonless, rainy night prevented her from determining the color, but she knew from the pictures it was a deep claret, with contrasting trim in the myriad ornamental details. Her eyes widened as she took in the narrow lawns at the sides of the house, the long sweep of landscaping in the front. "How did you get a lot this size?"

"I purchased it not long after the earthquake."

Of 1906. "I'll keep that in mind if I ever decide to acquire property: the best time to buy is after a major natural disaster."

He seemed to soften a little. "Yes."

She bit her lip, studying the line of his profile. A little wasn't enough. How much damage had she done with her thoughtless question at the restaurant? Her heart climbed into her throat as he braked in front of the main entrance and killed the engine. "Will you invite me in?"

Oh, god. She'd meant to sound sexy, sultry—to get through this moment on pure bravado. Instead a breathless vulnerability had crept into her voice, made it no more than a whisper.

His eyes closed. "I had good intentions, Savitri."

Her hands clenched on her lap. Her legs trembled, her lungs seized up. That sounded like the beginning of every I'm-ready-to-let-you-go speech she'd ever received. *I really like you, Savi. We get along so well, Savi. I thought it would turn out differently, Savi.*

It had never hurt before; but then, it had never really mattered before. "It's okay," she managed.

She'd known better than to wish for anything, even something as short as a month.

"I'm not bloody apologizing."

She glanced up in surprise at the anger in his voice, but he was already out of the car, around to her side. He hauled her out, dragged her up the front steps.

"I intended to let you sleep. You're fucking exhausted," he said as he unlocked the heavy wooden door and slammed it shut behind them. He dotted his hand three times on the symbols. Would they work on the entirety of the house? They must. "How many hours did you rest last night?"

She'd barely a moment to take in the marble floor, the vases and paintings decorating the dimly lit foyer before he was pulling her toward a large, curving stair.

"One or two," she said, running up each riser. Portraits flashed by on her right. "Oh, god, they're all you."

"Yes, of course," he said carelessly, then swept her up when she tried to stop and examine one, cradling her against his chest. "And I intended to make you swoon first—to give you the tour after you'd had several hours of sleep, sing to you in the music room, read poetry in the library. You've had a hell of a day, even by vampiric standards. A bit of relaxation seemed in order."

He was pissed with himself for his eagerness to get into her bed? "I'm swooning," she said against his shoulder, linking her arms around his neck.

"And then, then after that, only after that, did I intend to carry you into your room and . . ." He paused on the landing.

"Drink from me?"

"I drank," he said quietly. He lowered her feet to the floor, brought his hands up to cup her face. She didn't relinquish her hold on him; his chest was warm and solid against hers, his heart beating as fast. "From the vampires we caught. I don't need more blood tonight."

"Oh."

His thumbs smoothed over her quivering lips. "But I need *more*, Savitri."

Her fingers threaded into the hair at his nape. Even in the darkness, she could see the need burning in his eyes, but she didn't know . . . "More than I can give you?"

"Everything you can give me. I'm a selfish creature. Yet I intended to be a gentleman tonight." His left hand slid down her side, curved around her back, and found the zipper at her waist. Her skirt slithered down to pool at her feet.

"What will you be instead?"

He wouldn't let her pull his lips down to hers, so she rose up on tiptoe, pressing openmouthed kisses to his chin, his jaw.

"A beggar."

He tugged her sweater over her head, forcing her to release her hold on him as he stripped the sleeves over her hands. Already taut with arousal, her nipples puckered further in the cold air. She wrapped her bare arms around her naked chest, stared up at him. Shadows hid his features, but she knew she must be exposed to his preternatural sight—exposed in her freezing gooseflesh and white lacy boyshorts and the boots he'd admired.

She was standing almost nude in his house, and she didn't care that she was still wearing her shoes. "You don't have to beg."

"Apparently I do. You won't tell me what I most need to hear."

Disappointment speared through her. "You may as well tell me it's gravity that keeps my feet to the floor. Why do you need to hear from me what you know?" What every other woman told him.

"I don't know. I didn't hear your answer." His throat worked. His gaze searched hers, almost desperately. "Only that there was no future. Has your phase ended so quickly?"

Her knees weakened, but somehow she remained upright. "Aren't we speaking of your beauty?"

He stilled. "No."

"Oh." She moistened her lips. "You've never asked me."

The predatory smile that spread across his mouth was softened by an edge of humor. "I did. Have you already forgot?"

"No."

He took a step forward, lowered his head to skim his lips over hers. " 'Has your phase ended so quickly?' "

She laughed despite herself. "No. I'm still falling."

"Thank God." He rested his forehead against her brow. "Oh, sweet Savitri, how I need that. I can't remember the last time someone made love to me."

Neither can I.

But she clenched her teeth to prevent the question she wanted to ask, too afraid of the answer. And he must not have expected her to respond; his mouth covered hers, took a gentle sip from her lips before he lifted her into his arms again and began striding across a wide, dark room. It opened up to another through a wide archway, and she caught the gleam of a piano, the outline of artwork against the walls.

"The music room?" How strange to be carried through it—and how grateful she was, that she didn't have to run after him, avoiding unfamiliar furniture, and that the heat of his arms warmed her thighs and back.

She thought she'd resent it, feel like a little girl caged in by him, but somewhere between the stairs and the piano she was let out instead.

Falling, but she didn't have to hit bottom. Surely she couldn't with him holding her like this.

"The music room," he confirmed with a press of his lips against her temple. "Your rooms are just past it; my studio lies at the opposite end of this floor."

"*My* rooms?" She lowered her shields, felt the rumble of his approving groan against her cheek.

He stopped in front of a pair of floor-to-ceiling doors, adjusting his grip on her legs to reach down and depress the handle. His breath came more quickly now, and she smiled and tipped her head back to see him better.

"Yours. There is a practical reason for it."

"Because you rarely sleep?"

"No, I have a suite upstairs. This used to be mine, before I tore out the third floor and attic to make the new one." Shouldering through the entry, he glanced down at her. "But the open design makes it difficult to use the shields in that room, and the bed is directly above my studio. I fear I am very loud when I paint. There are likely vibrations."

She bit her lower lip before she ventured, "Opera?"

"If it strikes my mood. Lights on?"

"Yes. Isn't that a bit of a cliché?"

"Only if I pretended to be something I'm not." He moved to the wall, and she used the toe of her boot to tap the switch up. "It's not a cliché if you live it, Savitri."

The glow from the recessed lighting was soft, but still she had to blink her eyes, wait for them to adjust. He strode quickly through a sitting room: silk-papered walls in rich burgundy,

graceful sofas, and upholstered, deep-cushioned chairs. She
tilted her head back; an array of blues and golds in geometrical
shapes decorated the tray ceiling.

"This is amazing. Gorgeous." Had it been the same before
the fire had destroyed all of it? Had he tried to re-create the
original décor, or started over?

"You can change anything you like; make it your own. In
any room," he said, and his arm slid from beneath her thighs,
his hand catching her left knee and turning her, hooking it
over his hip. She wrapped her right around his waist, moaned
softly as the new position stroked his erection against her sex
with each step.

A huge canopied bed with royal blue satin draped on the
corners filled the circular room—the tower room. The matching bedspread was cool beneath her bottom, then her back, as
he bore her down into the mattress. Surrounded by him

He kissed her neck, her jaw. Quick, chaste kisses, if not for
the insistent presence of his rigid shaft between her legs. A
shiver tightened her skin, left her taut with need. She couldn't
see him, only the broad line of his back; she wanted to see
him. To feel his skin against hers.

She pushed at his shoulders, tried to pull up his sweater to
run her palms over his flesh; he drew her hands over her head
and held them there

"Let me touch you." Her back arched, and she dug her
heels into the mattress, tried to dislodge him.

And only succeeded in driving herself mad when the
movement of her hips ground her clit against his thick length.
She did it again, whimpering in sudden, desperate frustration.

Colin began laughing softly against her neck. "Another of
my intentions, gone to hell."

"What did you intend?" Her breath caught as he nipped the
skin above her pulse and his tongue ran a wet trail from her
throat to the point of her shoulder. Finally, she could see him.
His eyes, glittering with amusement and need; his blond hair,
darkened by the rain; his tanned skin against her golden
brown; the angular line of his jaw, and his soft, incredible lips.

"To do it your way first: directly to the fucking, if that
gives you the most pleasure."

Her only answer was an incoherent groan as he rocked

against her in demonstration. Releasing her left hand, he brought his down to cup her bottom, to prevent her from thrusting against him in turn.

"Then slower, later. Tasting you all over."

Fire slipped through her as he changed his rhythm, each languid roll of his hips taking her close to the edge. The delicious rub of fabric. Heat. His fingers slid beneath the seam of her panties, the lace soaked with her arousal. She gasped his name, a plea for mercy.

Much longer, and she would be the beggar.

"But I'd be a fool to waste this opportunity." He withdrew his hand from between them, brought it to his mouth, licked the glistening moisture from his skin with a long swipe of his tongue. His eyes closed, his face reflecting sheer erotic pleasure.

Oh god. She'd made him look like that; she'd be a fool to waste it, too. Her fingers clenched on his arm, his sleeve bunching in her grip. "What opportunity?"

His lids were heavy when he raised his gaze to hers. "No bloodlust. I'm completely sated. But for this need, this lust."

"How is that different?" His fingertips traced her lips. Both their scents lingered on his hand, and she opened her mouth, flicked her tongue across his skin. Her feminine flavor. The roughness of the pads of his fingers. Salt. She closed her lips around the tip of his middle finger, softly bit it.

He pulled in a shuddering breath. "It means this will last more than five minutes."

Her eyes widened. But of course it happened so quickly— he hunted for the purpose of feeding, not sex. And even if he tried to draw out the sexual portion, the bloodlust would rise and hurry it along. Then he put them to sleep, so they'd forget.

Would he want her sympathy? "It's comforting to know that you don't screw them again when they're unconscious," she said lightly, but the kisses she pressed to his fingers, the back of his hand told the truth. *I'm so sorry.*

The corners of his lips tilted into a smile. No, he wouldn't feel sorry for himself, but the soft gratitude in his eyes told her he appreciated her compassion. "Don't mistake me, Savi— those five minutes are bloody glorious. I'm very good."

The laughter rolled out of her from deep within. This time,

Colin allowed her movement as she pushed him over and straddled him, bracing her hands in the mattress on either side of his head. Her lips skimmed over his brow, his cheekbones, his smiling mouth.

"This month . . . if you feed first, and we have sex again right afterward, it won't be the only opportunity."

His breath caught, as if in anticipation. Then his eyes narrowed. "I still intend to take this one slowly."

"No woman would object to that," she said, and scraped his lower lip between her teeth, let it go to dip her tongue into his mouth. His body tightened beneath hers, and he made a sound of carnal satisfaction deep in his throat.

Her flavor. Was it just that he could taste her at all that affected him so strongly, or was her taste so delectable he couldn't resist it?

Did it matter? It had overcome his preference for hunting, his promise to Hugh, was the reason she was there now. Thank God for momentum—and the passenger who'd pulled on her skirt, made her accidentally swallow the venom.

She slid her tongue over his teeth, teased the tips of his fangs, moaning into his mouth as his palms came up to curve over her hips, then slide down the length of her thighs. His fingers curled, his nails dragging lightly over the sensitive tendons behind her knees. Her elbows weakened and she swayed forward. He tilted his head back, kept her mouth fused to his. Her nipples brushed damp silk.

She broke away, gasping. "Off. Your clothes."

He licked the soft skin beneath her chin, a hot, wet streak that immediately cooled in the frigid air. The exquisite contrast shivered through her. "Patience, love."

She didn't have any. "I want to see you. Taste you." She swiveled her hips over his cock, a blatant declaration of what she wanted to taste.

"Oh, Christ," he breathed.

"You won't come," she said, and sat up. Gathering the bottom of his sweater, she revealed the line of dark golden hair below his navel, his tautly muscled abdomen. Solid, lean strength. "We can still take a long time. Unless you bite yourself."

His gaze was riveted on her hands as she pushed the

sweater over his chest. "I'll not likely . . . Savi, wait." He rose onto his elbow, caught her wrists. "A condition."

Her eyes narrowed in mock anger. "You have a lot of those."

"I prefer to stack the odds in my favor." But his smile didn't reach his eyes. "You aren't to bite yourself, either. Let me. I'll not torture you, or deny your pleasure . . . not excessively."

She hesitated. "Why?"

"I can't come without your blood, and I'll not take it without your leave. It seems a fair trade, does it not?" He lifted his hand to her mouth and ran his fingertip along the inside of her bottom lip. "And because I will not be the cause of any more of your scars. I'll give you what you require; you need not inflict it on yourself."

She averted her face. Most of the small crescent scars were old, barely ridges in the smooth inner flesh, yet she should have known he'd notice them. "I just bit too hard sometimes. They wouldn't."

His fangs flashed as he grinned. "*I* will." He released her wrists, pulled the sweater and undershirt over his head.

Her fingertips circled his flat nipples. No hair on his chest. The smooth play of muscle beneath his skin fascinated her, and she slid her palms over his pectorals, his shoulders, his arms. "What do you like best? If I'm to make love to you, I want to do it right."

His hands stilled with his trousers half unzipped. She took over for him, rasping the tab down, tugging at the base to pull it over the rise of his cock. His undershorts barely contained him, the elastic stretching away from his abdomen.

"What I like best?" he echoed, his voice thick. He choked on a laugh as her hand encircled him through the silk. "Savi, you made me spend with a kiss. There's nothing you could do that wouldn't be the best I've ever had."

She smiled with pleasure, leaned forward to drag her tongue along the waistband of his shorts, then slowly lowered it. Freed, his shaft jutted out. She squeezed her legs together to ease the insistent, pulsing ache beneath her womb—reminded herself to be patient.

"I'll remember to keep my shields down if they have that effect."

"It's not the bloody shields." His hands fisted in blue satin. "It's you. Oh, good *God*."

She'd done nothing except lick her lips to moisten them, but she'd not considered how visually oriented he was. He lay back, propped up on his elbows. His eyes darkened further, as if just the sight of her gratification and her preparation to take him into her mouth was as effective as a touch.

Her heart pounding, she ran her nails up his length, swirled her thumb over the wide flaring head. How best to take advantage of it, to drive him mad with visual stimuli as well as physical sensation?

"Savi," he said hoarsely, "you're thinking too much."

"You'll like it." She swept her tongue around the base of his shaft. Hot, hard. His hips jerked toward her, his grip tightened on the comforter. "I promise."

"Yes, sweet." He panted as her mouth surrounded the tip of him. "I'm certain I shall."

He liked biting. He'd gone wild after she'd bitten him in Caelum; it might be too much now. But he'd also had a strong reaction when she'd touched herself, had wanted to see her do it . . . and, oh god, she needed some relief. His soft growls as she suckled him deeper, deeper, the lightly salty flavor, the taut flex of his abdomen as he forced himself to stay still were individual teases, combining to make her so moist and needy she could hardly believe she wasn't already riding him.

And *that* image, the anticipation of him inside her, sinking into her. She moaned around his length, shifting until she kneeled beside him in her boots and boyshorts.

She needed one hand to brace herself against the mattress, but her other was free and she slid it between her thighs, beneath her panties, burying her fingers in slick, soft flesh. Stroked in rhythm with her tongue, her mouth.

His growls abruptly stopped, and she darted a sidelong glance at him from beneath her lashes. His lips were pulled back, his fangs long and sharp against the line of his teeth. Desire and need burned hot in his gaze, his focus unwavering from her hand under the lace.

It seemed with effort, he unclenched his jaw. Met her eyes as she took him deep again, slowly, trying to gauge his response. The cords on his neck stood out. A groan rose from his throat. She suckled her way back to the tip, felt him shake. She raised her eyebrow in question when his hands lifted to her chin, pulled her gently up, forcing her to release him.

"Forgive me, Savi," he rasped. "I'm soon to be selfish. The scent of you, the sound—in those knickers—I shall die if I don't have my mouth on you within half a minute."

She stared at him, her fingers stopping in their motion between her thighs. "You have such an odd notion of *selfish*."

He grinned, pivoted up to catch her beneath her arms, turn, and push her back against the pillows. He sat on his heels, his trouser-clad knees forcing hers wide. "Once I'd failed in my intention to fuck you senseless, I intended to allow you the lead. But you proved too proficient. I shouldn't have given you time to think." Unzipping her boots, he tugged them off and threw them to the side of the bed. Hooked his fingers under lace and stripped her panties down her legs. "And I'll not allow you weapons such as these."

She caught her tongue lightly between her teeth, and her hands rose to cup her breasts.

Colin glanced up, froze. "Bloody hell. There's no help for it then. Death comes."

Before she could fathom his intention, he covered her body with his and lifted her leg over his hip, entering her in a long, powerful stroke. Her breath ripped from her lungs. Oh, god. She clutched at his shoulders, her nails digging into his skin.

"Savi, Savi," he chanted between kisses to her face, her lips. His hands were buried in her hair. "Did I hurt you? Was it too hard?"

She shook her head, unable to speak. Not hurt, but she felt like sobbing with the pleasure of it. Her inner thigh slid over his hip as she wound her left leg across his back, lodging him farther inside. A wordless cry for more escaped her.

"Hold on, love. Oh, *Christ*," he groaned as he slowly withdrew. She panted against his neck, her slick heat clinging along his length. Friction, though she was so wet she could hear it, too. "Hold on."

Not *wait*, she realized, but *grab on to him and don't let go*. He pushed back in. So deep. So thick. A perfect fit. No chance of letting him go. She twined her arms around his neck, felt the trembling in his elbows planted next to her shoulders, in his palms cradling the back of her head. Fighting for control. Her ankles locked together at the base of his spine.

She clamped her teeth on his throat.

He tensed, a rough growl tearing from his chest before he reared back, pulling her up with him. For an instant, she straddled him as he knelt on the bed, her weight resting almost wholly over his cock, and she took him in, deeper, wider. Pain in that full stretch, just under her womb, just a little.

Just enough.

He slammed her back down into the pillows, shoving hard, but she was already coming, unclenching her teeth as she cried out against his skin. Again as he thrust, dragging out the orgasm with each long stroke, faster as she reached another peak. His mouth found hers, and she helplessly sucked and bit at his tongue, his lips, taking all of him she could get inside her, and still he filled her, over and over.

She let him go, too shattered to hold on, but he followed and linked his hands with hers. And pushed her over again.

CHAPTER 19

S—— met with me at the port in Livorno; he was excited, eager for the transformation . . . as he approached all things. As you may have heard, it did not end well. A storm struck us—but it was already too late for S——. More when I return to Beaumont Court. It may be some time; I've not yet the stomach for open stretches of water. And if I never swim again, it will be too soon.

—Colin to Ramsdell, 1822

❧

"Colin?"

"I'm here," he said, smiling against her throat. Savi sprawled bonelessly atop him, a leg on each side of his abdomen, her feet tucked beneath the outside of his thighs. He'd been counting the minutes; it hadn't taken as long as he'd thought it would.

"You didn't . . . ?"

"No, love. You swooned." He didn't try to conceal the triumphant amusement in his tone.

"No," she said, her voice pensive. "I don't think I did. Evidence suggests I was fucked senseless. You are a gentleman, after all. Despite your intentions, you gave a lady what she wanted."

He laughed softly. "At that moment, it was my only desire, as well." He'd taste her soon enough. He ran his palms over her back, down to the swell of her small bottom, then swept back up. Smooth, naked skin, damp with perspiration.

Quickly cooling perspiration.

Bloody hell. Holding her against his chest, he rolled,

kicked at the blankets. Found the edge and yanked it up over them. She sighed, wriggling in closer to his side. Her thigh draped over his, rubbed up and down against the wool of his trousers.

"Are you still in your pants?"

"Yes. And though I am pleased I exhibited unmatched sartorial excellence whilst fucking you senseless, they have since rumpled to a mortifying degree. Thus I resort to a cover-up."

"Unbelievable. The only cover-up here is your cheap ass. I imagine heating this giant house must completely blow your budget." Her dark eyes sparkled with humor, and she pressed her bottom lip between her teeth before offering, "I'll pay for half of it while I'm here."

His chest tightened in desperate longing. Surely she must know a month wouldn't be enough. "All of it," he countered, his fingers running the length of her spine, tracing lightly over the large starburst scar alongside it. "I hardly need the heat."

"Your artwork runs the danger of mildew. Such a damp climate." She mimicked her grandmother at the last; whether unconsciously done or not, it charmed another smile from him.

As if drawn by the movement of his lips, her gaze lowered to his mouth. Beneath the blankets, her hand skimmed over his stomach and wrapped around the base of his erection. His teeth clenched at the exquisiteness of it.

"I have a condition," she said with a lift of her eyebrow, daring him to deny her.

"Heat in trade for lovemaking? I accept your terms," he said quickly. "Though I daresay you enjoyed it well enough freezing."

"It must be a secret desire of yours to have a woman whose skin is as cold as a vampire's." Releasing his shaft, she slid her hand up the side of his ribs, drawing a sigh of pleasure from him. Her lips curved into a slow, sad smile; he'd only seen that expression when she'd spoken of Caelum. "And I would have someone transform me and fulfill that wish, but—"

"No." The denial broke harshly from him, panic pushing it from his throat. "No, Savi. We could not even have a month if you did. You couldn't drink from me." She'd have to go elsewhere. And she wouldn't be with him if the bloodlust forced her to be with another; she wouldn't spread herself between two men.

He'd likely murder the other vampire—or completely remove himself from her life to keep from doing it. The first would be preferable, but the continual deaths of her food sources was hardly a viable alternative for her.

"I know." She blinked, then lowered her forehead to his chest. "And Michael told me that I probably couldn't, anyway. He doesn't know how the taint would manifest in me during the transformation. It would be too dangerous. The fever nearly killed me, and that was just ingesting a little bit of blood and venom; it's impossible to say what transformation would do."

"You asked him? When?"

She turned her head, lay her cheek against his shoulder. She glanced up at him, then looked away, watched her fingers tracing a pattern over the hollow of his throat. "Just after the fever broke—about a week after."

Before he'd returned from England. Before they'd made their agreement to try friendship. "Why?"

She seemed to contemplate the contrast of her skin against his for an extraordinary amount of time. "I want to see what happens," she said finally, and though her eyes remained dry, tears hoarsened her voice. "When I think of all you've seen and experienced in two centuries—and Hugh and Lilith, what they've seen . . ." Her hands fisted. "And I expect that if the demon doesn't manage to kill us this month, the next fifty years are going to be pretty freaking amazing. People are coming up with stuff all the time, changing all the time. But I want more than that. I want a hundred, five hundred, a thousand. Ten thousand. Can you imagine? I just want to see it." Her words slowly dropped to a whisper. "I would've eventually asked Lucas or Fia or someone to turn me . . . but then I took that flight."

She shrugged carelessly, but yearning emanated from her psychic scent as clearly as her desire had earlier. Colin brushed his fingers through her satiny cap of hair, unable to speak. If he'd had the power, he'd have transformed her at that moment. He'd never considered it, except to think of how it would deny him any future with her, but he should have realized . . .

someone with her extreme curiosity, with immortality all around her and the ability within reach—but then taken from her with an accidental swallow of blood and venom.

It would have been easier had she never known the possibility existed.

She forced a bright smile, flicked another glance up at him before her lashes lowered again. Her shields rose, as if to spare him from the pain of her need.

He should have been grateful; his pain was more than enough that he couldn't ease hers.

"And then I thought I could sacrifice myself saving someone's soul from a demon and turn into a Guardian, but Michael said no to that, too. Because of the taint. But that's okay, because I really don't want to be shot or stabbed or jump off a bridge or whatever it takes to sacrifice oneself. And I probably wouldn't have been a very good Guardian, anyway. In some ways, I'm too much like Hugh. I enjoy having free will. Though if I was a Guardian, we could . . ."

She didn't finish, but he could have if the tightness of his throat had allowed speech. As a Guardian, she could have fed him without having to feed from him. She would have been immortal and, even serving the Guardian corps, would have been able to make a life with him. As Selah and her vampire partner had together.

Swallowing, Savi began moving her fingertips across his chest, down over his stomach. "Anyway, your heating bill wasn't the condition I had in mind."

"Anything you want, sweet, and it's yours," he said, his voice rough. Anything but fidelity and immortality; devastating, that the two things she wanted most he could not offer. Yet it was more important than ever before not to give her false hope; he would not dangle anything in front of her only to take it away. But the first—there *must* be a way, even if he had to cut off his cock each night he fed from anyone other than Savi.

It would grow back. And after fifty or sixty years . . . he would live every single bloody day for her.

"You don't need more than a drop or two to come, right? You aren't going to feed from me tonight, just take enough for that."

"Yes."

"I don't want you to send me the . . . the . . . whatever you send them." When he stiffened, she raised her head and explained, "I have a feeling that I won't be too coherent if you're doing that to me."

Relaxing slightly, he tapped his forefinger against her mouth. "You won't be all that coherent, regardless."

She pressed her lips together, then buried her face against his neck, began laughing. After a few moments, she wiped her eyes and said, "I want to see you come. I watched you in Polidori's." She sighed sweetly in memory, her gaze on his lips. "It was beautiful. I want to be here for it."

His heart ached with need, as if it wanted to leap from his chest and enfold her within it. She would kill him before the month was out. "The bite is painful, Savi. The pleasure takes that away."

"It's not that bad." She waggled her eyebrows, probably to divert him away from recollection of how she knew that. "And I like a little pain. We'll do the rest when you feed from me tomorrow."

Her lashes fell, her smile widened, and a terrible certainty rose up in him. No, it hadn't been the bite in Caelum that had hurt her, but what had followed. She'd not have forgot it.

Was that why she postponed it? Curious, impetuous Savitri—stalling rather than discovering how good it could be.

He dreaded her answer, but he forced the question: "Are you frightened? Do you think it will be like Caelum?"

"Yes," she admitted softly, and Colin was quite certain Hell had descended on him. "But not for the reason you think."

He couldn't respond. What other reason could there be?

"It's because of Caelum, but not what you did to me. Just . . . Caelum itself. Or leaving it." Savi paused, and turned, propping her chin on the roll of her fist. Her brows arched. "Have you seen the Taj Mahal?"

He blinked. "Yes."

"I spent a week in Agra when I was in India last time. I was there on a perfect, incredible day." Her gaze unfocused. "A cerulean sky, the stone blindingly white. And the symmetry of it, the design . . . anyway, I've always thought even if some-one didn't typically like Mughal architecture, the dome, they'd have to agree that it's one of the most beautiful sites in the world. Maybe *the* most beautiful. When were you there?"

"Nineteen hundred and three. I toured the colonies after Emily and Ramsdell . . . after I left England, and before set-tling here." He lightly pinched her bottom when her eyes widened. "Savitri, I'll tell you of my travels another time."

She pressed her lips together and nodded. After a moment, she said, "It wasn't the same. I've seen the Taj before—and when I saw it again, it wasn't the same. There was wonder, and awe, but nothing like before. All I could think when I stood there was that I'd had something better, a million times better, and had to let it go. That I'll never have it again. And it *hurt*. You must know." It wasn't a question.

"Yes." Evidence of it filled his studio; she'd see it soon enough.

"Maybe it's even worse for you; you had two months."

"Perhaps it made it easier."

She shrugged. "How does one quantify and compare that kind of loss? It's impossible. Not worth the attempt." Ab-sently, she traced a circle on his chest, drew a square over it. "The anxiety attacks have been worse since I came back—the need to run. And running from you was easy, but from that loss?"

"It's impossible." His voice was rough.

"I try not to think of it, but . . ." She trailed off with a sigh. "And despite *knowing* how lucky I am that I went—and that I have this memory to take me back whenever I want—I wish it could fade, too. It's a blessing and a curse at once." She met his gaze and cocked her head. "Does that sound whiny? 'Woe is me, poor little rich girl'?"

"A bit," he said, his lips quirking.

She wrinkled her nose, huffed out a breath. "Yeah. So, any-way, last night when I realized I couldn't ever forget what you'd do to me, it freaked me out. Because how will anything else compare to it? It can't; it won't."

His relieved laughter disturbed her balance; she slipped from his side, sat up. "Oh, sweet—I'll not be sorry for that."

She wrapped her arms around her bent knees, stretching

the sheet into a tent over her legs. "Not men or sex. You ass. I'm talking about what I feel for you, and that I'll go into it knowing that I have to leave in a month. That it will be more to me than anything I've ever had; but unlike other women you've fed from, I'll never forget it. And that everything I feel in the future will be pale and insipid in comparison. It'll be like Caelum all over again. *That's* what I'm afraid of."

It seemed a simple solution to him: *Don't leave.* But he couldn't ask her that, couldn't ask her for a commitment when he did not know if he could offer anything in return.

Yet she *had* made a commitment. Had made this month-long bargain after she'd realized the consequences of it. "You're afraid, but you're not running. Is your curiosity so strong?"

"Yeah. But also because it's too late; even without your superpowered orgasm, this is already more than anything else I've ever had. And I don't know if I'll have another chance like this again."

"Then why wait until tomorrow?"

"Because I don't know how or why Caelum affected us like it did. And I won't know the reason behind your power, or how it works, or what it will do to me. Or if, even with this memory, it will seem like it isn't real." She turned, lay against his chest. "But *this*, I'm certain of. And when I leave I'll know that I'm pining over something that genuinely existed between us, instead of . . . magic. I just want to wait one day, so that I can say for certain: it was just you and me."

Nodding tightly in agreement, he drew her mouth down to his. Her eyes closed as he kissed her; the soft clinging of her lips, her breath, wrapped around him and rooted themselves deep. The rough stroke of her tongue across his. The play of her hands over his skin.

He eased her onto her back; her neck arched, and he licked a trail down her chin, her throat. Her muscles tensed beneath his hands, as if in anticipation of his bite. But he had not finished.

Allow me to give this to you.

She moaned as his lips closed over her breast, as he tugged her nipple between his teeth, as he licked and suckled the taut peak. Her fingers threaded into his hair, urged him to its opposite, and he eagerly followed her direction.

Anything you ask of me.

"I'm sorry," she gasped, and sweet, warm flavor flooded into his mouth through her skin. "I forgot."

He had, too. Hadn't cared for his pleasure over hers.

When had she effected this change in him?

Standing in the middle of a park, fearless and aroused? Across a restaurant, with her laugh and her playful smile? In a parking lot, her bleeding hand over his mouth? Outside a mirrored room, a kiss from her lips? Holding a sword over a wyrmwolf's neck, terrified yet determined to see it through?

Caelum?

I've fallen in love with you.

Of course he had.

"Don't apologize, sweet," he said against her belly. His tongue flicked into her navel. "It happens to the best of us."

With a strangled laugh she looked away from him, turning her cheek against the pillow. "Are you the best?"

"I'm exponentially greater than that."

As he'd hoped, she raised her head. Her warm, liquid brown gaze met his; her lips trembled. She blinked quickly, her eyes glistening. "You remember me saying that?"

"Yes. And you've enthralled me again, my sweet Savitri." He lowered his mouth, watched her face as he licked through her moist heat. Soft, slippery. Cinnamon and peach, the psychic scent of her arousal and the flavor that might have been from Heaven or Hell or Chaos, but that he would always associate with Savi.

Her thighs clenched beside his shoulders. She whimpered from between her teeth. She was tight around his fingers. Hot. He slid them deep. Closed his lips over her clitoris, stroked his tongue, firm, rough.

"It's too much," she whispered brokenly.

His fangs scraped alongside her sex as he dragged his tongue down to his fingers; she keened softly. No pain, no blood, only her surprise.

Her head tilted back, her teeth digging into her lower lip. Her small breasts rose and fell with each panting breath.

He stopped.

She looked at him. Released her lip. "I didn't bite—"

Colin did, gently. Soothed it with a lick. She cried out and her hips rocked, a hard involuntary thrust. Again. Her moisture slicked his palm, his mouth. His cock ached with need; his tongue didn't care.

Only for her. Always for her, everything for her, from this moment.

"Oh, god. Ohmygod." She averted her face, her hands twisting on the sheets.

Perhaps a little for him. He ceased all movement, waited.

With a frustrated laugh, she glanced back at him. He curled his fingers, angling up to rub against sensitive inner muscle. Her lids lowered. He stopped, hid his grin. She looked at him, then away so quickly he was caught in the midst of another lick.

"You ass!" she gasped, but she was laughing, and she held his gaze now, only glancing away from his eyes to refocus on the whole of his face, his mouth, the slide of his tongue. Then her laughter broke and ebbed into desperate cries as he pulled her closer, her thigh over his shoulder, and he tasted, fed from her, but hungered for more.

Her pleas took on a sharp edge; he bit but still drew no blood. He didn't need it, only the shuddering release that rolled through her, his name from her lips.

And this, too: he rose up, slid deep before the orgasm eased from her. Her sheath surrounded him, tiny contractions fluttering over his length.

Her lips parted beneath his. "I want to see you."

"I'm not yet done." A soft, drugging kiss. Another, taking her lips and body in the same unhurried rhythm, until she was moaning low in her throat and the sound filled his mouth, a dulcet echo of the flavor on his tongue.

Slower now. An immortal man could take his pleasure quickly, knowing there would always be time for more. But a dying man lingered, uncertain of another opportunity.

And if not death, this exquisite slow fall into oblivion, then love.

Longer. Watching as ecstasy coiled beneath her skin, watching as she watched him. Her rapid breathing matched his, paced the pounding of his heart. But outwardly he moved leisurely, each languorous thrust pushing him toward rapture.

Pulling her along with him.

Her feet rubbed flat against the sheets, her legs trembled. Her fingers clawed at his back, urged him faster, harder. "Colin. Please."

"Not yet. Don't run."

Tears gathered in her eyes, but she didn't look away. "It's too much."

He froze, a dark ache gnawing within him. *Too much.* He remembered that . . . here, in this bed, but by the fountain as well. "Don't cry. Am I hurting you?"

"No." It sounded like a sob. Her back arched, her head tilted as if in invitation. She still watched him, sidelong, like an indirect look into the sun. "I thought it was the enthrallment. Caelum. But it's you."

His throat closed, but he regained his measured pace. A great and terrible beauty. She hadn't looked at him in Caelum, never for very long. Did it remind her of what he'd done *now*?

"Are you frightened?" How could he bear it if she was?

"No," she breathed. Her hips rose to meet his again, her feet halted their frantic movements. "Overcome."

He laughed with relief, buried his face in her neck. Of course she wasn't afraid. "Oh, Savi. I am, too."

Turning, carrying her with him, he leaned back against the pillows, settled her over him with a long upward stroke. She stared down at him, her hands braced on his shoulders, using her knees to lift and sink. Slowly

Not afraid. What did she see then? His eyes searched hers. Passion, need—a reflection of his, though not of him. Yet it was easy to see his presence in the perspiration sheened across her cheekbones; her skin was flushed a deep caramel, her nipples hard and full. He leaned forward to taste them.

She rose, dropped, and he groaned against her breast. "Do you want me to tell you?"

Good God. Was he so transparent with her? "Yes."

She moved more quickly, but he was too far gone to protest. Dying, yes. In love, yes. But never an idiot. His teeth closed gently over her nipple. Each heated wet slide over his cock wound him tighter, threatened to pull him apart.

"You cover your mouth when you laugh," she said, her voice carried on panting breaths. "In public. Yet you never hide anything else."

Startled, his gaze flew to hers, his lips unmoving around her breast. She rocked from her waist, holding her torso still, her chin tucked against her throat as she watched him in turn.

"Not your vanity. It's out in the open, for anyone to take as they wish. I never thought I'd want to take it. That you'd make me laugh with it." Her fingers clenched on his shoulders, and she made a tight swivel of her hips. "And the way you move, as if the world is your ballroom. Oh, god."

His hands caught her waist, and he held her as he thrust deep, took over. Not what she saw. She was telling him why she was falling in love with him.

Don't stop, Savi. Please don't stop.

"And you live exactly as you are, without apology. I can trust your appearance; I thought I couldn't, but I can."

Only because she saw him as he was. Her hands cradled his head, and she suddenly pulled him forward, arched her back. His fangs scraped the upper swell of her breast.

Blood.

A drop against his tongue, but it hit him like a flood, a powerful deluge through his veins, repeated in the surge of his hips, of his cock. Pulsing, flowing. His eyes widened, held hers through sheer will. The rest of him was beyond his control.

I won't let you go.

"You're so beautiful," she whispered, and lowered her mouth to his, her flavor ripening and rushing headlong into him with the last traces of her blood, sending him over.

Incoherent with need, with love, with astonishment.

And still in his trousers.

CHAPTER 20

The Scrolls are in Latin, and contained in a library in Caelum. They contain information about each nonhuman race and a history of the Guardian corps, but I've only heard of them secondhand. I've never seen them.

—Savi to Taylor, 2007

Savi neatly avoided the morning after by sleeping through it. Was it possible to have the same awkwardness, rolling out of bed at four in the afternoon? It helped that Colin wasn't there; she could groan and shuffle and pretend later that she'd awoken fresh. Maybe even perky.

She stood under the shower spray for an eternity, letting the hot water ease some of her soreness, then stretching carefully against the tile to work out the remaining ache in her muscles. A citrus-scented soap helped invigorate the rest of her, though not as miraculously as television commercials suggested, and she discovered she was still tender.

It had been worth it.

There weren't any mirrors in the bathroom, but she didn't need one to see the silly, satisfied smile that wouldn't leave her lips as she brushed her teeth. Didn't need one to know that the thick blue towel left her hair a spiky mess, and that Colin wouldn't care. Didn't need one to see how well the scrape on her breast had healed, along with the tiny bite on the inside of her thigh.

She would have liked some clothes, though. The oversized towel worked well enough, covered her from chest to knees, but wouldn't make a fantastic afternoon-after impression.

At least she was warm; the marble floors in the bathroom were heated, her feet almost toasty. A strange luxury for a vampire who kept his house the temperature of a meat locker. Had he simply agreed to a suggestion by the contractor, or intended it for guests? She'd had the impression he didn't invite many people here—even before the fire had destroyed a good portion of it.

She sighed, unable to figure it out. She'd just have to ask him.

Weak afternoon sunlight spilled through the main rooms; he'd left the drapes pulled back. She found a white silk robe folded on the bench at the foot of the bed, and she slipped it on, studying the layout of the suite.

The windows faced east, out over the park. She'd fallen asleep in his arms, but he must have risen before dawn to avoid the sun. To paint? Evidence of it surrounded her, filled the walls. Portraits of men, women, and children in varying modes of fashion, though none of Colin. Landscapes. All photorealistic in their attention to detail, the execution. Absolutely incredible.

She rolled up the sleeves of the robe as she walked toward the door and brushed away the dried blood over the symbols. Rock music thrummed through the room.

If that came from his studio on the other end of the house, he hadn't been lying. He *was* loud.

She almost stumbled over Sir Pup, stretched out on his belly in front of her door, his paws over his ears. He looked up at her mournfully, then trailed behind her as she followed the pounding bass. The music room, with walls a soft tangerine, wooden floors, and thick rugs. More paintings. Another room, papered in lemon yellow—perhaps a parlor, as it seemed to have no use but to look beautiful, with spindly legged furniture upholstered with ivory damask. High, airy ceilings arched over delicate chandeliers. Though a side door, a glimpse of a billiards room.

Her feet padded against the hardwood floors, across a rug, quicker now that she approached the tall doors. Not running, though the beat of her heart and the music seemed to hurry her along. One of the wide doors was open—only an inch or two, but she took it as an invitation.

Her eyes had to adjust to the darkness. The windows in the music room and parlor had been uncovered; here, heavy drapes blocked the sunlight, left the studio in shadow. She hesitated, until movement and a red blinking light at the far end of the room caught her attention.

Colin sat atop a five-foot stepladder. The volume of the music fell—he'd turned to lower it with a remote control. The snowy white of his shirt shone through the dark, but the rest of him was in silhouette.

And the awkwardness she'd hoped to avoid descended over her, left her floundering for something to say. It would have been easier if she could see him, read his expression—easier if she wasn't aware of how he could see hers. She wrapped her arms around her middle, tried not to fidget, and was relieved when the click of the remote being set down against the ladder gave her something to latch on to: his recent obsession with British punk, but particularly this group. It seemed another contradiction that she couldn't parse into components that made sense.

"I wouldn't have thought you a fan of The Clash."

And the instant it came from her mouth she wanted to take it back. There was only one way he would interpret her comment.

"Because I'm everything they abhorred? An aristocrat who owns a large international corporation, exploiting the poor and underprivileged?" He said it lightly, but without seeing his face she couldn't tell if she'd offended him.

She closed her eyes. It didn't only sound insulting, but also hypocritical. Internally berating herself for her stupidity wouldn't accomplish anything, though, and she strove to match his tone as she replied, "I suppose I am, too. Of the Boston Murrays, creator of a game that I licensed to a corporation larger than yours—a game that rots young American minds, even as outsourced and underpaid foreign employees toil away to manufacture it. I may be worse, actually; no one has died because of Ramsdell Pharmaceuticals." She took a deep breath when he didn't respond. "I just meant it's something unexpected. And that I don't have you figured out yet."

She waited for what seemed forever, but must have only been a few seconds before he said, "And you surprise me as well, my sweet Savitri. I wouldn't have thought you'd be aware of their social agenda, as they disbanded when you were all of twelve years old."

"Well, I've been with a lot of guys." Oh, god. *Stop, Savi.* That wasn't exactly the best thing to say the afternoon-after. She rushed to explain. "I don't know why, but men seem driven to educate women about 'real' music, and to push their tastes on to our poor little brains. The Clash has been pushed on to my brain since I first started dating, and depending on the guy, warring with The Sex Pistols for The Greatest Punk Group Ever."

"I've no intention of—" His voice shook with laughter, and he broke off. Brief silence filled the room as the song track switched from "London Calling" to "Straight to Hell." "I vow not to push my tastes on to you," he finished.

Relaxing back against the door, she smiled. "They'd have been horrified by you, anyway. Is this a compilation—and on random play? You've ruined the artistic integrity of the original album." She rolled her eyes.

His teeth gleamed through the darkness. "I hardly give a thought to what another's artistic vision is. Ninety percent of every album is rubbish. I can't carry everything forward, or I'd have a basement full of vinyl trash. So I keep only what speaks to me, and only the best of it."

"Ah, the price of immortality: a music library stocked with Greatest Hits albums. Do you paint in the dark?"

"Yes."

"Do you mind if I open the lights?" Perhaps he preferred to keep his work hidden until it was finished. She knew a few digital artists who couldn't tolerate anyone seeing a work in progress—to Savi's regret, as the process of it often interested her more than the product.

"Please do. I shall be down in a few moments."

Anticipation quickened her heartbeat, and she found the switch in the same location as the one in her rooms. Were the upper floors of the house laid out symmetrically? This must have been a matching suite, before he'd renovated—

"Oh, holy shit." She turned a slow spin, her mouth dropping open, her head tilting up. Caelum surrounded her, hung in multiple frames of varying sizes, but there were more. So many more—large canvases stacked six and seven deep around the room, leaning against the walls. And not all of Caelum.

Moving to the nearest, a wide landscape that stood as high as her chest, she pulled it forward, looked at the one behind it, and burst into laughter. Hugh and Lilith, as they'd been before she'd known them: a crimson-skinned Lilith in her horned and winged demonic form, standing next to Hugh, her forked tongue snaking out to tease his ear. Hugh, appearing all of seventeen but for the long-suffering expression on his face, wearing a brown robe belted with a rope, his arms crossed over his chest.

Her laughter died. She *had* seen him like this, and with his wings. Once, when he'd thrown himself in front of her, then flown with her to the hospital, leaving her parents and her brother behind. There'd been nothing that he could have done to help them.

She forced that memory away.

"I'd intended to give it to Castleford," Colin said from beside her, wiping his hands on a towel. Attired in a white dress shirt and black trousers, he gave the impression of immaculate elegance—despite the casual touches in the two buttons undone at his collar, the unfastened sleeve cuffs, and his bare feet. "But I'm not certain if Lilith would kill me."

She tore her gaze from the hollow of his throat. "You're incredibly good," she said, and moved on to the next. A smiling woman with coiled blond hair and an empire-waisted dress, holding a baby on her lap.

"I ought to be after two hundred years. That's Emily and their first boy, Hugh. I protested the name; I thought it should be mine." Amusement deepened his voice.

"You didn't paint this in the nineteenth century." The edge of the canvas was brilliantly white, the staples shining.

"No. Most were destroyed; this is what I've managed to produce since the fire. Some others, as well, but the majority of the paintings in the house I had shipped from the attics at Beaumont Court. These have been brought from Polidori's and storage in the past week; I've not yet sorted through them."

Her eyes widened, and she glanced around the room again. "All of this in eight months?"

"I'm limited only by the oils' drying time. I can paint very quickly. But most of these I'll toss; they aren't worth keeping. Even I can produce rubbish."

She shook her head in disbelief as he gestured to the next canvas. It seemed perfect to her. "That's the house at your family's estate; I've seen pictures of it on the tourist website." A stately mansion, set behind rolling lawns and framed by gardens. "Nani's going to love it."

"Yes. It's difficult to do otherwise."

Swallowing, she said, "I'm sorry about what I suggested last night."

"As you should be. It is my nature to be vain and selfish, but it is not a reflection of my family or my class. I would have been the same had I been born in a poorhouse."

"How do you know that?"

His brows drew together. "Look at me."

She grinned, but still felt the need to explain, "The one time we ever visited my grandparents, it was only because my grandfather laid a guilt trip on my dad because of all the money spent on his med school, the nice living he'd received. And the visit was a disaster—they had this huge place, but we got stuck in the guest house, and only my dad was invited up to the main house. My dad was infuriated by the insult to my mom; it was one of the few times I'd seen him really pissed."

"So you assumed my family would only accept Auntie into their home out of obligation for my financial support, resent it, and then—unwittingly or deliberately—insult her? Savitri," he said, "for all of your intelligence, you can be incredibly blind where your *nani* is concerned."

"I know. I should have remembered what you'd said: That you're their beloved Uncle Colin. That it wasn't obligation, but a willingness to assist a member of the family when he asked them for help."

"Just as you would for Auntie."

"Yeah." With a sigh, she pushed the canvases forward. "I need to call her, let her know we're okay, and make sure she's settled."

"I did this morning; it's after midnight in Derbyshire now. She's well." A triumphant smile played around his mouth.

"You recognized the house; you've searched the Internet for information related to me?"

She refused to blush. "Yes. If you can eavesdrop, then I can use Google."

"It seems a fair trade. Though I would answer anything you ask; you need not turn to a computer."

"I wasn't exactly happy with you at the time; a computer was safer."

"Yet you still looked."

"Yes." She met his gaze. "I couldn't help myself."

His eyes closed. The hand towel dropped to the floor, and his palm cupped her chin, tilted her mouth up. His left arm wrapped around her waist. "Neither could I, Savi." A soft kiss to her forehead. "Each visit to Castleford's was a new torment. How you ran the moment I arrived." Her cheek. "I could hear you in your flat when you didn't leave, and how I listened for your return when you did." Her lips. "Your scent everywhere. Torture, but I couldn't stay away."

Her chest aching, she caught his mouth before he could say more; it would be worse after a month of this. Much worse. She hadn't wanted to hurt him, too.

Think, Savi. But she didn't see a way out of it. Nor did she want to waste this opportunity, live with the regret. What was she going to do when the month was up, if they survived the demon?

Better to worry about surviving the demon, first. The rest would hardly matter if they didn't.

She broke the kiss, tucked her face against his chest. "I almost contacted you once, after you gave Lilith the painting of Caelum; I was going to commission one."

His hands smoothed the length of her back, sending shivers of awareness down her spine. "Had I but thought you'd accept anything from me, I would have showered you in them. Any you wish are yours to keep; you've only to tell me which are your favorites."

"I'll pick one out later." She stepped away, checked the robe's belt to make certain it was still in place and her neckline closed. It wouldn't do to tease him—or herself. "Will you show me what you're working on now?"

"Of course. Are you well? You're walking like a sailor just landed."

This time she couldn't halt her blush. "A little sore."

Colin turned and led her toward a giant canvas, at least eight feet tall, ten feet wide. No wonder he'd needed the ladder. "I intended to stop after the second time."

"I'm glad I disrupted every one of your intentions, then." She studied the canvas. He must have recently begun this one; sepia tones and dark shadows created shapes, but not any detail. Four prominent vertical lines, with the bottom half blocked out. "I'm not impressed."

Laughing softly, he collected a sketch pad from the shelf beside the ladder, flipped it open. "I'm working from this. But if it makes you uncomfortable, I'll not finish it. Not where you can see it and protest, that is."

She smiled, but it faded as he showed her the sketch. Not even a sketch—though in pencil, it was as detailed as a black-and-white photograph. He must have drawn it that morning as she slept lying on her stomach, her fingers curling into the pillow just beneath her chin, the pale sheet draped over her hips. Her limbs were sleek and toned, the material surrounding her luxurious; textured by his pencil, even the scars on her back appeared lovely, as if they'd been designed for her skin.

Her lips parted on a sigh, and she glanced up at his face, saw the hopeful glint in his eyes, the uncertain half-smile.

"I suddenly understand why you have so many self-portraits." To be seen in such a way; it stole her breath. "Can I have this sketch when you're done?"

"Yes. Or I can paint two."

"Will you put yourself in mine?"

He stared at her. "You've no idea the effect you have on me. If I trusted the bloodlust not to make its appearance, I'd kiss you senseless."

But he did not, taking back the sketch pad and flipping to the next page. His pencil flew across it before he turned the page toward her. The same scene, though more crudely rendered—and this time Colin was in the bed, dressed in a cape and tuxedo, leaning over her sleeping form with a rapacious grin and his fangs glistening.

She bit her lips to hold back her giggles. "Naked." And couldn't contain them when his hand moved in a blur, drew a penis extending from the tuxedo's now-open fly.

Grinning a bit like his double in the sketch, he slapped the pad closed and tossed it aside, then took her hand. "I shall paint us reenacting the whole of the *Kama Sutra*."

"Or we can just reenact it."

"Both. Come along. We've much to do, and I have much to show you before night falls."

❧

After the attack from Beelzebub and the nosferatu the previous year, Colin had apparently rebuilt with defense in mind. Every room and closet on the first and second floors had the symbols ready for activation and weapons hidden behind wall panels and in cupboards—even in the furniture.

In the basement, once Savi had finished panting over the theater and shelves of DVDs, he led her to a small room that could have doubled as a bomb shelter, and that served as the heart of his security system.

She took in the bank of video monitors, the computers, and fell in love all over again. "Does this work with the spell?"

"The monitors and the security controls, but no outside communication. However, the spell shouldn't be necessary; no demon could break through the steel walls or the door. Perhaps you might need it if you don't have time to engage the locks, but even if the power's cut, a generator will provide the backup." Colin pointed to a metal cabinet. "Enough blood for three weeks, food for six. Oxygen tanks, if air runs low and the intake has been compromised."

"You've prepared for humans?"

"Lilith, Castleford, and you. Anyone else I'd shove out the door." He paused. "But for Auntie."

She chewed on her lip, thought it over. "So at night, when we are home, we have the symbols active over the entire house so that Sir Pup is free to protect Lilith and Hugh. And we'll keep my bedroom spelled if I'm sleeping during the day, and Sir Pup available to you as a backup if Dalkiel decides to attack you." That thought made her uneasy; she didn't like that the demon would ever have access to Colin. As a human, she only had to fear the vampires; Colin had to protect himself from demon and vampires, night and day. "Can't we leave the spell active at all times when we're home?"

He shook his head. "For portions of the day, perhaps, but the cleaning service needs access, and we should have a window of availability for Auntie or SI to reach us."

"I can clean. What if the demon shifted into one of their human forms to trick you?" She couldn't imagine a demon doing something like that—it would consider a cleaning woman too low-caste—but then she hadn't thought one would concern himself with the likes of her, either.

With an arch of his brow, Colin said, "No."

"Snob."

"Yes." His lips twitched, and he leaned back against the smooth steel wall. "And you'd be too exhausted after cleaning a house of this size for me to take advantage of you as I intend."

"Well, I wouldn't do a very thorough job. You saw my apartment. Do you drink from your cleaning ladies?"

"No. It's bad form to eat the help. Would you prefer that I engage a cook for the duration of your stay?"

"I can do it; I like to, actually." She returned her attention to the monitors, saw Sir Pup strolling through one of the parlors. "So, if something happens, my first response should be to run down here and lock myself in?" The demon could set fire to the house and she'd still be safe; she wouldn't have the same protection if she was locked in one of the rooms, or a closet. When Colin nodded, she said, "How will I know if I can come out? Or if you need to be let in? You won't appear on the video."

"If I do, don't let me in." But he frowned thoughtfully as he strode forward to stand next to her. He tapped a few keys, brought up the feed from the theater. "The portrait of Mary Shelley, here—" He pointed to a painting beside the large plasma screen. "—I'll remove it, place it behind the sectional sofa."

"Okay. I'll also get us panic buttons, and link them via satellite to SI. Maybe a personal alert for Michael to wear when he's not in Caelum. If the shields are down, they should receive a signal, and he or Selah could teleport in. I might be able to incorporate them into our watches, or maybe a pendant, so that they're always on us."

She rubbed her forehead, mentally running through the

security, looking for any holes she could plug. There were holes, a lot of them, but short of imprisoning themselves in the room and waiting, there was little else they could do to prepare. Fleeing—to England or elsewhere—was tempting, but would make it more difficult to protect themselves.

And it would allow Dalkiel to return underground. If they remained in San Francisco, it gave the Guardians a better chance of locating him.

"Is it too much?" Colin said quietly.

"No. I'm just frustrated, because no matter what we do, there's going to be something we've missed. And I'm a little scared."

"Scared? Bloody hell, Savi, I have tried for months, and it is my gangster demon double who manages it?" He shook his head in mock exasperation, but his smile faded as soon as her laughter tapered off. "Don't lose that fear, sweet. It'll keep you sharp and aware. We know where we are vulnerable, and where we are secure—but to take either for granted is to court disaster. Our moment of greatest vulnerability will be leaving the house and traveling to Polidori's every evening. We'll vary our schedule, but they'll eventually know to look for us."

"Does Polidori's have a similar security system?" This one resembled the setup at SI; Colin had probably contracted with the same firm who had installed the security at the warehouse.

"No. You'll use the symbols in the suite and watch through the monitors. We'll have Sir Pup with us; I'll instruct him to remain with you."

She nodded, looked around the small shelter, and released a long breath. Half of her life spent avoiding the urge to run in order to protect herself, and now it would be her best defense.

"So what exactly will we be doing at the club?"

He heaved a great sigh and tilted his face toward the ceiling, with an expression close to pain tightening his features. "Conforming."

❧

But for his hair, Colin's life-sized portraits could have been a study in men's high fashion from the early nineteenth century to the turn of the twentieth—and a study in his moods. Savi trailed slowly down the stairs, memorizing each one and trying to ascertain the cause of the niggling sensation that each one was not quite right.

The third: Colin in fawn breeches and emerald waistcoat, smiling close-lipped; the proportions of his face and body were exact. Perfect. The eighth: The line of his jaw as he seemed to laugh at himself—or the observer—his fangs a startling counterpoint to the conservative black suit. The tenth: His angry glower tightening the skin around his mouth, his brows heavy and dark over his eyes.

And the very last: Situated at the base of the stairs, and the only one in which he wore modern clothing—though his hair still overlong and curling at his nape and around his ears—cruelty in the icy gray stare, the mocking tilt to his lips.

"Is my nose too long in this one?"

Startled, Savi turned her head. Colin stood on the riser above her, leaning casually against the banister, looking up at the painting. Her mouth dried, and she took a few moments to let her gaze travel the length of him before she managed, "No. It's exactly right."

A black shirt clung to his torso, the long sleeves loose at the cuffs; black leather jeans and boots finished the ensemble. Conforming, but not outside the boundaries of his personal taste. The metal rings studding his belt might have been a concession to Goth sensibilities, but she thought it fit his own; he looked lean, strong, dangerous—and ridiculously chic.

She clasped her hands together to prevent herself from touching him. Though they'd spent the past few hours together, first in the kitchen as she prepared her meal, then in the studio as he painted and she set up her computer equipment in the adjoining tower room, he'd not approached her.

She didn't mind waiting until after they'd returned from Polidori's; the anticipation would be almost unbearable by then, its own sweet pain.

He slanted an amused glance at her. "Lilith lied to me, then. Are any of them wrong? But for the hairstyle."

She eyed his hair in silent envy; it looked as if he'd pushed his fingers into the thick strands, tugged them forward, and left it sticking up in a haphazard, golden tangle. Why wouldn't she be surprised if that was all he'd done? And it had taken her nearly twenty minutes to gel and mess her hair to her satisfaction in front of the single mirror in the house: in her bathroom, hidden behind a wall panel.

He'd retreated to his upstairs suite—the one set of rooms he hadn't yet shown her.

With a sigh, she turned back to the paintings. Again, that feeling of *not quite right* hit her, and she hesitated before she shook her head. "Not really. Not wrong, exactly."

"It's important to me," he said quietly. "You'll not damage my artist's ego by telling me I've done it incorrectly."

"No, it's not that." She stepped forward, studying the pitiless curve of his mouth. "Everything's technically right. You've even captured your expressions, like in this one."

"You've seen me like this?" Dismay colored his voice.

"In Auntie's, the night we first met. A couple of times in Caelum. At Polidori's. In the parking lot two nights ago." Had it only been two days since he'd told her she was falling in love with him? How far she'd gone in that short time.

He was silent, and she turned, lifting her brow in question. His lips quirked, but no humor touched his eyes. "I'm not always a kind man, Savitri, and I cannot apologize for it. But I'm sorry I directed it at you."

"I know. I'm not fishing for an apology." She ran her hands over her arms. "It was there last night, too. When you saw what had happened to Nani and told me who'd done it. And I didn't mind—was glad of it even—because I felt the same way."

He hauled in a deep breath. "Perhaps you won't be once I've told you what I did to them."

Them. Three teenaged boys under the influence of a demon. He'd told her they'd been caught, that they were in SI's custody, but not spoken of anything he'd done specifically.

What could be so terrible that he was concerned about her reaction? "What did you do?"

His gaze held hers, his features without expression, but she could almost feel the tension holding him still. "I punished them with Chaos. The same way I gave it to you."

"Oh." She blinked up at the portrait again, tried to imagine their terror. Tried to weigh it against hers, and what Nani must have gone through. "I think I'm glad of that, too. It's appropriate—though it must have felt like shit for you."

"A bit. I'll not likely use it often." His voice, his posture relaxed slightly. "With luck, we'll convince the vampire community not to test me . . . or my consort. You look edible, by the by. I chose well; you carry the image spectacularly."

She blushed, glanced down at herself. She'd felt a little ridiculous when he'd given her the low-slung, white miniskirt, the boots that laced up to her knee, and a matching top that covered her arms and neck but left everything between her navel and hips bare. And doubly idiotic when he'd topped the pile of clothing with a pair of sai sheaths that strapped to her thighs, and a long white coat that fluttered behind her like a pair of wing tips as she walked.

But wearing it was oddly comfortable, not ridiculous. Like his clothing, this wasn't her typical style . . . but it wasn't *not* her, either.

"You realize I'm dressed almost exactly like Angelika from DemonSlayer?"

He nodded, and his eyes rose from the strip of skin at her waist. "Yes. We'll use it to our advantage. They will be able to sense that you are human, but once it's become known you created the game, and after you've demonstrated in some small way your strength, they won't know exactly what to make of you—and will likely fear challenging you. For all they know, the character and her powers are based on you. The game and Castleford's book have achieved something of a cult status amongst the community, their one source of information about their origins; knowing that you produced both will be an added protection."

She bit her lip, somewhat uncomfortable with finding security in something that killed two of her friends—but forced that discomfort away. "Okay."

Colin sighed, reached forward, and pulled her against him, dropping a quick kiss to her mouth. "If I could leave you here, Savitri, I would."

He must have mistaken the reason for her hesitation. "I'd rather go with you. Aside from that small display, I just sit there?"

He rubbed his cheek against hers, his shadowed jaw rough against her skin. "No; I need you to look and talk, establish yourself as a source of knowledge. Tell them any truth they want to hear, answer any questions but for my connection to Chaos and the extent of your abilities. And keep your shields as high as possible."

His mouth drifted toward her ear as he spoke, down. The neckline of her shirt rose almost to her jaw, the white silk clinging to her throat; his tongue moistened the skin along the edge. Her knees weakened. Her heart thudded against her chest.

"I will," she whispered.

He pulled back abruptly, breathing hard. "Oh, Christ. Not yet. We'll not leave the house if I give in now." His hands clenched on the banister behind him. He offered her a strained smile. "It would be easier if I didn't want you so desperately. Though not quite as pleasurable."

She stepped away, raised her psychic blocks. They'd been partially down, her natural state that he seemed to enjoy for its presence, though not an overwhelming one. He made a low sound that could have been relief or disappointment. Perhaps both; if so, it echoed hers—the disappointment that they'd had to put the arousal between them aside, the relief that he could. It wouldn't have boded well for the evening if he was constantly tormented by her scent.

"Will I be too much of a distraction at Polidori's?"

"No. And I need your eyes; you've seen the two vampires who followed us, and your memory is an advantage I'd be a fool not to use. I need to catalogue the vampires there, and who talks with whom. I doubt the demon will show, but his lackeys might." His mouth flattened as if he'd recalled something unpleasant. "Will it hurt terribly to re-create those memories later?"

"No. Not if I'm paying attention." At his questioning look, she explained, "I only have to anchor to the emotion when it's something I didn't notice—like the license plates. I saw them, but I didn't really *see* them. If I'd read the plate, it would have been no effort to remember the number without narrowing it down by tripping through my brain. It's the same with connecting one bit of information to another; if I'm actively doing it, I'll notice similarities. Otherwise, it might never occur to me—it's just random trivia. Like your house. I never thought of the house in the picture I saw on a website five years ago as being the same one listed in your data, though I knew both addresses . . . but if I'd considered it even once, I'd have immediately known."

She glanced up at the painting again. Two hundred years, and he still had a precise memory of his features. His long line of portraits couldn't account for the accuracy from the different angles, the expressions.

"I frequently observed myself in the mirror," he said, obviously guessing the nature of her thoughts.

She smiled, but looked at the portrait with new eyes. "Perhaps that's the difference—what's wrong. You've only seen yourself as a human. They're all . . . flat, I guess. There's something missing. This is more like Dalkiel than you." Unsure she could elaborate better, she shrugged and said, "No one dropped anything when he came into the café."

"I've seen myself as a vampire. I know what you're speaking of—it's an effect of the sword after the transformation. What you saw last night is, I imagine, a focused version of it—Lilith said it was psychic in nature. So you are likely correct; a painting can't produce the same effect." His brows drew together when she turned to him, her gaze searching his face, her lips parted in surprise. "I've always been splendidly handsome, Savitri, but I've not always been *this*."

She shook her head, certain she'd misunderstood. "You've seen yourself in a mirror? After you were turned?"

"Yes." Was that embarrassment in the casual lift of his shoulder, the tilt of his smile? "I'm no stranger to moments of idiocy."

"When did you begin seeing Chaos?"

"The summer of 1816. June fourteenth, to be exact—after a house party in which the houseguests thought a séance and invoking a curse purchased from a Gypsy would be a brilliant diversion. We determined that as a vampire, and a member of the paranormal set, I was the most appropriate person to recite it. Idiot that I was, I agreed—and finished it up with the dramatic use of my blood to write the necessary symbol. In hindsight, it was an embellishment I should have refrained from making."

Her eyes widened. "A Gypsy curse? What did it say? What

language was it in? What was the symbol? Have you tried to find a way to reverse it?"

Colin briefly caught his tongue between his teeth and grinned at her, his gaze bright with humor. "No. I'll not answer these; such things ought not to be played with, Savi. I've learned that lesson well."

"Have you asked Michael? Or Hugh? Do they know how it happened?"

"I imagine so, as Castleford was there directly after." His face darkened slightly. "No matter. The anchor to Chaos is from the sword, and has been in me since the transformation; the mirrors are a minor inconvenience compared to being there."

Minor? She could not believe that, not after experiencing the emotions of it, seeing his aversion to the Room, and hearing from Jake and Drifter about the effect it had on him. And it had forced him into seclusion for almost a century. Why should he carry the burden of it? "But maybe—"

"No, Savi." He softened the denial with a kiss to her fingers, and led her across the foyer. "No. The consequences of that night were heavier than simply mirrors and reflections. I'll not risk you to them, even to satisfy your curiosity."

"What other consequences were there?"

He wiped away the blood from the symbols, turned to look at her before opening the door. "Three men dead by my hand; not intentionally, but dead all the same."

She held his gaze. "You can't protect me from that; I've already killed three people with my stupidity. I've just not paid for it."

CHAPTER 21

On the Continent, finding one or two companions and living amongst a community has become all the rage. They have come to resemble poets huddling about in self-congratulating and, at the same time, melancholy societies. I do not know how they manage to be both—only that they do.

—Colin to Ramsdell, 1823

The younger son of an earl, with no ambition to take orders or serve in the Foreign Office—and after his transformation, unable to marry—Colin had had two options to maintain his lifestyle: to kill his older brother and his brother's heir to gain a title and fortune, or to be so handsome and his manners so engaging that, even if his family disowned him, even though he might become destitute, the rest of Society would welcome and support him out of simple appreciation for beauty. But though Colin had little affection for his brother Henry, his nephew had been too adorable to strangle; despite his status as one of the bloodsucking undead, his family had not cast him to the dogs—or the duns; and Society had never rejected him, though eventually he'd left it.

He determined he was either the luckiest sod alive, or he was simply that charming and beautiful. Perhaps both. Savi falling in love with him he ascribed to the first—but to win over the vampire population, he intended to utilize the latter.

Colin couldn't defeat the demon in combat; he hadn't the strength. He could, however, fortify himself with the vampires' loyalty, by playing on the very thing the demon would never recognize in them, would never *think* to recognize: modern vampires did not want to be led, particularly by a figure who would raise himself above them.

They wanted order; they wanted protection. They wanted knowledge. They didn't want a barbaric hierarchy based on physical power and age.

But they were too entrenched in vampiric tradition to know it yet.

Fia met them at the private entrance to Polidori's, carrying a tranquilizer pistol and accompanied by her partner, Paul. Two more vampires stood just inside the door, their guns trained on Colin's head and chest.

Savi apparently hadn't been expecting such a greeting, and he'd not thought to warn her of the preparations he'd made; her left hand found his, and her right rested near the weapon at her thigh. Colin reassured her with a squeeze of his fingers, but his amusement died when one vampire shifted his aim.

"Mr. Levitt," he said softly, "if you cannot immediately determine a demon from a human, I am quite capable of sending you to Hell to better learn the difference."

Levitt quickly retargeted Colin's forehead.

Paul slanted a glance back at the pair, then frowned at Colin. "Dalkiel could impersonate her, too."

Sir Pup flopped down at Savi's feet, panting from his run. Obviously considering the hellhound proof of their identity, Fia holstered her gun. "Or take a partner and throw us off-guard by impersonating the both of you, when we only expect one."

Savi's gaze was assessing as she studied the vampires. "I can make more of the handheld IR detectors to augment door security; they'll be useful inside, as well. Inside," she repeated with a lift of her brow, "where a vampire sniper might not pick me off from a rooftop."

Bloody hell. Colin had her through the entrance within moments.

"I can't believe I said 'vampire sniper' with a straight face," Savi said as he led her down the corridor to the private suite.

Colin couldn't believe he'd been so careless. The thick red

carpeting muffled their steps, but the quick beat of her heart raged in his ears; if it ever stopped, he'd be completely lost.

"In the future, you'll wear a Kevlar vest and helmet in and out." Sir Pup carried them for Lilith and Castleford; a simple protection that he'd overlooked.

"That'll be sexy," she said dryly, but he didn't hear any objection beneath it. Surprised, he glanced at her, but she only shrugged. "I don't want to be shot. I remember it too well."

His lips firmed as he nodded and escorted her into the suite. Sir Pup lay down in the hallway; if someone tried to take them by surprise whilst they were inside or planned to ambush them upon exit, they'd have to go through the hellhound first. Colin waited for Fia and Paul to follow them into the room, then activated the symbols.

Only drops from his fingertip, but the odor of his blood sent a dull, throbbing ache to his fangs, mirrored by a tightening of his groin. Christ. He released Savitri's hand, and she immediately moved across the main living area, toward the bank of monitors on the far wall.

These monitors showed the same images the guards in the security room would see. Redundant as they were, Colin had kept the cupboard closed and the doors hidden behind Savi's portraits when he'd stayed in these rooms—but those paintings had been moved to his gallery, and it served Fia and Paul to keep the security feed uncovered.

Just as well, he thought; she glanced back at him, and his talent seemed inadequate. Gold shadow glimmered across her lids; she'd lined her eyes with a smoky gray, emphasizing the exotic tilt at the corners. Her glistening, full lips were sultry, berry-stained perfection.

Paint, on a canvas far more enticing than any he'd ever worked—and the result much more beautiful. Good God, but he would give anything to take his brush to her skin.

With effort, he forced himself to look away from the picture she made. She'd been psychically and verbally distant since they'd left his house, holding herself rigid as if trying not to tempt him in the small confines of the car—and likely mulling over the revelation he'd made about the curse. But even with her shields up, she was an irresistible temptation.

He'd have preferred to tease himself with her nearness and

his arousal, heightening their anticipation through simultaneous pursuit and self-denial, but they had too much at stake for him to lose his focus.

And so with a sigh, he focused. "Did Castleford learn anything useful from the boys?"

Shaking his head, Paul took a seat on the sofa and rested his elbows on his knees. "They talked, but had nothing that might help narrow down the demon's location, or even any names of other vampires."

"Dalkiel only met with them at Denver's apartment. No motel rooms, no restaurants, nothing that might give us a place to start," Fia added.

The demon had likely cultivated them for the single purpose they'd served, then. Too young and weak to be true assets, but desperate enough to be useful, even if their use was of short duration.

"You've got metal detectors at the front doors?" Savi said, peering at one of the monitors.

Fia nodded. "We'll be carrying, but no one else is allowed through with anything sharper than a nail file." As if reminded by the mention of weapons, she unbuckled her holster, replaced it with a sheath that would carry her sword on her back—more for show than for use, and less dangerous than a gun to carry around in the crowded club. Even if a vampire got hold of the sword, he'd have to move close enough to Savi to use it.

Close enough to Colin.

"If I were one of Dalkiel's vampires, I'd snap off the stem of a martini glass and stab it through my target's throat. Or use my fangs; they've got to be good for something." Savi glanced over her shoulder at Colin, her dark eyes sparkling with amusement. "But that's just me. Hopefully they'll be reliant on their guns and swords." Her gaze shifted to Fia. "You've got your security guy walking a circuit of the cameras to make certain the video isn't compromised, but he's using the same 'OK' thumbs-up each time. It's too easy to loop. The first thing I'd do is record about ten minutes of that, then hack into your feed and send it back. By the time your guys in the security room noticed something was off, you'd have a breach."

She should have been a criminal. Smiling, Colin wiped his fingertip with his handkerchief; the puncture he'd made had already healed. "What do you suggest, sweet?"

"Song lyrics," she said, turning to study the monitors again. "Have him sign a line at each camera, using a different song each round. Some firms use the time, but if Dalkiel has enough patience, he can just record one day and use it the next."

Paul stood, gathered his sword from the low coffee table. "Do you know the Guardians' sign language? If we need to talk to you, can we?"

Though Colin couldn't see her face, couldn't sense her emotions through her psychic blocks, he could feel the blood rising to the surface of her skin as her cheeks flushed.

"No. I haven't been paying attention. It's visual, so it should be easier for me to pick up than something verbal." She slanted a glance at Colin before looking away. "Can you teach me a basic vocabulary tomorrow?"

"Yes. We'll use Hindi or Latin until then." Both languages were somewhat obscure; there'd be little chance more than a few—if any—vampires at the club knew them.

"Paul and I don't know Hindi," Fia said.

"And I don't understand spoken Latin." No embarrassment colored Savi's voice this time; her attention was fixed on the monitors. She pressed her finger to one of the screens. "We need to talk to this woman. Do any of you recognize her?"

Colin crossed the room, careful not to touch her, not to contemplate what lay beneath the white silk making a marble column of her slender throat. She pointed to a thin female with short, platinum hair, but it was impossible to determine through the small video if she was vampire or human. "No. Fia? Paul?"

"Yeah," Fia said. "That's Raven. About twenty years plus seven as a vampire. That's her partner, Epona." She indicated the bosomy brunette rubbing her pelvis against Raven's bottom. "I've chatted with them a couple of times. They stay pretty low-key. I think Epona bartends on the weekends at The Thirst, down on Folsom; Raven works the night desk at a hotel in the Tenderloin."

"The last time I was here, Raven was dancing with the guy with the mullet—the driver in the Navigator that followed us from SI on Friday. She might know his name," Savi said, then pointed to another monitor. "And this guy, too. The blond talking to the *Vampire Princess Miyu* wannabe. He was Mullet Boy's passenger, though he's traded in his suit for that fishnet shirt. Do you know him?"

"No," Fia said, blinking rapidly in surprise before glancing at Colin. He gave a quick shake of his head, a hard knot forming in his stomach.

Savi's stiff silence in the car apparently had a different cause than he'd thought: she'd been searching through her memories of that night. Painfully, he imagined—she'd been drinking too much to have paid such close attention to those around her.

And he'd no doubt Caelum—and Chaos had been her emotional anchor to access those memories.

"Do you want us to bring him to you?" Paul asked.

"No," Colin said. "Watch him, see whom he speaks with. If he leaves, take Varney and follow him."

"And if he meets up with Dalkiel?"

"Run." Colin saw Paul's surprise. "If the demon senses you, he'll kill you. Once you're secure, contact my phone or SI immediately."

Savi continued searching through the faces onscreen. Finally, she shook her head. "I don't see anyone else I recognize. Does the club keep the security tapes more than a month? Maybe we can track down Mullet Boy that way, get a name."

Colin's teeth clenched. They might have, had he not ordered them erased after two weeks: only enough time to use them in case of an investigation or a crime committed at the club. He'd not been able to hide his absence from the club employees who worked security, but he hadn't wanted it archived and filed away interminably.

"No."

"It'd be nice to have a name when I hit the computer tomorrow. I can do a lot with a name: find locations they've visited, movements, purchases." She stepped back from the monitors and turned, her coat hem swirling around her ankles. "Do you know Raven's name?"

Fia's mouth quirked into a smile. "It's really Raven. Raven Thorne. Shall we ask her to join you at your table?"

Good God. Her parents had essentially birthed her with fangs in her mouth, giving her such a name. Colin glanced at the screen, and shook his head. "No. Invite Epona. I have a proposition for her."

❧

Colin was the most accomplished flirt Savi had ever seen. She watched in amazement as, with a few choice compliments, Epona's and Raven's expressions transformed from fear as they hesitantly approached the table, to stunned admiration as they took their seats on the low sofa adjacent to Colin and Savi's, then to easy, slightly girlish enjoyment.

And though she'd known he'd use this tactic—and why— she'd feared jealousy would unwittingly rise within her and ruin the evening, leave its insidious ache.

She needn't have worried.

He flirted outrageously, but never indicated his affections lay anywhere but with Savi. Though his eyes shone with interest as he looked at them, when he turned to her to gauge her reaction or seek her response, either they darkened with heated intensity, or his lips curved in a delighted smile he reserved solely for her.

And she'd guessed where the conversation would eventually lead, but she was surprised by the skill with which he guided them all from a discussion of the tattooed Gaelic knots decorating Raven's wrists, to their desire to visit Ireland, to pubs and San Francisco nightclubs. And, when a note of disillusionment entered Epona's voice when she spoke of The Thirst, Colin pounced.

"I must confess that when I invited you here, it was to discover any secrets my competition has; The Thirst is quite the success." Colin raised Savi's hand from her lap, pressed a kiss to the back of it, and stared contemplatively at Epona. Sitting so close must have been torture for him, but he'd kept Savi against his side since they'd sat down. Likely weighing her need for protection against his bloodlust.

Protection—and appearance—won.

Epona laughed shortly and shrugged. "I'm only part-time. Barely that. Just Fridays and Saturdays."

Raven patted the brunette's thigh, her black-tipped nails stark against Epona's white skin. Her own thin legs were tucked underneath her on the sofa cushions, her high heels lying tumbled on the floor.

It was a gesture that spoke of a long relationship, and with a familiarity to it—it wasn't the first time Raven had given her that encouraging caress.

Difficulty in finding a better position when she could only work evenings? Or did it arise from another complication?

"Forgive me for prying, but you don't sound as if you're satisfied with your employment. Surely you can do better."

Epona's lips twisted into a hard smile. "Are you offering me a job?"

"Yes," Savi said. "If you are looking for something full-time. We could use more help at the bar, and we prefer to hire within the vampire community."

"I applied when you reopened, but I didn't get a callback. You have pretty stringent background checks."

"It's a necessary evil," Colin said. "But an easily circumvented one. What name did you use? I'll ask my manager to pull up your file."

She glanced uncertainly at Raven, who nodded. "Epona Smith."

Smith? It clicked into place. The weekend employment, the frustration, the unfulfilled dream vacation. Had Colin already realized? "You were passed over because of a lack of ID?" And probably without the necessary Social Security number for above-the-table employment.

Bad enough that vampires were limited by their daysleep and a need to hide their nature from humans, but legal requirements made finding a suitable job doubly difficult.

A grimace briefly pulled Epona's red-slicked mouth tight. "Yeah. I've hit the age where my birth certificate is useless. The DMV won't issue me ID, and trying to get a passport is impossible. I don't look seventy."

Savi's brows drew together as she glanced up at Colin. He watched her, a smile lurking at the corners of his lips. "Who did yours?" she asked. His identification and backup documentation were perfect. "Was it someone here in San Francisco?"

He nodded slowly. "Stephan. An elder."

Raven heaved a long sigh. "Yeah. Who isn't much help now."

"The nosferatu killed him last year? Here, at Polidori's?" Savi guessed. Apparently Colin was rebuilding more than just a structure. Too many of the community's sources for help and businesses had been disrupted by the nosferatu's slaughter of its elders, then the subsequent flight of the younger vampires from San Francisco.

Savi suddenly grinned up at him. "This feels like a big 'fuck you' to Dalkiel. This is what got me in trouble in the first place, you know." Before he could respond, she leaned forward and said to Epona, "E-mail a picture to me—preferably a passport photo—and I'll set you up."

Colin slipped a business card onto the table in front of her, and Savi scrawled her address across the back. It disappeared into Epona's generous cleavage.

His fingers played with the hair at her nape as he added, "And should anyone else require the same service, we'll provide it for them." He pulled Savi back against his side again, his arm wrapped around her waist, his hand at her hip.

There'd likely be no need for Epona and Raven to tell others; Savi could feel the change in the attention they'd been receiving from the vampires who'd listened nearby.

Suddenly, Colin wasn't just a beautiful vampire oddity—he and his human consort were useful.

With luck, now Raven would prove to be, as well.

❧

"That didn't work," Savi muttered in Hindi, and took a sip of her water. The faint citrus of the lemon slice combined with the fragrance of her soap and her natural feminine scent, making an intoxicating perfume.

Doing his best to ignore his own thirst, Colin smiled into her hair, the short, gelled strands stiff against his cheek. "We accomplished something almost as important," he said softly. Even if someone could understand the language, they'd likely not hear him over the music.

His gaze skimmed the lounge on the second level; Fia

stood near the railing, looking down at the dance floor, Sir
Pup at her heels. He raised his voice and said her name. She
glanced at him, shook her head.

She quickly signed, *Fishnet Shirt slipped out about ten
minutes ago with the woman he was with—probably his partner; Paul and Varney are following them. Raven didn't know
the name? And do we need to have someone watch the women
to make sure they aren't targeted for your questioning?*

No, Colin signed. *Raven remembers him, but he was just a
random bloke. Send the pup down, and order the DJ to lower
the volume a bit.*

He turned to Savi. "Are you up for a tour?"

With a nod, she downed her drink and set the glass on the
table. For just a moment her brow quirked, as if she wanted to
make an observation. Then she hesitated, her lips pressed together, and she rose to her feet.

He allowed her to pull him up, kept his hand clasped in
hers. "You're correct," he said, leaning forward to speak
against her ear. "You can say it."

"It just occurred to me that you were holding court." Her
voice was amused . . . and somewhat apologetic.

"Yes," he agreed easily. "It came naturally." He drew back
to search her expression, found humor and relief. "I've since
realized it isn't the right tactic."

"More like something Dalkiel would do."

"Yes."

Her gaze moved past him, surveyed the dance floor. "Perhaps half and half. I think some appreciate it; others would be
swayed by your coming to them." Looking back at him, she
rose up on her toes, pressed a kiss to his jaw.

Oh, sweet heaven. The soft touch of her lips. The warmth
of her skin. And all too quickly gone as she lowered back to
her heels.

"I'm still feeling my way around. I never expected you to
care what I thought or said."

To respond as he'd like would be to take her there on the
sofa. He fought the flare of resentment that they couldn't
leave, that he still had too much to do before taking her home,
where they wouldn't have to speak in whispers and guard
every word against the ears of those he meant to win over.

He only nodded, his mouth tightly closed, refusing to draw breath. Bless her perspicacity. She stepped away from him, stooping to pat Sir Pup's head.

"Pup," he said quietly. "Grow up a bit."

The hellhound sat down and licked his front paw. When he stood up, Savi didn't have to bend to reach him. Subtly done, though someone watching carefully would have noticed.

"Stay at her feet, and kill anyone who tries to touch her." Colin hesitated before taking her hand. At times, the hellhound followed commands too well. "But for me."

Sir Pup grinned at him, then fell into step beside her as they began a round of the tables. They stopped to chat with the humans, playing the club owner ascertaining his clients' satisfaction.

With the vampires, he dropped the pretense, though not the charm—and had to fight his frustration again when he didn't find the resistance he'd hoped for from the first few groups. Worse, they asked few questions, despite the myriad leading statements Savi and he made.

Any brainless sod could herd sheep; he needed to find the wolves, and bloodlessly tame them.

While Savi told four vampires how to access a hidden level in the DemonSlayer video game, Colin searched out Fia again, caught her eye. *Who likely resents my presence here more than any other? Someone with influence.*

Darkwolf and his consorts, Arwen and Gina. You've seen them before. He was the one who questioned your feeding from humans that night Paul and I met you.

Christ. *Darkwolf?* His exasperation must have shown on his face; across the club, Fia began laughing at him. He couldn't hear it, but he could easily sense her psychic amusement.

Fia's not my real name, either, she told him, grinning, and then signed Darkwolf's location on the second level.

§

On the stairwell, Colin pushed Savi against the wall and buried his face in her neck. Her surprise and arousal broke through her carefully constructed shields; he stiffened against her, but his gaze was approving when he pulled back to look at her.

"Just like this, sweet," he murmured. "Keep them down but slightly, so they feel your need for me. They don't have the ability to look deeply, but they'll sense this."

"What about the wyrmwolves?"

"They've only appeared when you've been completely open." His lids lowered, and he stared at her throat for a moment before shaking himself. "And if one does make its appearance, it will only help our cause when I demonstrate my magnificent fencing technique, defeating the slavering monster, saving all and sundry."

She bit her lip to halt her automatic protest. It would also make it torturous for him. He hadn't yet fed.

As if reading the cause of her distress, he said, "We'll leave directly after this; for now, my hunger is an asset, but I'll not have control much longer with your shields down. Keep the pup by your hand. And we've still to expose your strength; if you find an opportunity for a display, take it."

She tried to think of a subtle demonstration as they climbed the stairs, but the new tension in Colin's form distracted her from all but the most melodramatic scenarios. Sir Pup licked her palm reassuringly as they approached a table in the corner of the lounge; somewhere between the first and second floors, he'd grown another couple of inches and his appearance took on a wolfish cast.

Three vampires sat around the table; two of them, Savi deduced, must be Darkwolf and Arwen: the tall male with dark skin, a clean-shaven head, and a howling-wolf tattoo on his left forearm, wearing a leather vest and spiked wristbands; and the fragile, ethereal brunette, who wouldn't have been out of place in Rivendell. Beside them, a female who didn't hide the suspicious anger tightening her full lips.

Like everyone else Colin had spoken with, they had a brief moment of disconcertment as he moved close enough for them to really see him. Anger quickly replaced it on Darkwolf's and Arwen's faces, coupled with slight unease.

The suspicious female was more outspoken in her reaction. "What the fuck did you just do to us?"

"Gina," Arwen admonished softly, but her gaze remained hard as amethyst as she stared at Colin, then at Savi. "We're his guests. If he chooses to exercise his power over us for his pleasure, we've only ourselves to blame for accepting the invitation."

"There's no need to blame anyone. He can't help it," Savi said. She turned and dragged an empty chair from the next table. Breaking the metal frame in half would have made a fantastic show of strength, but would have likely been misinterpreted as an attack. Not to mention, beating up a chair would look ridiculous. "It goes away the better you know him."

Colin nodded. "Please accept my apologies for your discomfort. It is unwittingly done, and my consort speaks the truth: the longer the acquaintance, the less effect it has."

She allowed him to pull her down onto his lap, straddling his right thigh. His hand rested on her hip; the weapon strapped above her knee would be immediately available to him.

She doubted they knew Sir Pup had countless others in his hammerspace.

Darkwolf's mouth was closed, but she saw the movement of his tongue beneath his lips, as if he was running it over his fangs. Telling Colin that he was not without his own weapons, Savi realized.

A vampire who wouldn't rely on blades and bullets. It was oddly reassuring.

"You speak as if you expect our acquaintance to be of a long enough duration that it would matter to us," Darkwolf said. "It doesn't. We've no use for a vampire who flaunts the very tradition and law that has kept us safe for centuries."

Colin smiled lazily; his manner still easy, but no longer flirtatious. "You're mistaken," he said. "Nosferatu and demonkind would have eradicated or enslaved us centuries ago had not Guardians held them in check; your safety has come neither from tradition nor law, but from Caelum."

The word elicited neither surprise nor puzzlement in their expressions—but then, they could have read Hugh's book or played DemonSlayer. Probably had done both.

And the dubious glance Arwen and Darkwolf exchanged indicated they knew very well it wasn't a fictitious place.

"We have Guardians to thank for our continued survival?" Arwen shook her head. "I think not. Except for the nosferatu last year, the only beings who've ever posed a danger to vampires have been the Guardians."

That was likely true—but twisted in such a way Savi wouldn't have been surprised if Dalkiel had been the one to bring that truth to their attention. "You personally knew vampires who've been killed by them?"

The color had to be the result of contact lenses, but the effect was still striking when Arwen leveled that purple gaze at her. "Yes, little human."

"And what kind of vampires were they?" Savi asked. *Little human.* Hobbits had saved Middle Earth; Arwen should really know better. "I bet not someone you'd like to have over for a sip from your neck."

Arwen blinked quickly and looked away from Savi, toward Darkwolf.

"They were all assholes," Gina said. "Mostly rogues. Taking blood from humans, killing others. The kind of vampires the elders—if we'd had any left—would have convened a court for and judged." She snarled and turned to Darkwolf when he made a motion for her to hush. "I told you fuckers this after the blond demonfucker told us all that shit, but you stupid assholes wouldn't listen, were all 'Vampire Power!' and—"

"Gina," Arwen said softly.

Savi had to hide her grin when she felt the tiny tremor of Colin's laughter against her back. Her amusement quickly died when his fingers skimmed over her hip, across her bare stomach. A light shiver of arousal ran over her skin.

"You knew he was a demon." Colin gave no indication of his triumph, though Gina's outburst had helped them enormously.

Savi fought to keep her thoughts coherent as he raked his nails up the inside of her thigh. Why? She could have held her shields, never given indication of his manipulation—or his lies, if he used them—through psychic scent or expression.

Then Darkwolf drew a deep breath, shifted in his seat, and Savi saw the purpose behind the tactic: they'd be distracted by her need. By Colin's escalating bloodlust.

"We'd watched you for months. Your habits. Nothing matched up." The tattoo on Darkwolf's forearm undulated as he drummed his fingers on the table, and he leaned back to sling his left arm over Arwen's shoulders. "And suddenly you're interested in leading us? Willing to share blood, and to stop feeding from humans? It didn't make sense." He flicked a glance at Savi before returning his attention to Colin. "It still doesn't, but at least there's no doubt you're a vampire."

No, not just a distraction, she realized. The bloodlust was a tie, a commonality which the demon could never share.

"I've no intention of giving up human blood or sharing mine," Colin said. "And I'll admit my first impulse was to let him drag you all to Hell with him."

Oh, god. Apparently, he was not going to lie or attempt to charm them. A breathless tension hovered over the table for a moment as the vampires seemed to decide whether to take offense—or to take his blunt declaration as an indication of his readiness to have honesty between them, even if that honesty didn't endear him to them.

Finally, Darkwolf's eyes narrowed. "What changed your mind?"

"I find the demon's use of my face and my name most disagreeable. Offensive, even."

"Why doesn't that surprise me?" Gina muttered.

"I've no idea." Colin's tone held a hint of amusement. "But my vanity is nothing to my willingness to accede to Miss Murray's determination not to let you fall slave to the demon's yoke."

A smile touched Arwen's lips as she cast a speculative glance at Savi; the sharp little points of her teeth made an appearance. Savi repressed her shiver. With Colin, with Darkwolf, the fangs fit. In Arwen's pretty mouth, they were unexpected, and all the more sinister for the surprise.

"Do you intend to become like us, little human?"

Colin's thigh tensed beneath her, but she rested her hand on his knee, squeezed lightly. Biting back her anger was difficult, but anger wouldn't serve any purpose. Nor would asking Sir Pup to eat Arwen's face.

"I hope not," Savi said. "I've got enough issues and my own prejudices to work through without adding 'condescending vampire bigot' to the list. What's the point of that, really?"

Remembering Gina's outburst, she said, "Vampire Power? Let me guess: you want what Dalkiel had to offer you, but without Dalkiel attached?"

Arwen waved a slim white hand toward the dance floor. "We're stronger than them. Will outlive them. Yet we're forced into the underbelly of the human world—and the Guardians' and demons' worlds. Why should it be that way? We should not have to beg for scraps from human society and mercy from the Guardians' swords."

Savi shook her head. "It doesn't have to be that way. But putting yourself above humans is the last thing you should do."

"So we should put ourselves below your Guardians?" Darkwolf's gaze slid over to Colin. "Live by their whims and command? Serving the government, acting as informants against our own kind?"

"Do you imagine we're suggesting a trade? The demon's yoke for the Guardians'? You mistake us." Colin slid one of the sai blades from the sheath at Savi's thigh, placed it on the table. As one, the three vampires stared down at the weapon. "If you want to follow tradition—and if your partner insists on insulting Miss Murray—you're welcome to test your strength against mine. I'll have no compunction smashing each of you beneath my heel, nor, by tradition, should you resent it when I do. As the most powerful of us, it is apparently my right to have those weaker than I bowing before me. So, please, prostrate yourselves. I prefer you do it smiling."

His voice took on a hard edge; his expression had the same cruel cast she'd seen before. Frustration lurked there, too; she didn't need psychic abilities to read the tension in his body— a tension likely fed by the bloodlust.

Would his patience have worn as thin if he hadn't needed his hunger to establish that tie between them? His attempt to exploit their prejudice toward their own kind proved a double-edged sword.

And though she knew he didn't want to, if they left him no other alternative he would make his point with bloodshed. Not one vampire—or even several together—would have a chance against him. As no one moved to pick up the blade, they must have realized it, as well. Perhaps they'd seen him fight the wyrmwolf; if so, there could be no doubt of his ability to take out anyone who challenged him.

Their fear wouldn't engender their trust, though.

And raising her shields might have eased his frustration and helped him regain control—but it also might lead them to think she was lying or hiding.

Savi placed her hand on Sir Pup's ruff and said in her halting Latin, "Remove knife table."

The sai disappeared; Darkwolf's eyes widened and Arwen visibly startled, probably attributing it to her words, as if it had been a spell Savi had cast instead of Sir Pup's hammerspace.

Although to anyone unfamiliar with hammerspace, it would likely have been as amazing as a vanishing spell.

"The problem is not power," Savi said. "Not your lack of it compared to Guardians and demons, or the humans' lack compared to you. Physical power means very little. Do you have any idea what happened last year? One human managed to trick Lucifer—*Lucifer*—into closing Hell's Gates. Another found a way to rid the city of the nosferatu who slaughtered your elders. Guardians—and Colin—assisted, but it was humans who defeated them."

Colin released a long breath against the back of her neck. "What Miss Murray is trying to tell you is that your ignorance is dangerous by itself; but if you seek truth from demonkind, those answers will kill you. Or I will."

Gina's eyes flashed with anger, and her lips pulled tight over her fangs. "It's not as if you've been all that forthcoming with answers."

"No," he agreed easily. "And I was in error."

As if deflated by his admission, she sat back and frowned at him. Arwen did the same. Not, Savi noted, looking to Darkwolf for his reaction, as they had only minutes before.

Darkwolf's wry smile told her he saw the difference, as well. "So this is your offer? To raise us from the depths of ignorance? I find it hard to believe, considering that you're connected with an agency that has been nothing but secretive."

"Raise you?" Colin's brows winged upward, and he shook

his head, laughing softly. "No. I'll make information available, and assist in reconstructing the community the nosferatu destroyed. But I'll not prod you into action, or pat your head in reward. Dalkiel preys on this community because it is weak; I'll give you the tools to strengthen it—and to resist any other demon who would take advantage of you."

"But he's still powerful enough to kill us," Arwen pointed out.

"Yes. And so relations with the Guardians and Special Investigations must be maintained—they would kill any demon or nosferatu regardless, but with communication we can identify threats and remove them more quickly. Their secrecy is not aimed at you, but to prevent the general public from panicking."

"At least for now," Savi said. When Colin glanced at her in surprise, she clarified, "I don't mean that Michael or SI will eventually keep things from vampires again. It's too late for that, and the communication is too valuable." Particularly with Guardian numbers still so low. "But that it won't be long before humans find out. I imagine not more than a decade, at most."

"We've done well thus far, sweet. We're not more than a dream to most, fiction in books and movies."

"Yes, but that was before satellites that can read license plates from space, and before Regular Joe could access those images from his home computer. Before the explosion in the vampire population. Before security cameras on every corner. Before hundreds of rogue demons fled Hell, and are—for the first time—acting for their gain rather than Lucifer's. And how long do you think it'll take before they stop fearing the repercussions of Lucifer's anger if they are worshipped for themselves? The Gates are closed for five hundred years. Someone's going to get cocky—already one demon grabs for power here. On a small scale, sure, but it's still something he'd never have attempted if Lucifer had access to Earth."

Colin nodded thoughtfully. "If that's the way it's to be, then far better to align ourselves with beings who look like angels, and once were human."

"Yeah. Protection from demons and nosferatu is fine in the short term, but it's humans and their reaction you'll have to really worry about." Savi glanced at Arwen, then Darkwolf. "And it's important not just to have that link to Caelum and SI, but to keep the current partnership and bloodsharing structure. Now, feeding from humans isn't allowed, but primarily for reasons of secrecy and community security. But if you start to think yourselves above them, feeding from them or thinking it's okay to kill them, you'll appear nothing more than parasites. The panic and the backlash upon public exposure will probably be bad enough—but add in vampires who think like demons and nosferatu, treating humankind with disdain, and you're going to have seven billion people hunting you down. Those aren't good odds."

"You think about this far too much," Colin said, pressing a kiss against her temple.

She smiled, arching her brow as she turned to look at him. Though his voice had been teasing, his gaze was dark, speculative. "Someone has to. It's going to happen. And though it will help that vampires were once human, and some might have family living who'll stand up for them, the only real defense is to set up the vampire communities like they are model minorities: self-sustaining, yet still economically valuable in the greater human society. And, to all appearances, safe."

"That's fucked up," Gina said.

Colin grimaced, tilting his head back to stare up at the ceiling. "It will chafe, won't it?"

Savi patted his leg. "Don't worry. With luck, it'll only be that way for a century or so."

He looked down at her and grinned, but it faded when Arwen asked, "And will you be feeding from humans in a century or so? Are you going to turn her?"

"No," he said softly, holding her gaze. "I can't transform her; my blood would kill her."

She sighed and leaned back against him. Every vampire in the club likely felt the hollow despair in her psychic scent, but there was no point in concealing it. "And I can't be transformed; I'd probably die."

Gina looked between them, a furrow of confusion on her brow. A touch of pity around her lush mouth. "That's fucked up, too."

"Yes," Colin agreed.

CHAPTER 22

Humans are anchored to Earth, but may be teleported to Caelum or Hell. It takes a ritual or sacrifice for a human to resonate with a Gate, allowing them to move between realms without being teleported. The same may be true of nonhumans, but I haven't been able to convince anyone to tell me exactly how—or to show me the symbols that complete the ritual.

—*Savi to Taylor, 2007*

Colin waited with barely restrained impatience as Levitt checked the exterior security cameras in anticipation of their exit. All in all, their first foray had gone well. Eventually, he'd have to thrash someone rather than simply threaten it, but it wouldn't be that evening. When Savi and he had left Darkwolf's party, they'd still been tense and slightly confused; Colin imagined they'd discuss the situation the whole of the night, agreeing on what an ass he'd been, but eventually coming to the same conclusion: he'd be more valuable helping the community than fighting them.

It was unfortunate he'd resorted to the threat of violence; unbelievable, how quickly his control had deteriorated.

Apparently, Savi had come to a similar conclusion. Beneath the bulletproof headgear, her eyes were amused—and dark with anticipation. "Charm and bloodlust don't mesh well," she observed.

The corners of his lips lifted in a wry smile. "No, indeed." Luckily, it was a tactic he only needed to use once. They'd no doubt he was a vampire. "In the future, I'll feed prior to leaving the house."

Levitt gave his all-clear signal, and the locks clicked open. "We could do it in the car."

Christ. He was so desperate for her, he probably wouldn't last the distance to his house. But he refused to succumb to his bloodlust in the parking lot, where Levitt would see Savitri tupped by an invisible man on-camera.

He shouldn't have given Paul and Fia the suite as their living quarters. He shouldn't have—

The odor of fresh blood struck him a second after he opened the door and stepped outside, Savi's hand in his. He paused, his body blocking hers from attack. At her heels, Sir Pup barked a warning and shifted instantaneously into his three-headed form.

But death had already come; there was nothing to fight. A woman's severed head had been impaled on the Jaguar's hood ornament, her mouth open and her fangs exposed by a twisted grimace. Her eyes had been ripped away.

Tension dug its claws into his spine; Colin tore his gaze from the macabre display, opened his senses, and scanned the lot.

Nothing.

Savi's hand flexed against his, and he felt the slide of fabric against his back as she rose onto her toes, as if to look over his shoulder. Bloody hell. He pushed her back in and slammed the door closed, but not quickly enough.

"Ohmygod," she whispered, then began gagging.

The thick, heavy scent of the vampire's lifeblood saturated the air within the small room; despite his hunger, his fury overwhelmed his bloodlust.

She wouldn't forget.

"My sword, pup." The blade appeared in Colin's palm; he turned toward Levitt.

The vampire glanced up from the monitors, horror etching his features into a stark mask. It rapidly changed to terror.

"It wasn't there a second ago! I fucking swear, man!"

Johnson whimpered softly, backed up against the wall, and closed his eyes, his arms rising protectively in front of his face.

"Colin." Savi's hand tightened around his, her slim fingers surprising in their strength. Not strong enough to hold him back, except that she wanted him to wait. "Colin, don't."

Footsteps pounded along the corridor, and Fia burst into the room. Confusion slid over her expression as she took in Levitt's and Johnson's frozen panic, and she glanced askance at Colin. Her eyes widened; her sword fell from her hand.

Savi made a small sound of distress. "Put up your shields, Fia—all the way. Hold them. Has Paul come back?"

Savi's arm came around Colin's waist as she spoke. His grip on his sword tightened before he forced the fury away, redirected it. She hadn't mentioned Paul to help Fia center herself.

The female vampire was the same Paul and Varney had followed.

Fia shook her head, bent to pick up her sword. "Not yet. Whose blood do I smell?"

"Give him a ring, Fia," Colin said softly.

For just a moment, her psychic scent trembled with fear. Then she pulled out her cell phone.

Savi looked up at Colin and, apparently satisfied he wouldn't slaughter the security team, strode over to Levitt's desk and frowned at the monitor. "Can you ask the guys in Security to get the video of the parking lot ready for us to look at? If we slow it down, we should be able to see who put the head there."

"Straight to voice mail," Fia said, snapping her phone closed. "He's turned it off. He'd only have done that if he was worried a ring or vibration might be overheard. What happened? What head?"

"They killed Fishnet Shirt's partner," Savi said. She pointed to the screen.

Fia walked across the room to look and blanched. "Oh, God." She met Colin's gaze. Either the effect of his anger had passed or she was too frightened for Paul to let it affect her. "I'm going."

"No. I need you here."

"But—"

Colin firmed his lips, shook his head. "I'll find him. We need a name, Fia. This woman, and the partner. Someone in Polidori's will recognize them; bring them in and Savi can give me the rest. I'll find him," he repeated when she began to argue.

She swallowed, and her jaw clenched briefly before she said, "It'll be Darkwolf, most likely."

"Fine." It didn't matter, so long as they knew who the woman was.

The jingling tones of Savi's computer drew his attention as it booted up; a small pile of electronics sat on the desk in front of her, and it grew with each softly voiced request she gave to the hellhound.

She picked up a headset, plugged the wire into a slim radio. Colin stood motionless as she hooked it onto his belt, then slid the earphones over his head, adjusted the microphone at his chin. She discarded her helmet, then donned a matching contraption and tested the connection.

"Q," he teased quietly. "As well as Curry Delicious."

Her smile was brief. "Take Sir Pup," she said.

"He's to stay with you. You cannot use the symbols *and* communicate with these." He gestured to the radio. "I'll not leave you unprotected."

Her dark eyes searched his, and he saw the moment she relented in the frustrated twist of her lips, the crease between her brows.

"Take a shitload of weapons then?"

He grinned. "You've such a wonderfully filthy mouth," he said, and kissed it. He called in another sword and a pair of pistols, and headed out into the night with her flavor on his lips.

A trail of fluorescent paint would have been less obvious than the scent of the female vampire's blood. Colin easily followed its odor south across Market. Foolish of the bastard. Unlikely that it had been Dalkiel—the demon would have been better served escaping by air, and the blood held the physical tinge of a male vampire beneath it.

Another of the demon's lackeys? How many had he persuaded—or forced—into his service?

The scent disappeared in the middle of Folsom Street.

Clenching his teeth in frustration, he cast around for another thread, but only smelled rain and oil and metal. The fading odors of humans who'd passed through. Litter and sewage. The pavement glistened wetly beneath the streetlights; aside from the sparse traffic and the background noise from within the surrounding flats, all was quiet.

A car drove slowly by, then stopped. Colin tensed, but allowed himself to relax when it began backing into the single free space along the curb. The woman who emerged looked at him; her gaze didn't rise above the pistol rig and his swords. She fled into the nearest building without glancing at his face.

Amused, he thumbed a button on the radio. "Savi, I need a direction. He must have had a vehicle waiting here; I've lost the scent."

"Where are you?" She repeated the address he gave her, then added, *"Okay, the woman was Guinevere, a.k.a. Jennifer Branning. Arwen says she and Fishnet Shirt live together. I've got an apartment listed under her name in Daly City."*

Eight miles south. An easy distance for Colin in the time they'd been gone, but not for a normal vampire. "Paul and Varney are on foot."

"Yeah. Hold on; the guys have the video from the parking lot up. I'm going to check it out."

Colin bit back his immediate protest. She'd been sickened by the violence, but had recovered quickly. Had it only been the shock of it that had affected her so?

No matter. If she thought herself capable of seeing it again, he wouldn't coddle her.

"It was Mullet Boy," Savi said. *"I've got a name: Peter Osterberg. According to Gina, he moved into the community three months ago. He had a partner—a woman. A redhead, but they don't know her name."*

And Colin hadn't bothered to ask it before he'd slain her. Bloody, bloody hell. "Moved to where?"

"Just a sec, I'm pulling it up."

A police cruiser turned in at the end of the street; a searchlight penetrated the darkness as the car rolled slowly toward Colin. He slid into the shadows between the buildings, leapt soundlessly onto a fire escape platform.

A fat white cat hissed though the windowpane near his elbow, its claws digging into the sill, fur bristling. Even with its back arched, its belly skimmed the wood at its feet. Plenty of blood in that pampered thing. Colin contemplated taking a sip to tide him over, then decided it was too much effort when a push at the sash proved it locked.

The searchlight illuminated the alley beneath him; the cruiser continued on.

Another minute passed before Savi said, *"He just leased a condo on Nob Hill. Swanky little place. And probably with your money—he had a huge influx of cash three weeks ago."*

Colin smiled grimly. "Then he'll not mind if I call on him."

"Are you at the same location? Darkwolf and Gina are offering to provide backup."

The suddenly cheerful note in her voice alerted him to her unease; he knew its cause, but could see no way to deny them without damaging the nascent trust he'd built with the vampires. "Have them meet with me at Osterberg's building; I've attracted a bit of attention here."

"The swords?"

"Yes." He jumped from the fire escape, landed quietly on the pavement thanks to the finest leather Italian bootmakers could produce. Unfortunately, a journey across downtown would do little for their shine.

"People should really be more accepting of vampires running through the streets armed like ninjas. I've given Darkwolf and Gina a few guns with venom-laced bullets. They're going now."

Guns, not swords. Clever Savitri. Colin would much rather be shot in the back than stabbed or decapitated from behind. He could recover from a bullet wound, even one to the brain; he didn't want to test his capacity for healing without a head.

"How long will it take you to get there? Can I talk dirty to you on the way?"

His brow creased as he began jogging north. She was too aware of her effect on him—and the effect of his arousal on his control—to risk distracting him with such sexual play. "Please do."

In Hindi, she said, *"I had sex with a monkey and it gave me herpes."*

He let out a shout of laughter, then replied in the same language, "That is quite all right, sweet. I'm immune to such diseases. I daresay I'm fortunate in that, given my history."

"Very fortunate. Okay. I just wanted to make certain no one here could understand me, but they didn't even blink." Her voice was breathy, her tone sensuous. *"I'm going to send either Fia or the hound to watch your back. Your only choice is which one I send."*

He gritted his teeth, glanced heavenward. Above the skyscrapers, the moon peeked through the thinning clouds. "Savi, if I don't know you are safe—"

"I'll stay in Security with Arwen and the guys from SI. Sir Pup is in his demon form; no one's going to challenge him here. If nothing else, I'll drop my shields and bring a pack of wyrmwolves down on them." She sighed, and he could easily imagine her liquid brown eyes, their expression caught between amusement and gravity. *"I don't like Arwen, but I don't think she's going to try anything; she was pretty shaken up when she saw the present Dalkiel and friends left on your car."*

"But you're worried that Darkwolf or Gina might try something."

"Not terribly worried, because if they do anything to you I'll tell Sir Pup to eat their friend here," she said. *"I'm simply less trusting than I used to be. Or less stupid. And I want to know you are safe, too."*

How could he resist that? "Fia, then."

"Okay," she said in English a moment later. *"She's going. When you get there, you'll find Dalkiel on the roof terrace. I think it must be him; he's in his demon form. Osterberg's there, too. It looks like they're just waiting, but it's hard to tell; the video is kind of fuzzy."*

Good God. "Have you hacked into a spy satellite?"

Her voice trembled with laughter. *"No. That'd take a lot more skill than I have, and a much better system. This is from a KRON WeatherCam."*

"A decade suddenly seems a bit generous, Savitri."

"Well, I've isolated the feed and taken the camera offline— but, yeah, there's too many ways people might see something they shouldn't."

He shook his head in disbelief, but only said, "I've arrived. Are Dalkiel and Osterberg on the roof still?" No reason to be quiet; the demon must know they'd come.

"Yeah. You'll wait for the others? It's the only way I can see where you are, if you're with them."

"I'll wait." His position near the entrance was relatively safe; he focused his senses upward to guard against attack from the roof, and caught the faint threads of two familiar psychic scents. "Paul and Varney are here. Alive." For now, at least. There was no mistaking the bitter trace of fear—and pain—they hadn't managed to block.

"I'll let Fia know."

Three figures dipped between the shadows across the street. "No need, sweet. She's here, too."

❦

"How will they get in?"

Savi's fingers didn't stop moving over the keyboard as she glanced over at Arwen. The vampire had apparently conquered her fear of Sir Pup; despite the sharp-toothed grin he trained on her from his left head, she'd sidled close enough to the hellhound to angle her neck for a view of Savi's monitor.

Sir Pup watched, too, from his middle head; his third, he'd turned to keep an eye on the security team behind them.

"He'll probably just smile at the guy," Savi said, and pushed away from the desk with a kick of her foot. Her chair rolled back, and she grabbed a phone from the adjacent table. A twist and another kick, and she was at her computer again, trailing the phone cords behind her.

She plonked the phone onto the desk, took a deep breath. This wasn't going to be easy.

Engaging the speakerphone, she dialed Hugh's home number.

On her monitor, three small blobs crossed the street and congregated near the front of the building. The silence from Colin's radio and the absence of background noise told her he'd turned off his microphone while talking with the others. Savi silenced hers, as well, but kept the earpiece on.

"What?"

Oh, crap. "Hey, Lilith," she said cheerfully. "Can I talk to Hugh?"

Arwen's purple eyes grew large in her thin face; she must

recognize both names from Hugh's book. Hadn't the vampires known who was in charge of SI? Or perhaps just hadn't expected to have direct contact with them.

There was a pause, in which Savi had the small hope the phone was being transferred.

"No," Lilith said. "You sound like you're smiling. What's wrong?"

She *was* smiling. She'd overcompensated. Dropping the pretense, Savi said, "Not wrong, yet. Dalkiel had a vampire killed, and put her head on Colin's car. We're pretty certain he's holding Paul and Varney. Colin, Fia, and two others from the community have gone after him."

"Do they have a location?"

"Yes. They're set to go in now."

"Tell him to stand down. I've got ten Guardians at SI; Hugh's on the other line with them. What's the location?"

Savi swallowed past the tightness in her throat. "I'll give it to you when Colin asks them to help. We just need them ready to come in, when . . . *if* he wants it."

The brief silence might have as well been filled with Lilith's angry cursing. "Savi, this isn't your fucking game. Colin isn't as strong or as fast—"

"I know that." Her fingers clenched on her lap, and she stared at the demon's dark form on the screen. "It's not a game. That's why he *has* to go in. He has backup. They've got venom-laced bullets; those will slow Dalkiel down."

"Untrained backup. They'll be completely unprepared. Goddammit! Did he turn off his phone?"

"Darkwolf was Special Forces," Arwen said softly. "And Gina was LAPD."

Savi shot her a grateful glance before returning her attention to the monitor. "Send a couple of Guardians downtown, Lilith, or here to Polidori's. But let him go in first. Let *them* go in first. If they can make a statement now, it'll make all the difference."

"Colin doesn't have to defeat a demon to cement his leadership," Lilith growled.

"It's not about his leadership. It doesn't even matter that it's *him*. If we call the Guardians at the first sign of demon-trouble every single time, the community here will look weak.

And the next demon will take advantage of it. And the next. Caelum isn't strong enough to stop them every time."

"And this is what he told you to tell me? That he intends to martyr himself for the cause? Fucking coward."

"You know Colin doesn't risk his life like that," Savi said. "Dalkiel only threatened us yesterday; he's not done playing with us. If Colin thought he'd be in real danger, he'd have called you in. And he didn't tell me this. He didn't have to."

"You've known about vampires for eight months and you think you're qualified to make that decision? That you know anything about demons and how they think? *What's . . . his . . . location?*"

Savi closed her eyes. Each sharply bitten word made her feel like a recalcitrant—and stupid—child.

Lilith could make a rock doubt itself, but her words weren't necessarily true. She'd simply say anything to get her way, particularly when someone she loved was in danger.

But Savi knew her argument had gotten through—Lilith had struck at a personal level.

Luckily, Savi knew Lilith's soft spot: Hugh. "Not eight months, Lilith. I grew up with Hugh. Even when he isn't aware of it, he's teaching and lecturing, about fighting and manipulation and making things permanent. Not just winning a short term battle, but making certain the effects last. I learned very well; I just didn't listen until now And I've *known* for a long time—I saw Hugh with his wings when he saved me. I remember him flying with me to the hospital. I just thought I was crazy."

Stop, Savi. She shouldn't have given Lilith that last bit. Weakness against weakness only dragged it out. But it was too late.

"Crazy? I suppose it didn't help when the fugues began. Those were because you'd seen Hugh?" Lilith's voice changed; the anger underlying it dropped to amused disdain. This was her strength, bolstered by two thousand years of practice: finding the deepest hurt and fear within a person and digging into it. Savi wouldn't stand a chance. "And I thought they'd started because you saw your family murdered in front of you. Are you so eager to see Colin—"

Savi cut off the speaker and hung up before Lilith could

finish. Colin had been right: sometimes, fleeing was the best option.

Sir Pup whined softly, and she patted his head. Arwen stared at the phone, then looked at Savi.

"Did you win?"

Savi shook her head. "I don't know." Lilith might be angry, but she'd do as Savi had asked. The Guardians would be in place to offer quick assistance.

Then she'd probably come down to Polidori's and kick Savi's ass, and start in on Colin when he got back.

The light from the monitor wall cast a blue tinge over Arwen's pale face. "You guys really are trying to do what's best for us. Not just working for the Guardians, I mean."

"Well, it's not all about you," Savi said, and watched as the building door in Nob Hill opened, seemingly by itself. "We're trying to save ourselves, too."

❧

A dazzling smile through the front glass got Colin inside; the doorman slumped over a second after buzzing him through.

Disappointed he'd not needed to drink from the poor bugger to put him to sleep, Colin held the door open, let the others through. He took his weapons and shoulder rig back from Fia, checked the pistols, and disengaged the safeties before sliding them back into their holsters.

Darkwolf did the same with his guns. His efficiency suggested he'd have no trouble using them. "How long is he going to stay like that?"

Colin had no idea; it was magic, not science. "Long enough," he said.

"Better no one else sees us, though," Fia said, glancing at the corner of the ceiling, where a camera recorded the lobby traffic. "Stairs or elevator?"

"Stairs." Too easy to be trapped in a lift.

"You'll want to take the north stairs up to the roof," Savi said, and Colin quickly moved in that direction. *"His condo is on the tenth level, three floors below."*

Was her voice shaky? "All right, sweet. I'm silencing the radio until we reach the roof. Are you secure?"

She didn't hesitate. *"Yes."*

He scanned the space beyond the stair door before shouldering through. A soda machine hummed softly in the corner. The stairwell was sparse, utilitarian; no carpet muffled their footsteps.

Though impossible to see upward beyond the current flight of stairs, the psychic scents of several vampires—unfamiliar, arrogant—reached through the distance, despite their attempts to block his probe.

He signed the information to Fia, then pointed to the ceiling and held up four fingers to relay the same to Gina and Darkwolf. They wouldn't be able to conceal their approach from the waiting vampires, but Colin preferred that the idiots thought themselves with the advantage of surprise.

"I don't sense anyone," he said aloud, then took the stairs, his blades ready at his sides. He paused just below the final flight, turned and gestured to Darkwolf's and Gina's guns, then shook his head. It wouldn't do to alert the building residents with gunfire at this stage. "Wait here," he mouthed silently.

He took a glance at heightened speed around the stairwell wall. Apparently, Dalkiel had thought the same; each of the four vampires held a gun with a silencer, swords sheathed at their hips. One female, three males. They stood shoulder to shoulder, their guns leveled at chest height toward the landing below.

A clever tactical decision—so long as the enemy didn't get too close. Either Dalkiel didn't care to protect these vampires, or he'd no idea of Colin's swiftness.

Colin hoped it was both.

He stepped onto the landing. A near-simultaneous click and fire from the four vampires, but he was already ducking below the bullets' paths, clearing the stairs with ease. He sliced through the legs of the middle two, rose up between them and took their heads before they could scream. The third's gun clattered to the floor, her finger still clenching around the trigger. His blade was through her neck before she knew her hand was gone.

He finished off the last as the vampire turned toward him, desperately trying to pull his sword from its sheath.

Blood spread and trickled down the stairs. Colin wiped his

face and neck to remove the worst of the spray. What a sodding mess.

"Come on up," he said quietly, and frowned when he saw the horrified expressions on their faces. They'd been softened by their natures; blood wasn't always appealing, even to the hungriest of vampires. It was best they learned now.

Sorry, Fia signed weakly. *We know them.*

Colin forced away his pity; he couldn't allow his regret for their pain to get in the way of protecting them. If he hesitated in the future, wondering whose partner he might be cutting down, it endangered them all.

What had they thought fighting Dalkiel would entail—killing faceless strangers? A demon would always use friends and acquaintances against his opponents; it made the despair slice more deeply.

Colin cast a measuring glance at the solid metal fire door; he couldn't hear anything from outside. It was possible Dalkiel hadn't yet realized his defensive line had fallen. "Savi, love, we're at the terrace. Give me a picture outside," he murmured. Though Dalkiel must know they were coming, he might not realize they had the advantage of her eyes.

"Oh, thank god. That was a lot faster than I expected; I thought he'd have someone guarding the stairs or something." She didn't try to disguise the relief in her voice. He looked down at a vampire's head, at the blood soaking his sleeves, and didn't tell her she'd been correct. *"You're going to come out in the middle of the north wall. I've got a blind spot just to the left of the stair housing. The right side is clear. About ten feet in front of the door is an artificial pond. Just beyond that is a gazebo; that's where Dalkiel and Osterberg are. They went into it about a minute ago, just after you turned off your radio."*

"Do you see Paul or Varney?" He met Fia's gaze, gestured for her to replace the gun she held with her sword. *Once we're through the door, go around low and check the left side,* he signed.

"No, but the gazebo roof is blocking most of its interior. It's about fifteen feet in diameter, I'd guess. The sides are open."

"If we need to take immediate cover, which direction should we go?"

"There's a big concrete planter on the left side of the pond. About four feet high. It would block any shots from the gazebo."

"Have you alerted SI?"

"Yes. They're headed downtown, but I haven't given them a location yet—not until you need it. Or until I have to. Lilith is . . . angry," she said, and Colin could almost see her grimace.

"Bloody hell." Best to do this quickly, then. "Hold her off. We're going out."

CHAPTER 23

I am inclined to let him rot in his sickbed. I daresay you will not find such a response acceptable, but that is why I abhor vows—they compel me to action. Both Hippocrates and your Guardian mentor would have done well to leave the hopeless and the cursed alone. Alas; to Greece we go? Perhaps I shall force him to finally admit that I am the more beautiful before I offer him my blood.

—Colin to Ramsdell, 1824

Colin thrust open the door and stalked to the edge of the pond, armed with his gun and a sword. Behind him, he heard a vampire's cry as Fia struck one down in his hiding place, heard Darkwolf's and Gina's running steps as they fell into position behind the concrete box and took aim over its bulk. Their eyes widened with horror.

Fia's psychic distress swamped his mind before she caught herself, cut it off.

Paul and Varney couldn't have run; Dalkiel had taken their feet. Their blood formed a dark pool on the gazebo floor. They were still alive, their wounds already closed and their shields strong—likely for Fia's sake rather than their own—but they desperately needed to feed.

Colin flicked a glance at Osterberg before returning his attention to Dalkiel. "As fond as I am of fangs—and as much as I despise pinkie rings—you were much more pleasant to look upon in the café."

Much more. Colin had thought he'd known demonic, but Lilith's form had never been so inhuman. Though the wings and curving obsidian horns were familiar, crimson scales glittered over Dalkiel's body instead of skin, his knees articulated in the reverse, and his feet ended in cloven hooves.

The stuff of nightmares—but Colin's reality had been worse.

"I shall adopt that form again when it suits," Dalkiel said. His voice slithered over Colin's skin, and the vampire had to repress a shiver. The demon's glowing red eyes lit on Fia; his enjoyment in her pain was no doubt as great as it had been when he'd amputated Paul's feet. "And I shall make improvements."

Colin snorted humorlessly. "Don't be absurd. Shall we bargain, then?"

The demon's attention was riveted on him; pleasure pulled his lips into a thin smile. In Colin's ear, he heard the tiny catch of Savi's breath.

Do not fear, sweet. He'd no intention of making a bargain. One who did, and failed to meet its terms, risked an eternal torment: his face frozen in Hell and his body dangling—continually devoured—in Chaos.

Colin couldn't imagine any gain worth that risk.

"What have you to offer that I cannot take?"

The crippled vampires sat propped against the left wall of the gazebo. Colin held the sword lightly in his right hand as he began circling the pond counterclockwise; his gun—the weapon Dalkiel feared the least—he kept between them. "Your life," he said simply. "I'll not kill you . . . tonight . . . if you return those two to me without further harm done to them."

He knew Dalkiel only played with him when the demon did not laugh at Colin's assumption that he *could* kill him. A demon hunter, luring the vampire prey close by letting it think it could defend itself.

Colin hated being prey.

"Two lives for one? Hardly an equal bargain," Dalkiel said. The demon had to turn his back to Paul and Varney to keep Colin within his sight; in his arrogance, he wouldn't feel threatened by them—but nor would he turn away from Colin to further mutilate them.

"You equate your worth with a vampire's? I once heard a

halfling demon say that a vampire's life was nothing to her; what must you be, that two are worth more?"

"The inequality is theirs, not mine." Dalkiel studied him through radiant slitted eyes. He stood with his arms crossed over his chest; not a defensive gesture, but one that stated he'd no reason to prepare himself. His hands had transformed into razor-tipped claws. "We cannot bargain with these terms, vampire. I believe I shall kill them, after all."

He'd never had any doubt of the demon's intention. Colin stopped halfway around the pool, giving himself a view of those inside the gazebo, as well as Fia, Darkwolf, and Gina. "Why bother to kill them if they are nothing? They hardly seem worth the effort."

"Their *lives* are not, but their deaths?" With a smile, Dalkiel uncrossed his arms, reached out and clamped his hand over the top of Osterberg's head. The vampire's skull cracked. He shrieked, but Dalkiel had no mercy: he did not finish it. He held the vampire there, his head half-crushed. "Pain and fear. The most powerful currency in the world."

Christ. Colin preferred to take Osterberg alive. He raised his pistol, held it on the demon's face. After he'd sufficiently weakened and distracted Dalkiel, and given a signal, Fia and the others would rush in to retrieve Paul and Varney—but as soon as he fired, the Guardians would hear it, swoop down on them.

Osterberg screamed again.

Bloody fucking hell. They'd hear that, as well. Colin squeezed the trigger. Dalkiel's head rocked back with the impact, but he remained standing. Blood poured from his missing eye.

The demon laughed softly, his lack of concern serving better than mockery. "You threaten me with a *gun*? Do you truly think these vampires will follow you when they see what I can do to them? How I easily erase liabilities?" He glanced toward Darkwolf with his one burning eye, and another sickening crunch sounded from Osterberg's skull. "And any who resist me or expose me, I'll consider a liability."

"Not just a gun," Colin said coldly. "Hellhound venom. Let him go."

Surprise flickered over Dalkiel's face.

Colin fired again; a hole appeared over the demon's right eyebrow. He'd missed, but it'd have to do—the first eye had begun to regenerate.

Colin traded his pistol for his second sword; Dalkiel staggered backward, blinking. The two bullets had been covered with a minuscule amount of venom—the demon was at normal vampire speed, most likely, or just above that. Colin's weapons switch must have looked instantaneous. "Let him go; you'll need both hands to fight."

Dalkiel glanced over at Osterberg swaying in his grip, and tore off the vampire's head.

"Get them," Colin growled, and cleared the pond in a single jump, running after the demon when he turned and fled. Footsteps pounded behind him, splashing—then Fia's soothing murmurs.

Colin sped through the gazebo, across the rooftop, his gaze fixed on the demon's back. He'd catch him within a second or—

Dalkiel's wings unfurled, and he leapt into the air.

Fucking coward. But shouting the insult after the demon only earned him Savi's muttered, *"Ouch. My ear."*

"Sorry, love." He watched Dalkiel's form until the demon disappeared amidst the grid of skyscrapers downtown, then swore again and swiped his blade through the air. He'd *had* him.

A subtle psychic pressure had him tipping his face back; overhead, a phalanx of fledglings arrowed silently after Dalkiel.

"Were those Guardians I just saw?" She sounded slightly awed.

"Yes." He turned back to the gazebo; Michael was there, likely healing the amputations. "Did you see him run from me?"

"Better yet: I recorded it. You can't really see him until he comes out, but the sound is there; it'll make lovely propaganda. Though it'll also appear as if he ran from the others, not from you."

"That's quite all right, so long as *you* appreciate how

fearsome I was." The tension of battle released, his hands began to shake with need. He was starving. If he didn't go now, he'd begin sucking the blood from his shirtsleeves. "Can you drive with a standard transmission?"

"Yes. Kind of. Just don't ask me to go up Telegraph Hill."

She'd likely lurch all the way home and burn out the clutch. No matter. "Take Sir Pup, and I'll meet with you at our house." He could be there long before she could drive the distance, even taking the time to speak with Michael.

"Oh, thank god. I'll leave now."

"So keen?" His body roared to life with pleasure, with anticipation.

"Lilith's on her way here."

"Leave quickly, then." They'd face the consequences of this together . . . tomorrow. "Keep your radio on until you are in the car and have engaged the spell's protection."

Stepping into the gazebo, he met Michael's eyes. The Guardian looked the ancient warrior with his ridiculous toga and impressive black wings, but he'd been the Healer that night.

Both Paul and Varney were standing. In response to Colin's observation that hazard pay might be necessary for Polidori's employees, Varney danced a light-footed jig. Fia slanted Colin a grateful look before wrapping her arms around Paul's neck.

Satisfied that nothing more needed to be done, Colin continued on through, heading for the stairs. "You've a mess to clean up in here," he told the Doyen.

"Of your creation," Michael said. "Do not impede us again."

"Impede?" With a disbelieving laugh, Colin stopped and swung around. "I've served your fledglings a venom-weakened demon on a silver platter."

"We cannot protect you if you hinder us."

"You can't? Or you won't?"

Savi must have known Michael would hear her through Colin's earpiece; Michael's mouth tightened, as if her question reminded him that he could not interfere with Savi's will—and she had been the one to hinder them.

"Cannot."

"As comforting as it is to know you won't abandon us, you'll do well to learn to protect the community despite us. For it's become quite clear that we lack—" Colin paused, searching for the word.

"Underworld izzat," Savi supplied. *"Demons wouldn't care for personal honor, but vampires' lives must be given value in a currency the demons understand."*

Colin nodded. "Yes, *izzat*—and that lack is more detrimental than the lack of protection. We are neither human nor a threat; but we must be one, or the demons and nosferatu will continue to kill us with impunity."

"Demons and nosferatu will never assign any value to a vampire."

Colin shrugged. "Then the honor will be for ourselves, so that we know we do not have to accede to the demands of pain and fear. That is how you can best help us; by allowing us to be a threat, and assisting us if we fail." His jaw firmed as he studied the Guardian's expressionless features. "When did you last ascribe value to a vampire? Do you slay this demon for killing us, or simply because he is a demon?"

Michael sighed. "There is no difference."

Perhaps not to him. Colin had made this clear to the vampires, but now he had to explain it to the Doyen as well? Lilith and Hugh understood it. The vampires would follow the Rules, but they'd bow neither to the demons nor the Guardians.

"If there is no difference, then you should begin amending those Scrolls. A redefinition of 'vampire' seems in order."

❧

The house blazed with lights when Savi pulled into the drive. Most of her concentration had been on making it there without stalling the engine at each stop and shift of the gears, but now that she'd arrived, stark reality hit her with gut-clenching fists.

Colin would feed from her. And give her—*something*—in return.

There was no going back from this. There was nothing

impulsive about her decision, and it wasn't a means to a simple end or to satisfy her curiosity.

And there would be no simple end; only a painful one. This could only make it worse.

Colin waited on the porch, speaking into his cell. He'd showered and changed, his hair dark and wet beneath the lights. He closed the phone and tucked it into the pocket of his cream linen pants when she turned off the car.

It was probably a good thing she liked pain, because she wasn't going to run from this.

Though the indefinable quality that had been missing from his portraits made her certain it was he, she allowed Sir Pup to exit the car first. Her legs were unsteady as she joined them, her pulse racing. He watched her with unconcealed hunger.

"Was it—" She had to pause, clear her throat. Why was she so nervous? He'd fed from her before, and she'd survived. "Was it their blood you had to wash away, or yours?"

"Theirs. Of course."

She gave a little headshake. "Of course."

His lips quirked, and he held out his hand. "Go on home, pup." His fingers clasped over hers when she slid her palm in his. "I've just spoken with Lilith; Dalkiel evaded the fledglings."

"You're joking."

The frustration in his gaze answered her before he did. "No." He released her hand to set the alarm and activate the spell.

God. She could just imagine what Lilith had said to him.

Savi automatically bent to remove her shoes, and braced herself against the wall as she unlaced her boots and yanked off the left. The marble was cool and hard beneath her bare foot. "It's not your fault, you know." She dropped her right boot to the floor.

"I rarely blame myself for anything; I'll not begin with this."

She froze, her heart thundering in her ears. His voice had deepened to a soft growl. She straightened and turned to face him.

He was staring at his hands. They trembled, and the blood

that beaded on his thumb began a thick slide. He raised his eyes to hers; they burned with need.

So did she.

"Are you frightened?" His tone begged her to say no.

"A little." He'd know the truth of it when he took her blood; she wouldn't lie to him now. She shrugged out of her coat and grasped the hem of her top. Her neckline was too high. "But mostly excited, and really *really* turned on. You like to hunt; what happens if I run?"

A voracious smile spread over his mouth; his gaze fell to her breasts as she bared them to his view. "I chase you."

"How far do you think I'd get?"

"Not far; I'm *dreadfully* hungry." Colin's response was as playful as hers had been, but there was no mistaking its truth. "I'll allow you a handicap."

"A head start? That hardly tips the odds in your favor." She covered her breasts with her hands as she edged along the wall of the foyer, toward the stairs.

As if the movement was a true attempt to escape, some of the humor left his expression, replaced by predatory intent, the bloodlust taking hold, despite his apparent aim to ease her fears through this game.

"Run, Savi," he rasped.

She didn't; she walked backward, and watched him stalk after her. His every step was a thing of grace and beauty. His focus narrowed on her throat, then drifted down. And down. His lips parted; his teeth gleamed.

Oh, god. Her nipples tightened beneath her palms; moisture slicked her inner thighs. Her heels hit the bottom riser. She dropped her shields.

And he was on her, his care as he cupped her head and protected her from the impact against the floor at odds with the rip of her panties, the ravenous sounds that rose from his chest. He shoved her skirt up.

She clutched at him to pull him inside her, but he slid out of her grasp. "Forgive me," he said, and his mouth was on her, his tongue in her. Her back arched, her gaze skimming across the ceiling decorated with fat cherubs and lazy gods. She looked away. That wasn't Heaven.

This was. The sharp slide of his fangs into her flesh. His blissful moan, reverberating against her. He surveyed her from his portraits, laughing and cruel and beautiful, and she thought, *Look at me. Look at what you do to me.*

But they were the parts, the sum much less than the whole—and what she thought had been exquisite pleasure had only been Colin.

There was more.

His hands tightened on her hips, holding her in place as he tore through her blood, ripped a scream from her throat. This was beyond ecstasy, beyond momentum, out of control and spinning her along with it, falling and ascending and *impossible* to feel like this without dying.

And her brain couldn't process it, but her body knew what to do—rid itself of it, it was too much, and she twisted and clenched and tried to keep hold, but it slipped away with the orgasm, blinding bright and extinguished as soon as Colin lifted his head.

Already, she raced along her memory, pulling each thread and examining it for what she'd missed the first time: the cold marble beneath her, the brush of his hair on her thigh, the suction of his mouth, the sound of his pleasure as she rocketed into hers.

He'd not taken much; when she came back to herself she found him watching her with the need still hard upon him. He licked his way up the length of her torso, and she wrapped her legs around his waist, reached down to guide him.

"Oh, Christ, Savi. On the *floor.*" He pressed frantic blood-scented kisses over her mouth, down to her neck. "I'm so sorry."

"Don't apolo—" But she didn't finish.

He sank into her, filled her. Rapture streaked along her veins, greater than before, as if his physical pleasure fed it, increasing with each heavy stroke, suspending her between the thrust of his body and the fire in her blood.

This couldn't be real.

He stiffened, his anguish pushing into her with the euphoria, and she realized she'd spoken it. Or he'd heard it within her. It didn't matter; he'd misunderstood. Angels and demons and vampires weren't real, either.

"I won't forget," she said to all of them staring down at her, begging her to see him, to remember. Or she thought she did, but he must have heard her—the pain vanished. *I'll never forget,* she promised.

Tremors shook him. *Stay with me*, she thought she heard him say.

Yes. For this. For now.

She dared not hope for more.

❧

Colin apparently didn't know that most blood donations only netted juice and a cookie. Food enough for a village had been delivered from the local grocer, most of it perishable; she'd barely made a dent in it that afternoon.

"Why does a vampire have a gourmet kitchen?" Savi wondered as she turned away from the enormous glass-front refrigerator, unwrapping yet another package of fruit.

"I'd an obsession for The Food Network; I briefly entertained the notion of learning to dice and sauté." He leaned his hip against the counter, watching as she washed a small pile of strawberries and transferred them to the cutting board. "But this is just as pleasurable, and far less effort."

The berries' sweet fragrance released with each slice of her knife, the juice as red—if not as thick—as blood.

"What does it taste like? When you drink from someone."

"Never as I expect," he said. "I don't believe I truly taste it—it's nothing like the few times I bled when I was human."

"Metallic? Salty?"

His gaze fell to her throat. The punctures had closed by the time she'd run upstairs to change into her little T-shirt and pajama pants; they'd stopped itching before she'd come down again.

"The texture is the same, but the flavor is . . ." He shook his head. "There's nothing with which I can compare it. I daresay it's more of an experience than a taste."

"A bloody glorious one?"

His laughter rolled softly through the kitchen. "Yes."

"It was," she admitted, and his delighted grin sent a delicious quake through her stomach. "Though it wasn't near five minutes. More like two. Does everyone taste the same?"

"No. Elements of the flavor are similar, but it's influenced by temperament, by mood. Animal blood—and human blood taken outside the body—have no flavor at all."

Nor could they sustain a vampire for long; perhaps the physical properties of the blood weren't enough.

"So the taste is probably psychically based."

He made a sound of agreement. "Much like your scent, though no one else perceives it that way."

"Except for the wyrmwolves."

"Yes." His face hardened slightly.

"How deep can you get? Into my head, I mean," she quickly added the last.

Though amusement softened his voice, he only said, "Not as far as I'd have liked. Your shields were down, so perhaps it is the structure of your memory that prevents me."

"But you heard me. The surface thoughts."

"Yes." With an expression almost achingly tender, his gaze roamed over her face. "And they gave me more pleasure than your blood, your taste, or your scent. I could not have hoped for more, Savitri."

She had to speak through the tightness in her throat, the swelling in her chest. "I heard you, too." A berry liquefied under her knife, and she fought to control her frustration.

It wasn't as if she wished for forever—just the rest of her life.

"I'd no idea you could," he said quietly, and she realized he wouldn't have asked her to stay if he had known. Was he trying to protect her? Far too late.

He tilted his head to the side, and added, "I suppose I'm a right cad. I typically don't think at all during the feeding, let alone stay to chat about it afterward."

She bit her lip against her laugh. With the flat of her blade, she scooped up the strawberries and dumped them into her yogurt bowl atop blueberries and mango slices. When she turned back around, Colin had an orange waiting.

She shook her head. "I can't eat that much."

"It's my favorite." His ridiculously charming—beguiling— smile made its appearance.

"Oh, god." She wiped her fingers onto a paper towel, leaving a bright pink stain. "You're trying to stuff me with food. Nani does this to me."

"I have good reason. You're eating for two."

She braced her palms against the countertop, her body shaking with laughter. "That's the worst joke I've ever heard," she said when she could breathe again.

"You lived with Castleford too long for me to believe that." He fluttered his lashes. "In any case, you'll forgive me."

"Not likely; it was really bad," she said, but reached for the orange and sliced it down the center. His lids lowered fractionally, and he inhaled—he truly enjoyed the burst of fragrance. She found a glass, set it in front of him with both halves of the orange. "Squeeze the hell out of it."

He arched a brow.

She arched hers. "I've earned my juice. And you're stronger than I am."

"It seems that I am not," he said as he pushed his sweater sleeves over his forearms and picked up the orange. "How have you manipulated me into performing manual labor? I shall have to weaken you, put you wholly under my glorious vampiric power. Oh, good God, this smells incredible."

She stared at his wrists, his flexing fingers. "Did I mention that the sight of your hands drives me absolutely *insane*?"

He looked up from the pulped orange, his gaze heated. "Then I shall pulverize fruit by the ton."

She rolled another toward him. "Six ounces will do. I'm easy."

"Sweet Christ, you will grind me beneath your heel. I love nothing so much as easy women who worship my hands."

"And lips," she reminded him.

He tossed the orange carcass into the sink with a flick of his wrist. "Let us see if I can put both to good use." Her heartbeat quickened, but he only cast a wicked grin her way before lifting her glass and bowl from the counter. "Come along. I intend to drive you mad."

"With hunger?" She trailed after him, admiring the line of his back. He began climbing the stairs, and she sighed with pleasure. Every bit of him was gorgeous. "Do you mind if I objectify you?"

"Please do," he said over his shoulder. "Particularly my knees, as they are oft-neglected."

"Maybe if you ever got your pants off, they wouldn't be."

"It hardly matters, sweet; once they've come off, the attention isn't likely to center on my absurdly handsome knees."

She almost tripped over her feet laughing, and was pleased when she noted Colin wasn't too steady, either. "We'll have to experiment tonight, and see what draws my attention," she said as she followed him into the music room. "I promise not to remove any variables."

He grinned in response, but it ended on a slight grimace. Turning away, he set her bowl on a side table that flanked the wide bay window.

"What is it?" She accepted the juice and sank into the window seat. Pulling up her feet, she leaned back against the cushions. A view of the street and front landscaping stretched out to her right. Colin sat at the piano.

What could her remark have reminded him of? "Was it something Dalkiel did?" She hadn't seen most of what had taken place in the gazebo, only heard it. "To Osterberg?" His screams had sent chills down her spine.

He sighed. "No."

Of course not; Colin wouldn't be overly concerned with that vampire's death. Savi found she hadn't been, either—not in comparison to her relief that the others had made it out alive. "To Paul and Varney, then. That's why you mentioned hazard pay. Michael healed them?"

"Yes."

She was silent for a moment; her imaginings might have been worse than the reality—but they might not be. "Dalkiel won't allow us the advantage of the venom next time, will he?" And his humiliation would make him all the more determined to kill them both.

"No." His profile was starkly drawn against the piano's black veneer.

"Perhaps I made a mistake; I should have called the Guardians in immediately."

He turned to face her; his gaze was fierce. "No. If he'd sensed the Guardians' approach instead of being distracted by ours, he'd have killed Paul, Varney, and Osterberg—and still he would have fled. Only his certainty that we posed no threat and his desire to torment us kept them alive. You acted exactly as you should have, Savitri; Castleford taught you well." His throat worked before he seemed to shake himself. He flexed his hands over the piano keys. "I take requests."

She sighed and dug her spoon into her yogurt. "Nothing depressing."

"My exquisite fingering and magnificent voice will lift your spirits," he said, and launched into a jaunty rendition of The Beatles' "When I'm Sixty-Four." When she protested she couldn't eat for laughing, he segued into a lively minuet.

She was scraping the bottom of her bowl when he abandoned the piano. He opened a violin case and lowered himself onto the opposite end of the window seat, his posture mirroring hers. The moonlight played over his features; he closed his eyes, tucked his chin against the instrument, and tore open her heart with a simple, poignant melody.

Colin looked up as the last note faded; she stared at him, not bothering to wipe away the moisture shimmering on her lashes.

"Is there anything you don't do beautifully?"

He slowly shook his head, his gaze never leaving hers. "No."

It was so easy to believe him; how much evidence had she seen? Silk damask whispered beneath her as she slid forward across the seat. The violin thudded against the thick rug, the bow scraping discordantly over the strings. His hands circled her waist as she scooted between his legs, lowered her head against his chest. She met his mouth in a soft kiss; and yes, he did this beautifully, as well. He didn't demand more, but allowed her to melt into him.

With a sigh, she lay her cheek against his shoulder, watching the half moon set over the houses across the street, absorbing the warmth of his solid length.

Until she could bear it no longer.

"Colin," she said. "It's *killing* me."

He pressed a kiss to the top of her head; though his body shook and amusement deepened his tone, he did not give voice to his laughter. "I'll not believe it; you've been too distracted this evening to think of it overmuch. Let it alone, Savi."

"I won't ask about the curse," she said, looking up at him. "Even I know better than to mess with the symbols; I just want to know why you're so certain you can't transform anyone. Are you sure your blood would kill me?"

"It's a moot point, as *your* blood makes a transformation uncertain."

"I'd risk it; if I thought there was a chance that I could transform and drink your blood and stay with you, I would. Are you sure?"

His head fell back against the cushions, and he stared up at the ceiling. "Yes."

The strong line of his throat called to her; she traced it with shaking fingers. "They all died?"

"Yes." His eyes closed. "One would have regardless, but the other two were young. Men in their prime."

"Three humans?" Her voice was rising; anger coursed through her. Not at him. Why did this have to be so fucking impossible? "The nosferatu drank your blood and are surviving just fine in Chaos. Has another vampire ever taken blood from you?"

"Yes." His fingers tightened on her waist, and he shook his head and continued before she could give voice to her surprise and question him. "Compared to the nosferatu, vampires are weak; they may as well be human. And the minuscule amount the nosferatu had does not signify next to what a partner would need." His gaze was like iron when he looked at her, his frustration apparent in each clipped word. "Do you think to have another vampire attempt to transform you despite the taint in your blood, then return to me to drink my blood? Risking your life doubly?"

"I don't know." She couldn't catch her breath. "No. That's not what I'm thinking—I'm just trying to figure out if there's any way I can keep from dying when I leave you."

His lips softened and parted; his eyes darkened before he clutched her to him, his mouth against her ear. "Don't leave me," he said roughly.

"I don't want to," she whispered. "But I can't think of a way—I can't see how—" She buried her face in his neck; her hands grasped wildly at his shoulders. "Please don't let me cry. I promised myself I wouldn't."

He gently tilted her chin back; she shivered as his tongue ran the length of her jaw. "Don't think, Savi," he said against her throat.

And for the first time, she didn't.

CHAPTER 24

Lucifer rules over Hell, but Belial and his demons have rebelled against him. Whether they follow Lucifer or Belial, however, demons aren't to be trusted.

—Savi to Taylor, 2007

When Savi awoke, the silk beneath her cheek was caramel, not blue. Heavy velvet curtains shadowed the bed. She'd fallen asleep in her room, but Colin had apparently brought her to his.

A packet of yellowing letters lay on her pillow.

The acrid odor of smoke clung to them; the string tying them was new. The aging paper felt fragile under her fingers, and despite her curiosity, she hesitated to open them.

A shaft of light fell across the bed; Colin pulled back a curtain and threw himself onto the mattress beside her. He propped his elbow on his pillow, his indolent smile a match for his posture.

"I have Lilith to thank for their existence; they'd have burned if not for her scheme to forge Polidori's letter and deliver it to the detectives. Though some of the credit belongs to me: I was too lazy to carry them back upstairs after copying his handwriting. Which, I'm pained to note, is nearly as illegible as yours. It shall be easier for you if I simply describe the events related therein."

Her brows drew together; his manner had not been so insultingly careless since the night she'd attacked him in the parking lot.

"Are you *nervous*?"

"Don't be absurd," he said. "I'm terrified. You will think very ill of me when I've finished."

"I began falling in love with you when you were a complete ass; I doubt something that happened two hundred years ago will change that."

His eyes widened with pleasure, his smile became genuine, and he plucked the letters from her hand. "If you will love me regardless, then I'll not bother—"

"You ass!" She tackled him, laughing when he caught her and rolled her beneath him. She was naked, he was clothed; she was becoming wonderfully accustomed to this. "I'm dying to know; you can't tease me this way."

"Oh, but I can—and that is why I shall. Hold still. The sight of you in my bed is enticing on its own; I'll drain you dry if you squirm. I'll *not tell you* if you squirm," he said, resorting to the greater threat. "Do wrap your legs around me, however, for I like that exceedingly well."

As she did, too, she complied. "Why are you telling me? You don't have to."

"You want both my recitation and my reason for giving it?"

"Yes."

"Choose."

"Your reason."

For a moment she thought he'd refuse. He stared down at her, his amusement fading. He swept his thumb over her right eyebrow, caressing the delicate arch. "So that you know I don't deny you without cause, or based on flimsy conjecture, and that I truly would transform you if I could. This is the only evidence I have to give you; I cannot provide an explanation, but I can offer a—somewhat—documented history. I doubt your conclusions will differ from mine."

She shook her head, her gaze locked with his. "You don't have to; I trust you."

"*And* because if anyone on Earth can see something I've not, and draw a conclusion different than I have—you are she."

She took a slow, painful breath. "I love you."

His boyish grin soothed and swelled the ache within her

chest, and his mouth pressed against hers in a brief kiss more teeth than lips.

"Savi, you will soon have me spouting romantic poetry as tortuously wrought as . . ." A wry expression tightened his smile.

"Shelley's?" she guessed.

He dropped his forehead to hers. "John Polidori's. You've already deduced most of this, haven't you?"

"Only that the three men who were at Lake Geneva when you were cursed died not many years afterward. All very young, and the first of whom was your friend. Were the others?"

"No," he said flatly.

"When did you meet him—Polidori?"

"In Edinburgh, 1813, whilst the good Dr. Ramsdell and I attended a series of lectures on the medicinal use of leeches." He lifted his head and arched a brow. "I had something of an obsession for it at the time."

She was immediately diverted. "You went to medical school? Did you drop out?"

"My obsession burnt itself out," he said, narrowing his eyes. "A peer's son does not 'drop out'; the lectures failed to hold my attention. The medical properties of my blood no longer fascinated me, and we learned no more about the reasons behind it than when Ramsdell returned from Caelum—except that it sped the healing of whomever I bled over."

Ramsdell had utilized the healing knowledge he'd gained in Caelum in his practice as a physician? "Didn't you risk exposure?"

"Even if the accuser would not be named mad, who would dare level such an accusation at me? Certainly no one from the lower classes. And if someone of higher rank had attempted such, they'd likely have been ousted from Society. Beauty has always garnered far more invitations than virtue. I cut a dashing figure through many a ballroom; so long as I did not smile too boldly, no one was uneasy."

Was he being facetious? "Not everyone could have been so blind; some must have known."

"Yes. We were not quite as shallow as that, but the moral implications so important to the underclass hardly mattered to many of those in my set. And at that time, vampires were the ragged undead—a papist's myth, most popular amongst the peasantry on the Continent, therefore easily dismissed. I could not be lumped with them." He paused. "You are revolted."

She forced herself to admit, "Perhaps it is best two hundred years have passed; I wouldn't have liked who you were then. I'm sorry."

"I'd not have cared for the opinion of a foreign female, so we are equal in our hypothetical disdain." The warmth in his gaze softened the words. "I'd have charmed you into my bed."

"That's probably true. So I would've slept with you because you're gorgeous, and then discarded you for your condescension," she said lightly, and rocked her hips beneath his when he laughed. "What of Polidori?"

"Ah, poor Polidori," he said. His smile falled, and he shook his head. "No, he does not deserve that epithet. He was brilliant, Savi, and exceptionally young for a man in his final year before his physicians' exams. Engaging, humorous—if not dripping with wit—and more than willing to bestow his admiration on those he deemed worthy. And though he was given to tedious bouts of melancholia and brooding, I liked him very much. Of course he soon deduced that I was not all I seemed."

"What was his reaction? Why melancholia?"

"Much like yours: curiosity. He wanted to know all, and Ramsdell and I could see no danger in telling him how I was transformed—though we left out details such as the Doyen's sword. He knew I was different from the usual sort of vampire, but we explained the difference by my status as one of the nosferatu-born. There were—are—few other nosferatu-born vampires to which he could compare me to determine the truth of it."

And even if Polidori had, he would have found them much like Colin: stronger, faster, with greater psychic capabilities, though unable to wake or walk in daylight. Savi knew of one—Lucas, Selah's partner. Though her body quivered with the need to ask about the others, she bit her tongue to prevent it.

"Hold still. As for the melancholia, he admired and loved nothing more than poetry, but unfortunately had little talent for it. Equally unfortunate was that though he was aware of his lack, he could not accept that he would always be mediocre. His employment with Byron—and his acquaintance with Shelley—allowed him close to everything he wished to be, gave him a glimpse of it, but also prevented him from forgetting his own lack. Byron, particularly, took care to mock his efforts."

"Should they have been mocked?"

"Yes." Colin flicked her nose in reproof. "But he could have told Polidori the truth without resorting to cruelty, simply to exercise his wit."

She bit her lip, but couldn't help herself. "So why didn't you like Byron? Because he was so handsome? So talented and brilliant?"

"It is true that I despise handsome men more clever than I—whereas I adore beautiful, intelligent women—but primarily I disliked him because he was a self-absorbed ass. His only redeeming quality was his eccentricity. One could never be bored near him. Don't laugh; this is not about *me*. And hold still."

"So you were all together in Lake Geneva, where you read the curse." At his nod, she squelched her need to ask about the details of it. For now, anyway. "When did you see Hugh? You mentioned he was in Switzerland shortly after that."

His face hardened. "I did not *see* him; I heard him. Deciding whether to slay me, and then bargaining with Lilith for my life when she threatened to rid the world of one more bloodsucker."

Savi's mouth dropped open; her stomach knotted. "You're joking."

"No."

"Why? He made a vow to protect you."

"Yes, but there had been deaths in the region, seemingly vampiric in origin. If I'd have been the cause, he'd have executed me. His specific words were to the effect that he'd allow me to live, and to take blood from humans as I needed, so long as I was not cruel, and so long as I did not kill."

She stared up at him. No wonder he'd harbored such resentment; though she couldn't argue with the conditions Hugh had set, Colin must feel that he'd essentially lived for two hundred years by Hugh's leave.

Colin sighed. "It was not all as bad as that, Savi, and I am grateful, in some respects. Without that warning, I don't know what I might have become—especially once the curse took effect. Without Ramsdell and Emily, without Castleford, I could have easily been not much different from Dalkiel. If I am not the more corrupt for the increase in power my transformation gave to me—particularly in those initial years—it is only due to the people surrounding me."

She squeezed her legs more tightly around his waist; there was nothing to say, no response but to hold on to him. "Did you leave Switzerland after that?"

"I thought the curse would fade, but after several weeks it did not, and I returned to Derbyshire. Eventually, I moved on to London, where the hunting was better. And I was not as likely to upset my family; my adjustment to the curse was . . . difficult."

"How did you get through it?"

"I developed an obsession for oil and canvas. A long-lived one, as it turned out." He smiled slightly. "I am too eager to talk of myself, Savitri. You must not encourage me. By God, hold still."

"Don't blame me; it's not my fault you're fascinating." Her quick grin held no apology, but she stopped moving. With more seriousness, she asked, "When did you try to transform him?"

"Five years later. I'd met with him in Brighton for a holiday, and shortly after we returned to London, he asked it of me. He'd been practicing law, under a different—" He grimaced tightly. "—less *foreign* name. He'd had a succession of failures, professionally, artistically, personally . . ."

Pressing his lips together, he stared at the headboard for a moment. His gaze flattened, cold and bleak; gently, he disentangled Savi's legs and sat up.

She scrambled to her knees and pulled the sheet over her breasts; there was no rejection in him—only, she sensed, a refusal to take enjoyment or pleasure of any kind while he related the last.

"He'd also accumulated a mountain of gambling debts—but one did not talk of such, Savi. It was vulgar. And I don't know that I could have helped him—if I *would* have helped him—if he'd asked me. His depression and embarrassment were severe, but he was certain that the transformation would allow him to renew his fortune—mentally, financially. And so I drank his blood, and slit my wrist for him to take mine. Before he'd taken half of what he'd need for the transformation, he began screaming. It didn't stop until he fell into the daysleep."

"Was it Chaos? Did he see it?" Savi whispered.

"No. He said his blood burned like hellfire within him. I could detect no fever, however, and the next evening, he was no longer in pain. Only morose and weak, and he determined that we would continue the process. He'd not taken more than a couple of sips before he simply . . . flared out. I could not revive him."

"What did you do?"

"There was nothing to do; I wrote to Ramsdell—and we both thought the failure had been an indication of some hidden reluctance on Polidori's part. Creating a vampire is very easy for most. Foolproof. Despite the taint, there was no reason to think the fault lay with my blood instead of Polidori— after all, I transformed without incident, though I suffered from weakness caused by a month-long starvation. And so when Shelley wrote to me, I did not hesitate."

Her brow creased. "Why? He wasn't a friend to you."

"No, but he was not all that terrible—indeed, in some respects he reminded me of Emily. Very romantic, sometimes overly sentimental. There were other reasons. Appreciation for beauty and talent. And I thought Polidori would have wished it, his admiration for Shelley was so great, so perhaps it was guilt as well. This time, I made certain the blood was taken all at once, very quickly." He swallowed, his jaw clenching as he stared down at the mattress. "His screams did not last until daytime; within minutes, his skin had blackened as if he'd roasted from inside, and he was dead."

Savi scooted forward, wrapped her arms around his shoulders. "You don't have to tell me any more," she said, her throat aching.

He slid his hand into her hair, dropped a kiss to her forehead before sitting back to look at her. It seemed with effort, he smiled; ice lingered about the edge of it. "It's no hardship, sweet. I'll finish—and I rather like the last one."

❧

Yet another reason not to obsess over the past, Colin thought; not only did it transform one into a brooding maniac, it made one forget the present. He hadn't guarded his tongue—how could Savitri not be offended at such a statement?—but she neither recoiled nor appeared startled by his admission. A contemplative frown touched the corners of her lovely mouth, her eyes darkening to the same rich velvet brown surrounding them.

"Byron had already been turned, hadn't he?"

Colin blinked, his hesitancy to continue—and the bitterness the recollection had revived—dropping away in his surprise. "Do not try to convince me you've deduced that from what I've told you today."

"No." She shrugged. "I read a biography once, and you said last night that a vampire had fed from you. Byron had strange eating habits, uncertain health toward the end of his life, and a beautiful face. And he was considered a hero, a celebrity. Why wouldn't he have sought true immortality if he knew he could? But not from you."

"He did not seek it at all; it was forced upon him by a vampire who admired him and wished to give him eternal life and beauty. It did not take well."

"Because he didn't choose it?"

"Yes. And the doctors around him mistook his affliction, kept him bled out, weakened and starving. He wrote to me in desperation, deciding that even vampirism was preferable to death." Colin grimaced. "Good God, but he'd have been an intolerable sort of immortal, constantly lamenting his existence. An eternity's worth of brilliant poetry wouldn't have compensated for such dreariness."

"It's fortunate, then, that most choose it."

"Yes." He watched her carefully as he admitted, "I'd have refused his entreaty; I'd have left him to rot. Only at Ramsdell's insistence did we travel to Greece."

"You didn't leave Varney and Paul to rot last night. I'll

weigh the two events, and decide whether to hate you." She tilted her head, as if considering. "No, I still love you."

There was but one response: to kiss her senseless. Her lips were smiling beneath his, ripening with hunger and need as he continued.

Only the onset of the bloodlust made him stop—he'd had more than he should've the night before, and dared not take more—but he found his pleasure in the knowledge that she was, indeed, senseless, her gaze soft and unfocused, her skin flushed.

Irresistible.

Best to finish quickly. "His end was the same as the others: he took the blood—which should have strengthened him immediately—and his life was snuffed. We felt the heat emanate from him, though his skin did not burn; a difference caused, most likely, by his transformation and the manner in which the blood is processed."

Her expression sharpened. "A normal vampire transformed him?"

"Yes. Ramsdell returned home, and I hunted her down."

"Did you kill her?"

"No. I warned her."

Savi's lips pressed together, and her eyes sparkled with amusement. "Taught her a lesson?"

"*Suggested* that she might refrain from forcing the change onto humans, and find a companion. Which she did, transforming him with no complications. That letter is included as well." He took a long breath. "There was another vampire. A female. Osterberg's partner."

Her mouth rounded in surprise. "When?"

"Thursday evening, after I left you in Castleford's house."

"Oh," she said. Her shields weren't up; he could feel the spin of her emotions as she worked it through. Confusion, realization. "I'd heard that you had to slay a vampire who'd broken the rules—who'd killed a homeless man. That was her?"

"Yes."

"She fed from you? And she died the same way as the others?" At his nod, her brows drew together and she looked down at her hands.

His throat felt swollen. "It wasn't a . . . kind way to do it, Savi."

"No." She raised her dark gaze to his. "Perhaps next time you should use your swords."

Relief rushed through him, but he held himself still. "Yes." He swallowed thickly. "She was old, Savi. Perhaps a hundred years or so. Strong."

Her eyes unfocused as she thought it over. "So perhaps vampire blood can't overcome the taint; it has to be nosferatu blood. But you'd have thought of that."

"Yes."

"So even your blood, from the strongest nosferatu-born vampire alive, isn't enough to overcome it during transformation. Or feeding, in Byron and the female's case."

A confirmation of what he'd already determined: both transformation and feeding, too much the risk. "No."

"But there are a lot of variables," she said quietly. "Polidori's transformation was interrupted; Shelley was strong, but . . ." She glanced down at the letters. "I don't know. I'll read these and talk to Hugh and Michael."

"I've already—" He couldn't finish; she raised her eyes to his again, hope glimmering within them. He shouldn't have put it there, but he couldn't crush it. "I've already made arrangements for us to meet with them at the warehouse today."

It wasn't a lie, but she'd likely protest his true reason. Nor was he looking forward to another visit to the Room—but the wyrmwolves' connection to Savi rather than himself made discovering the reason behind it vital.

She nodded and pressed a kiss to his mouth. "I need to phone Nani before we go." Wrapping the sheet around her, she crawled toward the foot of the bed, reached out to pull back the curtain. "You'll have to lower the shields around the house; should I call from the room in the basement?"

He gave an automatic assent; distracted by sight and sound of the silk sliding over her bottom, he'd barely an instant in which to remember what she'd see. But an instant was all it took to crouch behind her, cover her eyes.

"Wait, Savi," he said urgently. He felt her body tremble, as if in laughter—then still when she realized he'd not detained her for play.

His heart pounded in his chest, his blood racing through

his veins. He should ask her to shut her eyes until he carried her from the room; she would, he'd no doubt—but his request would only torturously pique her curiosity.

And hadn't he brought her up here so that she would see? So that she would know why he'd given her the letters? He'd told her his reason . . . but he'd not told her the whole of it.

He needed to prepare her, though—and himself. He'd not thought he'd be anxious. "They're not intended to . . . I hope you do not think them *creepy*."

She blinked rapidly, her lashes tickling his palms. "Let me look."

He inhaled the warm skin at her nape, held the sweet scent in his mouth. Then he lowered his hands and waited.

She clutched the sheet to her chest. The drape of the material at the bottom of her spine swayed gently with her steps; the silk trailing on the floor made her seem to glide rather than walk.

He did not tear his eyes from her as she stared up at herself, enthralled and beautiful. Or as she moved on, examined her wary expression when she encountered him outside Castleford's home the night of his return from Caelum—and at the next, the curiosity and confusion in the glance she'd given him when she'd turned to leave. As she placed her palm against a small study of her hands, measuring the likeness.

"Was I so judgmental—disdainful?" she asked suddenly, coming to a halt in front of another.

The tension holding him frozen on the bed dissolved, and he crossed instantly to her side. "I believe I'd just said something to the effect that there were few things I enjoyed so much as women who walk alone at night—"

"—but finding two eager to bend over a park bench after they've had a glimpse of your face is better. You deserved it, then."

"Yes. For its banality, if nothing else. You always ran so quickly; I found myself saying the most ridiculous things to make you stop for a moment and look at me."

He heard the effort it took her to swallow before she whispered, "Is it just an obsession?"

"I thought it was," he said quietly.

Her eyes glistened; she averted her face and dragged in a

trembling breath. "The one from Caelum is wrong," she said, her voice hoarse.

"No." He didn't need to glance at the painting to confirm it. "I perfectly remember your appearance; do not be modest and protest you could never be that beautiful."

"Not me; I wouldn't know what I looked like, only what I see. It's the water—you've depicted it reflecting me, the obelisk, and a few of the spires surrounding the courtyard."

"The angles are correct," he said, turning to scrutinize it. He'd not sketched the water, but he'd been certain of the perspective.

"Yes, but *I* was the only thing that reflected—the sky did, I guess, because the surface of the water was so incredibly blue. Nothing else. It *should* be as you've painted, but it wasn't."

"Bloody marvelous," he said, though the familiar, giddy wonder rushed up within him. "Caelum is cursed."

"You would choose the most melodramatic interpretation. More likely, the curse is made of the same magic that holds Caelum together," Savi said, leaning back against his chest. His arms circled her waist, and she tilted her head to look up at him. "*Or* Chaos and Caelum are made of similar stuff. *Or* it's impossible to see what it truly is."

Surely it was equally impossible—and melodramatic—to love a woman this much. "What would you choose?"

Her brow lifted and she glanced over at the painting. "Lacking evidence, I'd play the odds and choose 'All of the above.'"

ᕦ

Hypothesizing that the curse might be more of Heaven than Hell did not make it easier to experience—or to watch its effect.

In the dimly lit observation room, Savi's heart lodged in her throat as Colin slid one foot slowly in front of the other, inching along the mirrored floor. The effort whitened his lips; his face was set in a rigid mask.

"When you said you wanted to conduct an experiment, I didn't think you meant *this*." She forced the words out; if he heard screams, even inanity must be a welcome respite.

A smile flickered over his mouth, quickly erased. He

closed his eyes and swayed, then braced his hands on his knees as his body heaved violently.

Her eyes burned. Could he smell it, as well? Taste it? She turned to Hugh, who met her panicked gaze with a reassuring nod.

"He's doing well this time, Savi," he said.

This was *well* in comparison to other times?

Colin lifted his head and looked in their direction. "Yes, sweet, I'm quite alright. Smashing time to be had in here."

His ragged breathing, his sudden recoil from an invisible threat told her better than his flippancy how much the words were a lie.

She felt like breaking the glass in frustration, but settled for clenching her teeth. He was doing this for her, and she didn't know whether to be angry with him for torturing himself, humbled by it, or sickened by the realization of what he'd gone through so many times before.

She only knew she wanted him out. "Do you see the pack yet?"

"No." He shuddered and retched.

Lilith drummed her fingers on the glass. "You know, Colin, when we said you should accept some responsibility, we didn't think you'd embrace the concept so wholeheartedly. It's disgusting. Somewhat plebian, as well."

"Sod off, Lilith," Colin said harshly, but his eyes opened again. How many times must have Lilith drawn the focus away from Chaos for him in that manner? "It's philanthropy, which is a privilege of the upper classes."

Savi added, "And entirely for self-serving reasons, not out of any moral obligation." He'd never have gone into that Room for anyone other than the few people there: Michael and Selah, Lilith and Hugh.

And her.

"Precisely." Colin slid forward another inch, then two.

"So Savi must be a charity case," Hugh said.

"I'd have thought you were Savi's. The homeless Fallen angel."

Savi frowned; a sneer had worked itself into Colin's voice. *Not himself when he comes out,* Jake had told her. Was this part of it?

Hugh only looked amused, as if the banter had not taken on an ugly cast. "Aye. Desperate for a family, I took advantage of the girl who'd just lost hers."

"Ah, yes. Desperate. Little wonder you did not tell her—"

Savi jumped in surprise as a sharp slap against the glass cut him off.

"Colin," Lilith ground out. "Don't."

Tell me what? Her mind screamed for answers, but she forced herself not to ask. Hugh's hands were fisted in his pockets, his legs braced apart as if readying for a blow.

Colin's eyes narrowed at the glass for an instant, his gaze almost silver in his anger. Then his chin dipped and he said quietly, "My apologies, Castleford. I could not bear to lose her, either." He blinked and stared downward. "I've found the wyrmwolves."

Savi's hands shook, and she willed them to stop. What the hell had just happened? What did they think was so terrible that she couldn't forgive Hugh for it? She forgave fucking *everything*.

She looked to Hugh, but he only said, "We're lowering the spell around the Room, Colin. Block as much as you're able."

Not now. Savi drew in a deep breath. Selah's wings rustled as she erased the symbols from the door; Michael stepped forward, spoke for the first time.

"Are they in the same formation? One large group?"

"Yes." It came out as a hiss, and Savi stifled her cry as Colin flinched and dropped to his knees. Sweat beaded on his forehead; his mouth drew back in a grimace of pain, his fangs slicing into his lips. His eyes lost their focus.

"Colin! Goddammit."

"Come back, Colin," Michael commanded, and his voice took on a melodic resonance. "Come back *now*."

Savi flattened her palms against the glass. Colin kneeled there, unmoving, unresponsive. "What's happening?" The vagueness of his gaze tickled a memory. "A hallucination?"

"Yes," Hugh said quietly.

"Can we go in there? Help him?" She was already moving toward the door when Hugh caught her arm.

"No, Savi." The understanding in his voice did not soften his implacable grip. "We've each tried; even Selah, who was

in Chaos with him. He has attacked—and attempted to feed—
from us all. Lilith barely survived, and only because Michael
was here to heal her." He let go her arm. "He'll come out of
it."

She started to protest—he'd hallucinated before and hadn't
hurt her, but this wasn't Caelum.

"Okay. Okay." This time, she gave in to her frustration; the
glass rattled under her kick. Still no reaction. "What happened
to him?"

Silence greeted her, and that frightened her more than anything they could have said. When he'd fed from her at the
fountain, she'd *felt* the horror he'd gone through, but only the
emotion; she didn't have a memory to go along with whatever
had caused it. Was he reliving it now?

"Savitri, your shields are failing," Michael said. "If you do
not hold them until he is ready, his pain now will be for nothing."

How many times had they asked him to go in? Had it ever
been good for *anything*?

"Sorry," she bit out, but carefully rebuilt them.

Thirty endless seconds passed before he dropped forward
onto his hands, a harsh sound tearing from him, a scream
muffled only by clenched teeth and will.

"Colin." She was shaking as hard as he was. "Let's do this
and get you out."

Panting, he wiped the blood from his chin with the back of
his hand and nodded. "Do it slowly."

She'd have preferred to lower her psychic blocks all at
once, get this over with, but it was best to be thorough now. At
her natural state—high for normal humans but unconsciously
shielded for her—she paused. "Anything?"

"No." Colin absently licked the blood from his skin.
"Though it is a pleasant distraction for me."

Breathing a sigh of relief, she continued. Colin climbed to
his feet, his brow furrowed as he watched the wyrmwolves in
the flat, empty mirror. The tension had eased from his expression; though he still shied to the side now and again, once
muttering of a dragon, he seemed to hold on to her scent as
armor, using it to keep the rest of Chaos at bay.

She was almost completely open when he frowned and

said sharply, "Stop, Savi. They're moving. Toward the mountain." He took at step forward, turned to look behind him. "I'm there—they still come this way. All of them. Piling over one another like rats in a bin."

Wet, exposed flesh sliding against scales and fur. Savi fought her involuntary gag, immediately pushed the image from her mind to prevent adding her revulsion to what must already be a bombardment of psychic and physical sensations.

"Are they headed to the caves?" Selah asked, coming to stand beside Savi.

"No, they're running up the side of the—" Sucking in a harsh breath, Colin fell to his knees again, stared intently down. "A symbol is carved into the stone. Near the peak."

"From the nosferatu? Are there any still there?" Perhaps they'd practiced writing the symbols before they'd moved to the frozen ceiling.

"No, sweet." Colin wiped a shaking hand over his face. "Oh, good God."

"Draw it into the air," Michael said softly.

Colin hesitated, then clenched his jaw and traced a design in front of him. As soon as he finished, he swatted his hand through it as if to erase the invisible mark he'd created.

"'Reflect'?" Lilith turned to Michael for confirmation. "That symbol could not work alone to cross the realms. The nosferatu would have returned long ago, if it were that simple."

The Doyen was shaking his head. "Colin, did you write it as you see it, or reverse it so that we see it correctly?"

"I reversed it." He stared down at his palms, his fingers curling into fists. "I've not the courage to write it again."

"Fuck me," Lilith breathed. "Written the other way, it's 'bridge.'"

The blood against her tongue alerted Savi to the force with which she'd been biting her lip, desperately trying to put the pieces together. They wouldn't fit.

"You wrote it?" When? Hadn't he and Selah fled to the caves? *Inside* the mountain?

"Yes, sweet. I do not remember doing so, but I must have. Perhaps in the hope the curse that had brought me there would take me away." His hands lowered to his sides. "They're tearing into one another now."

Michael did not seem surprised. "Likely an instinctive response; the blood will activate the bridge."

Hugh frowned. "Did you not see the symbol when you retrieved him?"

"They'd dragged him to the base," Michael said.

"Most of me." Colin flinched, then added with forced humor, "Oh, sweet, do not despair. They didn't eat the choicest bits."

CHAPTER 25

*She was certain that B—— had written that blasted
story, rather than P——. I convinced her that she
ought to conform to Continental fashion, and take a
companion. I, however, am more certain than ever that
I never shall. My blood will not allow it. I do not
lament the loss, of course; where on Earth shall I find
a companion who can command my attention away
from myself? Furthermore, why should I want to?*

Colin to Ramsdell, 1824

❧

"Are you well?"

The list of Osterberg's recent credit card transactions
blurred in front of her, but Savi didn't glance away from the
monitor. Not that it had helped; keeping busy hadn't kept her
from thinking.

"Not really," she said as Hugh sat on the edge of her desk,
crossing his arms and ankles in his professorial talk-to-me
pose.

"Are you running?"

"A little. But productively." She pointed at the screen.
"Both Osterberg and Fishnet Shirt—Ken Branning—have
several gas purchases in St. Francis Woods, within two blocks
of each other. I can't find any reason for them to be there; they
don't have any other transactions, and it's out of the way for
their usual routes."

"So we'll pinpoint Dalkiel's location thanks to the Navigators' low gas mileage?"

"That, and because an aide employed eight months ago at
the German Embassy in London—in Belgrave Square—quit a

couple of days after SI captured the nosferatu. That took me a little longer to access; I'll keep digging at that angle now that I'm finally in. It's funny how governments are secretive about things like that."

"Very funny," Hugh said, smiling. "Lilith and Colin are returning from their wyrmwolf hunt. It was successful."

Daylight streamed through the window; she envied Colin the ability to take out his frustration on something almost as much as she worried for him. "Where did it come up?"

"In the bay, just north of Alcatraz."

"Did it eat any tourists?" she said, and immediately felt sick. "Oh, god. Never mind. That's not as funny as it should have been. Did you kill James Anderson?"

His soft gaze was the same color as Caelum's skies; his body was as rigid as the marble. "Aye."

Her stomach roiled. "You used your Gift—forced Truth on him? And he shot himself?"

"Aye."

"You thought I'd hate you for that? So you let me think he was just crazy? Even after I knew you were a Guardian?"

His brow furrowed. "No. I never thought you'd have turned from me."

"Did you think I couldn't handle the moral dilemma?"

"No. If I did, I'd never have allowed you into SI. You think I see you as a child, Savi; I haven't since you returned from Caelum."

Her eyes widened. "But you did before that?"

"Yes." Lines appeared at the sides of his mouth, as if he was repressing his grin.

Was the change hers or his? But she couldn't think of that, not when— "Why did he do it?"

His smile disappeared, and Hugh sighed. "Savi, don't."

She heard the door latch click open but didn't look away from him. The room wasn't shielded; everyone in the warehouse would hear anyway. It didn't matter where they stood when they heard it.

"But Anderson told you, right? He had to tell you the truth."

"Yes."

"Then why? He'd already taken the money." Her parents

had known better than to argue when someone pointed a gun at them. "He never looked in the purse; he didn't know there wasn't much in there, so it wasn't because he was pissed about the amount. And the jewelry was worth a couple of hundred dollars. Was it because they'd seen him?"

"No. That was why he shot *you*, but not them." He uncrossed his arms and clenched his fingers on the edge of the desk. "You always look for a reason, but there isn't one, Savi. He just wanted to."

Her brows drew together, and she shook her head. "Just wanted to? He liked the power in it?"

"No."

"He hated interracial couples? And their kids? He liked the sound of gunfire? He had a shitty childhood? A bad fucking day?"

"Savi—" Hugh choked on a humorless laugh, passed his hand through his short hair. "No."

"It was completely random then? He just wanted to, for no reason, and pulled the trigger? Three times?" More than three. She could remember each loud—*don't think, Savi.*

"Aye."

She couldn't breathe. "I don't know what to do with that."

"I know," he said softly.

Slowly, she forced her legs to stop their trembling, pushed air into her lungs. "That's why you didn't tell me? Because there was no reason? And you thought I couldn't handle it?"

"Yes."

She swallowed hard. "I think . . . I think eight months ago—maybe even yesterday—I couldn't have. As it was, I was making up all kinds of stuff in my head: justifications, rationalizations. That's not any better, is it?"

Hugh relaxed slightly. "Hardly."

Lilith said from the doorway, "Do you know why I adore him so much? Because he doesn't say anything retarded like, 'It's so that I could come into your life, and you'd eventually translate my book, which in turn would lead to us kicking Lucifer's ass' or 'So that eventually the most beautiful bloodsucker in the world would be your sexual plaything.' As if it were a trade."

"It'd have been a poor exchange," Colin said. He was leaning against the door frame, the hood of his Guardian-made jacket pushed back. His gaze locked with Savi's. "I apologize, sweet. I ought not to have mentioned it. It cannot be pleasant to re-visit those memories."

"I think we're equal then." He'd revisited his own hell for her.

"That was not a trade, either. Only demons keep tally."

The rustle of paper and the shift of Lilith's and Colin's attention beyond where she and Hugh sat alerted Savi to Michael's arrival.

"That's not precisely true," the Doyen said as she turned. He held a rolled parchment. "I do, too."

His tone lacked threat; it was the others' reactions that made it seem ominous. Lilith sucked in a sharp breath; though it was difficult to tell, Savi thought Hugh tensed with disapproval.

But Colin's demeanor became carelessly nonchalant as he unzipped his lightweight jacket. She'd never seen him truly bored; he only affected it when he was at his most interested—or frightened. "If that Scroll is an accounting of mine, pray do not tell me the balance. A credit is a boast, a debit an embarrassment—and to acknowledge either exceedingly vulgar."

"It is neither. I tally; I don't demand payment. *That* is de-monic." Michael stepped to a workstation in the middle of the room, vanished a computer from the tabletop, and spread the Scroll open. "Shield the room."

As Colin pricked his thumb and dotted it to the symbols, Savi rose from her chair to study the parchment. She slid her hand over its pale cream surface, tested the edges. The paper between her fingers was as thin as onionskin, but she could hardly bend it. "Is it blank—or can I just not see the writing?"

Lilith joined Hugh at the other side of the table, stood with her arms folded beneath her breasts, frowning down at the Scroll.

"There is nothing yet written. I've not yet heard anything of this curse to record."

Startled, Savi glanced over at Colin, found him standing beside her. The crease of his brow betrayed his own surprise; he met her gaze, blinked, then looked from Michael to Hugh. "You must have known. It was in Switzerland."

Hugh shook his head. "I saw that you'd covered your

mirrors; I'd no reason to think it a curse, or different from anything you'd done in the five years since your transformation. I'd not seen you in that time."

"And when he came to me later, related the lack of reflection, we thought it an effect of the sword. You gave no indication that you saw something within the mirror until you returned from Chaos."

"I'd no idea such a place as Chaos existed," Colin said. "I assumed it was Hell, or a nightmare reflection of myself. The curse was supposed to show us our inner selves; we thought it a joke."

"So did I, until a minute ago. This really was a *curse*?" Lilith looked between Michael and Hugh. "You aren't serious."

"They're exceptionally rare; typically, they don't work, except in an accidental convergence of symbols, blood, and items with a particular resonance," Michael said.

Lilith frowned. "But Lucifer told no one of the symbols; I learned how to use the protection spell by luck. And except for that, I've never taught anyone those I do know, because I daren't write them. Have you?"

"No. They are too powerful; too dangerous. But it is inevitable that a human eventually stumbles onto a particular symbol. And perhaps knowledge of a few is left over from before, but their power rendered inert except in unique circumstances."

"Before when?" Savi asked.

Michael glanced at her, his mouth a hard, straight line. "Before I began writing the Scrolls in Latin."

She compressed her lips to stop herself, and focused on the more important question: "Can it be broken?"

Savi slipped her hand into Colin's as Michael said, "No. Once done, some things cannot be reversed."

Colin's fingers clenched on hers, but aside from that small movement, he gave no response.

"Then what is this for?" Savi said dully, indicating the Scroll with her free hand.

"Some things cannot be undone; however, they may be altered. But I cannot go forward without knowing what has gone before. Do you recall the words you spoke with it?"

"Yes." Colin's brows lifted when Michael looked at him expectantly. "You cannot expect me to repeat them?"

"I can."

"Bloody hell." Colin closed his eyes, and his body tensed as he recited a string of words in a language Savi didn't recognize. He half-raised his lids to peer about, then smiled down at her. "And I'm still here."

She grinned in response, letting out a breath that she hadn't realized she'd been holding. "What was that?"

"Romany," Hugh said. "Roughly translated, a command to reflect a true nature hidden within."

"The language matters less than the meaning and intent behind it." Michael raised his hand over the Scroll; a blade flashed and disappeared. Blood thinned and spread in rivulets over the paper, sliding into an arrangement of letters and words. Latin—yet another translation of the curse.

Savi read the first lines, fascinated. "Are you moving it into place with your mind, or does your blood make the letters on its own?"

"There's no difference," Michael said quietly. He turned his arm; the bronze skin had healed flawlessly. "And the symbol—how was it written?"

"In blood, on a mirror," Colin said. "Neither was required by the curse; I thought it more appropriate to the mood that night."

Michael nodded. "I will note it, but not record the symbol. Particularly not in my blood." Even as he spoke, it slid like red mercury across the surface of the Scroll, leaving glistening sentences in its wake. "Was there anything unique about the mirror or its frame?"

Colin shook his head. "I believe it was gilded wood, Louis XIV perhaps."

"So writing the symbol on the mirror made it both *bridge* and *reflect* at once? And that's probably why he sees Chaos in the mirror?" Savi guessed, and after a brief hesitation, Michael nodded. "But why does it work as a bridge for the wyrmwolves? It's written on rock in Chaos, and he didn't write it in blood."

Hugh looked up from the Scroll. "What did you use to carve it?"

"Selah left weapons for me; perhaps it was a dagger." Colin lifted his hands. "I was bleeding. Some might have dropped onto the symbol."

"But you aren't certain?"

Colin shrugged, a tight smile around the corners of his lips, his eyes. "No. I'd delayed my daysleep for days, and hadn't fed in almost a sennight. I wasn't supposed to be awake after Selah left, let alone fleeing the caves for the top of a mountain."

Oh, god. "You knew the wyrmwolves were coming when you sent her away?"

"Yes, sweet."

"But you woke up."

"Yes."

He wouldn't have wanted to; he'd have wanted to go easy . . . like his sister and Ramsdell had. And he'd been starving—weak. The instinct to survive might have driven him to fight the wyrmwolves, but how had he managed the strength to do it, and to run? Where had he gotten the—?

Her eyes widened. "You drank from them? That's why you were certain the wyrmwolves were connected to you when they first appeared. And why you can sense them. Not just because you are an anchor to Chaos; you ingested their blood."

"Yes, but the buggers took most of it back," he said and looked at Michael. "She's likely correct; yet they respond to her psychic scent, not mine."

Michael's dark gaze narrowed thoughtfully. "I'd be surprised if venom and nosferatu blood had such an effect alone. Did you take her blood the night the first wyrmwolf appeared?" When Colin shook his head, the Doyen met Savi's eyes. "Have you taken in his blood?"

"No. I bit him, but I was careful; I'm positive I didn't swallow any." Her cheeks heated slightly.

Colin glanced down at her, his fangs exposed in a brief, teasing grin before he said, "It arrived directly after—too soon for it to have been the bite."

"And the fever began long before that."

"In the plane?" Lilith said.

"I first noticed it in the car. Not long after . . ." Her voice broke, and she stared up at Colin. "Not long after you healed me with your blood."

The last traces of his smile faded. "That is also when I first noticed the scent. But I've used my blood to heal thousands of people—everyone I've fed from, even after I returned from Chaos."

"But none of them had hellhound and nosferatu tainting their veins." Her mind raced. "Or it was the henna—all over my hands. What if there was a symbol in the design somewhere?"

"It could be any of those things," Michael agreed. "Or a combination of them all, or something we've not considered."

"In the hospital, was my room protected by the spell?"

"No," Hugh said.

"My shields were down from the fever, but no wyrmwolves came. For two weeks."

"Because I was not near enough to sense you," Colin said slowly. "It's not you or me, but *us*."

"Yes." She saw the despair in his gaze, the tightness around his lips. "It doesn't matter," she added quickly, though her stomach knotted. "I can keep my shields up. And I'll only be here for a few more weeks anyway."

Hugh said quietly, "Michael, are there any alternative food sources for a vampire? Blood—but not from humans, or that isn't accompanied by a sexual urge?"

"No." He ran his hand over the parchment and the liquid stilled, sank into the paper. "If there were, I'd have given vampires that choice long ago."

The tight clasp of Colin's fingers on hers grew painful; she held on, uncaring.

The Doyen's crimson blood covered the Scroll with a list of all of the reasons they should—*had to*—let go, and dried into lines of obsidian.

❧

After such a morning, it was a relief to spend the latter part of the afternoon in Colin's basement, lounging on the sectional with him as Lon Chaney Jr. lurched across the enormous screen.

She lost count of the times he buried his face into her hair, laughing—and even if his commentary resembled something out of *MST3K*, she heard the fondness beneath it. He apparently adored monster movies, and judging by the DVD titles stacked two-deep in the shelves, the era and medium didn't matter. *The Wisdom of Crocodiles* sat between *Frankenstein* and *Blood: The Last Vampire*; he'd offered up *Vampire Hunter D* and seven versions of *Dracula* for consideration before they'd settled for *The Wolf Man*—the only one Savi hadn't seen.

It was too much to hope for a happy ending, but at least a werewolf died at the end instead of a vampire.

"That *is* the happy ending," he reminded her when she said as much a few minutes later, after they'd retreated to the kitchen. He absently shook the decanter of blood he'd pulled from the refrigerator. "The ungodly creature wiped from existence, the Earth restored to its natural order. And, indeed, any man so hirsute should be treated as a perversion. Will this disgust you?"

Her mouth stuffed full with rice from the takeout they'd picked up earlier, she could only shake her head. He poured the blood into a tall glass; it frothed at the top, like a cappuccino.

He grimaced and set it aside. "I'll wait; I detest foam. That smells incredibly good. Perhaps I will hold it below my nose as I drink, and pretend it is red coconut curry."

"Do you miss eating?"

"Not when I'm feeding from you, sweet. But compared to swine? Yes."

"I'm flattered." She poked at a carrot with her fork. "You'll let me know when it starts to affect you?"

"Not it if hurries your leaving."

"I'll be able to tell," she said quietly. "You'll be shaky, stupid, tired. No libido. If my choice is between your weakness when Dalkiel's still out there, and my staying—" She shook her head. "It's not a choice."

"And if Dalkiel is dead?"

"Shaky, *stupid*, tired," she repeated, and hated the tremble in her voice. "With no sexual drive. Do you want to live like that?"

His jaw tightened. "No. Bloody fucking hell." He unclenched his fists. "I'd still be beautiful; you could bounce upon me now and again whilst I lie in my daysleep."

She snorted with amusement, but it didn't last. Her laughter ended on a sigh. "Talking to them didn't help us much, did it?"

"No."

If anything, it had only raised more questions. "What did you expect Michael to say when he popped into the tech room earlier? When you said you didn't want to know the balance of your accounts."

Colin stiffened; though the bubbles hadn't disappeared, he took a drink from his glass. Delaying his answer?

She forced another smile and waved the carrot in the air. "I know the balance of all your accounts; does that make me terribly vulgar?"

The glass clinked sharply against the countertop. "I daresay it makes you practical, sweet. Every woman should calculate her suitor's worth."

"After calculating it, I daresay I must be brilliant."

"Disagreement would insult your intelligence and my vanity."

"You're insulting it by pretending there was nothing; even Hugh looked as if he was ready to argue with Michael, when usually I can't tell if he's upset." Savi tried to hold her smile when he didn't answer; she failed. Her stomach ached. Shoving the curry away, she said, "I'm sorry. Not stopping again. You don't want to tell me; it's none of my business. A different topic then: You thought the same thing I did, didn't you? That Hugh didn't tell me about James Anderson because he was afraid I wouldn't forgive him."

"Yes." His gaze was steady on hers, dark as iron.

"When I was sitting alone in the tech room, I was thinking: All of this time I've been telling myself that Hugh *understood* me when I did that shit with the IDs as a kid, and that was why he never disapproved of me or lectured me about it. Because Nani sure as hell did."

"As she should have." He took another drink.

"Yeah. But then I realized he used his Gift on Anderson, and my first reaction was: He didn't understand me. He's just got such a screwed-up sense of morality that anything is okay; that his idea of what's right is so wide, it encompasses even the unforgivable shit. So what was a little bit of forgery to someone like him?"

Colin's brows drew together; he shook his head. "That's exactly opposite of what it is, Savitri."

"I know; I remembered what you said of his warning to you, and I realized it's so *narrow* that the only thing that matters is that no one is cruel if they can help it, or interferes with someone's free will if they can help it, or kills if they can help it—but if it has to be done, it will be. So by the time he came in to talk to me, I was thinking that what he'd done to Anderson had to be done, and I wasn't comfortable with it—but I was okay with it. But if I hadn't spoken to you this morning, I never would have been okay with it; would have never seen that other way of looking at it. And I don't think I could be like Hugh or like Lilith, but at least I can see better how they decide those things." And how, as head of the vampire community, Colin would have to make similar decisions. "And then I realized he does understand me, maybe better than I do myself."

"It's an exceptionally annoying trait of his." He downed the remainder of the blood.

"Yeah." And a trait of Colin's—despite his tendency to talk about himself in any other circumstance—was to barely respond when something about Chaos came up. He didn't like to brood over the past, or things in the present he couldn't change. And he probably didn't want to worry her, either.

But she was worried *for* him, dammit.

She took a deep breath. "So when Hugh wants to argue with the Doyen about something that pertains to you, but stops himself, it scares the shit out of me. Because it means something that he doesn't want to happen needs to be done. And whatever it was, it scared you as well. And I only know two things that do that: wyrmwolves and Chaos. But the wyrmwolves are pretty much under control. So it's Chaos, right? You have to go back for some reason, and finding the bridge today made it the more urgent. Probably because of the nosferatu; if they realize what's going on with the wyrmwolves, they might try to copy it and break out of Chaos."

"You deduced that from half a second's reaction?" Colin stared at her, his face a rigid mask.

"No. It was a combination of things. Something you said in the parking lot, the way you responded to Michael last week in

the hall, seeing a new side to Hugh, thinking about the nosferatu and his execution."

But she hadn't wanted to be right. Would Michael try to
take Colin against his will? Was there any way she could stop
it? She was human; Michael couldn't go against *her* will, even
if he could a vampire's.

Sighing, she felt her frustration slip away; just once, she'd
have liked to hold on to it—but she couldn't solve anything
now, anyway. "It also helps that my freak brain remembers
that half second really well."

His expression softened but slightly. "I love nothing so
much as morally conflicted women with freakish brains."
With slow, deliberate steps, Colin stalked around the counter
and braced his arms on either side of her chair. Sudden heat
built as he shoved himself between her legs. He lowered his
nose to hers and said through gritted teeth, "But if you do not
use your freakish brain to discover a way to stay with me, I'll
hunt you across the Earth. I vow it."

Her chest heaved; a flush of excitement spread over her
skin. "Will you fuck me senseless when you catch me?"

"Yes. The first time, for you." He nipped sharply at her bottom lip, and she opened her mouth, tried to catch his in turn.
He evaded her easily. "Then slowly, for me."

"I love it when you're selfish," she said, and her back
arched as he lifted the hem of her T-shirt and his teeth scraped
her breast. Her hands threaded through his hair.

"This is completely selfish. An experiment to ascertain
that my libido still functions."

"I daresay it does," she moaned as he rocked the evidence
against her.

"I daresay."

❧

Two days later, Colin had to admit that although regular sex
and blood were more conducive to charm, the damage had
been done—his physical prowess had won over more of San
Francisco's vampires than his smile. And Savi's video, Fia
and Paul's oft-told description of the chase, Varney's open appreciation for his raise, and Darkwolf's quiet support had

made the venture more of a success than Dalkiel's escape warranted.

"There's Darkwolf," Savi said quietly. Her margarita sat untouched in front of her; though she'd not taken much alcohol of late, Epona had discovered her favorite drink, and seemed bent on showing her gratitude for the position by continually supplying Savi with a fresh glass. Another success, and one that had kept her busy with an influx of requests for IDs and documentation.

It was just as well; there was not much else she could do to flush out Dalkiel. Colin studied her face beneath the changing lights from the dance floor, the soft glow of the sconces above them.

Though her shields were up and her gaze alert, exhaustion seemed to hang about her; a touch of lethargy deepened her voice. The stress of Dalkiel's constant threat, combined with work and their nightly visits to Polidori's? The change in her sleeping pattern?

Or had he been taking too much? He'd not fed from her but once. There was little danger in taking a small sip while making love to her . . . except he'd made love to her with desperate frequency.

A subtle tension gripped her; Colin glanced away from her face as she said in Hindi, "He has Fishnet Shirt with him."

Not in his Goth clothing any longer, Colin noted, but a pair of jeans, a heavy jacket, and a wide-brimmed hat . . . almost as if he intended it as a disguise. The vampire appeared haggard, hungry.

Grief emanated from his psychic scent.

"Ken Branning," Savi reminded him beneath her breath. Her fingers played at her neck, hooking in the slim chain and around the pendant that doubled as an alarm.

"Mr. Branning," he said, and his gaze shifted to Darkwolf. "Do we need privacy?"

"No." Branning shook his head; his shoulders were hunched, his fists shoved into his pockets. "I'm going to say this and go."

Darkwolf slid into the adjacent sofa; Sir Pup lifted his head to make room for him. "He came to Arwen. She sent him here."

"She wasn't close to Guinevere, but Arwen was the first when we came here to—" Branning choked, pressed his hand to his face. "Fuck, I can't believe he did that to her. I can't believe it."

"Do you know where we can find him?" Colin asked quietly.

With a shudder, a clench of his fists, Branning nodded. "Yeah. There's an office on Lawson—"

"Between Funston and Fourteenth?" He saw the other vampire's surprise, and sighed. Taylor had contacted him earlier in the day, reported that one of the Navigators had been parked in front of the building. Lilith had led the raid on the office and come away with two vampires, still caught in their daysleep.

And when they'd awoken, Colin had found it difficult to punish them in wake of their effusive thanks for their capture.

"And another in St. Francis Woods—a residence."

Colin felt Savi's immediate interest. "Do you have an address?" She pulled out her cell phone as soon as Branning recited it.

Castleford answered on the other end; Colin refocused his attention on Branning. "Will you flee the city?"

Branning nodded, swallowed hard. "He's told us too many times that he'll kill us for deserting. I'll go back to my first community—I've got friends willing to take me in until I can find . . ." His countenance smoothed, as if he simply couldn't think of taking a new partner at that time, and pushed it away. "We heard about what you did. A few of us have been trying to get out, since things started going bad—they want to know if you can help them. Keep them safe if they run."

"Yes. It may require relocation until Dalkiel has been slain, but if they come in, we'll provide them protection." Colin held his gaze. "If they lie, or come to me with the intention of using my promise as a way to hurt anyone in the community, I'll know it." Castleford would question anyone relentlessly; they'd not be able to deceive him. "And I'll not be merciful if they do."

Darkwolf waited until Branning had left. "Is he lying now?"

"If he is, I'll kill him; if he's not, Dalkiel will."

"Lilith and Hugh are taking a few Guardians to check out that address," Savi said, closing her phone. "You don't think he'll make it out of the city?"

"Perhaps if he leaves immediately. The longer he remains and tries to contact those still following the demon, the lower his chances."

"He doesn't look as if he cares all that much."

"No."

Darkwolf slid his hand over Sir Pup's ears. "Dalkiel is using threats against their partners to keep them in line. For some, it's not effective—some partners are together because there's no one else, and they just have to feed." He glanced at Savi, then back to Colin. "I am not one of them. I won't bargain with a demon to save myself, but I will Arwen and Gina. I have refused him once; the three of us have. Gina witnessed his humiliation. We were already in line of Dalkiel's anger, but we may be more so now."

"So we are perfectly clear: I will destroy you if you try. And if I ever need make a choice between Savi and the lot of you, I'll choose her." He smiled slightly, took her hand to ease her sudden tension. "But there are alternatives."

"I don't want to flee." Darkwolf's mouth twisted in a wry smile. "Not again."

"It may be what saves you," Colin said. "But you'll not have to run far. The nearest room typically suffices."

Savi blinked. "You're going to show him the symbols?"

"We've told the employees; it'll hardly stay secret for long. It's a temporary measure," Colin told Darkwolf as he took out his card, a pencil. "Though the three of you could stay within its protection indefinitely, you'll only need the extra time for help to arrive."

"It's fleeing," Darkwolf said, though he leaned forward with interest. "I'm not a coward."

Amused, Colin lifted a brow. Did he think it made him seem weak? "It's survival," he said. "We're prey to a demon. And a warren is a more attractive choice than an eternity frozen motionless in the putrid bowels of Hell."

"Well, god, when you put it *that* way . . ." Savi rolled her eyes and burst into laughter.

Colin grinned and began to sketch the symbols on the card. The line of the first wobbled. The pencil shook in his hand.

He swallowed, concentrated. Forced it to steady.

Perhaps he was a bit tired, too.

❧

It was eerie, how still he was.

For a few moments, Savi's own breath seemed to stop as Colin slipped into his daysleep. The rise and fall of his chest ceased; his features took on the waxy, bloodless cast of the newly dead.

The subtle radiance that differentiated him from Dalkiel died, like a film of grease over a lens. He was still beautiful, but she decided that bouncing on him in this state wasn't the least bit appealing.

It'd be hours before he awoke. There was nothing she *had* to do that she could. The symbols protected the house, but prevented her from working online. She wasn't hungry, and there wasn't anything to clean.

Days like this were why video games had been created. DemonSlayer it was.

She planned her strategy in the Seventh Level of Hell as she arranged the curtains around the bed. It was Savi's favorite level, full of violent sinners and harpies that had to be killed before moving up to the Sixth Level. Her gaze skimmed the room. Why didn't he put drapes on the windows? He painted in the dark; surely he didn't need natural light for his gallery. Perhaps he just preferred it—

She stifled the scream that threatened to tear with jagged fingernails at her throat.

Outside the turret, Dalkiel hung upside down, grinning though the glass. His scales gleamed dully in the sunlight, his eyes glowed scarlet. In his talons, he held a twelve-inch cardboard box.

Her hands fisted in the heavy velvet, her gut clenching. She was safe. Colin was safe. Dalkiel couldn't break through the spell.

Despite that reassurance, clammy perspiration snaked the length of her spine. Naked. She grabbed for her robe, pulled it on.

As if in response to her sudden fright, her discomfort, Dalkiel shape-shifted into her form. The box disappeared, and he twisted and clutched at his breasts and crotch in a disgusting parody of masturbation.

Anger rose to take the place of fear. Yanking the belt tight around her waist, she stalked into Colin's dressing room. A pistol lay on a pile of neatly folded undershirts.

She could shoot through the glass; the symbols only prevented things from coming in.

When she returned to the bedroom, the gun in hand, Dalkiel was gone. Her breathing rapid, unsteady, she cocked her head and waited. And immediately berated herself.

Stupid. She was *listening* for him; she couldn't hear him any more than he could her.

A red blur had her spinning around, aiming the gun at the eastern window. Nothing. Another blur, across the bay window. She whirled.

Nothing.

He's just trying to scare you.

And doing a good job of it. He was too quick; she imagined him skittering around the exterior of the house like a spider, all grasping fingers and clinging feet.

The hair at the back of her neck prickled. Fighting to keep her arms steady, she looked at the turret window again. In his demon form, Dalkiel beckoned her with a crook of his claw, then sliced a fingernail over the tape sealing the box closed.

She didn't want to know what was in there; he liked to rip off heads too much. But if he had killed someone, she needed to know who.

She swallowed and stepped forward, until she was only a couple of feet from the glass.

Dalkiel flipped open the lid, lifted out the head by a tangle of blood-matted hair. Eyeless. In the instant before the sun disintegrated it to ash, Savi recognized him.

Ken Branning.

The gassy *pop!* of the silencer was louder to her ears than the snap of glass, the fissured hole in the window.

She'd missed; he was too fucking fast. Her teeth grinding, she made a slow turn. Her heart skipped, raced.

His wings slowly flapping, Dalkiel hovered at the side of

the house and flicked open a lighter. A tiny flame leapt from the igniter.

Savi jumped onto the bed, rolled the sheets around Colin's body, scooped him up, and ran.

❧

Colin woke, fear and exhaustion heavy in his lungs and mouth. Savi's psychic scent.

He opened his eyes to smooth steel walls: the shelter in the basement. He sat up, silk falling to his waist; Savi turned away from the monitors, offered him a strained smile.

"Dalkiel. He didn't burn it; I thought he was going to burn it," she said in a near-babble. "But I think he just wanted to freak me out. Branning's dead, and I shot out one of your windows."

Oh, Christ. She'd been trapped in here, prevented a call for help by the very thing that protected them. Even the pendant around her neck had been useless behind the spell. Colin wrapped her in his arms, tucked her head against his chest.

"Is he still out there?" His voice was rough.

"I've been watching, but I haven't seen him pass any of the security cameras in a couple of minutes. Not since the sun set, and the thermal sensors aren't picking him up anymore."

"Inside or outside?" She could have escaped without fearing for herself—Dalkiel couldn't hurt her, even if she'd abandoned the house—but it would have left Colin alone, vulnerable.

"Outside. I'm not paying for the window."

He tried to drum up a smile as his palms swept the length of her. No injuries, but he *needed* to touch, to be certain. His fangs ached to taste, to feel the truth of it from inside—to completely erase the fear. He kissed her instead, a sweet slide of texture and scent against his lips.

The tension in her slim form slowly eased; her muscles quavered lightly beneath his hands, as if she'd held them too tight for too long.

She breathed his name when he drew back. Arched her neck in a wordless plea.

Oh, sweet Savitri. No need to ask for this; *he* would beg for it. Her blood: a shock to his tongue, a burst of light and color.

She gasped, panted as he slipped in, around the thick spiraling vault of memories, sampled the emotions spinning over its surface, found the right notes to strike.

Awe. Fear and delight. Passion and enthrallment.

Caelum.

He could give her this. If only this.

It was hardly enough.

CHAPTER 26

Before the Guardians were created, angels protected humans from demons and nosferatu—but mankind never mistook them for humans, even though, beautiful or not, their forms must have been perfect replicas. So what gave them away? Are they beings of light who transform to matter when they shape-shift? Is it energy they couldn't obtain? A psychic presence? I don't know . . . but I think I've seen something like it in Caelum.

—Savi to Taylor, 2007

This was not a course he should have been taking—not with Savi. And yet Colin still found himself sitting on a bench outside the new glass-and-steel Federal Building in the middle of the day, waiting for a man who could kill him with little effort.

Probably would kill him for daring to manipulate him in this way.

"I should have expected this of you," Michael said as he sat beside him. "But I'll admit I did not. Do you need a covering?"

Thick gray clouds hung low in the sky; there was direct sunlight enough to make him squint, not enough to burn. "No."

Michael leaned back, observing the busy human foot traffic, the flow of government employees in and out of the building. He wore linen trousers and a tailored shirt as a concession to the public, but his sandals appeared castoffs from a poorly produced gladiator film.

"Before I left, Lilith informed me that the latest raid was successful. Seven vampires; there cannot be many more under his control. You have taken the community well in hand."

"I'll add my self-congratulations to yours when Dalkiel has been destroyed." Colin studied the Doyen's profile. Savi's efforts had uncovered almost every avenue of concealment the demon had taken, and his only remaining hold on the vampires was their fear. There was little left for Dalkiel to do in San Francisco but to pursue his revenge. "If he manages to destroy me, however, you'd do well to ask Castleford to continue training Fia and Paul. They could take my place, with assistance from Darkwolf and his consorts to form a council."

"And if Dalkiel does not?" Michael's gaze moved from the people to the bubbling fountain in the concrete courtyard.

"I will stay sixty years, perhaps." He could not think beyond that time; Savi would age beautifully . . . and he could not conceive of a life here without her. "And if what Savi fears comes to pass, and we are exposed, I'd be an unlikely spokesperson for any community. So I will establish a council regardless; cameras do not flatter me as well as they do others."

"Others, such as a demon who was elected to human government office because of his performance on-camera."

"Yes."

Michael turned his head; his eyes were hard, his gaze like onyx. "You would not."

"I am myself surprised by the lengths I'd go to to keep her with me; a demon has no sexual need. There'd be no danger of the bloodlust forcing from me what I don't want to give anyone but her."

"So you would take his blood, and your blood would be the trade? He'd most likely find a way to kill you. Rael is adept at bargaining; you are not."

"I may die, yes. His liege is embroiled in a war against Lucifer; he would accept the power it can provide Belial. I would have five hundred years, I think, before he would kill me. That is time enough. "

"Are you attempting to force my hand?"

"Yes. It would be unfortunate if you lost your only access to Chaos."

Michael smiled, and it moved like ice through Colin's veins. "You are mistaken; Belial wants nothing of Chaos. Only to return to Grace. Rael would probably kill you the moment you stepped into his office, or play with you for his amusement."

"We shall soon see."

"Perhaps," Michael said after a moment of silence, "you are not so poor a bargainer. But you did not have to go to these lengths."

Colin relaxed slightly. "You denied Savi's request to visit Caelum. You don't have to honor my free will, and may take me to Chaos at any time; but I know Guardians too well. You prefer choice over force. So I'll go willingly, if you allow her access to Caelum whenever she wishes it."

"Caelum is not for humans," Michael said. "Nor for vampires."

"I daresay that in essence, we are not truly vampire or human. And it did not affect her poorly when she was."

"Perhaps." Michael watched him; without waiting for an invitation, he sent a psychic probe through Colin's mind, then eased away. He could have no doubt of Colin's resolve, no doubt that this was not a bluff. "Very well."

"Take her for her protection upon my next daysleep," Colin said. "I'll not have her terrorized by Dalkiel again."

"A pair of novices can be sent to the house."

Colin shook his head. "I confess it is not only for protection; I need to make amends before she leaves. It is best done there, where the injury was given."

The Doyen's hard mouth softened. "For that reason alone, I would have agreed to this." Michael stood, lifted his face to the sky, his eyes closed as if soaking up the weak sunlight.

"Would you have forced me?"

"Yes." With a sigh, Michael looked at him again. "A Guardian prefers not to impose upon the free will of any being, but when it is a moment of necessity and it does not break the Rules, we are often more men than angels—and perhaps more demonic than human."

Colin nodded, and watched as the Doyen walked slowly across the courtyard and disappeared beyond a concrete sculpture.

What would he be if he forced a commitment from Savi?

Demonic came to mind. So did *selfish*. But they did not concern him as much as they might have, if the alternative for Savi and him was not *alone*.

❧

The first time Michael had teleported Colin to Caelum, the Guardian had dumped him unceremoniously in the middle of his temple, and disappeared immediately thereafter.

And as pleased as Colin was not to be thrown to the floor, he'd have preferred Michael left as quickly. Instead the Doyen walked with him, nattering on about the effect of the realm seeming to lessen over time—and indeed, Colin noted with idle curiosity, he was not as overwhelmed by it. He'd attributed it to his eagerness to see Savi, but when he stopped and looked, he saw the same beauty, the same perfection . . . but it did not bring him to his knees.

Nor did it seem a tomb. The faint sounds of Guardian life reached his ears: conversations, practice, movement. Only a few Guardians now—not enough to populate the realm, nor to protect Earth without human and vampire assistance—but it was *life*.

"Perhaps I am better prepared to see it this time," Colin said as he crossed the courtyard. The archway Savi had declared impossible rose in front of him, and his heartbeat sped to an equally unlikely rhythm. He could hear her, scent her. So close.

She'd teleported with Selah almost three hours earlier; Colin had remained behind to collect the few gifts he'd kept hidden from her since his conversation with the Doyen earlier that week.

"Perhaps," Michael agreed. "Though I maintain you were both fortunate. With an anchor to Chaos in your blood, your passing through the Gate could have had a much different outcome."

Colin's brows drew together, and he hesitated for just an instant. "A Gate?"

Michael cocked his head toward the archway. "If I—or any other Guardian—passed through, we'd emerge in a Vietnamese village. I can teleport into that part of Caelum, but not walk."

Though his stomach was slightly unsteady, Colin grinned. "I must confess it gratifies me exceedingly, knowing there are *two* things I can do that you cannot."

"An orgasm with a kiss," Savi said, poking her head into view beyond the left side of the archway, "and walking through a Gate. What's that?" She nodded toward the case in Colin's hand, curiosity widening her eyes.

"One thing," Michael said without expression. "I'll return for you in two days." He disappeared before they could respond; a sound like a dainty thunderclap echoed through the courtyard.

Savi blinked. "Did you hear that? The vacuum filling. It works up here. What's in the bag? I brought food. And a digital camera, but nothing appears on the display except the sky, me, and the Guardians. Oh, and Selah showed me the apartment we'll stay in during your daysleep tomorrow; it looks terribly uncomfortable. How do they regulate time when the sun always shines? I wouldn't have minded a trip to Vietnam," she said as he stepped beneath the archway. "I imagine I'll be traveling a lot pretty soon. I've been thinking."

The soft despair in her psychic scent told him before she did. His tongue felt thick as he led her toward the fountain. "Will I hunt you across the Earth? Or will you stay?"

"Neither," she whispered, and her breath hitched in her chest.

The case fell from his grip, the paintbrushes and bottles rattling together. Her weight was nothing; he lifted her onto the wall, pressed his forehead to hers.

"Stay," he pleaded. "Stay with me, marry me, be with me." It was selfish to ask; he didn't care. If it took manipulation to force her to commit to him, he would manipulate.

"I think about it," she said, and her voice was hoarse. "I get to the point where I almost convince myself I could do it. Because my head *knows* you can't help it, that you won't really want to have sex with them, that it's the bloodlust. And how many people have you been with—have *I* been with? They don't matter. Why should any in the future be different?"

They won't be, he almost lied. But he could not. In the past he had wanted them; now, there was no one else. They *would* matter, because their very existence would hurt her.

"I try to tell myself it's just feeding, like stopping for takeout. And I think you'd be careful. You'd shower before you came home. But then I'd know when it happened, because you'd be in different clothes; so maybe you'd shower every day before coming home so that I don't know exactly when, but it would still be a constant reminder. Eating away at me. At *us*. And not just the sex—you'd feel like shit because it hurt me, and I would feel like shit because you felt guilty for something you can't control. It would ruin—*taint*—everything good between us."

She was right; and she saw far too much for him to hide anything from her. "And so your solution is to run? To avoid this for the remainder of your life? Do you think that will hurt less?" His tone was harsh, but not cruel. Still he saw each word striking her, the depth of his pain reflecting hers. "You love me, Savi. You will always love me."

"I know." She drew in a shuddering breath. "I'll come back. A day or two at a time. Once a month. More frequently, if I can."

His throat closed. Like a blood donation schedule— enough time between feedings that it wouldn't endanger her. But even once a month would take its toll. Hope warred with misery, anger. "Must you leave San Francisco?"

Her hand cupped his cheek; her gaze searched his. "Yes. It would kill me to have you so close, but not to have you to myself." She forced a smile. "And I'm rich, but don't have much time compared to an immortal; I might as well spend some of both seeing the world. I can perform most of my responsibilities online: work, help out with the community stuff, the information and IDs. I can come back to check on Nani—and be with you as much as I can. And maybe once a year or so, when you've built up your tolerance to animal blood, we can have two weeks. Or three."

His chest constricted painfully. This would be their life? Was their situation so hopeless that a stolen moment here and there was the only solution; that her gaze brightened as if *three weeks* per year was a bloody miracle?

Yet it was a solution—far from perfect, but he would take it. Take anything she had to offer him. "There will still be others," he said softly. "How will your leaving make that different?"

Moisture pooled in her eyes; she blinked it away. "Because it's not as real if I don't see it."

"And I'll not be the only one who pretends things I don't like don't exist," he said ruefully.

Her smile was watery, but genuine. "Yes."

"You'll ring me every day?" And he *would* hunt her down when he couldn't bear the separation.

She nodded. "And instant messenger. And text message."

"I'll be fastened to my computer and cell phone in anticipation. Only I hope not to receive more e-mails whilst you are aboard airplanes, unless they are to inform me of your flight home," he said. "I will live for your every return, Savitri, and die upon your departure."

"That's so melodramatic," she said, but she kissed him frantically, as if her leaving would be in the next moment and death imminent.

He slowed her, soothed her with lips and hands until her breathing regained its steady rhythm and his eyes no longer pricked with tears.

With a sigh, she leaned back to look up at him.

"So . . . what's in the bag?"

§

The paintbrushes he laid out on the fountain wall didn't surprise her; the airtight bottles of prepared henna did. Colin poured the mixture into a wide-bottomed bowl; the fragrance of tea tree oil, lavender, and lemon saturated the sterile air. The dark scent of *mehndi*.

Mesmerized by his hands as he stirred and smoothed the mahogany paste, she belatedly realized, "The consistency's too thin." Like pudding, when it should have been like frosting.

"For cone application, perhaps." A half-smile curved his lips as he selected a line brush. "But I've no intention of decorating you as one ices a wedding cake. Lift your arms."

He stripped her T-shirt over her head, then picked her up to slide her skirt and panties over her hips before setting her on the wall again. Stepping back, he surveyed her as he did a canvas before he blocked out the underlying shapes. Her skin tightened; her nipples hardened beneath his slow, assessing gaze.

"What do you intend?"

His lashes lowered, and he took her right hand in his. "My

intentions," he dipped the brush into the paste, turned her palm up, "were completely destroyed. Do not move."

She couldn't, not when he rapidly traced a tiny flower in the center of her palm, reapplying henna to the bristles every few seconds. Over her fingers.

In less than a minute, he covered her skin with a complex design that would have taken a skilled *mehndi* artist an hour or more. He released her hand, lifted her left.

Stunned, she examined the petals of jasmine, the scrolling lattice and delicate leaves. Her stomach hollowed when she recalled where she'd seen it before.

"Where did you get this pattern?" Did he know the significance of it? Or did he just think it attractive?

"In your flat, from a book of traditional henna designs." His breath swept as lightly over her palm as his brush. "Intended for brides. If you do not want it, wipe it away before it dries. Before the stain sets."

Colin pulled a white tea towel from his case. The thick terry was soft against her thigh, waiting.

Never. She stifled the urge to curl her fists protectively, stared at his bent head. He held her hand in his, but didn't continue painting; a fine tremor transferred from his fingers to hers.

Ohmygod. Caelum swallowed her whisper.

He'd remained in this realm for two months after she'd left. And the month before that, he'd lived almost wholly on animal blood—unable to hunt while the nosferatu had roamed the city. What had she imagined he'd done, fed from the Guardians here? Hunted them? She'd been so stupid; she hadn't thought.

Three months . . . and less than a year to recover from it, to build up immunity again. Now he was shaky. And only three days had passed since his last daysleep; he'd take another at the end of the night.

His jaw tightened, and the trembling stopped. His brush moved over the heel of her hand, then began a bracelet around her wrist.

"What did you intend?" she asked softly.

"To manipulate your emotions." The backs of her fingers now. "To force you to commit to me; to bargain for more time."

"For how long?"

"Until Dalkiel was dead, but that could be tomorrow. Hardly as long as I'd like. Perhaps until the henna faded."

"Two more weeks. A month."

"Yes. Still not enough." He paused, cleaned the bristles before setting the brush down. From his trouser pocket, he withdrew a small box. "Until these wore thin."

He met her eyes as he opened it; two rings lay nestled in velvet—a band for her, a thicker one for him.

Her breath caught on laughter or a sob—she wasn't certain. "Platinum doesn't wear."

"I'd have invoked your promise to Auntie, and wept pathetically if you'd said no. The tears would have been sincere, but quite calculating. I find, however, that I prefer what you give without manipulation."

Her gaze dropped to her palms. "Then why the henna?"

"Because, my sweet Savitri, you asked what was in the case." Colin tilted her chin up, caught her lips in a soft kiss. "And I've ached to paint your skin for weeks. Months. Your hands, done quickly, was for you. The rest is for me."

"I wondered why I had to be naked," she said breathlessly.

"That is for me as well. What shall we do with these?" He gestured with the jewelry box; the rings gleamed silver beneath the sun. "Toss them into the fountain and make a wish?"

"You should never pay more than a penny for a wish. I'll put mine on until it wears thin."

"As I will." His eyes closed briefly; when he opened them again, he smiled at her, his fangs flashing. "I'm pleased you are so practical in budgetary matters. Now, turn around and brace your elbows against the wall; I'll begin with your back. Take care not to smudge your hands—good God, you've the sweetest arse."

A perfect reflection of her face laughed up at her; she rose up on her toes to see better. If a penny could allow him to see his after so many years, would it disappoint him or please him?

"What would you wish for?" she wondered, then sighed in pleasure as his lips skimmed over her spine. The rasp of his zipper was loud in the silence of the courtyard. Her back arched, her hips pressing into the cool marble.

"This. Forever." He spoke against her shoulder, his skin bare against hers. "Ah, Savitri, look at you. What you do to me."

She watched as he slid deep, as the ecstasy unraveled over her features. Twice she forgot herself, closed her eyes, and tilted her head back; twice he reminded her to look. And she saw the need he created within her, spiraling, twisting ever tighter.

She couldn't let go. She didn't want to do it herself.

"Colin. Please." Her teeth clenched; she shook under the easy glide of his body into hers, his gentle thrusts.

"You're open, love. Your shields are down." He whispered it against her ear; in the pool, the tips of her hair fluttered as the strands caught his breath. "You're already there."

She was . . . she was but she couldn't go over. "Please."

"No pain. Not this time." His lips touched the back of her neck, but only to kiss, to lick. His hand pushed between the marble and her sex, worked at the slick, taut bud. At delicate flesh, stretched around him.

A sob lodged in her throat, but she rocked back against him, took more and more. "Help me."

He cupped her chin; his thumb pressed against her panting mouth. "Hold on, love." And he eased the side of his palm between her lips, her teeth. "Take what you need."

Not her pain, but his; she bit down, heard and felt his groan against her skin. She did that to him. She was the reason for his breathless chant, the swaying of her breasts, the excitement and heat and wet. The fullness deep within her. And there was only him inside her, pushing and pushing . . . pushing her painlessly over. His hand captured her cry, her wonder.

And then finally pain, though she didn't need it—the delicious sting accompanied the two punctures in her neck. Her blood rolled across the shape of his tongue, then disappeared from the reflection when he took it in, made it his.

And her last coherent thought was that if anything in Caelum abided by sensible rules, she'd have vanished, too.

§

If Michael thought it strange that Savi wore a mahogany painting of Caelum over her arms and shoulders—and guessed that, beneath her strappy backless top and long skirt, it covered the rest of her skin—he gave no indication.

It had taken most of twenty-four hours for the color to fully develop, with Savi wrapped up like a mummy for a good portion of it. The color would fade—first from the long stretches of fragile skin on her back, torso and legs, last from her hands and feet—but now, Colin thought it perfect.

And he couldn't tear his eyes from it. The beauty of Caelum surrounded him, and yet it was the spires rising over her forearms that held him captive, the tower braced by her spine, the curve of a domed temple on her shoulder. The fountain's wall ribboned around the base of her throat; he'd painted no higher, and it served as an ideal frame for her slim neck, the delicate structure of her face.

It was, he thought as he took her hand and readied for teleportation, well worth the price.

She smiled up at him as Caelum dropped out from beneath their feet . . . and then he clutched frantically at her wrist, trying to keep her from falling. The iron band of Michael's arm around his chest held him dangling above a nightmare. Screams split the putrid air like an overripe corpse.

Chaos.

The bodies hanging above them, rotting—their faces frozen into the ceiling.

A loud snap cracked through the shrieks as the Doyen's wings unfurled from nothing. The rush of freefall jarred to a stop. From the corner of his vision, Colin saw pale skin, membranous wings. Heard a shout of surprise in the Old Language as the nosferatu recognized Michael. The dull shine of their weapons.

"Don't look," Colin begged, and grabbed for Savi's left hand, hauled her up against him. But she *was* looking—her gaze had focused over his head, her eyes widening. Then vacant and staring, as horror settled in. Her body shuddered, and she kicked wildly at him, tried to yank her hands from his. "Savi, don't run, don't—"

"Dragon," Michael said quietly in warning, but the tone made it a near shout. "Prepare yourself; hold her."

A flash of scales, the stink of sulphur—the impact ripped Colin and Savi from the Doyen's grip.

Falling. Rivers of molten rock below; it would be quick and painless and Savi was somewhere else, not running now, and she would never know they burned and burning was better than being eaten, thank God—

"Colin," she said against his ear, and her arms tightened around him. "He's coming."

The dragon? God, no, *please* no.

He scented Michael's blood before the Doyen collided with them, a rush of black feathers and bronze skin.

Glass splintered around them into slicing, biting shards. Savi grunted as he landed on her, as they crashed through the Room and skidded into the observation area, the friction of the carpet like fire against his hands.

Savi's blood. His blood.

The shrieks multiplied, a million different pieces and voices. *Chaos wouldn't let him go, wouldn't*—

"The mirrors," Savi gasped. "Get rid of them!"

Silence.

Then the rapid beating of her heart, her frenetic breaths. She stifled a sob when he lifted his body from hers. But even as he gingerly rolled her, cried out when he saw the shredded ruin of her back and shoulders, a burst of power knitted her skin and muscle together again.

A psychic touch slid quickly over Colin's form, and his wounds sealed up.

Michael. Colin's gratitude died, overwhelmed by rage. Bloody fucking bastard. He wouldn't need a sword; he'd tear the Doyen's head from his shoulders.

But when he turned, shock held him immobile.

"I apologize," Michael said evenly, but he staggered as he climbed to his feet. Crimson soaked his white linen tunic in rough arcs: the shape of the dragon's bite. The blood still flowed; the wounds didn't appear deep, and hardly fatal—but even a vampire's would have stopped bleeding by now. "I had not anticipated how strong your combined anchors to Chaos would be."

The Doyen frowned down at his side. Behind him, the Room gaped open and empty, blank white walls where the mirrors had been. Vanished into Michael's cache.

"You can't heal it?" Savi asked, standing with her arm crossed over her breasts. Holding her shirt on, Colin realized. The glass had sliced the straps.

Freshly repaired caramel skin streaked like scars through the painting of Caelum.

He didn't trust himself to speak; he'd weep or scream, and either reaction would likely frighten her. He moved behind her, untied the bow dangling useless on one side, and used the extra length to knot it closed.

Simple courtesy—and it was all that held him together.

"Apparently, I cannot," Michael said. He blinked; obsidian obscured the white and amber of his eyes. "That is . . . not good."

Her ribs expanded beneath his hand as Savi sucked in a harsh breath; her small frame shook with sudden, hysterical laughter. Not amusement at the Doyen's understatement, Colin knew; like him, she was overwhelmed and had either laughter or tears as a release.

Or both.

She wiped her eyes, leaned back against him. "I saw what they were writing," she said. "The nosferatu, on the ceiling."

Michael's head jerked up, his gaze narrowing. "You can remember them—replicate them?"

"Yes. Though not today; I'm not quite ready to go back there yet. Even if it's just in my mind. But Colin won't have to take you to see them."

Christ. Colin forced the tension from his arms, wrapped them around her. "There's still the bridge, sweet."

"Use a freaking nuclear bomb," she said. "In and out, two seconds. Blow the whole place to Fuckville."

This time Colin let himself laugh, pressing his cheek against the top of her brilliant head, inhaling the scent of her spiky hair.

"That may be a solution, but we'll not do it today."

"No," she agreed. "Not today. Home?"

"Yes." He could think of no other place he'd rather be with her.

"It is probably best that I do not teleport you," Michael said. Though he looked a bit steadier now, his lips were taut with pain, his face stonier than typical.

The sod was the bloody *king* of understatement.

§

The taxi driver probably assumed Colin was sick or sleeping, but whatever concern it might have engendered didn't prevent him from remarking several times that he'd never experienced such a quiet rush hour. Savi just hoped that he wouldn't notice the symbols she'd scraped into the rear passenger door.

Colin's hands were firm on her hips, his head in her lap. The hooded jacket Michael had made protected him from the sun, except for his face.

But Savi thought he held her so close out of a much deeper need than avoiding a burn—and she clutched him as tightly, though she had little to fear now.

Death had been so near—and the danger hadn't come from Dalkiel, which they'd expected and prepared for, but something within them.

She glanced down at Colin's fingers. Was the shaking a delayed reaction, or the animal blood? Hard to say, when hers trembled, too; the henna seemed to shiver, barely anchored by the band of platinum.

The light glinted off his ring, and she slid her skirt up, used the cotton to cover his skin.

"Shameless hoyden," he said, his voice muffled against her now-naked thigh. And he remained down there the rest of the slow trip, though the sun descended past the horizon. Twilight hung a violet backdrop against his house when the taxi dropped them off in the street. She punched in the code to the gate, then, grinning, challenged him to a race and darted through.

Did he let her win, or had he slowed so much?

She forced the question away; as soon as he stepped through the front door, tension stiffened his body. He inhaled, a long draw of breath.

"Dalkiel?" she whispered. The house had been locked, but not spelled. The demon could have come in at any time.

He nodded. Two swords were in his hands; apparently, he'd let her win. He'd retrieved them so quickly his movement had seemed a blur. "Two days old, perhaps. And three vampires—I don't recognize their physical odor." He tilted his head, relaxed slightly. "No psychic presence."

She glanced quickly around; Dalkiel hadn't destroyed anything. "Taking inventory of what he wants to claim?"

Colin smiled. "I'll accompany you to the basement, then I'll make certain the house is secure before I lock up with the symbols. Once you've gone in the room, ring Lilith. Ask her to send the pup over."

"Okay."

"Don't open it until I move Mary."

The portrait in the theater. "I remember," she said, and followed him down the stairs, her heart thudding. The vampires couldn't hide their psychic scent from him, but Dalkiel could. "Why don't you go in with me until Sir Pup gets here?"

"That," he said as he crossed the theater, "is a splendid idea."

Colin reached the door; it was half-open, but when he tried to walk through, he slammed into the empty air as if it were solid. He stumbled back.

Two scarlet eyes flared bright from the darkness within.

Oh, god. They'd discovered how to use the symbols.

"Run, Savi—" Colin's ragged warning broke off as Dalkiel rushed through the door. Their swords clashed, sparking with the force of each blow; within a moment, Colin was at the other side of the room. Drawing the demon away from her, she realized. Or falling back.

Think, Savi. Get help; get weapons. She turned, fumbling for her pendant as she began to run. But she wasn't as fast as a vampire.

And there were three of them.

❧

This was hell.

Colin sensed the presence of three vampires as they left the shielded room—hungry . . . starving. Heard Savi's quickly stifled scream, felt the burst of her psychic scent as her shields dropped. In pain.

Holding her arms, they dragged her into the security room. When the fragrance of her blood and the wet sucking sound of vampires glutting themselves tinged the air, it descended beyond hell.

And Dalkiel was *playing* with him.

The demon could have killed him. He effortlessly parried Colin's increasingly desperate thrusts. Dalkiel's sword had drawn blood from his arms, his chest, his face; each strike potentially debilitating, even fatal.

But he only made certain Colin didn't get to Savi.

Her scent was fading. Her heartbeat fluttered like a hummingbird's. Low blood pressure, from exsanguination.

Everything blurred. Sweat or tears or his own blood, dripping into his eyes. Even if he got to her, how could he save her? How could he—

Dalkiel fell back. Fear erupted from his mind, was quickly shielded. And for just an instant, the demon stopped toying with him.

Colin streaked past him. The vampires fed from Savi's still body; they'd no opportunity to defend themselves.

Had he more time, he'd have gutted each one slowly. Instead, his blade sliced through their necks; Savi's lifeblood splashed useless to the floor.

"What in Lucifer's name are you?" Dalkiel stood in the door, his sword dripping. "You did not appear on the monitors as you came in; we thought she came down the stairs alone. I'm pleased that she wasn't—though torturing her with your face would have been entertaining."

Colin ignored him, kicked the bodies aside. He fell to his knees, gathered her up; she was limp in his arms. Her throat had been ravaged, her inner thigh. Her breath was thin, bubbling with each short draw.

"Stay," he said, though he could barely manage that simple word. *Don't leave me here alone.*

She heard him; her body shook with the effort she made to speak. He hushed her, curling forward as hollow agony tore through his gut, and rocked soundlessly. He couldn't think; couldn't breathe.

He forced himself to do both. He sat up and his gaze fell to her throat—the chain of her pendant snagged on the torn skin. Her gadget; she wouldn't have forgotten it was there. But had she time to call for help? Had the Doyen been in any condition to teleport?

The signaler button had fallen behind her neck; her eyes opened when he reached for it.

Her brows arched infinitesimally, an unmistakable question. *What took you so long?*

Good God. He couldn't live without her.

"You can save her if you transform her." The glee in Dalkiel's voice made it a hiss. "Are you so certain your blood will destroy her?"

So this was the demon's game—not enough that she died, but that Colin had to have hope enough he could save her, only to see his blood kill her anyway.

But he'd nothing to lose; and what other choices had he? He brought his wrist to his mouth, severed the vein.

Michael appeared beside them, his sword in hand. A blood-stained bandage wrapped his bare torso. He glanced down at Savi; healing power knocked Colin forward.

Dalkiel turned and fled.

Savi shuddered, heaved. Her heart stopped for an endless moment before beating a rapid, impossible pace. He clenched his teeth and held on to her; tears itched over his cheeks. Michael had repaired flesh and skin, but he couldn't give her blood. And too much had been taken. There was no hope—no hope except—

"A Guardian," he realized. She'd have to serve, but she'd *live*. "You must make her a Guardian."

Michael lowered to his heels beside them. "I cannot."

Her breath rattled to an end. A thin moan rose from Colin's chest. "The taint—"

"The Rules. She did not sacrifice herself for another," Michael said softly. "You must try to transform her. With *their* blood, if not yours." He gestured to the vampires lying dead around them, but his face was set with concentration as he stared down at Savi.

Colin stilled. Not these vampires. They weren't good enough.

"Colin—you must *hurry*." The Doyen's voice was strained. "I can keep her brain cells oxygenated but a short time; if they die before she is transformed, they cannot be repaired."

"No," he said, resolution lending him strength, and he lifted her. "I'll not do it here. Can you teleport us together?"

Michael rose; his gaze never left Savi's face. "Yes."

It didn't matter if he was wrong—Chaos couldn't be worse than failure. "I need a weapon," Colin said.

🍃

The nosferatu had no chance. Colin fired the venom-filled dart into Ariphale's neck before it had time to react to their appearance in the detention cell.

The second dart hit its chest as it fell to the floor, paralyzed except for its mind. Its psychic scent burned with rage.

Nosferatu hated nothing so much as vampires; Ariphale would have likely rather died than be used to create one—particularly the human woman who'd humiliated him. A fitting punishment, if not preferable to execution.

And now Colin could only thank the stubborn Washington bureaucrats for delaying it. He shoved his knee into the nosferatu's throat to hold it down—he'd no idea how powerful the venom was, and Michael needed to attend to Savi—and glanced up.

She lay in the Doyen's arms. Colin couldn't hear her heartbeat.

His voice was hoarse. "Give her to me."

Her slender frame felt heavy without life flowing through it. Awkwardly, he reached for the nosferatu's wrist; Michael lifted it to his questing fingers.

"Colin, you must prepare yourself if it does not work; the changes in her blood may interfere with the transformation."

His only reply was to tear open the cold skin, to take in a mouthful of exquisite, dark liquid. An electric storm swept across his tongue—so incredibly strong.

Nosferatu blood had overcome his taint; it would overcome hers.

It quite simply had to.

Her lips were slack. He massaged her throat, forced her to swallow.

No. Not force—she'd want this. She'd want immortality.

He didn't let himself consider that it couldn't include him. Surely contemplation of it now—when she still didn't move and her open eyes were devoid of curiosity—would push him beyond a threshold of agony, and there was only so much he could bear.

Another draw from the nosferatu's vein, given like a kiss past her lips.

Why didn't she respond? Less blood than this had allowed

Colin to survive for a month, though his transformation had been incomplete.

Panic settled over him; he sealed her mouth with his and breathed, pushed the blood down with the strength of the exhalation. It didn't matter where it went, her lungs or stomach, as long as it went *in*.

Her lashes fluttered; she blinked. Beneath her rib cage, her heart thundered into life. Her startled gaze flew to his, but he silenced her questions by pressing Ariphale's arm to her lips.

She didn't hesitate; she drank quickly, and her psychic scent rose around them, unbelievably aromatic.

Sweet, fearless Savitri. She'd make the best sort of vampire.

Michael inhaled, his brow furrowing. He turned, and at his signal, the fledgling who'd stood guard outside the cell opened the door. "You and another to Alcatraz; a wyrmwolf may traverse the portal."

Surprised, Colin glanced away from Savi. "Could you detect it before now—the fragrance when she lowered her shields?"

Michael frowned. "Her mind is open; that is how I knew she was not shielding. This odor is not psychic—it is the hellhound venom in the nosferatu's blood."

His gut clenched. Oh, Christ; he'd not even considered that risk. "Has she taken enough?"

"Yes."

Savi clung to the nosferatu's wrist when he tried to pull it away; her eyes had closed as she drank, but now they opened wide. Colin jerked back, his knee slipping from Ariphale's throat.

No longer velvety, chocolate brown, the whole of her eyes burned crimson with hellfire. Like a demon's.

Like a hellhound's.

Heat rolled in waves from her flesh.

A horrifying sound raced along her body: the deep splintering of bone, the wet tear of muscle. Her skin bulged as if a creature inside tried to leap out. Her fingers stretched and buckled, reformed into gnarled claws.

He hardly heard himself calling her name over the noise of it—couldn't hear anything at all over her screams.

❦

Colin didn't feel the crash into Castleford's living room, only the sudden, disorienting teleportation that preceded it. Savi writhed on the floor; his arms were around her, but he dared not hold her securely for fear of hurting her.

"Give her to me, Colin," Castleford said. His chest was bare, heaving. His gaze riveted on Colin's face; his psychic shields snapped up. "And look away from us until you control it—I can help her, but you *must let her go*."

"I can't." His body shuddered. His grip tightened and Savi's shrieks intensified.

Lilith sped into the room, Sir Pup at her heels. Her gaze dropped as Savi's back bowed, her vertebrae popping the length of her spine.

"Oh, motherfuck. Sir Pup, my sword," she said, and launched herself at Savi.

Colin's fangs were in Lilith's neck less than a second later, but the shock of her blood prevented him from ripping her throat out. Sense returned.

He'd let go of Savi. Lilith had deliberately provoked his protective instincts, and now she lay beneath him, unresisting.

Castleford's soothing murmurs rose beside them. *Listen to me, Savi; don't fight it. You must concentrate.*

Her screams ebbed into panting, whistling breaths.

The calming words were effective on Colin, too. His body shook, and he slid his teeth from Lilith's skin, rose up on his knees. He didn't need to close the wounds; Michael's power swept across the room in a low, focused pulse.

His hand trembled as he helped her up. "God, Lilith. I'm sorry."

"That's a good boy, you beautiful fucking idiot," Lilith said, and slapped him sharply across his face before twining her arms around his shoulders—to support him or hold him in place. Probably both. Her tone gentled. "Her body's trying to shape-shift. Michael's keeping her brain from turning to mush, so don't distract him by making him heal me again. Hugh will talk her through the rest of it."

And indeed, the convulsions had ceased—but her frame was misshapen, broken. Her feet had elongated, her shins and ankles fused at an angle almost lupine. She'd turned her face toward Castleford, but the visible side of her jaw was malformed, heavy.

"You've seen this before?" Some of his terror drained away.

Lilith's tight embrace loosened. "It happens sometimes with fledglings if they don't have a strong mental image of their forms to anchor themselves."

Savi's shields had served as a block between her mind and body for over a decade. How would she know to reform it?

She wouldn't, Colin realized . . . but Castleford would. He'd mentored and trained novice Guardians for centuries.

"Think, Savi. Remember." The other man's hand brushed over her face. Her hair had grown; Castleford lifted ebony strands from her eyes, from her cheek. Dark fur formed a patchwork over her arms, her back. "The first year at Stanford, your anatomy class—you came home and told me you were going to cut the rest of the term because you'd memorized the book in three days. You know where everything goes, where it belongs. You've got to put it back."

Savi groaned—her *flesh* groaned as her legs pulled into a human form. But not hers; the skin was too pale, the bones too thick.

"That's good, Savi," Castleford said, though the glance he gave her feet betrayed his concern. "Just like in the textbook—now remember the last time you bathed, the last time you soaped your legs. The texture, the shape."

Her shivering increased. A high-pitched whine sounded from between her clenched teeth.

Castleford quickly said, "Your first kiss. You remember it perfectly; go back, Savi."

The tortured noises faded. Behind him, Lilith breathed a sigh of relief as the line of Savi's chin smoothed into a contour unmistakably hers, though fragile, immature.

Michael's focus on Savi lessened; he looked away from the pair on the floor and signed, *Lilith, contact SI. I left the nosferatu paralyzed, but unsecured. I had no time to alert them before we teleported.*

Lilith released Colin, reached for the phone.

Colin crawled forward. Castleford was searching for something more personal, more intimate for Savi to cleave to. Her first kiss had likely been before he'd taught her to block the anxiety attacks. In the shower, she'd have had her shields up. In bed, she did until she used pain to get past them.

He did not want her to rebuild herself with memories of pain.

"Savi, love." Her face turned toward Colin's whisper. Her eyes still shone red, though not as brightly. Her mouth and jaw were a young girl's. Colin grasped her hand. Her once-slim fingers had thickened, curled; the platinum band cut into her knuckle. "Go back to Caelum, by the fountain. My paintbrush on your palm. Do you feel it?"

She sucked in a harsh breath; her wrist cracked in his grip. Colin couldn't make himself look.

Castleford glanced at her hand, nodded. *More*, he signed.

Vaguely, Colin was aware that Michael vanished—that Lilith was arming herself, preparing to leave.

He pushed those distractions away. His fingertips trailed up her forearm, over the delicate veins and muscle. "The henna, here." Her skin rippled and softened. "My lips, here." He brushed his thumb across her mouth and watched in awe as it widened, sliding into the lovely, full shape he'd never taste enough. He continued, traced every inch, recalling her to his paintbrush or his touch—and to the pool reflecting her face, her hair. Her skin slowly cooled . . . and cooled, until he feared the contact might burn her.

Finally, her eyes cleared to a rich brown and locked with his. "I love you so bloody much," she said. Exhaustion deepened it, but her voice was her own, her accent still horrid.

She kissed him before his relieved laughter died, and she threatened to make him lose all sense—until he felt the sharp press of her fangs against his lips. She grinned against his mouth, broke away and reached up to test their length.

He smiled for her. She was a vampire—a powerful, nosferatu-born vampire. She'd live forever.

And he'd lose her within days.

❧

Savi hadn't known vampires *could* sleep during the night, but she must have done so; when she awoke, twilight had descended outside her apartment windows. Following her transformation, she'd slept the whole of the evening, and then throughout the day.

She sighed as she threw the blankets back. It was too much to hope that, like Colin, she'd be resistant to the sun and the daysleep. He'd have to occupy himself every day while she slept.

She stood up, and the floorboards screeched beneath her feet. She stumbled forward; the swish of her cotton pajamas roared as loud as a storm-tumbled ocean, her breath a monsoon. Paint, varnish, the month-old scents of spice and incense scorched her mouth and lungs.

Oh, god. She bent over, covered her ears to the sandpapery scrape of her palms against the fragile cartilage. Now the wet pulsing through her veins, the beat of her heart.

Footsteps approached like planets crashing together, but in space it was silent, not here, not here.

"Shh," Colin said, as if it were her instead of everything around them. "Just as you would use your shields, Savi—block it out."

Block it out. She panted against his chest. His cologne clung to his shirt. It smelled wonderful, each note perfectly realized, some she hadn't scented before.

And his skin . . . god, *Colin's blood.*

Silk shredded under her fingers. Heat streaked from her mouth to her nipples, her belly, her sex; her fangs ached and she rubbed her tongue against them. She was so slick and wet and she could almost taste it in the air.

His palms cupped her jaw. "No, Savi." His grip was gentle, immovable. "You can't. We can't."

She tried to rise up, to kiss his neck, to bite that strong beautiful throat. "I need this, I need—" Blood and fucking.

But the urge died when she lifted her gaze to his face. "I know," he said brokenly, and pressed his closed mouth to her open lips, a kiss flavored by mint and salt.

I can taste you. It hovered on her tongue, until she realized why he'd stopped her from tasting him fully. Why he didn't drink from her.

"Oh, god." Her hands ran over his face, his hair. Memory of the aborted shape-shifting ripped through her; even now, her body felt oily, her joints and muscles loose beneath her skin.

And Colin hadn't seen himself for two hundred years.

She couldn't risk feeding him even a day or two a month; he couldn't feed her at all. Both tainted. They'd both have to take blood elsewhere, and she'd never be able to pretend that the sex didn't go along with it. "What are we going to do?"

He had no answer.

❧

"Look, Sir Pup, you're a daddy now," Lilith said when they came downstairs to the kitchen. The hellhound hopped in place, grinning hugely with his three heads.

Savi laughed despite herself and covered her nose; Sir Pup stank of sulphur and rot. She'd never noticed it before—had never noticed *any* smell from him.

"Is that his psychic scent?" Her palm muffled her words, but still they reverberated in her ears. She focused. Blocked it out.

Colin shook his head. "Wyrmwolf. Quite a few got through last night."

"And we had quite the hunt. Unfortunately, we didn't catch Ariphale." Lilith's voice darkened. She stood at the counter wearing leather and boots, food spread haphazardly in front of her as if she was stopping for a quick refuel before heading back out.

"He escaped?"

Lilith swallowed hard, her mouth a tight line. "And killed Sam and Vanessa on his way out. Not that Washington cares."

Two vampires. Savi's stomach churned.

Colin's brows drew together, his tone sharp. "Do *not* think that; it wasn't an exchange. It wasn't in trade."

"No, it was just a massive fuckup by Michael," Lilith said.

Hugh entered the room—to Savi's surprise, as his movements were almost soundless. "Though an understandable one. Even the Doyen doesn't make a habit of imprisoning nosferatu instead of slaying them, surviving attacks from dragons, and handling a shape-shifting gone awry—all the while holding a brain intact."

Lilith's lips quirked. "Then by me, for not killing Ariphale when I wanted to, and just lying to the assholes in the Pentagon."

"That, I agree with," Hugh said. He turned to Savi. "Are you well?"

How could she answer that? She was strong, immortal—and her heart ached so badly she wanted to tear it from her chest.

She *could* tear it from her chest; it was a startling realization.

"As well as can be expected. I can defeat a nosferatu on a plane, but not three vampires at a time. My odds sucked."

"Particularly as they were starving vampires," Colin said easily, though it seemed difficult for him to manage his light tone. "Dalkiel must've prevented their feeding whilst awaiting our return."

"Well, we should really have known better than to run to the basement, especially after he saw me take you downstairs last week. He *knew* I'd go there if anything threatened—and we rushed right on down. Stupid of me."

"Of us."

"Stupid of the golden boy; Michael should've killed Dalkiel when he was there." Lilith stole an amused glance at Hugh. "Even with the dragon bite."

"Forgive me for disagreeing," Colin said, "but I'm pleased he made Savi his priority."

"So am I," Savi said.

Hugh smiled; his blue gaze was steady on hers, assessing. "Have you eaten?"

"No."

"Do you need mine? You can consider it a wedding gift."

Of course Hugh wouldn't have missed the henna, the matching rings. Was he trying to offer them more time before they were forced to make a decision?

"He's rather dry, but edible," Colin said when she hesitated.

"No. It'd be creepy if I became—" Aroused . . . with her brother. She let her shudder speak for her. "I'm not really hungry yet, anyway."

Hugh sighed, but gave no other indication that she'd lied. "There's blood in the refrigerator; only use it if you must, Savi."

"You'll not use it at all," Colin said in a near growl. "Shaky, *stupid*, tired. You'll risk your brain? For what?"

She blinked. She hadn't intended to drink any, but— "One day. It'll give me time to think."

"To think—? Oh, bloody fucking hell, you'll have me dreaming of the impossible." Colin turned, stalked into the living room. She watched him, his head tilting back as he stared at the painting of Caelum, as he scraped his hand over the surface. When he returned to the kitchen, he looked at her—and relented with a short laugh. "One day. Think *hard*, love; without you, I'll surely become everything I despise. A melancholy maniac, lurking around Castleford in hopes I'll learn the most effective brooding techniques, donning a hideous friar's robe in effigy."

"You know, Colin," Lilith said, "Hugh saved her life last night. The least you could do is—"

Before she could finish, Colin was kissing him.

He could render in oil a flawless depiction of a face he hadn't seen in two hundred years; it shouldn't have been so difficult to garnish a glass of blood. The foam had dissipated minutes before, yet Colin still wavered between a sprig of mint, a slice of orange, or a twist of lemon.

How did Savi so effortlessly create a beautiful plate from a few lumps of food and leaves? He'd have appreciated her guidance now, but she'd shut herself away with her computer in the hours since their return to the house. Hunger must be gnawing at her, yet she hadn't sought him out—hadn't joined him when he'd abandoned his studio and ate in the kitchen.

He doubted it was the blood; she'd fed readily from the nosferatu, and had never been squeamish when he'd taken his in front of her. Perhaps it was too unfamiliar—a tasteless, un-attractive meal after an existence filled with rich flavors and textures.

Hardly an auspicious beginning to a life of blood-drinking, but he'd do what he could to ease her transition.

The mint, he finally decided, looked too festive; the lemon clashed terribly with the red. With the fragrance of orange in his mouth, he carried the glass upstairs and found Savi curled on the bed in her suite. Her laptop was open, the screen dark.

And it struck him that if he'd wanted to offer comfort and

familiarity, he'd have done better to stay with her than decorate a glass. Would have done better than leave her alone.

Would have done better than pretend they didn't have so little time remaining.

Her pajamas rustled as she turned. Her eyes tilted up at the corners with her smile of welcome, but their depths were solemn and dark.

He strode across the room to cover the sudden weakness in his knees, the ache in his chest. She scooted the computer aside and levered herself upright; she remained still as he sat beside her and carefully examined her face, her fangs.

"Did you look in the mirror? Do you like them?" Good God, but she was breathtaking.

"Very much, though I'll need to practice my public face." She pulled an awkward grin that puffed her cheeks like a squirrel's. "Am I disgustingly cold?"

He smoothed his fingertips the length of her jaw. Cool satin. "No. You're perfect." Why hadn't he told her already? Explored the novelty with her, answered her questions . . . eased her fears?

It hadn't occurred to him that she had any—particularly not concerning how he might see her now.

"Am I disgustingly warm?" He brought her hand to his chin, and closed his eyes when her palm curved, her thumb brushing over his lips in a delicate caress.

"No. You feel wonderful." Her fingers shook, her voice thickened. "You feel so good and I can't think of anything."

"Don't cry." He couldn't drink from her—couldn't help her as he had before. Desperately, he pushed the glass into her grip. "Eat."

Savi drew in a sharp breath. "Oh, god. Just like Nani." Her head bowed, and the bed began to tremble beneath her.

"I used a kitchen tool and made a spiral of orange zest," he said. "It was a lovely embellishment until it sank."

The blood sloshed; he quickly took it back.

It was with a long sigh that her laughter ended. The slice of orange sat on the rim, and she pulled it off. Holding it as someone taking a shot of liquor would a wedge of lime, she drained the blood in one gulp—then bent forward and, her throat convulsing as if she fought nausea, sucked the juice from the orange.

Colin sat frozen with astonishment. "You can *taste* it."

"I didn't think it would be that bad." She wiped at her mouth. "That was pig?"

He nodded.

"I'm officially a carnivore now. Excuse me."

Did she know how quickly she moved? In less than a second, he heard the sound of the faucet in the washroom, the scrub of her toothbrush. She returned a few minutes later, the sharp aroma of mint on her breath.

"It must be the hellhound part of me. I can't eat like Sir Pup, though—I had a piece of bread at Hugh's, and it didn't stop the hunger. But the blood did."

Crawling onto the bed, she laid her head in his lap and rolled around to look at him upside down. Her hair was silk beneath his fingers, and he vowed never to have anything less against his skin.

"It will be more pleasurable when you take it from a human or vampire." He hoped he would not be proven a liar. "Will you return to Castleford's home? There is no vampire like you, Savi; he's most qualified to help you adjust."

"I guess so. Until Dalkiel is dead, anyway."

And then what would she do? But he daren't ask; it was agony enough to offer: "I'll take you to Polidori's tomorrow night and teach you how to feed; it is the one thing I've more expertise in than Castleford."

"Just bite and suck, right?"

Her humor was forced, but so was his. "If you wish to be a bourgeois sort of vampire."

"No. Never that." She turned her cheek, rubbed lightly against him. "Your libido still functions."

He could have wept. "Yes. But I'd not be able to prevent you from taking my blood. You're exceptionally strong, with little practice at control—and the most beautiful vampire I've ever seen. I'd not be in my senses."

Her lips pressed tightly together, she nodded and sat up, linking her arms around her bent knees. "Will you stay with me until the sun rises?"

"Yes. Until it sets again. Until you have to leave." He memorized her profile. The curve of her back. The tips of her hair. The lay of her hands. "I love you, Savitri."

"No." Her shining eyes met his. "The evidence suggests that your feelings are exponentially greater than that."

Christ, how she tore him apart. He swallowed over the ache in his throat. "It never ceases to amaze me, how extraordinarily brilliant you are."

She sighed. "I wish I were brilliant *enough*."

CHAPTER 27

The Sunday crowd at Polidori's was thinner than it had been the previous week, the vampire-to-human ratio much higher. Savi had seen more than one human group leave, complaining of the temperature and rubbing their arms to warm themselves; others took to the dance floor with dizzying vigor.

She could hardly bring herself to watch them as they smiled and laughed and their blood pulsed through their veins like electronic music. Could barely see anything.

Perhaps she was enthralled—her heightened senses bombarded by light and sound and psyches, until Polidori's faded into a surreal backdrop.

How *could* this be real? This couldn't be how it would end: infinitely simple.

Infinitely painful.

She couldn't think. Blocking hadn't helped. She wasn't the least bit intoxicated, though Epona had sent Bloody Mary after Bloody Mary to their table. As a joke? As congratulations?

Savi didn't know. Didn't ask. She chugged them down, felt the burn of alcohol that couldn't assuage her thirst and didn't numb anything.

And she didn't want any of them, but she forced herself to ask, "Why not Denver?" She nodded toward the vampire signing lyrics at a camera. Colin had consulted with her about hiring the kid, and they'd agreed it would be easier to keep an eye on his activities—and protect him from Dalkiel—if he spent most of his evenings at the club. "He volunteered. His new partner doesn't care."

"He's too young; he'd not have enough control to prevent his feeding from you."

Her smile probably would have frightened a human.

"Good. I could conduct an experiment and see if my blood will turn his brain to mush."

The gleam of humor in Colin's gaze was the first she'd seen since they'd arrived at the club. "That is wonderfully unforgiving, sweet." He flicked a dismissive glance at the waitress gathering Savi's empty glass from the table, but his brows rose when it was replaced with a fresh drink. "Another?"

Savi shrugged and looked toward the bar. Epona caught her eye. Her fangs protruded over her red lips; her attention shifted to Colin and she turned away, fidgeting with a tall bottle of tequila. "Raven's not in her usual spot tonight. Perhaps Epona is volunteering. She seems kind of frustrated and hungry, doesn't she? Maybe they had a fight."

"If I'm to teach you survival, sweet, the most important lesson might be this: *Never* come between two women."

"Is that why you told Darkwolf no?" She tried to imagine herself fighting Arwen and Gina, and almost choked on her drink.

"No. He is not handsome enough."

She shook her head in disbelief. "What does that matter?"

"You prefer a pretty face, Savi." Colin rested his arm along the back of their sofa. Despite the casual pose, he radiated tension, his body rigid beneath his clothing.

"He's kind of hot. The shaved head, the tattoo."

"If your tastes ran to bald and brutish, I suppose he might be."

"My tastes generally don't run to blond and British."

"I'll not push you onto someone unsuitable just because they are available. And he did not want you; for that alone I should kill him."

"Will *anyone* be suitable?"

Music pulsed into the silence between them. Colin stared at her, a muscle in his jaw flexing. "No."

"Maybe I should do this alone." Her whisper was strained; any other vampire likely wouldn't have heard her.

"No. I have to know that you'll be well." He turned his face up to the ceiling before looking at her again. "I apologize, sweet. My jealousy is making this difficult. I did not want our time together to end this way."

"I know. I didn't either." She clasped his hand in hers. Tried to think of anything *good*. Her head buzzed, like a moth zapped in a buglight. "Do you know what I realized in the car? Tonight's the full moon. Not a whole month, but we proved Dalkiel wrong."

Smiling slightly, Colin said, "Perhaps Dalkiel will abandon his plans, humiliated that it did not rise over our graves. Just a moment, sweet. I have to take this."

Not her head buzzing—his phone. Detective Taylor. She could hear the other woman as clearly as if she'd been holding the receiver to her ear.

The detective interrupted Colin's polite greeting. "I've got about thirty seconds. A uniformed officer found two dead-on-scene when responding to a DD. I just arrived here; two male vampires. No humans. A Navigator—yours—is parked out on the street. We weren't able to open one of the closets, but Savi's infrared detector tells me that a vampire is behind the door—either knocked out or tied, judging by the position. Female, by size."

Colin frowned and looked at Savi. She shook her head; she couldn't understand it, either. A vampire might lock herself inside to avoid detection or capture, but it wouldn't be unconscious—and why leave one tied, except to starve if no one could get through the spell to reach her?

"What's the location?"

Taylor recited an address; Savi's eyes widened.

"That's Raven and Epona's apartment," she said under her breath.

"There's more; the male vampires aren't just dead, they're torn apart."

Colin stood up, his gaze searching the dance floor, the upper levels. "Torn apart? Or decapitated?"

"Ripped apart. Like those kids last year."

The nosferatu had slaughtered two of Dalkiel's vampires? In revenge, out of hatred—or with Dalkiel's consent?

Colin signed an instruction to Fia. A moment later, she and Paul were herding Epona away from the bar.

Two inches above the sofa, one foot in. Savi pressed the spring in the wall. So many drinks. And her partner not in her usual spot. A joke . . . congratulations . . . a taunt? A warning? Perhaps it would be nothing, a coincidence. Perhaps Raven had to work a different shift—

Oh god. The weapons hold was empty.

"Thank you, detective. I'll ring Agent Milton; she's out hunting it. With luck, it'll have left a scent for the pup to follow."

"For once, I'll be glad to see her. I've got to get—"

The call dropped. Fear slid icy through Savi's stomach, caught at her throat, and she met Colin's eyes. In the club—from only three or four humans, but it rose like a chorus around them: *Are you there?*

The signal lost, as if the spell had been activated around the club. To prevent a call for help from going out—or to prevent help from coming in?

It didn't matter: the symbols did both.

Colin didn't bother with silence, with signing; he shouted. "Varney! Darkwolf! Get them all out!"

He grabbed her hand and they darted across the floor; so fast that the dancers seemed to still around them, a 3-D music video in slow motion. The frozen rainbow of lights flickered, casting an odd shadow across the wall.

A naked white form scurried across the ceiling.

Nosferatu. Even with her shields up, Savi could taste the darkness in its psychic scent, the malevolent intent.

Ariphale dropped, falling faster than gravity could have pulled it. Its feet slammed against the floor; the polished wood shivered and cracked under the impact. Its pale, membranous wings snapped wide. God, had it been so big on the plane? In the cell? Colin slid, skidded. They couldn't avoid it. Momentum carried them forward; Ariphale knocked Savi aside with a brush of its claws.

The hands that caught her were warm—*too* warm to be human or vampire or Colin. Too strong and too fast to mean anything but death.

She watched as Colin stopped himself before crashing into the nosferatu, but the creature clamped its talons over his shoulders, turned him around and held him in place. Colin didn't fight. He stared at Dalkiel, his face tightening as heated fingers wrapped around her throat.

Not to squeeze, she realized—only to threaten decapitation. A sharp pull would kill her; strangulation wouldn't.

"Little Savitri," Dalkiel crooned into her ear with Colin's voice. "Listen to the worms scream."

They *were* screaming—and running. Humans, mostly. A few vampires. Their footsteps pounded up the stairs. Were they remembering how the nosferatu had burned the eldest of them the year before?

Or they were just smart. A beautiful demon was reason enough to flee; only an idiot would stay to see what a seven-foot winged-and-fanged nightmare would do.

Savi would have run, too, if fear hadn't immobilized her. If Ariphale hadn't been staring down at Colin with hungry amber eyes.

The music cut off. Colin's plea seemed a yell in the relative quiet.

"Let her go."

And echoed from the side: "Let *them* go." She couldn't see him, but she recognized his voice. Darkwolf. Savi felt Dalkiel's surprise; if Colin was surprised, he didn't show it. "Even if you kill them in combat, prove yourself strongest as by tradition, we won't follow you."

Her feet swayed over the floor as Dalkiel lifted her and turned—not far, keeping Colin in his sight, despite the nosferatu's hold and the threat to her life.

"Then I'll kill you," Dalkiel said. "Your friends, your consorts—you cannot fight me. And if you flee my rule, you will only prove yourselves cowards. Either way, I am satisfied."

Darkwolf's jaw hardened and he took a step forward. Gina, Arwen—others Savi didn't recognize. All moving, their psychic scents filled with determination.

The demon's fingers clenched, his nails digging in.

Blood. Savi's chest heaved; she couldn't draw a breath, didn't need it, but terror and pain wound themselves slick and greasy over her skin.

"Stop," Colin rasped, and though his command was for Dalkiel, the vampires immediately halted. "I'll bargain."

The demon laughed, dismissing Darkwolf and returning his attention to Colin. But he directed his response to Savi, in a low and triumphant rumble. "Your pretty young vampire knows I must consider the terms of the bargain, but he has no leverage and nothing to offer. I hold everything valuable to him in my hands; there is nothing I desire that equals his need to protect you. It is such a liability, these bloodsharing partnerships. They weaken vampires—but *I* am the stronger for them, the more powerful. I could have threatened to slaughter every vampire here and he'd have allowed it, but for your life he remains still."

Colin's mouth curved in a thin smile. "Ah, yes. A true leader sacrifices himself—not those around him—to preserve what he loves. I confess, I'd trade every worthless one of them for her." His gaze shifted to the side. "Darkwolf knows this well."

"Yes." Disappointment roughened Darkwolf's reply. "We have no use for such as you."

"You'd best run; you'd best go far. The foxes are inside the warren; there is no protection here for you and your partners, and no help will arrive. He will kill anyone who witnessed his humiliation, or he will force me to do it."

The warren? Savi forced herself not to think, not to give anything away.

A breathless silence hovered between them; then the sound of Darkwolf's boots as he turned and left. Arwen's soft slippers. Gina's heels. Dalkiel's laughter filled in the rest.

"You don't seek to control us," Colin said. "You allowed the nosferatu to murder two vampires; you cannot rule over those who are dead. What is it you truly want?"

Ariphale spoke for the first time, its voice guttural. "Chaos."

Savi was certain she misinterpreted the emotions that flashed over Colin's expression: surprise and dismay, she understood—but relief? How could it be anything but disastrous for a demon to know Colin was anchored to that realm?

Oh, god. Because he *did* have something Dalkiel wanted—and it gave Colin room to bargain.

"Eavesdropping," Colin murmured with a smile, "is a rather boorish activity. Don't you agree, sweet?"

She nodded as best she could, though her heart pounded an unnatural rhythm. *Don't bargain.*

How much had Ariphale heard through its cell walls? How much had it told Dalkiel?

Apparently enough.

"An open portal to Chaos," Dalkiel said. "Lucifer derived so much of his power from the dragons in that realm before he lost access to it, I'd be a fool not to take advantage of it. Five hundred years will be time enough to learn to wield it. When the Gates open, Hell will be mine, and I'll leave the Earth to Ariphale, and free his imprisoned brethren."

The nosferatu's eyes burned. Impatience surrounded him, like an electric blue fog. Not much trust existed between the two, Savi realized, but they'd formed a partnership out of necessity.

"You'll need Savi alive." Colin's gaze held hers. "The portal opens when her shields fail."

"Yes, but we don't need you," Dalkiel said. "Only your blood. If the other nosferatu were anchored to the realm by drinking it, so will Ariphale be. And so you will submit to him. Here, standing before those weaker than you. If your blood kills him, she will die. If you struggle before he's drained you, she will die."

Savi fought to speak. The demon had it wrong. The imprisoned nosferatu had taken Colin's blood, but it had been shed in a ritual, from specific symbols. And the portal depended upon the both of them—Ariphale couldn't have heard that. The room had been shielded when they'd realized it.

But Colin wouldn't correct his misassumption, as it probably rendered useless whatever bargain the nosferatu and demon had made. Their misconception that Savi alone was the key prevented Dalkiel from killing her.

From killing them both.

Colin shook his head—a tiny, almost undetectable movement.

And what came out instead was her laughter. *"You're afraid of him,"* she realized. "You have to threaten *me* to control him? You can't forget what he did to you on the roof, can you? He humiliated you." Dalkiel's claws pierced her side . . . and dug deeper as she continued, "You don't know what the hell he is, and he frightens you. Does he remind you of what you *used* to be? Two times you fought him, and two times you ran like a fucking cow—"

"Stop, Savi," Colin said desperately. "Stop."

She had to anyway. The pain swamped her vision, blinding her with crimson.

"Take him," Dalkiel said.

And she saw that, somehow. Though the red haze, saw Ariphale's fangs rip at Colin's neck, his mouth cover the wound. She scented the rich flavor of his blood.

Her blood, too. It leaked out of her, wet and sliding, and all of her seemed to be sliding and moving and pushing the wrong way.

"Hold on, sweet." He was losing strength, losing blood, but even now he was thinking of her, thinking . . .

Think, Savi.

Dalkiel's hand twisted before he yanked it from her flesh and slapped it over her mouth. Was she screaming?

Colin's knees buckled; the nosferatu held him up, sucking and sucking.

Oh god. *Think.* What did she have? No venom or hell-hound.

Should you leave and Sir Pup stay, no one could protect you from the evil creatures stalking the night—

No weapons.

A gun wouldn't have protected you if there had been two. You have to run—

Powerful hands beneath her chin and across her mouth forced her head back; Colin's features stared down at her, washed in the scarlet light of demon eyes. She wanted to snap her teeth at the demon. Bite his face off. Those beautiful gray eyes, corrupted by something evil and cold . . .

They were still gray.

"Let me go." It was a growl, tearing from her throat.

But that wasn't her. That sound wasn't anything human or vampire.

"What sort of ungodly perversion are you?" The demon's voice was filled with disgust . . . with horror. His hands tightened and shifted position, as if he was struggling to maintain his grip.

Why bother? Even if she could run, she wouldn't leave Colin here alone. She had nowhere safe to go.

If it comes to that, and you can't run—

Oh, god. Yes, she did.

—*grab the pup*—

Not out, not away, but in.

—*and hold on to him*—

Her memory waited; she plunged, ripped through it. Found fangs and fur and claws. Gathered them up. Grasped them tight.

—*and he'll run for you*—

And ran with them.

❧

Ariphale's hands slipped from Colin's shoulders, its frigid lips lifting from his skin; but even if Colin had had the strength to move, he wasn't certain he could have.

Nor was he certain who was the more astonished when Savi shape-shifted, and the slim woman became an enormous wolf: the nosferatu, who knew that nothing except Guardians, demons, and hellhounds could change their shapes; or the vampires watching, who'd been told nothing like a werewolf existed.

Or Dalkiel, when she ripped his throat out.

Clever Savitri. She'd always liked to bite.

The nosferatu's forearm around his neck strangled Colin's triumphant laughter. But he still shook with it when she went after Dalkiel's face, as the demon shrieked and rolled onto his hands and knees and tried to crawl away.

His wings sprouted from his back; his talons scrabbled against the smooth surface of the dance floor. A sword appeared in his hand, but he'd no time to use it. She pounced on him, her massive forepaws pinning his wings down. Her jaws snapped on the back of his neck. Silenced his screams.

She'd shown more mercy than Colin would have done.

Sleek black fur rippled beneath the colored lights as she turned her head to look at him. Her psychic scent rose around her, luscious and fragrant. Hellfire burned from her eyes.

Ariphale leapt into the air.

"You should let me go," Colin said. "She's less likely to kill you if you are kind to me. Oh, that crossbow will simply not do at all." It was absurd, how weak he was; but it took barely a kick to upset Ariphale's aim, hovering as it was with a beautiful vampire crushed against its chest.

The bolt passed several meters from Savi's pointed ears. She paced below them, her muzzle tilted up, her crimson gaze fixed on Ariphale as he fluttered across the ceiling like a bald bat trapped in an attic.

"She's probably thinking of a way to form wings," Colin told it. "You'd best release me."

But it wasn't the threat of Savi flying that spurred the nosferatu to action; it was the sudden psychic presence of vampires, of humans—of Guardians—from outside the club, as the protective spell surrounding Polidori's disappeared.

Fia, Paul, and Darkwolf rushed onto the floor below.

"Your idiot demon partner—" Colin struggled as the creature dove toward the suite. Savi raced along beneath them. "—used symbols activated by *blood* in a building full of vampires. Did you truly believe we wouldn't sniff out the location—oh, bloody hell."

Of course the sodding nosferatu didn't use a door; and reinforced as it was, the door might not have buckled under the force of Ariphale's body slamming into it. The wall did, and they crashed into the suite in a shower of wood and insulation.

The door rattled in its frame; the hinges squealed.

Before Savi could hit it again, Ariphale triggered the spell. Her scent vanished.

Colin rose to his knees, coughing to clear the plaster from his lungs. Epona sat on the sofa, her red-rimmed eyes wide with shock.

Ariphale stood by the door, its hand covering the symbols protectively. Not so arrogant now; before Savi, it'd have never feared that two vampires might have the speed and power to get around a nosferatu and erase the blood.

Unfortunately, at that moment neither he nor Epona did.

Colin smiled when he looked at Epona again, and she cringed back into the cushions. "Did you empty this room of its weapons, as well?"

"Yes. I'm sorry, I—"

"Don't apologize to *me*. I only refrain from killing you to avoid upsetting Miss Murray; she's much more reasonable and forgiving of such things. You made a bargain to save Raven's life?"

She nodded, her breath shallow. "I'm not sorry for that."

"I'd have done the same for Miss Murray." He adjusted his collar, tested the wounds on his neck. Raw, but closed. "It must have been quite the demonstration the demon gave you, when the nosferatu tore apart those vampires. They were your friends?"

"Yes." If possible, she appeared smaller than before, older. She darted a glance from his throat to Ariphale. "Do you need blood?"

"Yes." He strolled to the sofa, tipped her chin up and coldly studied her neck. She paled; her lips quivered. "But not yours. I will, however, take this." With deft fingers, he unbuckled her spiked leather choker and slid it into his pocket. "Once it realizes there is no exit the Guardians will not cover, that it is trapped, it will slaughter us; you'd do well to escape."

"How?" she whispered.

"It'll not leave the symbols unprotected to pursue you, for fear I'll destroy the spell. Leap through."

Colin pointed to the ragged hole in the upper half of the wall. Selah hovered outside, looking down at them. Her hands were moving as if she signed instructions, but he could not understand them.

The spell, taking its own interpretation of "silence" to prevent all communication.

"What about you?"

"If we both tried to escape, it would come after us. And even if I made it out, it could remain here indefinitely—until Polidori's fell down around it, or I set it on fire to flush it out. I've no intention to pay for the club's restoration again." He frowned as Ariphale fidgeted uneasily at the door, angling its head to look at Selah. "Go now, or I'll reconsider and take your place."

He should, regardless. Though Selah probably reported their location and safety within, Savi would be frantic with worry.

But he wearied of these intrusions into his homes; and if she had to leave him, he could at least give her a safe location to return to whenever she needed one.

Provided he survived, of course.

Ariphale's growl rumbled through the suite when Epona sprinted for the wall; its white naked body tensed as if to give chase, then stilled as it glanced back at Colin.

"I may have been weak enough that you could have caught her *and* returned to intercept me before I reached the door," Colin said, smiling. He approached the nosferatu at a slow, insolently careless stroll. "But it's difficult to be certain, is it not?"

"It is not."

The nosferatu could not be given accolades for wit and diction, but Colin was surprised that it had answered at all. He'd anticipated the creature would dismiss him as a nonentity.

"Ah, yes. You must know the limits of my strength. You've taken my blood; you know that many things which should be impossible for a vampire, I can do. You felt one of them—Chaos—whilst you fed."

But Ariphale had either withstood it disturbingly well, or Colin hadn't the ability to channel that realm as he could when *taking* blood. Savi had reacted with horror, and three young vampires had screamed in fear; Ariphale hadn't shown the slightest discomfort.

Not until Savi had destroyed his demon partner.

Colin touched the tip of his tongue to his left fang, let the scent of his blood tinge his breath.

Ariphale's nostrils flared.

The nosferatu had its own curse: bloodlust. A vampire would have been satisfied after taking so much from Colin earlier, but the nosferatu couldn't experience physical hunger, and so the bloodlust was not eased by feeding. And Colin couldn't mistake its effect on the creature's body.

Nor could he mistake the creature's self-disgust at its reaction.

Colin leaned his shoulder against the wall, crossed his feet at the ankles. "It is a terrible burden, a curse such as this," he said, his voice overripe with melancholy. "The endless need; the lack of control; the loss of one's will. The revolting urge to rut like an animal."

"Your lament would please a demon, who might assist you in ending your own existence and relieving you of your burden," Ariphale said. "But I do not care for it."

"I imagine you don't. I was not speaking of myself." His gaze swept the nosferatu's length. "At this moment, you must be certain of your impending doom. For though my consort awaits you, she'll not have the opportunity to kill you and end your cursed existence; the moment the shields around this room have fallen, the angelic Selah will teleport in . . . and will return you to your holding cell. But you've another option."

"To remain here?" Ariphale shook its head; its amber eyes glowed fiercely. "That is not another option; it is still imprisonment."

"You are mistaken; that is not what I offer. Chaos is not all that I contain within me," he said softly. "I also have Caelum. And I can make it very good for you."

Within his pocket, the spiked collar lay folded in his palm. Colin squeezed.

The tinge became a flood.

Colin withdrew his hand, and painted in blood a symbol on the wall. "My consort," he said, "cannot keep her psychic shields up whilst in her wolf form. You sensed them failing before her transformation; you know this to be true."

"Yes." Its response was guttural, the bloodlust raging fully upon it.

He wrote the reversed symbol below the first. "Also, that the portal to Chaos opens when her shields are down. You must have heard the experiment we conducted in the Room."

Ariphale stared at the symbols. "You are opening a portal to Chaos? Or to Caelum?"

Neither, but this ignorant bloodsucker had not learned that without Colin sensing Savi's psychic presence, the effect was inert. The spell prevented that.

Colin grinned and backed slowly away. Provoking a hunter's instincts. "The wyrmwolves should come through at any moment. And I shall lock myself in the suite's washroom, activate the spell inside, and wait for them to kill you. When you are dead, the protection around this room shall fall, the Guardians will sweep in and terminate the wyrmwolves . . . and I shall exit the washroom unharmed. And perhaps with my hair combed; I'll have little else to do as I wait."

Good God. He was more like Dalkiel than he'd thought; these monologues were quite entertaining.

And, as he'd hoped, infuriating.

With a cry of rage, Ariphale rushed him. Colin let him come—he couldn't have escaped by running. Nor did he want to: a nosferatu less overwhelmed by bloodlust might have drawn a weapon; Ariphale used his fangs.

So did Colin.

He only needed a sip. The nosferatu's hand over his mouth, holding his chin twisted to the side and his neck exposed, was just enough.

Ariphale's body went rigid, then quaked as Colin sent the rapture twisting through it. The creature's mouth opened, as if to cry out; the tearing pressure of its teeth in Colin's throat eased.

Release. A final pulse into the nosferatu's blood, to shift the odds in his favor; Ariphale already seemed better prepared for it. He was quickly losing his advantage, but Colin only needed a moment's head start, and an instant's clarity to recall that he shouldn't use his bleeding hand. And to hope that Selah was watching, and would be ready.

He swiped at the symbols; the nosferatu bore down on him, his weapon flashing.

Selah didn't transport in; she gave him a sword.

Colin stepped to the side and dropped. He cut Ariphale's running legs from under it, then stood and impaled it from behind, angling in between its wings and into the heart as it fell. And through the back of the neck, just because it was there.

Not very sporting, but fuck him if he wasn't as weak as a bloody kitten.

The suite door crashed open. Savi's fragrance filled his mouth, his lungs. He staggered, sank to his knees. Buried his hands in her fur as she pressed her cold nose against his throat.

Colin drew back and looked at her. "I'll not kiss you like this."

She opened her mouth in a wolfish, toothy grin; a moment later she lay quivering against him, still smiling . . . laughing.

Naked.

"I think I must have a hammerspace." She pressed a kiss to his lips. Another. "But I have no idea how to get my stuff back out of it."

Colin glanced down at her fingers; the henna decorating her hands was unbroken, but her ring was gone.

Her smile faded. Colin had no time to reply.

"Savi," Michael said from behind them, his voice eerily strained. "Raise your psychic shields."

His gut clenching, Colin turned to look. Beyond the plane of the wall, three nosferatu stared back at him. Wyrmwolves writhed and tore at each other. Chaos glowed silently around them.

Her scent disappeared; so did the portal. The crimson symbols radiated heat, and dried dark against the paint.

The Doyen unclenched his jaw. "That was . . . irresponsible," he said with quiet anger.

Colin glanced back at Savi. Her face was stricken, but her gaze rested on her bare fingers, not the symbols.

And Colin replied, "I must confess I find it very difficult to care."

CHAPTER 28

Bald and brutish.

His appearance suggested the latter, but Varney didn't seem to mind that a woman who'd been a dog sat on his enormous lap. Nor that Colin asked him to turn his lantern-jawed chin to the side, so that he could better explain to Savi the best locations to bite, the expected blood output from each vein and artery, and the proper method of healing the punctures and of opening her shields to return the pleasure of it.

Perhaps Colin had promised him hazard pay again? Or maybe he just had a very soft heart beneath that hard nosferatu-like exterior.

It was a heart that Savi couldn't stop imagining. Her fangs ached and throbbed in unison with its pulsing, steady flow of lifeblood, until Colin's voice faded beneath the incredible sound. God, she'd never been this hungry. Varney's pale, thick neck seemed the most beautiful thing she'd ever—

"Go on, Savi," Colin said quietly, but she was already leaning forward, already pressing her mouth and teeth against his throat.

It hit her tongue, raced through her. A flash of light behind her eyes, the heat and pleasure of willing blood in her mouth, her veins.

Electric. Heaven. Wonderful and sweet and luscious as it slid into her and he was thick and hard beneath her, and she was squirming against him, squirming and he was so big and she was so wet and the blood wasn't enough.

I don't want you.

She didn't want him, either.

But she couldn't stop. Her hands fumbled for her skirt. Oh god. Jeans, next time. Harder to get past. Wear jeans next time and shred them open at the crotch and just fuck fuck fuck—

Stop, Savi. I don't want you. Stop.

"That's enough, Savi," Colin echoed hoarsely. "You're taking too much."

Too much. She broke away and bit her tongue—more blood, her blood . . . and it tasted like blood. Varney's wounds were almost half-closed when she bent her head.

Practice, for when it wasn't a vampire she had to heal.

A flush of embarrassment spread over Varney's skin. His penis was solid between her legs. Oh, god—and she could smell herself.

Awkwardly, she scooted off. "Thanks."

I'll call you tomorrow.

She wouldn't cry. Not right now. Not when Colin's mouth was set and his gaze dark and he looked as if he'd just gone through seven agonies of hell.

"I didn't want him," she said as she took his hand.

"I know." His voice was rough. She stood still beneath his perusal as he studied her face, her mouth. "You've a bit here. I would kiss it away but I daren't." He raised their linked hands and brushed his thumb against the corner of her lips.

She stared at the smear of blood. Heard his heart quicken . . . could almost *feel* his hunger. He needed to feed.

And it shouldn't be animal blood—not after Ariphale had taken so much. Nor could it be half vampire half-hellhound blood.

"Will you drive me home?" She wasn't going to cry. "To my place?"

He closed his eyes. It was a long time before he said, "Yes."

❧

Five minutes after she exited Colin's car, with the painful silence that had stood between them still heavy in her stomach, he knocked at her door.

His golden hair had been mussed beyond its usual state—beyond what it had been when she'd seen him last. His collar was askew. The scent of a woman's expensive perfume eddied around him.

The fragrance of a woman's fear and arousal.

The door frame splintered beneath Savi's fingers.

His throat worked before he said, "I didn't." His eyes searched hers, desperation in the gray depths. "I didn't."

His face blurred in front of her. "I know."

"One more night, Savi. There's no bloodlust now. And you've fed. Just one before you leave." He came inside. No need to ask for an invitation. His mouth covered hers, sipping and tasting. His hands were at her waist, untying the belt of her robe. "Just one more."

A sound of protest rose in her throat. She'd taken off the clothes Selah had made for her the moment she'd arrived, but another man's odor clung to her skin. She couldn't make love to Colin like this.

But she didn't need to say anything; he smelled of someone else, too. He carried her to her bedroom, past the bed.

"There's a mirror," she said, but still he went in. His gaze never left her as his shirt fell to the floor, his pants. They stepped beneath the steaming spray together.

The tension in his body eased when she pulled the curtain closed; it heightened when the scent of her soap rose around them. He lifted her. The tile formed cold squares against her back, the individual shapes sliding together into one as Colin filled her.

It wasn't enough.

He braced his hands as if he intended to stay within her forever; hard and fast was best but now she loved slow, slow. How long had he been inside her?

It wasn't enough.

She writhed and pushed; her head fell back and the spray shivered like ice over her skin. Too tight. Too much.

Her shields were down. She couldn't break through. "Colin. Help me. Please."

His teeth closed over her nipple, his fangs scraped the softness surrounding. His cock thrust deep, every push and pull tearing a violent groan from his chest. And still . . .

"I can't." Panic gnawed at the edges of her arousal.

"It's the blood, Savi. You have to bite yourself." Water streamed over his face, dripped from his lips. He tucked his chin beside her neck; his body gentled against hers. Despair thickened his voice. "And I cannot even give you this."

She had nothing to give him, either. And though an orgasm

ground roughly through her when she sank her fangs into her bottom lip, there was little pleasure in it.

Except that it was with him.

❧

"Where will you go first?"

She barely heard him above the beat of his heart against her spine, the rhythm of his breath into her hair. For hours, they'd lain together in her bed, his arms surrounding her, her legs twined with his.

"Eastern Europe, I think. I'll learn Romany."

He pressed a kiss to her nape. "Do not invoke any curses."

"I won't. I just don't want to rely solely on Michael to figure out how to break yours."

"Savi—"

"It'll give me something to look forward to," she said quietly, "I like the idea that someday, even if you're still anchored to Chaos, you'll be able to walk outside without it screaming at you from a billion cars and their rearview mirrors."

"A billion? Such melodramatic exaggeration, sweet."

"I think it comes with the fangs," she said, and snuggled a little closer into him. She couldn't get any closer. "Will you help me take care of Nani? After a while, she won't be able to live by herself. I won't put her in a nursing home."

"Castleford may battle me for the privilege, but I shall relish both his defeat and Nani's presence in my home, wherever she deems it shall be. Will you not take a few weeks and visit with her at Beaumont Court? I should like you to become acquainted with my family. Even," he said softly, "if I am not there to perform the introductions. And Derbyshire produces some of the finest blood in the world; you'd not regret it."

"Maybe for a day or two, I could." Outside the window, the sky began to lighten. She should get up and close the blinds. Would he leave while she slept? Would it be easier that way?

"You'd be welcome to stay much longer."

"I know. It's not that." She tried to look at him, but his hands held her fast. Settling her cheek against the pillow again with a sigh, she said, "Varney wasn't *dazed.*"

He stiffened. "Dazed—?"

"He won't forget. Like Roberta did. Like all of yours do. I'll have to keep moving."

Horror strangled his voice. "No, Savi. Oh, God . . . no. You cannot live like that. If this is your alternative, you must stay."

"I don't have a choice, just like you don't. I can't share my blood with another vampire; I'd just be a burden, sucking on different members in a community without offering anything of my own."

"You can continue with the projects you've already begun, at Polidori's and at SI. No one questions your value. No one thinks you anything but an asset."

"All of those projects can be continued online." She gritted her teeth. They'd been through this.

"What of protection? We need you here; you destroyed a demon with little effort. We'll not be challenged again."

"I can't live like a glorified parasite off the employees at Polidori's—and do you want to go in every night wondering who I fucked and fed from? It would kill me. It would hurt you."

"There are humans," he said tightly. "You'll not have to see them again; neither will I."

"But humans will remember—I'll be able to heal them and they won't have any evidence, but they won't forget me. I'll risk exposing all of us if I stay in one place and feed from a different human every night. And the vampire communities aren't ready for—"

"Bloody hang everyone!" His teeth clenched; she could hear them grinding together in his effort to control his response.

"I can do it." Her throat ached. "I have money. I can create all of the necessary IDs and different identities so that I can't be easily traced. I can alter or erase any financial trail. Even if someone realizes there's a pattern, it'll be hard for them to pin me down. And once vampires go public, I won't have to."

"You'll run for a decade?"

"It's not running." She forced a smile. He couldn't see it, but it made it easier to lie to herself. "It's hunting. You were happy. Why can't I be?"

"Because, my sweet Savitri, you are not me."

"Then I'll be content knowing that you are happy. You

loved hunting for two hundred years, and when you go back to it, it'll be just as good as ever."

"That's a sodding pile of bullshite, Savi. I was not in love for two hundred years."

"So we're both going to be miserable?" She tried to move, and could not. She kicked her legs at him in frustration. "Why won't you let me look at you? I'm going to leave tomorrow and you won't even let me see you one more fucking time?"

"Because I need it more than I need the next beat of my heart." His breath shuddered against her neck; his chest heaved against her back. "What use is a reflection when I've you to see me and think me beautiful? And if you look at me again, I simply don't know that I could let you go. Oh, Christ, sweet—don't cry. I cannot bear your tears."

"I can't yours. I can't any of this."

But what other choice did they have but to bear it? His blood burned humans and vampires from within; her blood might physically transform him into something terrible, something unrecognizable.

The honey-gold sheet glowed orange. She covered her face, pressed the heels of her hands against her eyes. Nosferatu-born. Hellhound-born.

She'd already burned . . . had she been tempered by it or weakened?

"I'm strong," she whispered.

His eyelashes tickled the short ends of her hair as they swept down. "My vanity is immense," he said. "In two hundred years, there has been little that I've obsessed over as much as my appearance." Her heart constricted, until he added, "And there is nothing about which I've more certainty."

They lay in silence. She could not stop shaking. Her body would rattle itself apart. His mental image of himself was solid; his portraits were evidence of it. But would it be enough to save him? Would the method of her transformation be enough to save her? Or would it kill them? What hadn't they considered . . . what *couldn't* they consider, because they just didn't know?

There were too many variables; it was impossible to predict an outcome. They could only hope the odds were stacked in their favor.

"Savitri," Colin said softly, and she turned to him. "Perhaps we should see what comes next."

Her shivers eased. His cheeks were warm and wet beneath her questing fingers. "Are you sure?"

He nodded tightly. "It is well worth the risk."

It was to herself, but she risked him, too. Still, she rose up on her knees, and when he sat up against the headboard, she swung her leg across his hips, straddled him. "Oh, god. Oh, god." She kissed him, pulled back to look, then kissed him again. "We're so stupid. This is so stupid."

"Mad. Reckless." His mouth was warm against her frantic lips. "I love you, Savi. I love you." He pushed into her. Her back arched. So good. If she died, it would be like this.

But she wanted more. "Will you lower your shields?"

His eyes widened for an instant; then he laughed softly and a heady, textured scent flooded the air. Citrus. Sandalwood.

"Oh, god. It's just like your cologne. But better."

"My cologne," he said, "is just like me."

It would be. She inhaled; bliss rolled through her. She rocked with it. Euphoria spiraled from her sex, filled with him. Her lungs, filled with him. Her mind—"Let me go first."

She felt the icy slide of fear, the blunt denial in him before he said, "No. No, Savi."

"You're stronger than I am," she said. Her gaze dropped to his neck. "I can't do what you do—I can only make it feel good. But you won't be incoherent. If something goes wrong, you might be able to stop me."

"If my blood hurts you . . ." He shook his head. "No."

"If it does, it will whether I go first or last." Her thumbs smoothed over his cheeks. Crimson light glistened across the sharp angles, cast shadows in the hollows beneath. "And you've never had someone feed from you like this. Not to give you pleasure." Only nosferatu and wyrmwolves who'd offered pain; only men and vampires who'd wanted immortality and power from him and died of it. "I want to be the first. And if it's the only time . . . I'll just regret that I couldn't leave you senseless."

"You do. Kiss me again. And again. Bloody hell, we are mad. Your eyes are shining, sweet. Are you frightened?"

"Yes." Her blood roiled through her. "But more afraid of eternity without you."

"Oh, Savi. I am, too." And she could see it in his face, that enthralling beauty that came over him when he was overwhelmed—with rage, with fear, with passion or beauty.

With love.

A final kiss, and then his breath stilled as she touched her lips to his neck. Everything stilled—even, she was certain, her heart.

Her fangs pierced his skin.

I love you. It slipped over her tongue, and she didn't know if it was hers or his. Or if there was a difference.

Oh, god, and he tastes so good.

"Oh, sweet," he said, and his hoarse laugh rumbled across her lips. "It's better than good. It feels incredible." His hands gripped her hips, and he thrust.

It doubled within her, the pulse of Colin's pleasure through his blood, the tight clench of her slick heat around his shaft. His moan reverberated against her tongue. She swallowed, drew more. Opened her senses, and awkwardly tried to slide in.

His mind welcomed her. Oh, god. Everything beautiful, radiating an exquisite brilliance. Was this how he saw her? And there was darkness alongside it, unhidden. He tensed and breathed a denial as her mental touch flitted over it; she tasted, expected bitterness, but found it rich and thick and deep.

"Savi . . . tell me," he said, his voice strained. "Are you hurting?"

No.

This was the opposite of pain.

His relief rose through her like heated air. Gingerly, he set his teeth against the curve between her shoulder and neck. His palms flattened over her hips, up the length of her spine.

A trickle of blood, then gentle suction. Not the rapture.

Wait, Savi. I want to be certain. He drank slowly, measuring each swallow.

And in that moment of quiet, she felt the pleasure her blood gave him, flowing through his veins and uncoiling within her. Caution accompanied it, his careful test of her emotions, the tender probe against her memory.

Savi didn't know how to invite him in. *I'm sorry.*

His amusement melted like spun sugar on her tongue. *Don't apologize, sweet. Just hold on.*

It gathered beneath her skin—beneath Colin's skin—large and powerful and spinning toward her. Her hands clenched on his shoulders. His heart raced against hers.

She swallowed and it roared through her, familiar and just as impossible as before, and all the better for experiencing his through their blood link.

She writhed and shuddered, but there was more, and it shook from her, passed into him.

Colin growled and then she was on her back, and he burrowed deep, hard. Her legs wrapped him tight. His blood filled her mouth, and everything he gave her, she sent back.

He stiffened, thrust with fangs and his blood and his cock, and it hit her again, at a higher pitch. Higher.

A feedback loop. Painful, ratcheting and rising with each stroke, each draw. She couldn't let go. He grabbed hold of her mind, tore across it on a frenzied wave of pleasure.

And still higher. The tension spread her thin, long and taut and brittle. On the verge of fracturing.

But it was dawn that broke; the sun spilled through the window, across the far wall. Daysleep dragged her down, tried to take her from him, but Colin surrounded her body, shielded her mind with his. Didn't allow her to fall; didn't allow her to burn.

Don't be afraid, sweet. Don't be afraid.

But even he was swept along by it, and she tasted his fear just below the ecstasy. His body plunged deep and deep, and the orgasm spread through her again, wound her higher. And then his as he came, pulsing into her, his rapture into her blood, back into his. Cycled again. And again.

Too much.

She shattered out from beneath him.

❧

Brilliant, sweet Savitri. How perfect her mind was; how clear and detailed every memory.

She'd claimed it hadn't hurt, and their mental link had confirmed the truth of it—but Colin was relieved when the fractures began to close, to heal. He had an eternity to repeat the process, to slip through the fissures and examine everything that made up Savi.

That was, when she stopped showing him images of himself.

His hair was a terrible mess, but he wasn't surprised it looked so bloody spectacular that way. And she apparently adored it, so he'd not change it anytime soon.

Exhaustion quickly enveloped her; the few remaining cracks surrounding her memory sealed shut, pushing him outside. She'd been using her fangs to reopen his punctures, to keep the blood flowing . . . but now even that effort seemed too much.

Colin floated along with her until he couldn't hold her up, and let her sink into the daysleep.

Then, to his astonishment, he'd barely a moment to pull the blankets over them before it took him down as well.

❧

Savi woke from dreams almost as lucid as life . . . and they immediately began to slip away. No surprise in that; even her memory could not hold on to them—had never been able to.

Colin lay on his stomach next to her, his face in her pillow. Not breathing; his heart beating a sluggish tempo. She slid her hand across his shoulder. Warm.

Daysleep.

Early for it, but perhaps the past evening had taken its toll on him. The past weeks, drinking the animal blood. She wouldn't worry yet; it was just after sunset, but he'd always been terribly lazy, never waking the moment the sun dropped below the horizon.

She had.

Curling around him, she waited. Nothing felt different, though it was difficult to tell: she'd barely had enough experience with her body as a vampire. But there was no pain. Her skin was still cold. She waved her hand in front of her face; her eyes weren't glowing, but perhaps they only did that when her shields were down, or she was afraid.

Her ring was still missing.

She spent fifteen minutes trying to feel around her mind

for her hammerspace before she gave up. Hugh could teach her. Or Sir Pup could. What had she looked like as a wolf? Could she talk to other dogs?

This was killing her.

She slipped out of the bed. It would only take her a few moments. Almost sliding across the slick bathroom tile in her hurry, she stopped and stared at the mirror in surprise. Everything was the same.

Not for long. She activated the symbols; the bedroom was spelled, and it extended into the bathroom, but this way Colin wouldn't be disturbed when she lowered her psychic blocks and maybe even howled—

Her reflection wavered; she faded. The shower curtain's bold diagonal pattern appeared *through* her, like a double-exposed photograph. Silent screams ripped through the small room.

She didn't see herself transform.

❧

Savi prepared the breakfast out of habit, rather than hunger. Orange juice. A frozen blueberry waffle. She didn't want to eat it.

Why hadn't Colin woken yet? In three minutes, she would fetch Hugh and Lilith. Two.

She heard his first deep draw of breath, and sagged back against the counter. Listened as he shuffled into the bathroom, pulled on his pants. As the water ran, and the sound of him brushing his teeth.

And his strangled cry of surprise.

He was still faster than she. Before she'd taken a step, he was standing in the kitchen, looking wildly about. Her toothbrush dangled from his mouth. He pulled it out, grabbed her orange juice and gulped down half of it.

"Colin—oh, god," she said, and covered her face, began giggling when his lips turned down and he stuck out his tongue as if to rid it of a terrible taste. "Orange juice after mint is *bad*."

He tore off a bite of the waffle, chewed. Grimaced again. "That's revoltingly tasteless."

She pointed toward the syrup.

His gaze narrowed on her. "I've something sweeter in mind." His kiss was flavored of orange and mint, and she clung to him until she was breathless. And continued, because she didn't need to breathe.

Finally he pulled back to stare down at her. "Are you well?"

She nodded. "I can still turn into a wolf."

His thumbs brushed over her cheeks, her brows. "Your shields are up. Can you lower them without transforming?"

"Yes." Her throat tightened. "Did you see the mirror?"

"That you'd covered it? I do like to perform morning ablutions without the screaming." Despite his light tone, his body tensed against hers. "Why?"

"Will you go look at it?"

His jaw set. "Why? What are you not—"

"You can taste," she said. "I think I got something of yours, too. I can still see myself," she added quickly when he paled, his skin drawing taut over his cheekbones. "Just go look."

His fingers threaded tightly through hers; he led her back to the bathroom. Her heart was in her throat as they stood before the mirror. She'd tacked the shower curtain across it.

His bare chest rose and fell on a deep breath, and he ripped it down.

He wasn't there. Still not there. She tried to pull him out. He didn't move. "I'm sorry   I'm sorry."

"What did you think it would be, Savitri?" His brows drew together, and he tilted his head as if studying his missing reflection.

"I didn't know. I dropped my shields, and I saw it—"

He whipped around to face her. "Chaos?"

"Yes. But only when my shields are down."

"Bloody hell." He stared at her for a moment, his throat working. "I'm sorry, Savi."

"Don't apologize. I'm okay now. More than okay." Whatever price she had to pay, it had been worth it.

He glanced at the mirror again, his lips parting slightly as if in wonder. "So am I."

Her breath caught. "You can see yourself?"

He shook his head. "No. Just you. The shower behind me. Not Chaos." His voice thickened. "Like the reflection in glass, or water."

"What if you lower your shields?"

The scent of papaya, of orange; he cringed, and it disappeared. "That is not as pleasant," he said softly.

She looked at the mirror. "But still . . ." He wouldn't have to be alone in it. Wouldn't have to suffer it, except by choice.

He pressed his lips together as if to hold back tears or laughter, and nodded. "But still," he agreed.

❧

Surprisingly, Michael followed Savi's suggestion—though they didn't use a nuclear bomb, uncertain of the effect of such a powerful weapon.

In and out within seconds, and she watched in the Room as Michael and Colin appeared at the top of the mountain. The charges had been prepared; Colin simply had to set them against the rocks and start the timer.

Fifteen seconds later, Colin was in the Room with her, holding her hand as the explosion obliterated the symbols, a good chunk of the mountaintop, and a few curious wyrm-wolves.

"It's done," he announced, and held her gaze as he pressed a kiss to her fingers. She raised her shields a moment after he did; she reflected infinitely in every mirror, each successive image decreasing in size. Dizzying.

"Well," Lilith said from behind the glass. "Despite all of your whining, that wasn't bad at all."

Colin rolled his eyes; his fangs flashed with his grin. "Sod off, Agent Milton."

❧

Flying, Savi determined, was still much safer than teleporting. Especially when one hired a private jet, and the pilots didn't raise a brow when Colin demanded they fly west around the globe, rather than taking a shorter route east.

And Beaumont Court looked exactly as it had in his paintings—if slightly darker, lit by moonlight.

"I'd rather not tell her I can turn into a wolf," Savi said as they pulled into the drive. "I think having a vampire for a granddaughter is a big enough shock."

Colin slanted her an amused glance. "You've dashed my

hopes, Savitri; I'd imagined you entertaining my family for hours, chasing a stick or some such nonsense."

"Oh, god. Is that all of them?" There must have been fifty people wating near the entrance, but it was the slim dark woman in the bright turquoise sari that drew her gaze. "She looks really good. Relaxed."

Three hours later, Savi couldn't determine how it was possible to be refreshed when so many children vied for Nani's attention, when they chased Colin around the drawing room with crucifixes and garlic, and she had to explain several times over that her education wasn't nearly as haphazard as her translation of Hugh's book suggested.

She wasn't at all ashamed when she finally fled to Nani's rooms with Colin in tow.

Colin stood by the window, looking out over the gardens as Nani examined Savi's face, her hair, her teeth.

The henna and the platinum ring.

"Oh, *naatin*," she finally said. "You will make me cry. This is not how things are usually done."

Colin smiled, leaned against the sill. "But the way things are usually done is so tedious, Nani."

Her own eyes starting to burn with tears, Savi shook her head. "Don't cry. Watch. Watch." She had to concentrate, recall everything she'd ever read about hair follicles and growth—but it was an image of her mother that made it simple: a moment later, her hair fell in a heavy cascade down her back. "I said it would be long for my wedding. I kept my promise."

Nani covered her face and began to shake with laughter.

"I think we'll have one wedding here," Colin said. His gaze slid the length of her hair; his eyes were heated when they met hers again. "One in Bombay, and one in San Francisco. We shall shock all of your friends and relations with the extravagance and expense of it." He scratched his jaw and added with studied innocence, "It is the bride's family who traditionally pays for such things, is it not?"

Nani pursed her lips. "Yes, *beta*. But the way things are usually done is so tedious."

"I fear," Colin said minutes later as they exited the room and Savi followed him to his suite, "that I shall soon be a poor man."

He pulled her inside his rooms, tossed her onto his bed, landed on top of her. Wrapped her hair around his fist, and inhaled its length. "Good God. I love it short, but . . . good God. I shall slide it all over me. Tell me what I need to do for you to keep it this length for a month."

She licked his jaw, his throat. "I want a spaceship for my five thousandth birthday."

"Done. I'll begin budgeting for it now." His breath caught, then stopped as her fangs sank into him. "I shall traipse across the heavens with you, Savitri. You'd best start working on your accent; British public school is best for colonizing, even in space . . . oh, bloody hell, sweet, how I love you."

That's the one thing that I've never doubted, she whispered through her skin. *That I never had to ask.*

She'd just had to look at him.

"Do not mistake me for a kind man, Savitri."

She wouldn't. Not again. "What are you going to do?" She pushed at his chest.

"Taste you. Only your mouth, and only if you agree."

Heat coiled through her stomach; he was like a fever inside her, a sickness. "What if I don't?"

"I'll carry you to my suite and do it there." There was no apology in his tone now. "I don't intend to take your blood, Savi. I simply want—*need*—to taste you. I think I will die if I do not."

She would not believe that; only poets and horny teenagers did. But her gaze dropped to his lips. Her fingers buried in the hair at his nape. So thick and soft.

"This must be because I'm drunk," she whispered as she lowered her mouth to his. "I know better."

Titles by Meljean Brook

DEMON ANGEL
DEMON MOON
DEMON NIGHT
DEMON BOUND
DEMON FORGED
DEMON BLOOD
DEMON MARKED

THE IRON DUKE
HEART OF STEEL

Anthologies

HOT SPELL
(with Emma Holly, Lora Leigh, and Shiloh Walker)
WILD THING
(with Maggie Shayne, Marjorie M. Liu, and Alyssa Day)
FIRST BLOOD
(with Susan Sizemore, Erin McCarthy, and Chris Marie Green)
MUST LOVE HELLHOUNDS
(with Charlaine Harris, Nalini Singh, and Ilona Andrews)
BURNING UP
(with Angela Knight, Nalini Singh, and Virginia Kantra)
ANGELS OF DARKNESS
(with Nalini Singh, Ilona Andrews, and Sharon Shinn)